OPEN WOUNDS

A DI HARRISON BAIRD NOVEL

ALEX SMITH

RELENTLESS
MEDIA

OPEN WOUNDS

Published Worldwide by Relentless Media.
This edition published in 2025.

Edited by Jacqueline Beard MBE

1.1.3
PRINT ISBN: 978-1-913877-21-7

www.alexsmithbooks.com
relentless.media

ALSO BY ALEX SMITH

The DI Harrison Baird Thrillers

A Long-Dead Thing

Open Wounds

Mad Dogs

The DCI Robert Kett Thrillers

Paper Girls

Bad Dog

Three Little Pigs

Whip Crack

Run Rabbit Run

Stone Cold Dead

Every Mother's Son

Sweet Briar Rose

Jaw Breaker

Knock Knock

King Rat

Knuckle Bones

Lucky Number Seven

Unholy Saints

Truly Madly Deadly

Every Last Devil

Red Line

Cold Iron Kills

Tin Soldiers

Other Books

Six Days, Six Hours, Six Minutes

The Harder They Fall

For Morag,
thanks for introducing so many people
around the world to DCI Kett and DI Baird!

PROLOGUE

Saturday

"What's the first rule of tug the pizzle? Don't drop the bloody pizzle!"

Lucas Bude hurled the words over his shoulder as he crunched down the gravel track, speaking loud enough that a geyser of spray exploded from his lips. It hung in the air behind him, the sun painting rainbows inside it, making it look like something from a fairy tale. As pretty as it was, Flora Arbon had no intention of walking through it as she trudged in Lucas' footsteps. She used one hand to furiously wave it away—the spit *and* the flies, who buzzed in their hundreds over the track. The hum of their wings made it sound like a Second World War bomber was inbound.

Flora's other hand was clasped on the giant wooden pole between her legs, an old broom handle that had already chafed her bare thighs and given her a splinter. She could barely walk because of the bloody thing, and it kept threatening to slide out of her sweaty fingers. But she couldn't drop it, because that was the first rule.

She clutched the pizzle hard, riding it like a broomstick.

"Say it with me," Lucas called out from up ahead. "The first rule of tug the pizzle?"

"Don't drop the pizzle," she said, a little feebly.

"Right!"

Lucas had a length of wood between his legs too, longer than a pool cue and maybe twice as thick. His had been immaculately waxed, with Avalonian runes carved into the side. Even though he was pushing twenty-five, he moved like a kid with a hobby horse, dainty cantered steps that kicked up plumes of dust. They seemed to suspend themselves for an impossibly long time, no breeze here to stir them. It was as if gravity had broken, and Flora pushed herself off the ground a little harder with her next step, almost disappointed when her pizzle didn't whisk her into the air like it did in the books.

"Try a little harder," said a voice behind her.

She glanced back to see Darcey Birch, still her best friend from university. She was bright-eyed and grinning as she clattered along with her own stick. Unlike everyone else, she was wearing the full royal regalia as described in the novels: a long, rose-pink dress, black boots, and a gleaming tiara.

Behind her was Anders Yarl, Darcey's other half, grinning at her with his distinctly un-British teeth, his Scandinavian eyes a shade of blue she didn't even have a word for. *Cobalt?* She half remembered it from an English class from years ago, but it didn't sound quite right. He also held a shaft of wood between his legs, strong hands on the hilt, firm, sweaty thighs clenching it in place beneath the hem of the shortest pair of shorts she'd ever seen.

Her foot hit a rock and she staggered, only a miracle of gymnastics keeping her from faceplanting. She almost dropped her pizzle from the shock of it, recovering in time to see Lucas spinning gracefully in a half circle, a reprimanding *tut-tut* visible on his face even if she couldn't hear it over the hammer-blows of her heart.

"The first rule of tug the pizzle," he said, waggling a pair of sweat-drenched eyebrows. "Don't drop the pizzle!"

The look he gave Flora was the look of a child eyeing up a pudding.

"Or you'll be punished," he said.

He spun around and continued on his merry way.

Second rule, thought Flora, the rush of adrenaline making her feel a little sick. *Jam the pizzle so far up Lucas' arse he could be a court jester's spinning plate.*

She focussed on where she was going, following Lucas along the path as it weaved through the countryside. The fields snoozed beneath snug blankets of flowering crops, nursed by the chattering songbirds that rose and fell. The air was hot, heavy with the smells of spring, as sweet as honey. Flora felt like she was getting drunk on it.

Drunk on *something,* anyway. As ridiculous as it sounded, given that she was trotting to the woods on a homemade pizzle stick with a bunch of nerds who were as weird as she was, she was *happy.*

It felt almost impossibly odd to even think that word, after the last two years. Her cat dying—even though, at twenty-one and almost as old as she was, it had been a long time coming. Then her nan. For a while, especially in the weeks leading up to Christmas last year, she'd found herself inside a locked box with no key. Dark, cold and extremely lonely, she hadn't been able to see a way out at all.

Then she'd picked up a copy of *The Court of Avalonia* from the lovely little bookshop in Southwold. A little light fantasy from a local author, a welcome escape. She'd fallen in love with the world, with the characters, with the landscape of Avalonia and the magic of its fierce and noble Princess Phenny LeFreene—the perfect antidote to her own joyless winter. It hadn't been long before Darcey was as obsessed as she was, and from there they'd found the *Avaloniaks* internet community, not just a handful of people but thousands of them, and plenty of those right here in Suffolk.

As strange as they were, she'd found her people. The kind of people who were into Live Action Roleplay, apparently. LARPing, it was called. Her only experience of it had been at the University of East Anglia, when she and her mates had laughed at the Quidditch players riding their brooms across the playing fields, chasing golden balls and pretending they were flying.

This was totally different, of course.

She adjusted her pizzle, her thighs burning.

No, this wasn't a game. She was about to sacrifice a victim to the Wild Man Vy'Agare, Lord Chieftain of the Avalonian forests.

Flora reached the top of a small hill, the woods appearing ahead—so big and so unexpectedly close that they might have been a wall of green water surging over the land. She gasped, nearly losing her grip on the stick again. These didn't seem like the woodlands of Avalonia, the quaint forests that surrounded the castle. This place was much older, the gaps between the trees full of captured night. A handful of people waited there, dwarfed by the crowning canopies, all of them trotting back and forth on their pizzle sticks.

"Onwards!" shouted Anders. He broke into a gallop as he overtook her, moving with an ease and an elegance that made her feel like a donkey.

She started to move as well, only to see that Lucas had barred her way with his enormous pizzle—held upright between his legs at an obscene angle. He gave her that look again, two parts hunger to one part lust, all drenched in more sweat than she'd ever seen on a person.

"You should stay close to me," he said, jiggling towards her.

"Ugh," she grunted, with no idea how to follow it up.

Lucas reached out and touched the end of her stick. It wasn't a part of her, but even so she had to lock the scream in her throat at the sight of his fingers there. She stumbled back, shaking her head.

Everybody in Avalonia knew you didn't touch another person's pizzle.

Lucas bared his teeth in a grin.

"Let me be your Prince, Flora," he said.

"No thank you," she said.

He left his lizard gaze on her for a while longer, then he shrugged, galloping after Anders towards the treeline.

Flora hesitated for a moment, some of the magic stripped from the day, the way it so often was because of arseholes like Lucas. She looked back, seeing the road where they'd parked, the cars shimmering in the sun like liquid fire. She hadn't driven, but she could easily hitch back to Southwold from here. It was ten minutes, max, and she knew most of the folks who came this way.

If she did that, though, then Lucas would win.

To hell with him, she thought. Phenny LeFreene would lock him up and throw away the key just for looking at her.

She headed down the hill, picking up speed. She tugged the pizzle the way they did in the books, making little whooshing noises beneath her breath. The little crowd by the woods welcomed her with a cheer, and she felt her spirits soar as she clattered down the gravel track.

Her people!

She was like the princess, riding down to Fair Isle to meet Captain Gavé Escon from his ship. The giddy thrill of it made her run with even more abandon, but she wasn't exactly built for speed even on the days she didn't have a broom handle wedged in her bum crack. Just ten yards from the end of the track, the tip of her pizzle stick hit the ground like a vaulter's pole, jarring itself out of her grip. The back end snapped up, whacking her between the legs with a gunshot crack while also catapulting her into the air. She croaked a gargled scream as she fell, managing to get one hand down a fraction of a second before her face hit the dirt. She did what felt like a full somersault, flopping down on her back, staring up at the branches overhead, and the blue sky beyond.

And there she lay. Her arse smarting, her ears ringing, her head spinning.

"Oh my God!" came a voice, heavy with an accent. Anders leaned over her, his beautiful face furrowed by a frown. "Flora, are you *okay*?"

"I'm fine," she grunted in a voice that said anything but.

Anders offered her a hand and she took it, surprised at the ease with which he pulled her up. Never mind the pizzle stick, she thought, Anders could make her fly—if he wasn't dating Darcey, of course. She smiled at him as much as her burning face would allow. Then she turned to the others, who all looked back at her like they'd just witnessed a Bulboid Tree Spider crawl out of her ear.

"Are you alright?" asked Darcey, brushing a hand down Flora's back.

"I'm okay," she answered. She noticed that one of her knuckles was bleeding and she sucked at the wound, tasting copper. "I tripped."

"Flo, you didn't trip, you *Buster Keatoned.*"

This got a smile out of her, at least, which lasted until Lucas approached, bobbing gently up and down on his pizzle stick. He used his free hand to wag a finger back and forth.

"No, you didn't trip, my dear," he said, his voice thick and oily. "You dropped your pizzle stick!"

A gasp of horror rippled through the small group, and they all clamped their sticks between their legs.

"No," said Flora, shaking her head. "I didn't drop it."

She bent down, collecting the pizzle stick that she had *definitely* dropped. She tried to slide herself onto it again, but Lucas—who, she was starting to understand, was a monumental twat in every single way—started shouting at her.

"She dropped her stick! She is the unchosen one!"

"Mate," said Anders, breaking character for a moment. "She tripped. Give her a break."

"The Gods of the forest have spoken. She is the one who will be sacrificed to the Wild Man of the trees."

The rest of the group muttered their agreement, all except for one girl who was looking at something on her phone.

"Go, child!" yelled Lucas, who was enjoying himself far too much. "Run! You do not have long to escape your fate."

Flora lifted her head and spluttered out a rasping breath.

"Can't we start over?" she said. "I don't want to—"

"Run!" Lucas repeated, this time a lunatic shriek. "If you are caught, you die!"

Flora groaned again, but there was nothing she could do. These were the rules, after all.

"Don't actually kill me," she grumbled as she turned her stick to the trees. The thick trunks seemed to lean away from each other, making room for her—the way a deep-sea predator relaxes its jaws to lure its prey. The creak of them was like a discordant choir, and for a moment the mystery of Avalonia was all too plausible. These were the woods that had inspired the stories, after all. It was right here that the author, Charlotte DeVere, had been inspired to write; as if, in her own words, "the magic had simply spilled out of the branches and into my skull."

What if that's exactly what had happened? What if there was a truth here, about the spiders, the trolls, and the Wild Man who feasted on human skulls? Because these woods were ancient, and there weren't just miracles to be found.

There were horrors, too.

"Run!" screamed Lucas, and the other members of the group took up the cry—a howl that sent her skittering past the treeline.

A giggle tumbled out of her lips, fuelled by adrenaline, surprising her. She ran as fast as the pizzle would let her, remembering to keep the tip well away from the ground in case she went bum over boob again. The trees creaked and groaned their celebration, leaves rustling, branches cracking. She imagined their woody bodies hauling themselves up from where they rested, roots uncoiling from the dirt as they prepared to devour her.

Or, if she was worthy, to serve her to Vy'Agare.

Another bubble of laughter, which she managed to catch in her fist. She allowed herself a look back, surprised to discover that she couldn't see the field any more. The woods had gobbled her up, and even as she thought it, she felt the trees crowding in, the canopy lowering, the ground softening to draw in her feet. She could taste her own fear in the back of her mouth, she could feel the electric charge of it, but she clamped her hand to her lips so she wouldn't cry out. She had to be brave, because this was her world now. Avalonia. These were her people and she their princess. It was *real*.

There was a faint whoop behind her, followed by a handful more.

The hunt had begun.

Flora moved deeper into the woods. She kept the pizzle between her legs even though there was nobody to see her here, counting on its magic to keep her hidden, to keep her safe. She thundered past the trees the way Princess Phenny might have, far too nimble for their twiggy fingers to snare her, far too fast for their clumsy footsteps to follow.

It could have been seconds later that she stopped again, it could have been hours. She skidded to a halt, kicking up dirt, wondering why it had grown suddenly darker. The trees in this part of the forest didn't even look like trees. They were giants that might have been hewn from rock, or molten shapes spewed up through cracks in the earth. Their branches had twisted into a ceiling over her head, and she had the idea she'd wandered into a building of some kind rather than a woodland.

She couldn't hear a thing other than the dry chuckle of

the creaking branches. No footsteps. No shouts. No laughter.

"Hello?" she said. "Darcey? Anders?"

Even the birds had fallen silent, as if they knew that this place was sacred.

Or cursed.

Shut up, Flora told her brain, feeling her stomach coil into knots like a nest of snakes.

"Hello?" she said again.

She was answered by a low growl from her left, a throbbing snarl that rose from a wall of dense vegetation. It was so unexpected, so terrifying, that she felt herself go liquid with terror—every bone melting, every cell dissolving. The growl ended with an ugly swallowing sound before immediately starting up again, louder than before.

Flora pulled the pizzle from between her legs, holding it like a club. She took a step away from the bushes, one she thought would be quiet. But her foot hit a twig and the crack was like a gunshot.

Whatever was in the bushes started to move towards her, branches rustling. Its growl seemed to make the entire forest vibrate, as if it wasn't an animal there but a piece of industrial machinery.

"Please," said Flora. "Don't."

Don't what? she screamed silently to herself. *Don't eat me? It's a wolf, it doesn't speak English!*

"Sorry," she shouted, as if that might make it better. "I'm going to... I'm just going to... you know... Bye?"

She turned slowly, using her free hand to wipe away the sweat and the tears, still clutching the pizzle. One step, another, a third, not looking at anything other than the ground. She prayed to everything she could remember the name of.

Please let me get out of here, please don't let me be eaten.

She even found herself praying to the Wild Man, the way LeFreene had in the books when she thought she was going to be sacrificed.

Please.

As she walked, the growl faded, eventually rattling into silence. It was going to let her leave.

Thank you, she thought. *Thank you, thank—*

A subtle shift in the air made her stop. She didn't know exactly what it was: a scent, perhaps. The taste of something other than her own terror.

Slowly, she lifted her head.

And she saw him.

The Wild Man.

He stood at the base of a monstrous oak tree, dressed in crimson robes. His body bristled with black feathers, hundreds of them, as if he was transforming into a crow. His arms were outstretched in welcome, and why wouldn't they be? He had caught her here, in his domain.

She belonged to him.

For a second, at most, she wondered if this was part of the game. If Lucas, or one of the others, had put this thing here to make their experience all the more believable.

Then she looked at the Wild Man again, and understood this was real.

He had no head. Not in the conventional sense. His neck was a disc of torn flesh, and above that somebody had carved an empty circle into the bark of the tree. There were no eyes there, but Flora could feel him watching her. There was no mouth, but she could hear his voice in the sudden rush of warm air. His body shook with silent laughter, the feathers bristled as if he was spreading his wings, and when his voice came, it was a cold whisper right in her ear.

"I've been waiting for you..."

The pizzle stick slid from her numb fingers, and she didn't even have time to acknowledge that she'd broken the first rule before something thumped into her back, as hard as a moving car. She fell to the dirt, hitting her head. There was only pain, pain and the inexplicable scent of lemons, so out of place here that she was convinced it must be a dream.

Then the Wild Man's darkness swallowed her whole.

CHAPTER ONE

"Are you sure you need the helmet, Connie?"

DI Harrison Baird leaned against the back wall of a warehouse, a takeaway cup of coffee held to his chest. The mid-morning sun was in his eyes, blindingly bright as it peeked over the roofs of the industrial buildings opposite. It was on his skin, too, burning his face and his scalp. In fact, it felt like it was everywhere, liquid fire that he would have happily extinguished beneath the heel of his shoe if it hadn't been a hundred million miles away.

The warehouse sat on an estate a few miles outside of Southwold, in the town of Reydon. The windows had been knocked through, the walls daubed with graffiti—including one of the longest and most detailed todgers he'd ever seen, which pointed up to the mossy guttering like a hairy rocket. Anyone would have assumed the place was abandoned, but according to Connell, there was a notorious kidnapper inside—as well as their victim.

Baird held a hand to the furnace of his forehead, peeking through his shadow to see Connell beside him. The young DC crouched at the back door, dressed in her usual shapeless grey suit. A ballistic helmet did its best to balance on top of her enormous nest of hair, looking like an upturned bowl of noodles. She had both hands pressed against the peeling wood, one eye to the keyhole.

"I said do you really need the helmet?" he repeated, wondering if she'd heard him.

"Hush, sir," Connell replied, her voice strangled by the thick strap. "I think I can hear something."

"You might hear it better if you take the helmet off," said Baird. "It's gonna cut off your circulation. Where did you even find it? A toy shop?"

She hushed him again, moving her other eye to the keyhole. Baird lifted his cup and took a delicate sip, the coffee still piping hot. They'd picked it up on their way out of town fifteen minutes ago, along with an ice cream for Connell, of course. He couldn't solve a case without a jolt of caffeine. She couldn't start one without seven teaspoons of sugar, a waffle cone, and a dollop of strawberry sauce.

Each to their own.

"I can definitely hear a squeal," said Connell, leaning back from the door and scrubbing the dirt from her plump cheek. When she looked up, the helmet tipped so far back it almost slid off her head. She trapped it beneath her hand.

"A squeal?" said Baird. "Define a squeal. That could be anything."

"Well it wouldn't be a sheep, sir," she said, as if that might help matters.

He thought about it for a second before conceding the point.

"Could be a chair being pushed over the floor," he said. "Or somebody in the throes of passion."

"It wasn't that kind of squeal, sir."

She stood, her knees cracking like she was a hundred

years old. She looked at him as if he owed her something, and she wasn't wrong. It had been three weeks since Baird had been exiled to the festering cesspit of England; since he'd been flushed down the toilet from his home in Aberdeen and carried through a sewer system's worth of foul-smelling cities and towns, finally coming to a stop on the very tip of Britain's eastern rump. Just over a fortnight since he and Connell had found not just one killer, but three.

The fact that he'd managed to wrap up his first case with Suffolk Police in breakneck time—ignoring, for the moment, the number of rules he'd broken along the way—had sweetened his old DCI in Police Scotland to the idea of him coming home early. And he had Connell to thank for that. Not just for the case itself, but also for the fact she'd helped him brush the fragments of some of those broken rules under the carpet.

Aye, he owed her big time.

"I just think it's crazy that we're risking it," he told her, looking up at the warehouse. "We have no idea what's waiting for us in there."

"Justice is waiting," she said, deadly serious. "Justice, and a young boy's broken heart."

"Och, aye, there's that I suppose. But what if they're armed? Maybe we should wait for tactical to show up?"

She gave her hat a tap.

"This is tactical."

"Your tactical unit's a single helmet?" he said.

"And Henry's homemade beanbag gun," said Connell. "But Briggs wouldn't let me bring it."

The sun was burning a hole in the back of Baird's head, and he moved to the other side of Connell to get a more even bake.

"We dinnae even have a constable with us," he said. "We're no armed, and don't you dare mention lollipop sticks."

She patted the helmet a few more times. Between that and the pounding ache in his head, Baird almost lost it.

"That hat'll be going in the skip if you're no careful, Connie."

"Sir," she said, as patient as she always was. "Ask yourself, why are you here?"

"Believe me, I've no stopped asking myself that since I got off the train."

"No, sir, why are you *here*? Why did you become a police officer?"

"It was the pension, Connie," he shot back. "That and they were giving oot those wee packs of Haribo on the recruitment stand, the good ones with the jelly babies. Look..."

He pinched his nose, screwing his eyes shut against the screwdriver of sunlight that was gouging its way into his prefrontal cortex.

"I get why you're doing this, quine, I do. This poor wee fella's been kidnapped, his family want him back. He could be dead in there, skinned and gutted and turned into bacon rashers. But honestly, do you really care enough to spoil my day?"

Connell's mouth dropped in shock. Baird lifted his hands before she could start, coffee spilling over his wrist.

"Alright, alright, you dinnae have to say it. I'm a horrible person. Just one more question: will it get me oot of this evil bastard sun?"

"Well, I mean, we'll be indoors, sir..." said Connell, confused. "So yes. And it's the same sun you get in Scotland."

"It's really no. This sun's brash and loud and in your face, makes you all angry and sweaty. It goes wherever it wants and it couldnae give a shite whether it's ruining your day or no. In other words, it's English. Our sun's a peely-wally thing that hides in the clouds so it disnae have to interact with anyone. Honestly, Connie, sometimes we dinnae see it for months on end, and when we do, we're so shocked there's something up there we think the world's ending. I've seen people diving into the Don in terror. So no, it's no the same sun."

The sigh that came out of Connell was the same sigh that comes out of a mother when her child won't stop talking.

"Fine," said Baird. "But I still say lose the helmet."

"I would, sir," Connell said, reaching for the handle. "But unfortunately, you have to come with me."

By the time he'd understood the insult, Connell had opened the door and walked inside.

"Hey!" he said quietly.

Baird finished his coffee and dropped the cup outside. He followed Connell into a dark, cramped corridor, a reek of what could only be rotting fish and chips hitting him in the face like a mallet. He pinched his nose with one hand, waving the other to waft the aroma away.

"Christ," he muttered. "That's awfie, Connie."

"It wasn't me, sir," she said from up ahead. She was approaching the only other door in sight.

"I ken, I'm just saying, what *is* that?"

"Animal feed. I'd know it anywhere."

Connell put her ear to the second door, hesitating for a moment before opening it. The creak of the hinges could have been heard by his half-deaf granny back in Aberdeen. A few seconds of silence followed, then the door squealed again—or at least Baird thought it was the door, until Connell turned to him, a grin on her wide face.

"A squeal!" she said. "I told you."

She jogged into the larger space beyond, still using a hand to keep the helmet in place. When Baird caught up, he saw that they were inside a large, double-height warehouse space that was absolutely crammed with wooden crates. Light poured through the broken roof windows, revealing no sign of life—if you didn't count the mould and the fungus that coated everything like decorator's sheets. The smell in here was even worse, a sickly sweet but undeniably rotting stench that coated him in cold sweat.

"Urgh," he said, his head spinning so hard he had to stop and plant his hands on his knees. "We're gonna get high."

He leaned over a little further.

"Or die."

Connell had reached the centre of the warehouse, seemingly unaffected by the air quality.

"Alright, Mo," she yelled, her voice echoing off the walls before heading to the ceiling. "It's the police. You can't hide him any more. Bring out Major Porkchop."

Baird straightened up and joined her in the middle of the room, by which time somebody was shouting back from the far side of the warehouse.

"He ain't here, Connie. Piss off."

It was the voice of a woman who'd eaten a pound of gravel, but it carried easily enough. Immediately following it was a squeal, and there was absolutely no mistaking it this time for anything other than a pig.

"Sure sounds like he's here," said Connell.

"Well he ain't."

The pig squealed again.

"Look," said Connell. "I know why you did it, Mo, but Callum really misses his pet. You know how close they are. This doesn't hurt Barney. It only hurts your son."

"I ain't trying to hurt my boy!" said Mo. "If *he* wants his pig, *he* can come get him."

"It isn't as easy as that, Mo," said Connell. "With the court order and everything. Last chance to hand him over, or we come and get him."

"And some of us are no as friendly as Connie," wheezed Baird, his lungs actually aching from the stench. "I'm gonna count to three."

He took a breath that made his stomach contract like a car in a compactor.

"Three," he said. "Time's up."

Connell gave him a look.

"I didnae say I was starting at one. Come on."

He set off in the direction of the voice, passing the stacked crates. Each one smelled worse than the last, and by the time the far wall came into sight he was sweating so hard he could barely see. He swiped his hands over his face, seeing a single door. It was open, but there wasn't enough light to identify the person who stood there. They were holding something in their arms, and obviously struggling with it.

"Fine!" yelled Mo. "You can bloody have him."

A pig flew through the door, hitting the floor with a skittering of feet and a monstrous squeal. It was the size of a Golden retriever, and it was obviously furious, because it started running, picking up speed.

"Get it, sir!" shouted Connell.

"Get *that*?" said Baird, horrified. "It's massive! I thought you said it was wee."

Connell barged past him, one hand holding the helmet

as she ran after the pig. It must have seen her coming because it turned, slipping onto its side. It squealed again, back on its trotters in a heartbeat before vanishing into the maze of boxes.

"Major Porkchop!" Connell called. "You're safe!"

"I must be dreaming," said Baird, rubbing his sweating face again. "This cannae be real."

The pig crossed an aisle with a thunder of hooves and another porcine shriek. Then it was Connell's turn, her feet slapping the ground as she lumbered after it.

"What are you even going to do with it when you catch it?" he said as she vanished behind the boxes.

The pig ran back the way it had just come, Connell right behind it. He could almost hear the Benny Hill music.

"Unbelievable," he muttered, and he would have added something else except Major Porkchop burst out of the crates again, his trotters scrabbling as he changed direction. He ran right for Baird, his black eyes bulging, his mouth foaming—looking every bit like a wild boar ready to skewer him through.

"Oh, shite," said Baird.

He ducked down, his arms out like a goalie before a penalty. Then he barked a couple of times, in the hope it might make the animal slow down.

It didn't.

The pig reached him in a heartbeat, then the bloody thing *jumped*, propelling itself through the air like a pink, wet-nosed missile.

Baird screamed. The pig screamed.

It was like being rugby-tackled by a ten-stone missile of jiggling flesh, the impact knocking him flat on his back. His head rung off the concrete, a tuning-fork whine breaking out between his temples. The pig's trotters dug into the soft flesh of his belly, stamping on his crotch. The smell of its squealing breath was enough to knock him out. But he held on for dear life, whispering sweet nothings with all the air his winded lungs had to give until the pig started to calm.

"Easy, pal. You're fine."

Connell ran up, gently pulling the pig away. She slid a carrot from her pocket, offering it to Major Porkchop. As it tucked in, she slipped a rope around its neck.

"Good job," she said.

"Aye," Baird replied, struggling to sit up. "I did alright."

"I was talking to the pig, sir," she said. "But that was a tremendous catch."

"I didnae even ken pigs could jump," he said. "Came at me like it had a rocket up the arse."

"They're little marvels," Connell said, offering him a hand. He took it, and she helped him to his feet. "You okay?"

"I'll live," he replied, massaging the back of his head. "Revenge for all those ham pieces, I suppose."

"You know what might have helped? A helmet."

He scowled at her, then he scanned the warehouse. There was no sign of the woman who'd unleashed the animal.

"Mo'll be long gone," said Connell. "That's kind of what she does. She and Barney have been at each other's throats for the better part of a decade. Poor Callum takes the brunt of it. Uniforms'll pick her up, sooner or later."

"Right," said Baird, fingering a hole in his trousers where a trotter had almost castrated him. "Long gone sounds like a good plan for us, too. You know somebody with a trailer?"

"No need, sir," said Connell. "He can just sit in the car."

She set off, giving the rope a gentle tug and making

kissing noises at the pig. Major Porkchop trotted happily after her, leaving a little trail of crunched carrot behind him.

"In the *car*?" said Baird.

They walked out the way they'd come in, the air hot but beautifully fresh. Baird inhaled deeply as he followed Connell and the pig across the yard at the back of the warehouse. Connell's sickly yellow Fiat Punto was parked by the gate, and she opened the back door.

"In you go," she said.

"It's no a dug, Connie," said Baird.

But the pig seemed to know exactly what to do, springing into the back of the car with a wag of its curly tail. Connell threw another carrot inside, which immediately vanished into the carpet of sweet wrappers and crisp packets, then shut him in.

"I'll drive us over to the Arnupp place," she said. "Callum will be over the moon."

She was about to climb behind the wheel when her phone rang. She almost dropped it as she pulled it from her pocket.

"Ma'am," she said when she'd answered. "Yes... we have. Yes, alive. Yes, he's still annoying... and yes, the pig is too. I was going to run him home."

She tilted her head as she listened, the helmet sliding sideways.

"Okay, sure. We'll be there in fifteen."

She hung up, looking at Baird over the roof of the car.

"Briggs needs us back," she said, wide-eyed. "There's been a murder."

CHAPTER TWO

Thanks in part to Connell's over-cautious driving, and in part because the pig wouldn't stop trying to leap into the front seat, it was more like thirty minutes later that the Fiat pulled up outside Southwold HQ.

The view from the top of the hill was as glorious as it always was, thanks in no small part to the presence of the sea—Baird's sea, which lay unbroken from here all the way to his home in Aberdeen. Even the fierce English sun was no match for the water, snared in the peaks of the waves where it cooled itself into a contented slumber. The tinfoil glow of it was so bright that for a few seconds after leaving the car, Baird could see nothing at all.

By the time his vision had returned, he was surprised to see Connell marching up the steps to the little fisherman's cottage that served as the command centre—surprised because she had the pig in tow. Major Porkchop was struggling with the steps, his little legs going ten to the dozen as he oinked his way upwards.

"You're no leaving him in the car?" he said.

"And risk him going AWOL again?" Connell called back. "No chance. Besides, Briggs loves pigs!"

"No in her HQ, surely," he muttered.

But he was wrong, because a second or two later DCI Briggs opened the door, grinning like she was welcoming home a much-loved relative. She ducked into a squat, gathering the squealing pig into a cuddle and planting a kiss right on the flat, wet pad of his nose.

"Eurch," said Baird, pulling a face.

"Congratulations, Connell," said the teapot-shaped DCI, using the doorframe to help her back up. "You got him."

Connell beamed.

"Well, once we knew it wasn't the vegans, it didn't take much to figure it out."

"You found Mo?"

"We did, but she scarpered."

"And this little guy came willingly?" asked Briggs.

The DCI gave Baird a once over as he walked up, taking in his filthy suit and the hole in his crotch.

"Ish," he told her. "I forgot my pig wrangling training in the heat of the moment."

"Easily done," Briggs said, giving Baird a smile. "You can clean up in your old room if you like."

He nodded his thanks, waiting for the two women and the pig to enter the cottage before traipsing in after them. He swung left into the part of the building that had doubled as his sleeping quarters when he'd first arrived—a single bedroom with a pokey *en suite* that Major Porkchop would have struggled to get into. He'd managed another two nights here after the end of the last case, but when he'd woken up one morning to Connell serenading him with a Taylor Swift song from the unlockable door while her dog humped a pair of his socks, he'd decided enough was enough.

His new digs were across town, a holiday apartment that belonged to some friends of the DCI. It was spacious, and comfortable, and if he stood on his tiptoes he could see the sea from the kitchen window. But he hadn't unpacked more than his suitcase, because in his heart of hearts he knew he wouldn't be staying long.

Home was calling him.

There were just a couple of things he needed to do before he left.

"Be quick about it, Harrison," called Briggs. "We're on the clock."

He washed his hands and splashed some water on his face, before using a wet towel to get the worst of the trotter marks from his suit. It was a poor effort on all counts, but he felt a little fresher by the time he walked back through into HQ. DI Henry Crump was in the kitchen, cooing and clucking with delight as he scratched the pig's head. Baird headed into the little dining space which served as their Incident Room, crashing into a chair next to Connell.

"Don't get too comfortable," said Briggs. "I need you both to head straight out again."

"Who's dead, ma'am?" asked Baird.

"That, Harrison, is a good question."

Briggs perched her cushioned rear end on the edge of the table, folding her arms across her chest.

"We're not sure who the victim is, because they don't have a head."

"Definitely dead, then," said Connell, with no hint of irony.

"Well, yes," said Briggs. "It's a man. He was found in

the Benacre woods an hour ago, tied to a tree. Somebody used him as target practice before they decapitated him."

"A gun?" said Baird.

"A bow and arrow, by the look of it."

"Ouch."

"He was discovered by a group of young people who were in the woods playing tug the pizzle."

If Baird had been drinking coffee, he'd have spat it all over the floor.

"Playing *what*, ma'am?"

"From *The Court of Avalonia*!" said Connell, obviously delighted.

"The court?"

"*Of Avalonia*," Connell repeated.

"The what?"

"The court," said Connell. "Of Avalonia. The book."

"The book?"

"The pizzle!"

His head was spinning.

"The book, called *The Court of Avalonia*," explained Briggs, exasperated. "It'll take too long to explain."

"You've been trying for aboot an hour, you might as well finish."

"It's a fantasy novel, by Charlotte DeVere. Princesses and swords and romance."

"And tug my pizzle," said Connell.

"I most certainly will not," he told her.

Connell snorted a laugh.

"It's the magic in the book, sir," she said. "Pizzle sticks are these floating logs they all ride around on. You have to tug them to get them going, because they've got a mind of their own."

He had literally no idea what to say. Connell made the motion of somebody starting a petrol mower.

"Tug tug," she said with a nervous laugh.

Baird ignored her, turning to Briggs.

"I think I'd like to go home now, ma'am," he said, earning an arched eyebrow from the DCI. "What the hell does a tugged pizzle have to do with the body?"

"Almost certainly nothing," said Briggs. "Benacre woods were the inspiration for the story, the author's local. We get people up there all the time paying homage, or playing games. Every now and again we have to send a uniform up when things get a little, uh, too romantic, if you know what I mean."

"Aye, ma'am, I'm guessing a different kind of tugged pizzle."

Connell snorted again.

"The young woman who found the body was attacked, hit over the head. She's in hospital, critical but stable."

"The killer was still there?" said Baird.

"We're assuming so. Nobody else saw what happened."

Briggs looked at the floor for a moment, her expression unreadable.

"I've never seen anything like this," she said, her quiet voice filling the small room. "Especially here. The deaths in the last case were bad enough, but this... It would seem you're something of a bad luck charm, Detective Inspector Baird."

"Aye," said Baird. "So I've been told."

"Declan and Fred are on site," Briggs went on. "They're waiting for you."

Baird's chair scraped as he pushed himself up.

"Then we'd better no keep them waiting," he said. "Let's go, Connie. And leave the pig here."

THEY RODE with the windows down, warm air whipping Baird's hair into a frenzy as Connell drove north. The car had no air conditioning, but it was the smell that was bothering him more than the heat. Sadly, it seemed to be coming from him—*eau d'pig*, thanks to his wrestling match with Major Porkchop.

Connell didn't seem to notice, craning over the wheel to better see the A12 though the filthy windscreen. She had a crust of ice cream in her hair, he realised. He could have sworn it hadn't been there when they'd visited the warehouse, but he couldn't fathom where she'd managed to find one, because she hadn't left his side since.

Outside, Spring was under the delusion that Summer was here. The fields were in full bloom, blanketed by crops. Hedgerows teemed with bird life, their songs serenading the Fiat as it trundled merrily along. Woodlands draped themselves over the horizon like sleeping cats, basking beneath the weight of their canopies. Baird could almost hear them purring. It seemed remarkable how much the landscape had changed in just a few weeks. Only the sky remained the same, an endless cerulean canvas dotted with clouds of peachy cream and lemon-zest yellow. If he saw a sky like this in a painting, he thought, he wouldn't have believed it was real.

"Pretty spectacular out there, sir," said Connell, glancing at him. "Isn't it?"

"Hadnae really noticed," he replied, clearing his throat to cover the lie. "Would be better with a few mountains. How much further?"

"Couple of miles," she said.

He sucked in the sweet-smelling air, watching the flint

and brick cottages roll past like schoolboys, their thatched roofs buttoned neatly to the top. Even the trees along the roadside looked smart, their swaying branches making them look like they were doffing their caps.

Christ, Harrison, he thought, rubbing his face. *If you dinnae get back to Aberdeen soon there's no hope for you.*

"Have you spoken to your father again?" asked Connell.

The question did a good job of taking his mind off the outside world, the same way a kick to the bollocks would have. He sat back, turning his head to the ceiling while he tried to think of a way of answering that wouldn't make him shout or cry or hurl himself out the door.

The reunion with his da felt like something from a dream, although the jury was still out on whether it was a good one or a nightmare. After twenty-four years apart—no letters, no phone calls, no explanation for why he'd just pissed off one day and never come back, no idea whether his old man was even alive or dead—he'd finally come face to face with him inside a care home just a handful of miles from the road he was driving on right now. Or face to face with some kind of Halloween parody of the man he'd loved so much growing up, that was, a skeletal, spectral ghoul who had lost so much of himself he was barely recognisable.

And all he'd got for his trouble had been an "alright, Harrison."

He'd almost walked straight back out the door, and even now he wasn't sure if it would have been a better choice. But they'd had their reunion. They'd cried their tears and hugged and shouted and pushed out every single drop of emotion from the last two and a half decades.

Only then had his father attempted to give him an explanation. An excuse. A reason for missing the lives of his son and his daughter.

Only then had he given him a *name*.

Robert Kett.

"Sir?" said Connell. "You okay?"

"Aye," he said, his stomach a cement mixer churning a brick. "I've no really had time to visit him, Connie. I've been busy."

Busy on the internet. Busy Googling the name, although Kett wasn't a hard man to find. Baird only had to see his photo to understand that he already knew him. He'd seen Kett a dozen times on the TV, and splashed across the front pages of the newspapers, even in briefings in his own HQ up in Aberdeen. Kett was about as famous as it was possible to be when you were polis, DCI Logan famous, even, and that really was saying something.

He was *infamous*.

As hard as he'd searched, though, he hadn't been able to find much about Kett's time as a copper in the Met, other than the fact his wife had been kidnapped by some fella in a pig mask—a fella who'd ended up with a hammer in the back of his head. What few files there were that promised to delve beneath the surface seemed to have been sealed, huge chunks of Kett's early career secured behind lock and key.

Or destroyed.

And that was all Baird needed to understand there was some truth to his old man's mad ramblings.

"You're being extremely quiet, sir," said Connell. "You're scaring me."

"I'm no being quiet, Connie," he said. "I'm thinking. Very bloody loudly, if you must know."

"Well, you can stop now, because we're here."

Sure enough, the landscape ahead swam with blue light from half a dozen IRVs, as well as the forensic van and a paramedic car. Most had been parked along a narrow dirt track that led into an enormous field, and a constable waved Connell through. There wasn't much space, so she poked the nose of the Fiat into a fence of wheat stalks.

"That'll do," she said, cutting the engine.

They got out together, heading up the track to where a PC fidgeted in the sun. It was Percy Albright, whose sweating face and gentle rotation made him look like a rotisserie chicken. He took off his hat as he watched them walk over, but only so he could fan his face with it.

"Hot," he said, nodding to the sky. "Sun."

"Aye," said Baird. "The sun is hot. Where are we heading?"

"I see your Scottish friend is still here," said Albright, speaking to Connell. He stopped flapping his hat, holding it over his face to conceal a yawn. "The body's up the hill. Just follow the track all the way to them woods. Fred and Declan are there already."

"Thanks Perce," said Connell. "Where are the witnesses?"

"Three of them went to the hospital with the girl who was attacked. The rest have gone home, didn't see anything."

Connell nodded her thanks as they set off along the track. It was rough going, every rut and pothole baked solid and carpeted with loose stones. Twice, Baird almost turned his ankle, and at one point Connell spilled onto her hands and knees with a noise like a goat falling down a hill.

"Could be worse," he said as he helped her up. "We could be on a boat."

They crested the hill to find an impressive woodland on the other side. More police mulled about, insect small against the ancient trees, their black uniforms contrasting perfectly with the white bodysuits of the forensic technicians. It looked a little like somebody had hurled a chess set into the forest.

"So, you've read this book?" asked Baird as they walked down the other side. "The Court of Something?"

"Avalonia," said Connell, a hand to her heart. "Gosh, yes. It's one of my absolute favourites, there's a whole series of them. So romantic. It's about this princess, Phenny LeFreene, who—"

"Phenylephrine?" said Baird. "Like the allergy medicine?"

"What? No, sir. Le*Freene*. She's this amazingly beautiful woman who spends her days in the court, but who turns into this kind of superhero at night. Nobody knows it's her, and she runs about the court fighting rebels, and outside, too, battling loads of monsters and stuff. She's in love with two men. One's the suitor her father wants her to marry, this handsome hunk called Captain Gavé Escon who can be a bit of an—"

"Gaviscon?" said Baird. "Those are the things you take for indigestion, I'm sure of it."

"Gavé *Escon*, sir. Pay attention. The other's this spirit who lives in the woods, but who takes the form of this hunk who runs around naked. The Wild Man Vy'Agare."

Baird stared at her.

"Viagra?" he said. "Now I ken you're messing me aboot."

"No, sir. They're really good. Swashbuckling murder mysteries that get..."

She looked behind her, as if somebody might be there, and when she spoke again it was in a whisper.

"A little NSFW, if you know what I mean."

"Right," said Baird.

"You should read them, sir."

"I will almost definitely *not* do that," he said. He took a breath and called out to the officers who milled by the treeline. "Yous lot seem to be struggling to find something to do with yourselves."

Everyone turned to look at him, but the answer came from between the trees. Fred Cheeseman, the ancient pathologist, wandered out, adjusting the cuffs of his tweed jacket. His face was even more creased and crinkled than it usually was, carrying an expression of deep concern. A younger man followed, this one wearing a set of pristine white overalls. The hood was pulled tight around his face, but Baird didn't need to see him clearly to know that it was Declan Bundy, the forensic technician—his inbuilt smug arsehole alarm had started blaring as soon as he'd appeared.

"Freclan," he said, addressing both men together to save time. "You finished already?"

Fred glanced at Declan, something passing between them. There was a definite sense of unease here, the coppers speaking in soft mutterings, nobody quite willing to meet Baird's eye.

"I'm afraid we haven't even started," said Fred. "We're waiting for animal control."

Baird stared into the woods, which seemed to hold far too much darkness for this time of the day. There was no birdsong, but somewhere, a woodpecker drummed its tribal beat. The trees themselves seemed to sing along, creaking and cracking in a breeze that he couldn't feel. He was used to the woods, of course. Scotland was full of them. But they were majestic bands of pine and moss that marked the hills and the glens, gentle and pure. There was nothing gentle or pure about these gnarled oaks and their grasping fingers.

"The forests of Avalonia," said Connell in an awed whisper. "Full of unspeakable beasts."

From close by, a pigeon cooed.

"Aye, unspeakable. Why do you need animal control?"

The two men looked at each other once more, and Fred sighed.

"Because there's something in the trees," he said. "And I think it's dangerous."

The pigeon cooed again.

"Not that," said Fred. "Your fellow officers heard growling. They think it might be a dog of some kind."

"Ooh, I love dogs," said Connell.

"Or a wolf," said Declan, picking his nails.

"I can tell you now, it's no a wolf," Baird told him. "I cannae hear a thing. They were sure?"

"They looked very shaken up," said Fred.

Baird stared into the woods, trying to make sense of the shadows that gathered around the twisted trunks.

"How much do you love dogs, Connie?" he asked.

She stretched her hands to her sides as far as they would go.

"Aye, me too," he said, setting off into the trees. "Let's go find one."

CHAPTER THREE

It was like stepping into another world, a universe of silence and stillness and shadow. The darkness closed around them as soon as they'd passed the first of the oaks, gathering them into the cloistered safety of the ancient woodland. A carpet of mulch muted their footsteps, turning Baird and Connell into ghosts as they filtered soundlessly past the mighty trees. Shafts of sunlight trickled through the dense canopy, sparkling dust caught in their glow. Where they touched the ground, the shades of green they woke were so vivid they didn't look real. It felt like some kind of church in here, thought Baird, complete with a choir of pigeons whose warbled songs sounded almost human.

It was undoubtedly magical. Everywhere he looked he expected to see a prancing unicorn or a frolicking elf.

Or a wolf.

"Just checking," he said, looking nervously over his shoulder to make sure he could see the way back. "There are no wolves doon here, right?"

"No, sir," said Connell. "Maureen at the Nelson has a huskie, but it's a fat old thing that doesn't have any teeth."

"Good to know," he said. "You have any clue where we're going?"

"No, but it won't be too hard to find. These woods only stretch half a mile or so in any direction. If it was the other side of the A12, on the reserve, it might be more difficult, but you only have to walk for a few minutes here and you'll hit the Bungay Road. Past that there's nothing but fields."

Baird carried on, taking care not to slip as the ground began to slope downwards. An army of bushes had gathered in the central section of the woods, impossible to see through or over. Coils of bramble snatched at his clothes and gouged his skin, harder to get past than barbed wire.

"Get off," he muttered. "Got enough bloody holes in my suit."

He cut to the left to avoid the worst of them, and here he stopped, because past the stench of mulch and rot he caught a whiff of something else, something worse. He sniffed, trying to work out if he'd imagined it, or if he was just smelling himself.

"Bingo," he said when he found it again, the unmistakeable smell of something dead.

He followed his nose through the maze of bushes, stopping again a few minutes later—not for a smell this time, but for a sound. It was low enough that he thought it might be a jet passing overhead, then he took another step and the sound settled into a distinctive, wet growl.

"Coming from over there, sir," said Connell. It might have been the light in the woods, but she looked ashen. She nodded to a wall of vegetation maybe ten feet from where they stood. "Maybe we *should* wait for animal control."

Baird licked his lips, wondering if she was right. After a moment, he took a step forward, then hesitated again.

"There are absolutely, one hundred per cent no wolves in Suffolk?" he asked. "You're sure?"

"I *was* sure, sir," she said. "Until just now."

"Right."

He waited a moment more, listening to the snarl of whatever was waiting for them behind the bushes. There was no mistaking its tone for anything other than a dire warning: *turn around and go away, or I'm going to eat you.*

"Do you want to go first?" he asked. "Seeing how you love dugs."

"No thank you," she replied. "You should go. As the senior officer."

"Senior officer in *Scotland*," he said. "We're in England. So technically, you're the boss right now."

The growl broke off, replaced by a furious chomping sound.

"I'm really not, *sir*," she said. "I think you should go. Lead by example."

"I caught the pig."

"Exactly. You're great at catching animals."

Baird groaned in resignation as he started walking again. He scooped up a branch as he went. It was rotten, and powdery, and the tip fell off when he swept it back and forth, but there was no time to replace it because the monster in the bushes was growling again.

Growling and *moving*.

Leaves rustled, branches shaking as it pushed through them. Baird froze, lifting the log, the electric taste of fear sitting at the back of his throat.

Something exploded from the bushes, fast enough that the scream was out of Baird's mouth before he could stop it. The creature ran right for them, barking furiously—a blur of wild eyes and sharp teeth. He couldn't make any sense of what it was, but it looked like it wanted to rip out his throat.

The only real mercy was that it was about the size of a shoe.

"Chihuahua!" squealed Connell.

The dog skidded to a halt when it heard her voice, planting its legs in the dirt and trying to make itself look as big as it was possible to be. It was barking its head off, each high-pitched yip making Baird's ears ring. He wasn't sure he'd ever seen an uglier dog. Chihuahuas weren't exactly nature's poster boys, but this one looked like it had been through a mincer and then Pritt-sticked back together again. Its fur was so matted it might have been wearing another, even less fortunate Chihuahua as a blanket, a pink collar around its neck. One rage-filled eye glared at Baird and Connell, the other bulged in an entirely different direction, as if it had a bone to pick with the pigeons overhead. Its underbite made it look like some kind of horror movie gremlin, and its yellow teeth suggested it smoked at least thirty cigarettes a day.

"Jesus Christ," said Baird, grimacing. "I think I'd have preferred a wolf."

Connell pushed past him, ducking down a few feet from the dog and opening her arms.

"Who's a gorgeous boy?" she said, making *coochie-coochie* noises. "Who's a handsome man? Who's a cutey-wutey?"

"No this fella for sure," Baird muttered.

The dog stopped barking, cocking its oddly shaped head. The growl was back in its throat, but it was gentler now, unsure. It scratched at the dirt, its poor excuse for a tail tucked between its scrawny back legs.

"Oh you poor little muffin," said Connell. She patted her thighs. "Come here. Come on. Come to mamma."

The dog's face twisted with confusion, its brow furrowing. A tiny pink tongue appeared, running over its teeth. Its good eye studied Connell, then Baird, like it had never seen a human being before.

"Don't worry about him," said Connell. "He's Scottish."

The dog answered with another bark.

"I know," she said, as if she was speaking to a baby. "He *is* a grump. He's a big grouchy grump."

"Can you stop bad-mouthing me to the dug, Connie," he said, lobbing his branch into the undergrowth.

Connell held out a hand, flapping her fingers. The Chihuahua eyeballed it for a few seconds and skittered over, its nose twitching. It gave her a few delicate sniffs, but it must have liked what it smelled because it began butting its head against her trousers, snuffling contentedly. Connell uttered a genuine laugh of delight, scratching the dog's matted fur until it flopped over onto its back, its chicken legs jutting upwards and jiggling like it was having some kind of medical episode. She turned her attention to its scabby belly.

"Oh you are adorable," she said, checking the collar. It was glittery, a little plastic tag hanging from it shaped like the letter D. "Doesn't say who the owner is. You want a tickle, sir?"

"No in any way, shape or form," said Baird. "Just make sure it disnae run off."

He skirted around them both, heading for the bushes where the dog had been hiding. There was no way he was getting through the dense foliage, so he cut to the side, tripping all the way. The smell of something dead was stronger now, but it might have been the dog. The animal did look like it had been run over and buried and brought back to life.

Twice.

As it turned out, it wasn't the dog, because ten seconds later, Baird pushed between the edge of the bush and a tree and saw the corpse.

"Crivens," he said, because he couldn't think of anything else to say.

The body had been tied to the trunk of an enormous oak tree, draped in robes that had perhaps once been white but which were now drenched with blood. It wasn't hard to see where the injuries had come from. A dozen or so long, black arrows protruded from the body, most of them impaled in the torso but more still in the arms and the legs.

Only the head had been untouched by this assault, and the main reason for that was it wasn't there any more. Somebody had removed it with force, replacing it with a circle carved viciously into the bark of the tree. Baird's skin crawled like he'd stepped on a nest of ants, his teeth chattering as the full horror of what he was looking at began to register.

The world suddenly tilted beneath a tidal wave of nausea, the sensation knocking him off balance. He reached out, grabbing the bush and instantly recoiling as the brambles bit into the flesh of his palm.

"Bastard," he hissed, pulling back. He looked away from the body for long enough to find his composure.

Long enough for Connell to catch up to him too.

"Oh my God, sir," she said as she staggered out from the bush. She had the Chihuahua in her arms, its trembling body clutched to her chest, its eyes bulging. It seemed happy enough to be there, straining its head up in an effort to lick her chin.

"Dinnae look too closely, Connie," he told her, pushing his fist against his mouth as another wash of sickness rode through him.

"Why?" she said, and he was about to answer when she carried on, covering the dog's eyes with one hand. "Why would anybody do that to a person? It's... that poor man."

"Listen, can you go find the others?" he said. "Tell them we caught the wolf, send them over."

Connell stared into the woods, which seemed to have grown darker even in the time they'd been standing here.

"Hurry now," Baird said. "The body's no getting any fresher."

She still didn't move, hugging the dog even tighter.

"The killer's long gone," he said. "You'll be safe enough."

She finally turned to him, the answer written in her expression.

"You dinnae ken the way back, do you?" he said.

"Sorry, sir. I'm no good with directions and stuff."

He pointed past the bush.

"That way, just keep walking."

Connell frowned, but she did as she was told, disappearing around the side of the bush to his left. Baird waited until her footsteps and her muttered curses had faded, then he turned back to the body. Some trick of the shifting light made it seem as though the dead man was closer now, as if the tree had pulled up its roots and scuttled towards him while he wasn't looking. He could see the body in more detail, every horror picked out in the golden light that trickled down from the canopy. Those robes, bound tight around his body and secured there with rope, leaving only his lower legs and his forearms visible. Bare feet. Hairy fingers. A tarnished wedding ring. The stump of his neck, a frill of severed skin and a nubbin of yellow bone.

Baird doubled up, making a growl of his own deep inside his throat.

"Bastard," he said again, quietly.

There was a crack to his right, loud enough to shake the bones from his body. He snapped upright, seeing a shape lumbering through the undergrowth. He had his hands up to defend himself before he realised it was Connell. She took a few more steps then stopped in shock, staring at him.

"Wait, how did you get here so quickly?" she said. "And *him*?"

She nodded over the quivering dog to where the dead man rested against his tree.

"We've no moved, Connie," he told her. "Try again."

Her frown deepened, and she vanished back around the bush.

Baird took a breath of stagnant air before turning to the corpse. There was no breeze here at all, no hint of movement in the clothes it wore, or the feathered tips of the arrows. It could have been a painting, and there was something in the display that made him think of a mural in a church. He couldn't work out why.

Another cracked twig, the rustle of leaves from deeper in the woods. He thought it might be Connell again until he heard her voice calling out from the other direction. He shivered, suddenly cold despite the heat. He'd told Connell the killer was long gone, but he didn't know that for sure. Somebody could be watching him right now, they could be drawing the string of their bow back, an arrowhead gleaming.

They could be sharpening the blade of their axe, ready to remove his head.

He held his ground for all of five seconds, then he scuttled around the bush.

"Connie?" he called out as he went, grateful that there was nobody else here. "Connie! Hold up, I'm coming with you."

CHAPTER FOUR

TWENTY MINUTES LATER, AND REASSURED BY THE presence of half a dozen uniformed constables, Baird stood in the same clearing watching Fred and Declan as they investigated the headless dead. Connell had elected to stay in an IRV with the little dog, who had definitely taken a liking to her.

The mood was uneasy, the coppers clustered together beneath the praying Mantis limbs of the oak tree, speaking in whispers. Nobody seemed to want to look at the corpse, but nobody could take their eyes off it, either. You didn't expect to see this kind of violence in the heart of London, or Glasgow, or Aberdeen, even when the gangs were at war.

Here, with the Suffolk coast a stone's throw away and the tourists already arriving for quaint, mid-spring holidays, it was unthinkable.

"Well," said Declan, who was leaning as close to the corpse as it was possible to get without planting a kiss on it. "He's definitely dead."

"Aye," said Baird, gesturing to his own head. "I mean,

he's missing all this bit, with the mouth and the eyes and the... brain."

"Indeed," said Fred, scratching his scalp. "The entire cranium and everything down to the..."

He cleared his throat, taking a step closer.

"I'd say the third cervical vertebrae."

"You think that's how he died?" asked Baird. "The heid bit?"

"It could have been the arrows," said Declan. "Did you notice them?"

Baird glared at the back of the young man's head, then at the forest of arrows that jutted from the corpse.

"*Arrows*? Jings, Declan, you're right. I'm no sure how I missed them."

Declan was oblivious to his sarcasm, gesturing to the feathered shafts that jutted from the corpse.

"Twelve of them in the body," said Fred. "Three more in the tree."

"And more back there," Declan added, jutting a thumb past the oak. "I found two, presumably the ones that missed their target. Although I'm not sure *how* they missed. Judging by the angle, the killer fired from about fifteen feet away."

He looked past Baird's shoulder.

"A little way back from where you are now."

Baird retreated carefully across the clearing, careful not to step on anything that looked like it might have been a footprint.

"His vestments are drenched in blood, and the ground too," said Fred. "It could have been from the decapitation, of course, but the markings on his skin where the arrows made entry make me fairly certain he was alive when he was shot. They're broadheads, designed for maximum damage. I'll have to get him onto my table, of course, to know the full truth."

"How long's he been deid?"

"My guess, in this weather..." Fred sucked on it for a second or two. "No more than twelve hours."

Baird checked his watch to see that it was coming up for midday.

"So midnight, then."

"Give or take, as always."

"We're pretty far away from the road," said Baird. "Screams probably wouldnae carry. But this place is popular, right? Folk come here for that book thing."

"*The Court of Avalonia*," said Declan with what might have been a wistful sigh.

"You are a fellow Avalonian?" said Fred. "Team Vy'A-gare or Team Gavé Escon?"

"You look like you could use both," muttered Baird.

"Gavé Escon, of course," said Declan. "Law and order must prevail."

There was a fair amount of undergrowth in this part of the woods, and it had clearly been trampled repeatedly. Baird stopped next to a circle of dirt, pulling out his phone and shining the light on it. The dusty ground was strewn with twigs and pebbles. Nobody had left a print.

"And what about you, Baird?" said Fred. "As a Scotsman, I imagine you would side with the Wild Man of the woods. Or perhaps you support Ven Tolin, with his cavalier brigands and his gay pirates?"

"Aye," he said. "Gay pirate. That's me all over. Anyone found any footprints?"

"You won't, in this weather," said Declan. "It's been dry for a couple of weeks."

Baird stood up, a sudden head rush almost making him lose his balance.

"Can you check our deid man's clothes, Dec?"

"Only if Fred says it's okay," he said.

"Fred says it's okay," said Fred.

Declan wandered to the edge of the clearing, opening his satchel. Somebody was humming their way through the trees from the other direction, and Baird turned to see Connell on her way over.

"How's your wee pal?" he asked.

"Oh, she, uh, weed."

She gestured miserably to her suit. There was a damp patch on her crotch, and when she arrived next to him the smell of urine was almost overpowering.

"You're sure it was the dug?" he asked.

"Yes!" she exclaimed, her face turning red. "I don't know how she had so much inside her. There must have been a gallon, it was coming out like a fire hose, spraying everywhere. By the time I got her out of the car... Urgh!"

She demonstrated with her hands, then slapped them wetly to her sides.

"Do we know anything about our victim?"

"Only that somebody didnae like him very much," said Baird. He pointed to the place where the killer had probably stood. "Watch your feet."

Declan was on his way back over, holding a steel tray. He passed it to Fred, then used his gloved hands to explore the dead man's robes.

"He's wearing some kind of dressing gown," he commented as he went. "An expensive one. It's pulled cotton, and I can see the loops for the belt. No belt, of course, just rope. He's, uh..."

There was a sticky sound as he pulled one side of the

robe away from the man's skin. Baird took the opportunity to look away, staring into the treetops. There was a buzz inside his skull that sounded like broken machinery.

"Definitely a he," said Declan. "*Most* definitely. Look, Fred."

"Oh!" said Fred as he leaned in to crotch level. "Glorious."

They ummed and ahhed a little, as if they were studying a famous piece of art.

"Anything else?" asked Baird.

"Quite a few greys down there, and a fair bit of testicular hangage," Declan said.

"Testicular *what*?" said Baird.

"How dangly his danglies are. We all know we get less firm with age. I'd estimate him to be somewhere from forty to fifty."

"From his danglies?"

"It's a fair assessment," Fred chimed in. "Mine just about brush against my knees these days."

"No, Fred!" said Baird, resisting the urge to put his hands to his ears. "Bad Fred. What else, Declan?"

"He's circumcised."

"Anything that isnae related to his todger?"

"It's very swollen," said Fred, and Baird was about to scream when the old man continued. "His torso, I mean. The swelling around his left side suggests his body was trying to repair the damage done by the arrows. He was definitely alive as he was being shot and..."

He pressed gently against the rubbery flesh of the dead man.

"I don't think it was a quick affair," he went on. "The attack might have lasted hours. See here, and here. There are more wounds on the body than there are arrows, which suggests that the killer ripped several of their missiles free *after* they'd entered, and then used them again."

He put his fingers to his nose, inhaling deeply. Then he offered the same hand to Declan, who indulged with a delicate sniff.

"Savlon," said the younger of the men. "Disinfectant. Somebody treated the wounds."

"Wait, somebody was trying to help him?" said Baird.

"Either that, or they were trying to draw out his death," said Connell, her face miserable. "Keep him alive so he'd spend longer in agony."

"A wee bit of Savlon wouldnae do much, would it? No when you've got a dozen arrows in you. And no heid."

"It would have stung like a bitch, though," said Declan. "We all know how bad it is when you put Savlon on a papercut. It's like acid."

"No sure I've ever Savloned a paper cut," said Baird. "But I ken what you mean. Anything in his pockets?"

Declan returned to the corpse, his arms out and his fingers twitching like a Dickensian tea leaf. He peered into the first pocket of the robe, then reached in for a rummage. When his hand emerged again, it held the core of a small, Cox-like apple.

"The core of an apple," he said, waiting for Fred to hold out the tray before placing it there. "Small. Probably a Cox."

Baird breathed out a long, impatient sigh as Declan went back in. He pulled out an empty purple and orange wrapper that was immediately recognisable as a Double Decker.

"One chocolate bar wrapper," he said. "From a—"

"Double Decker, aye," said Baird. "It's been eaten. What else."

"From a Double Decker," Declan went on, speaking even more slowly than he normally did. "It has been..."

"Eaten."

"Almost entirely..."

"Eaten."

"Consumed," said Declan, the corner of his mouth twitching into a smile. "There are a few crumbs left."

He popped the wrapper on the tray, pulling out another wrapper, this one golden.

"Crunchie!" barked Baird.

"One wrapper for a..."

Declan proceeded to tease the paper back into shape, taking his time.

"Crunchie," he said after a moment.

"You're gonna be getting a bloody Crunchie in a second, Declan," Baird said through gritted teeth. "Or at least that's the noise they'll make when my shoe makes contact."

Declan added the wrapper to the pile, returning to the same pocket. In an effort to stop the white-hot mess of his fury from leading to another murder, Baird turned to Connell instead.

"You ever seen anything like this, Connie? The arrows, the missing head?"

"It's funny you should ask, sir," she said. "I had a bit of a revelation on the way back from the car. I *have* seen something like this."

"Aye?"

"One Kit-Kat," Declan droned on. "A two-finger. Plastic wrapper, not foil. Consumed."

"Yes," said Connell, frowning at him. "There was a case a while ago, almost identical to this. Edward, I think his name was. He was tied to a tree and shot with arrows."

"You serious?" said Baird.

"It doesn't end there, sir. His head was cut off after the whole arrow thing."

"What?"

"They found it a little while later in the woods, being guarded by a wolf."

"Hang on... *what*?"

"And get this..."

She leaned in, speaking softly.

"It was still talking."

"The heid?" said Baird.

"No, sir, the *head*. It was still talking when they found it, calling for help." She adopted a ghostly warble. "'I'm here,' it said. 'I'm here! I'm here!'"

"Right," said Baird, who had no idea what else to say.

"It wasn't Edward," said Fred from beside the tree. "It was Edmund."

"That's it!" said Connell. "Edmund."

"Like Noel Edmonds?" said Baird, who felt once again like he might be dreaming.

"No, Saint Edmund," said Connell. "It was a little while ago."

Baird rubbed his face, pressing his fingers into his eyes.

"By a little while ago, Connie, do you mean a hundred years?"

"It was over a thousand," said Fred. "Somewhere around the ninth century."

"Right," Baird said again. "Helpful."

"It doesn't matter when it happened, sir," said Connell. "This guy, whoever he is, was murdered in the same way Edmund was. He wasn't strangled. He wasn't stabbed. He was tied up and shot with arrows, then somebody hacked his head off. Even if it's not the same killer—"

"No the same killer that offed Edmund a millennium ago?" said Baird.

"Then it's the same message," Connell finished. "Our murderer is a history buff, or a religious obsessive."

Baird nodded.

"That's actually pretty good, Connie," he said. "Well done."

Connell beamed.

"But it's no enough to figure out who this man is, and why somebody wanted him dead."

"This might help," said Declan.

The young man was holding up a small plastic card that he'd pulled from the dead guy's pocket. It looked like a credit card, but Baird couldn't see anything written on it.

"One key card," Declan went on.

"Really?" said Baird. "Where's it for?"

"From a hotel," Declan went on, studying the card intensely.

"Which hotel?"

"It's damaged," he said. "A crease in the middle, as if it's been folded in two, and it's taken a beating."

"Speaking of which," growled Baird, storming over.

Declan shrieked, holding the card out for Baird to see. There was a single word written there in ornate, flowery script.

"Denton's?" said Baird. "What's that?"

There was no missing Connell's groan of irritation.

"It'll take too long to explain, sir," she said, turning around and marching out of the clearing. "Just follow me."

CHAPTER FIVE

Southwold was buzzing in the afternoon heat, the streets full to bursting. Mobs of eager visitors crowded the shops like brightly dressed undead, pawing at the window displays and leaving trails of ice cream in their wake. Frustrated locals did their best to move through the town unimpeded, spilling off the pavements into the road, shouting at the cars that passed too close. For a little place, Southwold was making a lot of noise, and Connell had to lean on the horn more than once.

"Silly season has well and truly begun," she said.

In the back, the little Chihuahua barked her agreement. She was lying on a pile of old clothes and blankets that Connell had pulled out of the boot, quivering and fidgeting like a wind-up toy. Animal control still hadn't arrived when they'd left the woods, so Connell being Connell, she'd offered to take the dog with her. Baird had objected, of course, but it had been two against one.

The smell of the creature was eye-wateringly bad, and Baird was certain it had peed again. Not that it would have been visible in the rubbish dump that was the back of Connell's car.

"I'm pretty sure there are rules against transporting wild animals in your vehicle, pal," he said. "First piggy this morning, and then *pissy* here."

"She's not called Pissy, sir," said Connell. "I'm going to call her Diana until we know her real name."

"Diana?"

"Because of her collar. The D. And she looks like a princess."

Diana barked again, her eyes bulging in two different directions. There was a string of drool hanging from her lips.

"Aye, I can see the resemblance, now you mention it," said Baird. "Pure elegance."

"I'm just going to swing by my place," she said. "Get out of these clothes."

"Good plan."

"You want to stop at yours, too? Get changed?"

Baird looked at his suit, at the hole in his crotch, and shook his head.

"It'll only get dirty again."

"What about food? I'm a little peckish."

"You're hungry because you give your body nothing but heavy cream and sugar," said Baird. "It's crying oot for some vegetables."

"Fortunately, I know a little boutique place that does vegetable-based desserts," said Connell without missing a beat. "They use sweet potatoes instead of butter in their cakes, if you can believe it."

"I dinnae *want* to believe it," he said, and when her face fell, he added, "maybe when we're on the way back. I know one headless guy who wouldnae want us to dally. Where is this place we're going, anyway?"

Connell groaned again, the same noise she'd made in the woods.

"Denton's," she said, swerving to avoid another tourist. "It's a hotel and a private members' club, full of..."

"*Members*," said Baird. "Aye, I know the type. Posh knobs?"

"Not posh, definitely knobs. Carl Denton used to work for—"

"Och, dinnae say the Keebles, Connie," said Baird. "For the love of God, dinnae say that name."

She slowed down at a junction, indicating right.

"I mean, I won't say it if you really don't want me to. But yeah, them."

It was Baird's turn to groan. He'd met the Keebles already: Suffolk's most dangerous crime family—or at least they had been, until a bust had put away Ma Keeble and her two oldest sons. The third son, Tommy, and his daughter Sophie, had been right at the centre of his previous case.

"Carl never really got inside Ma Keeble's inner ring," Connell went on.

"Yuck," said Baird.

"That was too dirty even for Denton."

"What?"

"And far too tight for just anyone to slide into."

"Connie!"

She turned right, accelerating away from the main street, oblivious.

"But he was in the outer circle for sure. We suspect Ma Keeble used his place to launder the money from the drugs. It's not just the hotel, he's got a string of businesses across Suffolk, all cash, all under different companies, and all run by patsies. He used to run brothels, too, although he seems to have moved on from that in the last few years."

"You've arrested him?"

"Of course, but there's never anything to tie him to the operations. We'd build up a case on one of his employees and bring them in, but then nobody talks, and Denton denies all knowledge. If we throw them in prison, somebody else takes control of the operation and we have to start all over again. Denton's American, he's ex-army, an ex-boxer, and he's loud. He makes things quite unpleasant. He's clever, too, keeps everything at arm's length, and always somebody else's arm."

"He the sort of fella to cut a man's heid off?"

She thought about it for a little while.

"We've never found anything to suggest he's a killer. His hands are dirty, but it's ink, not blood."

"As long as it's no Ma Keeble's stinky ring," he muttered.

Diana let him know she felt the same way with a high-pitched bark from the back.

They stopped for ten minutes at Connell's flat so she could change into an identical shapeless grey suit, then they headed out of town. Slowly, the gaps between the little cottages widened to reveal glimpses of wide fields and, past them, the silver line of the sea. It was only just visible over the undulating land, but it was still reassuring.

That's your sea, Harrison.

Proof that at any second he could head north, go home.

He felt suddenly air starved and forced himself to breathe deeply, the world outside the car burning bright, like the sun had just exploded into a supernova. He rubbed his eyes again, feeling the itch of hay fever and the exhaustion of simply being alive.

"That's it up ahead," said Connell.

He opened his eyes, following her finger to see a slim, grey tower protruding from the woods on the side of the road. It had to be seven storeys tall, with a bulbous top that made Baird think of a thumb hit by a hammer.

"It's an old water tower," she explained. "Edwardian, I think. We've got a couple of them in town. Denton bought the old house round the back of this place back in the Noughties and converted the tower into apartments. It's the height of luxury."

"You've stayed?"

"Oh, sure," said Connell. "I turned up one day with Tom Hardy in my limousine and we got the top floor."

She snorted, slapping the wheel hard enough to make the car wobble.

"Bit out of a DC's salary, sir. Last I checked it was almost a thousand pounds a night, and that's just the rooms in the house."

There was a sign ahead, mounted on the crumbling wall of the estate: the same floral font as on the room key. *Denton's*. Connell indicated again, even though there wasn't another car in sight, then she pulled the Fiat off the road onto a tree-lined track. It wound towards a red-brick Tudor mansion that was bigger than Baird had been expecting. The grounds were mostly wooded, but lengths of perfectly manicured grass kept the gangs of trees apart, and numerous flowerbeds boasted impressive displays of colour. A handful of groundsmen kept themselves busy with hedge trimmers and lawnmowers, none of them looking up.

"Nice to see a criminal doing well for themselves, eh?" he muttered as Connell pulled into a gravel car park full of Mercedes and Porsches. "About time one of them got a break."

Before Connell could find a space, somebody came running out of the house's front door. They were wearing what looked like a valet's uniform, black trousers, a grey shirt, and a lurid red waistcoat that was so distracting it took Baird a moment to realise he knew the man.

"Hang on," he said, squinting. "Is that no your pal?"

"Oh yeah!" said Connell, opening her door and getting out. "Headcold Pauly!"

Diana sprung to her feet on the back seat, yipping her head off—each bark like a gunshot.

"Hey!" Baird said. "Enough."

The chihuahua leapt between the chairs, scrabbling onto his lap, her feet like needles as she trampled over his crotch.

"Och, enough!" he said again, hoiking her up. She was as light as a sock full of feathers, but wriggling so much he almost lost his grip. He held her to his chest, feeling the warm spread of drool through his shirt.

At least, he hoped it was drool.

"I thought I recognised the car," said Pauly as he walked over. Incredibly, he still looked like he was choked with the cold, his top lip caked with snot. A bumbag hung loosely from his waist, bouncing against his crotch as he walked. "Alright Connie?"

Baird offered a nod from inside the car. He'd had the misfortune of being acquainted with Headcold Pauly on his last case. He'd been wearing the bumbag then, too, and he'd thought it was full of cocaine until the man had admitted it was sherbet.

Pauly walked over to his open window, leaning in far too close.

"Who's the ugly little fella?" he said.

"DI Harrison Baird," said Connell. "You remember him?"

"I meant the dog," said Pauly, using the back of his hand to wipe away the snot. He pushed the same hand through the door in order to pet the dog, and Baird almost screamed.

"This is Diana," said Connell. "You recognise her?"

"No." Pauly gave the dog's head a firm massage, making her eyes almost pop clean out of their sockets. He glanced at Baird. "He's still 'ere then."

"Aye, it's hard to leave when everyone's so friendly."

"Eh?" said Pauly, his face gurning into a look of confusion. "What's he saying? Not learned English yet, I take it."

"I wouldnae put English in ma mouth if I was starving, Pauly," he said. "What're you doing here?"

"Huh?" said the man, looking to Connell for a translation.

"Why are you here?" she said.

Pauly broke into an enormous grin, resting his hands on the bumbag.

"Got a job," he said. "Head parking geezer. Denton gave it to me himself."

Diana had settled a little, her body vibrating even though it was roasting in the car park. Baird pulled his jacket around her to keep her warm, and she poked her face right out again, her little tongue squirming past her overbite.

"Pauly," said Connell, "I may be wrong. I *hope* I'm wrong. But haven't you lost your driving licence?"

The man's face began to turn puce, a bubble of snot popping out of one nostril. He scrubbed it away.

"No," he said. "You must be thinking of a different Pauly. There's hundreds of us."

"A different Pauly who drove his mum's car onto the

beach last winter, off his face on cold medicine and vodka, and left it there for the tide to carry away?" said Connell.

"Absolutely not me," he said, licking his lips. He glanced at the hotel. "Please don't say nuffink. You owe me, Connie. Besides, this is private land, you don't need a licence to drive here."

"That disnae quite work if you've been banned, pal," said Baird.

The dog barked, deepening Pauly's confusion.

"What did it just say?"

"She agrees with me," said Baird.

"Please," said Pauly, clasping his hands together as he looked at Baird, and then Connell, and then finally the little dog. "If Denton finds out he'll have me knackers off. I need this job, Connie. Sherbet's not cheap."

"You're still talking about actual sherbet, aye?"

"He here?" Connell said.

"Dent? Yeah, I think so. Probably in his sex dungeon."

"His *what*?" said Baird.

"I don't know what it is. In the basement, he's always down there with the birds. He won't want visitors."

"He won't mind me," said Connell. "I'm a bird. Come on, sir."

Baird got out of the car, still holding the dog. He didn't want to leave her, because technically she was evidence. Connell threw the Fiat keys at Pauly, who missed them entirely, scrabbling to pick them up from the gravel.

"I won't talk to Denton about you as long as you talk to me about him," Connell said. Pauly's brow furrowed as he tried to work out what she was saying. "Park it in the shade, mate."

He beetled towards the Fiat, diving into the driver's seat before Connell changed her mind.

"You might want to pinch your nose," she said. "Smells a bit in there."

"That man hasnae been able to smell anything for years," said Baird. "You could crack a vial of smelling salts under that nose and he wouldnae even blink."

Connell was heading for the door, and another young man opened it for them. He was wearing the same awful uniform, a nametag pinned to his red waistcoat: *Chris*. Baird nodded his thanks as he entered a large lobby, complete with an enormous staircase that led to the first floor. Half a dozen wingback chairs sat next to mahogany tables, a couple of them occupied by well-dressed men in their fifties who were engrossed in their newspapers. The smell of good coffee hung in the air, and he followed it to the grand reception desk on the far side of the room.

A woman looked up from her computer when she heard them, dressed the same as the others. The name badge on her shirt said *Tracey*. Her smile lasted for as long as it took her to see Diana, then it fell right off her face. Baird could see the gears of her brain trying to figure out what she was looking at.

"Oh..." she started, and the dog loosed a couple of barks.

"Oh is right," said Baird, patting Diana's lumpy head to calm her.

"Who... *what*? I'm really sorry, we don't allow... dogs?"

"She's no a dug, Tracey," said Baird. "She's a witness. And we're polis."

The woman stared at him in confusion, studying his filthy suit. Connell pulled out her warrant card and laid it on the desk.

"Police," she said. "I'm DC Constance Connell. This is DI Harrison Baird, and this is Diana."

Diana loosed another bark that almost made the woman leap out of her seat. She put a hand to her chest.

"It's leaking," she said, studying the line of spit that was hanging from the dog's mouth.

"Aye, Tracey, oot of both ends, which is why we should do this quickly rather than slowly. You recognise the dug?"

"Dug?"

"Dog," translated Connell as she returned her warrant card to her pocket. "Have you seen it in the hotel before?"

The woman shook her head, although she still didn't seem convinced she was looking at a real animal. Connell pulled out an evidence bag containing the key card they'd found on the dead man.

"This is one of yours, isn't it?"

Tracey looked at it with equal confusion. Baird wondered if she'd forgotten to put on her glasses.

"A key card, for a door," Connell explained, tapping the card with her finger. "It says Denton's, right there."

"Well, yes," said Tracey. "Denton's. I see it. It's one of ours."

"You mind telling me who it belongs to?"

"Uh, I really shouldn't say anything without, uh..." She glanced at a door behind her, but there was nobody there to help. "I should probably call for Mr Denton."

"In his sex dungeon," said Baird.

Tracey opened her mouth, trying to find a reply.

"You call him," said Connell, heading around the desk. "We'll just have a little shufti at the old computer."

"Uh..." said Tracey. "Can you just wait a second?"

Diana trembled in Baird's arms, making a noise that sounded like a kazoo inside a blender. She was contorting herself to try to escape, stretching towards the desk, and he barely had time to wonder what she was doing before she sneezed. The substance that came out of her nose had to have been some kind of ectoplasm, a bright green projectile that wobbled through the air and hit Tracey right in the neck.

He'd never seen the colour drain out of somebody so quickly.

"Oh, God," she said, frozen in terror. "Oh, I think I felt it on me. Is it on me? Something's on me, isn't it?"

"I cannae see anything," said Baird, trying not to look at the blob of mucus as it rolled towards her collarbone.

"I'm going to go now," she said. "I can take the... animal, too. I'll put her in the cloakroom until you've spoken with Mr Denton."

She reached out for the dog, and Diana tried to lick her fingers like she hadn't eaten in a month.

"I'll hang onto her for now," said Baird. "You may want to find a tissue. Maybe a towel."

Tracey walked away, managing to keep her composure until she was halfway across the lobby. Only then did she break into a run. Baird waited until she'd vanished through a door before following Connell around the desk. He gave the dog a gentle pat on the head.

"Good work, Diana. That was ingenious."

The chihuahua licked his fingers, cross eyed with pleasure.

"All polis should get one of these," he went on as Connell woke up the computer. "Perfect for clearing crime scenes, and firing projectiles at the bad guys."

He gave the dog a squeeze with his elbow, and she sneezed again.

"It's brilliant!"

He peeked into the small office that sat behind the reception desk. There was another door in the far wall, half open. Baird couldn't see anything other than darkness inside, but there was a hell of a breeze pouring through.

"Wait, that can't be right," said Connell.

She'd pulled the key card from the evidence bag, holding it by the edges in order to tap it against the reader. When Baird joined her at the desk, there was a name on the screen. She tried again and the same name flashed up.

"Gregory Brightwell," said Baird. "Why does that ring a bell?"

Connell put the card back in the bag, scrolling down the page of information. There was an address, as well as a phone number. The dates of his stay were next.

"He checked in on Wednesday," said Connell. "Not due to check out again until next Thursday. He's staying alone."

"Or he's the only one on the booking," said Baird. "What room's he in?"

"The Heron Suite."

"Then let's check it oot, before Snotty McGee comes back."

CHAPTER SIX

"You've really never watched *Cry Me a River*, sir?"

Denton's hotel was even bigger than it had looked from outside, and Baird and Connell were already lost. They'd climbed the enormous central staircase and turned left, quickly finding themselves in a maze of red-carpeted, mahogany-panelled hallways that seemed to have been designed by Mobius. There were plenty of rooms, and they were all numbered, but there was no sign of anything that might have been a luxury suite.

"No, Connie, I've no seen that one."

"*Bastion's Heartbreak*?"

There was a sharp bark from the chihuahua in Baird's arms.

"Diana's watched that one, but no me."

Another bark.

"She says it was shite."

Connell frowned, using the key card to unlock a heavy fire door and her body weight to shunt it open. Beyond was another corridor, which eventually led to a smaller staircase leading up. Another red-waistcoated member of staff passed them, his eyes so firmly fixed on the dog that he almost tripped over his own feet.

"He was in that series about Pompeii, did you see that?" said Connell as they made their way up to the second floor, passing an impressive suit of armour at the top of the steps. "He played the hunky Roman guy. I can't remember his name. He was naked most of the time."

She made a noise that might have been a giggle, then she shook her head.

"God, I hope it isn't him."

"Maybe if you show me a photie," said Baird. "I cannae remember where I've heard the name. Geoffrey Brightwell."

"*Gregory* Brightwell."

"Aye, that's what I said. You sure it's the same man?"

"He's huge, sir," said Connell, opening a door and entering another stretch of corridor.

"Aye, I was there when Freclan were investigating it."

"No. Ew, gross. I mean, like, Hollywood huge. But he's still local. You see him in Southwold sometimes, although he's not really one for a chat. He gets mobbed if the fans find out he's out and about."

"Can you tell if he's our dead man?"

"Not without his head, sir. Although, like you say, the... uh... other parts looked familiar."

"Christ."

"Oh, look, sir, that must be it."

The door she'd stopped next to didn't have anything written on it, but it did have an etching of a long, slim bird.

"Heron," she said.

"Are you sure?" Baird asked, leaning in. "Looks more like a penguin to me."

"Ah yes, sir, the famous Suffolk penguins. That's a heron, look at it. Long neck, long legs. Heron."

"I'll take your word for it. The card."

She passed the card to him, which had been touched so many times now he didn't think it was even worth checking for prints, and he tapped it on the reader. The light turned green, the lock disengaging.

"Heron," she said, with a decisive nod.

Baird turned the handle and pushed, but the door only opened an inch or so before snapping to a halt. He peered through the gap to see a security chain in place. He couldn't make out anything else except darkness, the curtains closed.

"Somebody must be in there if the lock's on," he said, tucking the key card into his wallet so he wouldn't lose it. He cleared his throat and called out. "Geoffrey?"

"Gregory."

"Och, right. Gregory? Can you open the door for us, it's the polis."

He put his ear to the gap, holding his breath—not that it made any difference, because the dog was snorting like a camel drinking from an oasis. He held the animal out like she was Simba on the clifftop.

"Here."

Connell plucked the chihuahua from his hands, doing her best to avoid her tongue as it probed at her face.

"Gregory, this is the polis," Baird said. "I'm coming in. You understand me?"

Still nothing. He took a step back, cricking his neck.

"I'm not sure we're allowed to do that, sir," said Connell.

"We are," he said. "Listen. Can you no hear that?"

He leaned in, speaking in a low, ghostly moan.

"Help me, Connie, it's Geoffrey, I'm—"

"Gregory."

"Aye, it's Gregory, and I'm in trouble, I need you to knock doon the door and assist me."

Connell gave him a stern look that he chose to ignore.

"I'm gonna count to six, pal, then I'm breaking it doon."

"Six, sir?" said Connell as he took another step back. "Why six?"

"Huh?"

"It's just usually three. Or five. Six feels a little random."

"One," said Baird, who had no idea what she was on about. "Two. Three. Four."

"Three just makes more sense," said Connell.

"Fine, *three*," said Baird, and he drove his foot into the side of the door. The pain clawed up his leg and into his back, but the chain didn't stand a chance, exploding from the frame in a detonation of splinters. The door crunched against the frame and rebounded backwards, Baird pushing past it before it could close again.

"Polis," he called out. "Nae funny business, alright?"

The room was pitch black, and when he mashed his hands on the various switches by the door nothing happened. He stumbled blindly across the room, heading in the direction of the window and cracking his shin on a coffee table.

"Argh, you walloper!" he roared, the pain unbelievable.

"Sir?" said Connell from the door. He could barely hear her over the yapping dog she was holding.

He thumped his knee on the corner of the bed, then cracked his other shin on a second coffee table. By the time he reached the curtains and ripped them open, he felt like both legs were on fire and he was about ready to pull the entire building apart brick by brick.

"What kind of muffin has two coffee tables in his hotel room?" he said, glancing through a wide-open window to a stone balcony and the hotel's back garden two stories below. "You can only drink one cup at a time."

He turned around, the room illuminated by the sun *and* by the lights, which Connell had managed to turn on by slipping a debit card into the cradle. It was an impressive space, a four poster, King-sized bed taking pride of place against the left-hand wall and a desk opposite that was almost as big as the one in reception. A wardrobe that looked like it might have led right to Narnia sat awkwardly in the corner next to an armchair. There weren't two coffee tables, there were *three*, ugly wood and iron monstrosities that had apparently been designed to double as street barricades during the French Revolution. He glared at them, mainly because there wasn't much else to glare at.

The room was empty.

"Somebody's definitely staying here," said Connell, carrying the dog into the room.

The bed had been immaculately turned over, but there was a suitcase beneath the desk and a jacket slung over the back of the chair. Two books sat on the nightstand, a four-inch-thick biography of Stalin and, even larger, a copy of *The Court of Avalonia*.

"Some coincidence," said Baird.

"Or not, sir."

He walked past the bed, heading for the bathroom door. It was unlocked, and led into a marble-clad *en suite* with not one but two baths. The walk-in shower was bigger than the kitchen in his new flat. A disposable razor and a well-chewed toothbrush sat in a cup by the sink, as well as a tube of what Baird assumed was toothpaste until he got a little closer.

"Lube," he said when Connell appeared in the doorway. "He's doing sexy stuff."

"Maybe he just has a dry mouth, sir," she said, shrugging.

"Aye, nothing fixes a dry mouth like a squirt of KY Jelly."

Baird pushed past her into the bedroom, heading for the wardrobe.

"Check the bags, Connie, will you?" he said.

"I'm not sure I should," she said.

"Geoffrey says it's fine," he told her, grabbing the handle. "He says—"

The solid wooden wardrobe door flew open, cracking him right on the bridge of the nose. He staggered back, the pain like a firework going off in his face.

"Fu—"

Somebody leapt out of the wardrobe, thumping into him like a demolition ball. He did a backflip over the coffee table, landing hard beside the bed.

"Oi!" he heard Connell shout from the *en suite* door. "Stop!"

"Argh!" he groaned, using the bed to haul himself back to his feet.

The person—a woman, he thought, with long, purple hair—was making a beeline for the window. Connell was chasing, but she still had the dog clutched in her hands, its eyes boggling with terror. Baird lumbered after them, cracking his shin on the other coffee table and practically somersaulting over it.

"Bastard!" he roared.

"Stop!" Connell yelled again.

The woman was halfway out the window, wearing jeans and a black hoodie. She glanced back at him, her face full of terror, her purple hair almost glowing in the blinding light of the day, then she dropped onto the balcony.

"Wait!" Baird gargled, back on his feet and limping after her. "We're polis, stop running!"

The woman had climbed onto the stone handrail. When she shot another look back, Baird saw that she was in her late thirties, maybe early forties. He couldn't get a good look at her face past all of the hair.

"Dinnae do it!" Baird shouted, reaching the open window and leaning out. He grabbed for her but she was too quick, leaping onto the balcony of the next room over. "I said *dinnae* do it!"

Baird looked back.

"Can you get her? I'm no a runner."

"Well *I'm* not a runner, sir," she said, gesturing at herself with her free hand.

Baird groaned.

"Then get some backup out here," he said. "And an ambulance, for God's sake. We're two floors up."

He climbed through the open window onto the balcony, the wind on his back like a hand trying to push him over the edge. He gripped the stone balustrade, telling himself not to look down and then looking down anyway, seeing the gardens forty feet beneath him.

"Nope," he said.

The woman had leapt effortlessly onto the last balcony, and she tried the window before looking back at him.

"Would you just stop?" he called out, the wind snatching his words away. "There's no place to go!"

Except there was. She leaned over the edge of the balcony, grabbing a cast iron drainpipe.

"You're gonna kill yourself!" Baird yelled. "Just *stop*!"

He braced a hand on the wall and climbed onto the balustrade, teetering there for a couple of seconds. The gap between the balconies was only about four feet, but the drop made it feel like the Grand Canyon.

"It's no worth it, Harrison," he told himself.

But the woman was descending the drainpipe with alarming speed, looking like an acrobat. She'd reach the ground before Connell got down the stairs, and then there was every chance they'd lose her.

Baird stepped over the gap, his stomach contracting, his bowels loosening—a moment of certain death before his foot connected with the balustrade of the next balcony. He dropped down, hoping nobody had heard the scream that had come out of his mouth. He crossed the balcony and scaled the handrail on the other side, feeling the wobble of loose mortar. Flakes of stone dropped earthwards, but he ignored them, making the leap and landing awkwardly.

"Ach, you jizztrumpet."

He limped to the far side of the balcony, feeling like he was about to chunder. When he leaned over, he saw the woman halfway down.

"Oi!" he shouted.

She glanced up, her face drenched in sweat and twisted by terror.

"You're in so much trouble," he said, pointing a finger at her. "Get back up here."

She kept going, pushing through the forest of ivy that grew up the side of the building, almost close enough to the ground to drop. There was still no sign of Connell.

"Unbelievable," Baird muttered, scrubbing his palms on his trousers to try to dry them out.

He got one leg over the balustrade, straddling it, hearing flakes of stone clatter to the ground below. The drainpipe was further away than he'd anticipated, and he had to lean out to grab it. The metal was rough, the girth of the pipe just right for him to get his hand around. He wedged his foot on a bracket and swung out, gripping it like a monkey at the zoo. He tried to move only for his body to lock up, paralysed by fear.

"Doon, Harrison," he ordered himself. "Towards the ground."

He lowered a leg, then a hand, then his other leg, everything scuffing and slipping. The drainpipe rattled alarmingly as he went, the screws threatening to pull out of the wall. He wondered how many years it had been since this thing had been installed, and the answer was probably centuries. The thought of it made him move even faster, and he quickly found his rhythm, crashing through the ivy.

There was a scream from below, and he looked past his own arse to see the woman in the flowerbed, sprawling backwards.

"Stay there!" he yelled.

No chance. She got to her feet and started to run, heading for the trees on the other side of the grass.

"Come on," he said.

He moved as fast as he dared, jumping the final six feet. The soft ground broke his fall, but did its best to slow him down as he chased the woman. She'd entered the treeline, surprisingly fast. *Too fast,* though, because her foot hit an exposed root and she went flying, bouncing off the trunk of a tree before hitting the dirt.

Baird sprinted as quickly as his cramping limbs would let him, making it into the trees in a handful of seconds. The woman was halfway to her feet by the time he reached her, groaning like she'd been winded. She had time to lift her head, a flash of frightened eyes past that crown of purple hair, before Baird grabbed her shirt.

"Stay still, you bawheid!" he said.

"I didn't...." she started, struggling to find the breath to speak. "I wasn't doing..."

Her head suddenly jerked to the side, looking at something behind Baird. He heard the crack of a branch, the thunder of feet.

"Enough of that!" came a booming voice, right in his ear.

Something the size of a small truck crunched into his back, hard enough to launch him off the ground. He landed hard, his wrist bending awkwardly beneath him. He tried to push himself up only to feel a knee in his spine, a hand on his neck.

"Stay down," said the voice, a growled American accent. "Or I'll make sure you never get up again."

"I'm—" he started, but the hand drove his face into the muck. Baird's ears roared, drowning out the world. He tried to push up, but the man must have been the size of a rhinoceros. "Polis!" he tried to scream, tasting soil. "Polis!"

He wasn't sure if the guy had heard him, but after a second or two the pressure left his back. Somebody grabbed his jacket and hauled him up like he was a bag of straw, and he understood why he felt like he'd been hit by a truck. The man in front of him was about seven-foot tall, and he looked like he'd been carved from a slab of dark stone. He had the squarest head Baird had ever seen, not helped by his military-style flat-top haircut, his hair black and greying at the temples. When he grinned, at least three of his teeth were gold.

"Shit, sorry buddy," he said. He used a hand the size of a shovel to brush the dirt from Baird's suit, hard enough to shatter ribs. "You good?"

Baird pulled free of the guy, taking a step back and nursing his throbbing wrist. Connell was jogging up from the house, finally, the dog still held to her chest. They both stared at him with wide, uncertain eyes.

"Are you okay, sir?" she said. "I can't believe you did that!"

He nodded, one hand to his back and one to his stomach, feeling for anything that might be broken. The other man was so broad Baird had to sidestep to see past him. He knew what he would see, though.

Or what he *wouldn't* see.

There was no sign of anyone else in the woods. The woman was gone.

"What are you doing, Carl?" said Connell.

"Didn't realise he was a—" the big man started, turning to Connell and seeing the dog. "Holy shit, what the hell is that?"

The dog barked, and Connell pulled her closer. The man turned back to Baird.

"I thought you were some sort of sex freak, pestering my guests."

"I wasnae pestering her," Baird wheezed. "I was *arresting* her."

"Oh," the man said, frowning. He scratched his head. "Whoops."

"Aye, whoops is right. Who the hell are you, anyway?"

"Sir, this is Carl Denton," said Connell. "Denton, this is DI Harrison Baird."

Denton offered a hand which Baird chose to ignore. The man pulled it back slowly, a flicker of irritation crossing his face.

"Well then, *Baird*," he said, spitting out his name like he'd swallowed a verruca in the pool. "Why don't we go inside, see if we can figure out what's going on."

CHAPTER SEVEN

THEY SAT IN A PRIVATE DINING SPACE INSIDE DENTON'S palatial club, a walnut-lined room whose mullioned windows looked out over the rear gardens where Baird had chased the woman just twenty minutes ago. A dozen red leather chairs occupied the space, looking like sunburned old men. They were surprisingly comfortable, though, and Baird was grateful for the opportunity to rest his battered body. The ache in his arms from climbing down the pipe was bad enough, the skin of his palms grazed. Worse still were the bruises that the coffee tables had left on his shins, his legs throbbing like there was a rave taking place down there.

And he still felt like he'd been in a wrestling match with a grizzly bear.

Denton *was* a bear. Even though he was well into his fifties, he was in incredible shape, his muscles bulging through his black turtleneck jumper and his grey chinos. He wore a heavy gold chain, a wedding ring resting between the slabs of his pecs like an Olympic medal. His hands were enormous, the knuckles permanently swollen from a lifetime of fighting. The only hint of weakness came when he walked. He limped on his left leg, and whenever he came to a halt he grabbed whatever was nearby in order to support his weight.

He was doing it now as he crossed the room, the briefest expression of pain on his stubbled face as he lowered himself into the chair opposite Baird. He barely fit, the leather squeaking as he adjusted his bulk. A woman in the hotel uniform walked after him, a tray in her hands, the cups clinking like she was playing a tune.

"Oh goody," said Connell, who sat in the chair to Baird's right. The dog trotted around the table, snuffling at crumbs. "Are we having cake?"

"No," said Denton. "Just tea."

Connell pouted. The waitress rested the tray onto the low table, passing out cups. Baird wondered, to his horror, if it was fruit tea, because the air was full of a sharp, citrus scent.

"Do you want me to pour, sir?" she asked as she set down the teapot and then the milk.

"No, Marie," said Denton. "You can go."

"You want me to take... *that* with me?" she asked, pulling a face at Diana.

"Leave the dug," said Baird.

Marie scuttled away without a backwards glance, closing the door behind her.

"You can have some cake when you tell me what's going on," Denton said to Connell, his voice like an angry headmaster's. He turned to Baird. "And when you explain why you were scaling down the side of my building like a fat, ugly Spider-Man."

Baird sucked in his gut.

"I'm hardly fat," he said. "And just to press the point, I wasnae assaulting anyone."

"You look homeless," said Denton. "What was I supposed to think?"

Baird glanced at his suit, which was ripped and filthy, the hole in the crotch certainly suggestive of some kind of pervert.

"That's no my fault," he said. "Blame the pig, the dug and the drainpipe."

"Huh?"

"The worst of the Narnia books," he said. "And I was climbing doon the wall because I was chasing a suspect."

They'd looked for the purple-haired woman, of course, scouring the woods and the grounds for a solid fifteen minutes until backup had arrived. There were Uniforms out there right now, still searching for her. But she must have been some kind of ninja, because as well as escaping out of the room using death-defying acrobatics, she'd managed to vanish into thin air.

"A suspect who was inside your hotel," Baird went on. "Rooting around in the room of a man we're investigating as part of a very serious crime. So how aboot *we* start with the questions, Carl?"

Denton leaned forward, the leather chair squeaking out a cry of alarm that sent Diana skittering between Baird's legs.

"You wanna explain why you were in the room without a warrant?"

"No, I dinnae. But for the record, the lass at the desk didnae say we couldnae, right Connell?"

"Uh," said Connell, struggling to remember. "I mean technically no, she didn't say we couldn't."

"And we had the key," said Baird. "And when we got to the room, we heard somebody. A voice."

He cleared his throat, catching Connell's eye. She'd gone bright red, the sweat gathering at her collar.

"Right, Connell?"

"I heard *a* voice," she said, omitting the fact that it had been Baird's.

"It sounded like an emergency," he continued. "So we broke the door doon. Your woman tried to kill me with the wardrobe, then she legged it. And the rest is history. Oh..."

He leaned forward too, close enough to Denton that the bigger man had to sit back.

"And whatever else is going on here, I feel like arresting you for those bastard coffee tables. They nearly killed me n'all."

Denton didn't comment, his sharp eyes never leaving Baird. Every movement, every word, made it clear he was a man who was used to getting his own way, a man who was used to being in control. Of course, it wasn't hard to feel that way when you looked like The Rock.

"So," said Baird, stretching his foot to try to relieve the ache in his shin. "Tell me aboot Gregory Brightwell."

The big man thought about it for a second, studying his immaculately manicured fingernails.

"I can't tell you anything you don't already know," he said. "He's one of our more distinguished guests."

"He arrived on Wednesday, aye? Due to stay until next Thursday."

That flicker of annoyance creased Denton's face again.

"You accessed our system?" he said.

"No," Baird lied. "He checked in on Wednesday?"

"I'm not sure," said Denton.

"You just said he was one of your most distinguished guests. Something tells me you welcomed him personally."

Denton lifted the teapot with sausage-sized fingers, delicately filling the three cups.

"We have a lot of celebrity guests," he said when he'd finished. "But yes, I greeted Greg when he arrived."

"He was alone?" asked Baird.

Denton nodded.

"Milk? Sugar?" he asked.

"No milk, no sugar, no tea," said Baird.

"I'll have some in mine," said Connell. "Sweet and milky, just like me."

Both men turned to her, and she frowned.

"I have no idea why I said that."

"He was alone," said Denton when they returned to the conversation. "Drove up around half four, went straight to his room. Came out for dinner about six, had it right here in the private room. Alone. Didn't see him again. As far as I know, he spent the night in his suite."

Baird waited.

"Alone," Denton added. "He's married. Melissa wasn't here, and neither was anybody else."

"You saw him on Friday?"

Denton shook his head, stirring sugar into his tea.

"I've been away on business a lot."

"What kind of business?"

"The kind you can keep your nose out of," he said, giving Baird another look, one that bordered on dangerous.

"That's the trouble with my nose, Carl," he said. "I cannae seem to keep it out of other people's shite. I must be part dug. This have anything to do with the business you used to do with Ma Keeble?"

Denton sighed.

"You wanna come at me, then come at me. I've got nothing to hide, but I've got a really good lawyer. And the first thing she's gonna ask is 'why are you harassing my client?'"

"We're harassing you, Carl, because we found a body this morning, in the woods just north of Southwold. He was wearing a dressing gown, and in the pocket was the key card we used to get into Gregory Brightwell's room. The card had a name on it, your name. Denton. That's why we're here."

The other man picked at his gold teeth, still glaring at Baird.

"It's Greg?"

"Well, that's what we'd all love to ken. But the jury's still out, because the fella we found didnae have a heid."

The confusion on Denton's face was obvious. He turned to Connell.

"Head," she translated. "He didn't have a head."

"A head?" he echoed, pointing to his own.

"Aye," said Baird. "A heid. Did Brightwell say why he was here this week? Did he mention any plans? Anyone he wanted to meet?"

Denton took a sip from his tiny cup, looking like a yeti at a child's tea party.

"No," he said. "Look, this body you found might not actually be him, correct? And I'm not going to talk about Greg or anyone else until you know for sure. We pride ourselves on our discretion, here, on our ability to keep things secret. No cameras, no questions. This is a safe space for all guests."

"It wasnae safe for him."

Denton slammed his cup down so hard that tea sloshed onto the table.

"Whatever happened to Greg, or whoever it is you found in the woods, it didn't happen here. You understand me?"

Baird nodded, giving Diana a scratch as she cowered between his legs.

"You recognise this dug?" he asked. "We found her in the woods, near the body."

Denton gave the animal a look like he'd have happily punted it out the open window.

"I'm not even sure that is a dog," he said. "We've had rodents bigger than that. And we don't allow pets in the hotel. Horrible things."

Connell gasped.

"You didnae answer the question," said Baird.

"I've never seen it before. I hope I never see it again."

"What about the woman?" asked Connell. "You must have got a look at her. Is she staying in the hotel? Does she work here? Have you ever seen her before?"

"I couldn't get a good look because *he* was on top, molesting her," said Denton.

"Wasnae—"

"And by the time I'd got him to his feet again, she was gone. As far as I know, I've never seen her. She certainly doesn't work here. I'm going to say it again, slowly, for the kids at the back. Whatever this is, it has nothing to do with me, or my hotel."

"You won't mind if we have a good look aboot, then?"

"I mind," the other man growled. "Come back with a warrant and you can do anything you like. Until then, you can kindly piss off."

He looked at Connell, then at the dog.

"All of you."

"What about CCTV?" said Baird.

"What about a warrant?"

"Guest logs?"

Denton pushed himself out of his chair, which was so tight that it clung to his buttocks for a couple of seconds before sliding off. He jabbed a finger at Baird.

"War-rant," he said, sounding it out.

Baird got up, nodding.

"Nothing says 'I'm innocent' like screaming 'warrant' at a polis officer, eh?" he said. "Come on, we're done."

Connell knocked back her tea, dribbling half of it down her chin. She scooped up the dog as she stood, giving Denton a nervous smile. He nodded at her.

"Sorry, Connie," he said. "But you know how it is."

"Yeah," she said. "I do."

She headed for the door, the dog licking tea from her chin. Baird followed, but after a few steps he stopped.

"She may know how it is," he said. "But I dinnae."

Denton stared at him, every muscle tense.

"Then let me explain," said the big man. "I didn't recognise you out there, Baird. Not at first, not when you were squirming about on that woman."

"Wasnae squirming—"

"But I do now. I saw you on the news, the press conference you gave last month, when you put Tommy Keeble and Graham Barron away."

"Aye? How did I look? They say the telly adds ten pounds."

Denton's lips peeled open into a golden smile.

"You looked like a man who doesn't know what's good for him," he said. "A man who doesn't know when to quit. Because what you did to Tommy? That pissed off a lot of people."

"I mean, technically I didnae do anything to Tommy

Keeble," he said. "That was all on his wee girl. But you're right, Carl, I dinnae know when to quit. I'm like Diana here. Once I've got something in my teeth, I won't let it go."

The chihuahua barked, baring her crooked yellow fangs.

"I'm a hunter," he added.

"That makes two of us," growled Denton, squaring up to him. He was taller than Baird by near enough a foot. "Only I hunt big game."

"Nobody hunts bigger game than I do, pal."

"I do," said Denton. "Biggest game you've ever seen."

They stood there, awkwardly gurning at each other, until Connell called out from the door.

"At the risk of ruining this testosterone-fest, sir, we should probably go."

"Aye," said Baird, grateful for the excuse to turn away. He could feel Denton's cold gaze on the back of his neck. "But keep my chair warm, pal, because we're no gonna be long."

CHAPTER EIGHT

"Big game?" said Connell as they passed through the hotel lobby. Other than Tracey behind the desk, it was deserted now, which might have had something to do with the parade of uniformed coppers that could be seen through the windows.

Baird laughed, although part of that was embarrassment. He glanced back to see Denton standing by the door of the private dining room, watching them go—smirking like a bouncer that had ejected them from a club. It took all his restraint not to jiggle a couple of middle fingers at him.

"Ach, sorry, I got carried away," he said. "It's men like him, they get under my skin. Their bollocks are bigger than their heids."

He opened the door, holding it for Connell.

"Although, in all honesty, that guy has the biggest heid I've ever seen."

"The hardest, too," said Connell. "He was a boxer for years, and before that he was a linebacker. One of the big teams, too. I wouldn't mess with him."

She carried the dog outside and Baird followed. The

sun found him instantly, a radioactive slap that threatened to sear the skin off his face. He shielded his eyes as they made their way towards the car park.

"Be alert, sir," said Connell, looking nervously at the wooded areas around the lawn. "There could be tigers. Maybe elephants. Better get your blunderbuss ready."

He scowled at her.

"Alright, pal, it could be worse. I could have said I was sweet and milky."

It was Connell's turn to blush. The dog broke out into a fit of high-pitched yaps as they made their way to the car park, probably because she could see Headcold Pauly, leaning on a Lotus like he owned it and taking grinning selfies on his phone. He was sweating buckets in the sunshine, making him look more like a victim of the plague than ever.

"Hey, Pauly," Baird called out. "Can you do me a wee favour?"

"Huh?" said the man as they crunched over the gravel. "What's he saying?"

"A favour," said Baird.

"A fever? No, it's just a cold. Can't seem to shake it."

"A *favour*," said Connell, yelling over the dog.

"Well why doesn't he just say *favour* then, for fuck's sake?"

Baird was starting to wish he *did* have a blunderbuss.

"Do you know Greg Brightwell?" asked Connell, guessing what Baird had been about to ask.

Pauly gave her a suspicious stare.

"Maybe," he said. "Maybe not."

"You've seen him here?"

Pauly sniffed as he pushed himself away from the Lotus. He looked left, then right, then leaned in.

"I, uh, notice you didn't give me a tip when I parked your car."

"I did give you a tip," said Connell. "I said it's probably not wise to offer your services as a valet to somebody like Carl Denton when you've lost your licence."

"I mean a tip," said Pauly, doing his best to wink but blinking instead.

"I'm about ready to give you the tip," muttered Baird. "Of a knife."

"What did he say?"

"He said maybe there's some money in it for you if you answer some questions," said Connell, struggling with the wriggling dog. "You know Greg?"

"Yeah," said Pauly, poking his thumbs into his waistcoat like a Victorian chimneysweep. "Me and Greg are mates. Now *he's* happy to tip, I'll tell you that much, even when I don't park his car for him. Nice guy, and nice car too."

"Which car?" asked Baird.

"What did he—"

"You heard me, Pauly," growled Baird. "Your ears aren't that jammed up."

"The Ford," he said, petulantly.

Baird scanned the car park, looking for a Ford and not finding one.

"Fiesta?" he said. "Mondeo? Help me oot here."

"That one," said Pauly, jutting his chin towards a light blue sportscar. "The GT40."

"*That* one?" said Baird. He walked over to it, listening to Connell continue her conversation.

"Greg was here this week, did you see him? Talk to him?"

"Like I said, I saw him drive in," said Pauly. "Wednesday afternoon, that would have been. Can't remember the exact time now. He gave me a twenty, let me take a selfie, asked me where I got my gear—I had to tell him it was sherbet, but I don't think he believed me."

"Did you see him again?"

"Yeah," said Pauly, unzipping his bumbag and taking a dab on his thumb. He sucked it like a baby, speaking with his mouth full. "Watched *Bernard's War* on Monday night, was on the telly, he was right there!"

"I mean did you see him in the flesh," said Connell.

"No! Stop that! I'm not into men."

"No, Pauly, did you see him in *person*, here, at the hotel?"

"Oh, right." He thought about it, jamming his thumb into the bumbag and then sliding it back into his mouth. "No. Can't think that I did."

Baird stopped beside the Ford, marvelling at it. The car was an old one, sleek and low and almost shark-like. It had a metallic, sky-blue paint job, the number 63 emblazoned on the side like an old-fashioned race car. He cupped his hand to the window, scanning the interior and seeing nothing at all on the leather seats.

"You know how much they go for?" yelled Pauly.

"A fair wallop," said Baird.

"Millions. And that ain't even a joke. Millions of pounds, for a car. His pride and joy, that. That's why he don't let me drive it, or anyone else. Insurance alone must cost him an arm and a leg. Keeps it under lock and key at all times."

It didn't need to be guarded. The door handle was so confusing Baird couldn't even figure out how to work it. He poked and prodded, hearing a crunch as Pauly jogged up.

"Don't fink you should be doing that, mate. It's my job

to keep these cars safe. Like I said, you want to get a closer look then you got to ask Greg. He's got the key."

Baird figured it out, giving the handle a gentle tug. The door popped, resisting a little as he pulled it all the way open. The smell of fresh pine wafted out, that and a burst of something floral and sweet.

"The hell?" said Pauly. "That ain't right."

Baird leaned into the car, seeing the key hanging from the ignition. He opened the glove box, but there was nothing inside except paperwork and a packet of Marlboro Reds. There were no rear seats, so he walked to the back of the car, searching for a handle.

"Anyone ken how to open the boot?"

"That's the engine, mate," said Pauly.

"Aye, I ken," said Baird, walking to the other end of the car so that Pauly wouldn't see the lie. "I meant the front boot."

"No boot at all," said Pauly, who seemed to be enjoying himself.

"Well where does he keep his bloody suitcase?"

"On the passenger seat," said Pauly. "Obviously."

"Obviously," said Baird, imitating the man's nasal voice. "You sure you didnae see him again? Yesterday, or this morning? Dressed in his goon, maybe."

"His goon?" said Pauly. "Fuck's a goon?"

"Dressing gown," said Connell.

"I told you, I ain't into fellas," he said. "I didn't see him with his clothes on, or with 'em off."

A car was driving down the track, a bright yellow Porsche. It revved its engine, completely unnecessarily.

"Wait," said Pauly, watching it approach. "That reminds me, I didn't see Greg, but I thought I heard his car. This thing sounds like a fucking dragon, you know? Like a bomber or something. Proper *brum brum*. Got a four-litre engine. V8. You can hear it coming from the other side of Suffolk."

"When did you hear it?" asked Baird.

"When he arrived," said Pauly. "Obviously. But I thought I heard it again last night. Hard to tell, cos I'm on the other side of the house."

"You're living here?" said Connell. "In the hotel?"

Pauly licked his scabby lips, keeping his voice low.

"In the old stable," he said.

"There are rooms in the old stable?"

"No, Connie, it's a fucking stable, but it's comfortable enough. Denton don't know, though, so don't blab. Got too much shit to deal with at home."

"Right," said Connell, frowning. "I mean, we should probably help you with that."

"Another time," said Baird, who was growing impatient. "You heard this car last night? What time?"

Pauly shrugged.

"Half eleven? I don't know. Took a bunch of pills to get to sleep, whole thing's a little blurry. Weird thing is, I thought I heard it again. In fact, I swear I could have heard it all night, coming and going. But maybe it was Cudge snoring. He's got a wicked snore, keeps me awake all night."

"Cudge?" said Baird. "He your roommate?"

"Yeah, but only when it serves him. Buggers off somewhere else most nights. Hops into my bed when he's lonely."

Baird caught Connell's eye and saw she was as confused as he was.

"Cudge is a person?" asked Baird.

"Nah," said Pauly, with no further explanation.

The man sniffed, wiping the snot from his nose then

plunging the same hand into his bumbag. The Porsche had almost reached them, a man behind the wheel, a woman in the passenger seat.

"Probably dreaming," he said, licking the sherbet off his filthy fingers. "Anyway, if you'll excuse me, I've got a job to do."

He met the Porsche at the entrance to the car park, opening the door for the passenger. Baird turned back to the Ford, gently closing the door.

"Nobody's gonna leave a million-pound car unlocked, right?"

"That depends, sir," said Connell. "On how drunk he was when he parked it. If he was out and about last night, there's a chance he might have been drinking."

"Aye, maybe," said Baird. "But there's a more important question. If this is Greg Brightwell's car, and he's our dead guy in the woods, then how the hell did it get back here?"

"His killer," said Connell, and Baird nodded.

"Call Declan," he said. "See if we can get some prints off the car."

He frowned.

"No from the door, though, because I just touched it."

"Yes, sir," said Connell, shifting the dog to the other arm in order to pull out her phone. "Then, if it's okay with you, I'm going to take this little lady to the vet, get her checked over."

"Aye, probably a good idea," he said, looking at Diana. She was more cross-eyed than ever, a string of drool hanging halfway from her mouth to the floor. "She looks like she had a heavy night. I'll give the boss an update."

He retrieved his phone from his pocket, heading across the car park as he searched for Briggs' number. He yelled to the nearest copper as he went.

"See that blue car? Nobody goes near it, alright? Nobody touches that sexy wee thing unless I give them permission."

"I have no interest in touching your sexy wee thing," said Briggs as the call connected.

"Sorry ma'am," he said. "We're at Denton's Hotel."

"So I understand," said Briggs. "And from what I've been told, you were climbing the drainpipe like some kind of Scottish King Kong."

"I wasnae *climbing* it..."

"I don't want to know, Harrison. If I don't hear it, then I can't lose sleep over it. The key card worked?"

"Aye, opened a room that was booked by Geoffrey Brightwell. The actor."

"I know who he is. And his name is Gregory."

"Och, aye. Gregory. There was somebody in it, a woman, and they didnae want to talk to me. She bolted, and Denton took me oot before I could catch her."

"Carl Denton? Took you out where?"

"Took me oot as in knocked me to the ground. Thought I was attacking her. She slipped away in the chaos. He isnae letting us back up to the room, says we need a warrant."

"Connell couldn't sweet-talk him?"

"She tried, but she wasnae milky or sweet enough. He's obviously hiding something. Trouble is, he knows we're after the room, so he'll be up there right now turning it upside doon. You want us to take some uniforms, force his hand?"

"No," said Briggs. "Don't give him the satisfaction."

Her sigh rattled down the line.

"You think Brightwell's our dead man?"

"I'm no sure, ma'am. I dinnae really know him from the telly. But there's a chance. He's obviously minted, and he disnae mind people knowing. Drives a million-pound car and leaves the keys in the ignition. He's a good target if you want to make some money."

"But you don't make money by shooting somebody twelve times with a bow and arrow and then chopping off their head."

"Fair point," he said. "But a guy in the public eye like that, he draws a lot of attention. Maybe it's something else. A grudge. An obsessive fan. I dinnae ken. There's no way of knowing unless we get something off the dead fella's prints."

"I'm working on it," said Briggs. "But there might be another way. Fred's finished his preliminary, and he found a tattoo on the dead man."

"Nice," said Baird.

"A handprint. On his arse."

"Not nice," he said. "How big is it?"

"Regular sized."

"No the arse, ma'am, the handprint."

"Also regular sized. Black ink on the right buttock. It's the only discerning feature we can find."

"So all we have to do is figure oot whether Gregory Brightwell had the same tattoo," said Baird. He started walking towards the Fiat, waving to Connell as he went. "Leave it with me."

CHAPTER NINE

"Who gets a handprint tattooed on their bum?" asked Connell as she drove them back into town.

Baird sat in the passenger seat, Diana the dog-like creature on his lap leaking dribble and snot and a variety of other bodily fluids on his trousers. She was still vibrating like a wind-up toy, one eye facing forward, the other boggling at the ceiling like she was worried about an alien attack. He gave her head a scratch, tickling her protruding chin and underneath her sparkling pink collar. She responded by making a noise that could have come from a chicken getting its neck wrung.

He had to admit, he was becoming quite attached to her.

"Somebody with a naughty side," Baird said when he realised Connell was still waiting for an answer. "Somebody who likes a slap on the arse."

"I've never heard about him having a tattoo," said Connell. "In the magazines and stuff. And I've seen plenty of pictures of him with his shirt off. Never seen his bum though, only the... other side."

She sighed wistfully.

"He always comes across as a nice guy," she went on. "Everyone has good things to say about him. Friendly. Generous. Quiet, off screen."

"It's always the quiet ones," said Baird, watching Southwold roll past the window. Most of the shops had closed for the evening, the pavements clear of everything except the seagulls.

"It's probably just a joke," said Connell. "The tattoo. He might have got it when he was a student or something. That's when I got mine."

"You've got a tattoo?" said Baird. "On your arse?"

"Pretty sure you're not allowed to ask that, sir," she said. "No, it's on my shoulder."

He stared at her until she caved in.

"It's a pickle," she said.

"A pickle?"

"Yes, a pickle. A few of us went out one night when we were at uni, in Ipswich. End of first year exams. We all got something to celebrate."

"A *pickle*?"

"Because of Pickle," she said. "The dog."

"You didnae want a tattoo of the actual dog?"

"Well, yes, but I didn't have any money, so I went with the pickle."

"Right," said Baird. "Can I see it?"

"No," she said.

"Please?"

Connell had slowed for a junction, and with another mighty sigh she pulled the collar of her shirt away from her shoulder. The thing that had been tattooed there was long and green and had a highly suspicious shape.

"Jesus Christ, Connie, that looks like Shrek's p—"

"Don't say it!" she said, both hands to her ears.

"Pickle," he finished, trying to keep the smile from his face. "I was just gonna say pickle."

She took the wheel again, turning left when the traffic was clear. They drove in silence for a while—or as close to silence as it was possible to get with the dog's wheezing breaths—heading north out of the town. The fields were drenched in honey-coloured light, swathes of long grass dancing in the breeze, countless meadow flowers puffing up their brightly coloured chests as an invitation to the bees. It was the kind of countryside that was designed for gambolling in, he thought, even though he couldn't quite remember what the word meant.

"Well, we probably didn't need his address," said Connell, nodding through the windscreen to a house up ahead.

The Brightwell residence was like something you might have found in the Hollywood hills, a white monolith with enormous glass windows that sat uneasily in the rolling countryside. A brick wall imprisoned the grounds, an imposing gate blocking the driveway. The Fiat crawled up to it, Connell winding down her window so she could jab the intercom. There was a buzz, followed by the crackle of static.

"I am in the wrong job, Connie," said Baird, staring at the roof of the house over the top of the gate. "I work ma arse off every day trying to bring law and order to the world, and for what? A wee flat in the middle of toon and about fifteen quid in my savings account. And this fella does a few movies and gets to live *here*?"

"To be fair, sir," said Connell, "I've never actually seen you work *that* hard."

Baird gasped theatrically, but he didn't have a chance to

reply before the intercom buzzed again and the gates started to open. Connell tapped the wheel until there was room for her to drive past, then she made her way up the driveway, parking next to a blocky triple garage with glass doors. A white Range Rover sat inside next to a little black Mercedes, plenty of space left for the Ford.

"What are we gonna do with you, eh?" he asked the dog. He glanced back to see the gates swinging shut. "Probably safe enough to leave you in the car this time."

Diana stared at him with one eye, loosing a single bark.

"You'll be fine," he said. "There's plenty of food on the floor of the car, knock yourself oot."

He lowered her into the back where she began rooting about in the carpet of empty packets.

"Your car is a bin, Connie," he said, lowering the window a crack before getting out.

Connell followed him, redoing her ponytail as they walked towards the house. The enormous front door was swinging open, revealing a striking woman in her thirties, her slim figure wrapped in a striped playsuit. She stepped onto the flagstone path with bare feet, shielding her face with a hand as she watched them approach. Baird knew her from somewhere, and he wondered if she was on the TV too.

"You're not Waitrose," she said.

"Sadly no," said Baird. He pulled out his warrant card as he reached the door. "My name's DI Harrison Baird, I'm with the police. This is DC Constance Connell."

"Police Scotland?" said the woman. "You're a long way from home."

"Aye, and I feel it in my bones. Are you Melissa Brightwell?"

"No," said the woman, planting her hands on her hips.

The Botox made her expression hard to read, but the concern was there. "I'm Melissa Stewart. But if you're asking me whether I'm married to Greg, then yes. Can I ask what this is about?"

"Maybe nothing," said Baird, the sun searing his scalp. "You mind if we come in? You could cook an egg on the back of my heid."

"Oh, sorry, of course," she said.

She stood to one side as they walked into a wide, shaded hallway, the polished concrete floor and white walls making Baird feel like he'd entered an industrial freezer.

"Straight through," she said, closing the door behind them. "We can use the kitchen. I've got some juice boxes in the fridge."

The kitchen was big enough to feed a campus, running the entire width of the house. Vast windows looked out over a neat patio and a football-pitch-sized lawn, the sunlight pouring through skylights and pooling on the marbled floor. The island in the middle of the room was as big as an actual island. It could have had its own postcode. Melissa trailed her fingers along its marbled top as she walked to a monstrous fridge.

"This is lovely," said Connell, her grin stretching off the sides of her face. "I don't think I've ever seen a nicer kitchen."

"Thank you," said Melissa. She rummaged inside the fridge, pulling out a pack of juice cartons and setting them on the island. "We had the house built a couple of years ago, after the *Star Wars* thing. Terrible movie. Great paycheque."

"I remember you building it," said Connell, leaning on the island. "There used to be a bungalow here, didn't there? Looked like a pebble-dashed shoebox."

"That's the one. We knocked it down. Planning was a nightmare, but Greg's got the gift. People like him. He can get away with anything."

She paused, studying Connell and then Baird, searching for clues in their faces.

"Orange or apple?" she said.

"Apple, please," said Connell.

"Aye, I'll take apple n'all," Baird said, walking to the island. Melissa slid two cartons over the smooth surface, returning the others to the fridge. She took a shuddering breath before she faced them again.

"You guys are killing me," she said. "Can you just tell me what's going on?"

"Do you ken where Greg is right now?" Baird asked.

Melissa nodded, bracing both hands on the island.

"He's staying at Denton's. The hotel. He goes there when he's got lines to learn, because he likes the quiet."

Baird took a moment to listen to the house. He literally couldn't hear a single sound from outside. He picked up the carton of juice, looking at the illustration of a grinning, bug-eyed apple.

"You've got kids?" he asked.

"No," said Melissa. "Greg never wanted them, and I..." She shrugged.

"You wanted Greg," said Baird. "I get it. He checked in on Wednesday, aye? You've heard from him since then?"

She shook her head.

"He doesn't like to be interrupted, not when he's working. He's... I mean, he's not a method actor, not like De Niro or anything, but he does really try to inhabit the role."

"What role is it?" said Connell, picking up her juice and pulling off the straw. "I'm a big fan. I probably shouldn't say, but I love Greg. He's amazing in everything."

"He is," said Melissa, offering Connell a cryptic smile. "I can't say what it is. It's all confidential, he's signed an NDA and everything. But it's big, and he's perfect for it. He's got an audition next week, so he decided to squirrel himself away in the hotel."

She turned to Baird.

"He *is* still at the hotel, isn't he?"

There was no point putting it off any more. Baird sucked in a breath, drumming his fingers on the top of the island.

"This is going to seem like a strange question, Melissa, and I'm sorry I have to ask it. But does Greg have any tattoos?"

She frowned, looking between them for a moment or two. Connell was oblivious as she tried to jam the paper straw into the hole on the top of her carton.

"A tattoo?" she said. "No."

It was impossible to deny the feeling of relief that passed through him. He nodded, glancing at Connell again to see if she was listening. Apple juice was raining from her carton onto the floor as she attempted to mush the crumpled straw into place.

"Blooming thing," she said.

"He disnae have any tattoos at all?" Baird went on.

"No, he's made it very clear that he doesn't," said Melissa. "He hates them. Won't let me have any either. Why?"

"No reason," said Baird. "Mistaken identity, I think. One more question, do yous guys have a dug? A wee chihuahua?"

"No," she said.

"Then we're really sorry to have bothered you, Melissa."

Baird turned to Connell again. She was still struggling.

"Connie, let's go, it's no him."

She glared up like it was his fault the juice box wouldn't let her in. When his words sunk in, though, she smiled.

"It's not?"

"No tattoos," he said. "You want me to do that?"

Connell passed him the juice box and the straw. He nodded to Melissa.

"We can show ourselves oot. Sorry again to worry you." He glanced at the puddle of juice by Connell's feet. "And sorry aboot the mess."

The woman didn't reply, chewing on her bottom lip like she hadn't eaten in a month.

"It was a pleasure to meet you," said Connell. "Can you tell Mr Brightwell I'm a fan?"

Melissa still didn't say anything. Baird led the way out of the room, trying to get the crumpled straw into the wee hole in the box. His hands were sticky with juice.

"His *biggest* fan," Connell added.

"Alright, Annie Wilkes," said Baird. "Are you coming back later with a sledgehammer?"

"Wait," came a shout from behind them, one that echoed around the kitchen like a ricocheting bullet.

Baird turned back from the hall, hearing the patter of apple juice on the floor. Melissa Stewart was framed perfectly in the kitchen door, her arms spread, her hands still gripping the island. A halo of sun had formed around her hair, making her look almost saintly. It could have been a photo in a celebrity magazine, Baird thought, a snapshot of how the other half live.

This was something else, though, he knew. This was the final image of a life that was about to be destroyed.

Connell understood it too, puffing out a sad little breath.

"What kind of tattoo does he have?" Baird asked. "The

kind he wanted to keep secret, aye? The kind he wouldn't want the world to see."

"It's a stupid thing," said Melissa. "From his first movie, the awful one about the fraternity students. He was drunk, the tattoo shop never should have done it. But like I said, he's a persuasive guy. He gets what he wants."

Baird and Connell waited for Melissa to find the words.

"It's a hand," she said. "On his, you know. His bum."

She studied Baird's face, seeing the inevitable truth. She put a hand to her mouth, shaking her head.

"I'm very sorry, Melissa," he said, walking back into the kitchen. "We dinnae ken anything for sure yet, but we... we found a body in the woods up by Benacre today. A man. He's got a tattoo of a handprint on his backside. Black ink. Right buttock."

Melissa was shaking her head harder now, her knuckles pressed against her lips like she was trying to hold back a scream. Her eyes were wide and wild.

"We havnae confirmed his ID, because..." He wasn't sure what to say. "Because of *complications* with the body. The handprint is all we have to go on."

"It's Greg," said Melissa, her voice so choked that Baird couldn't work out if it was a question or not. "Please. I can... Can I see him? Can I make sure?"

Baird met Connell's eye, and Melissa must have seen the horror that passed between them because she whirled around to face the fridge, a guttural cry exploding from her mouth.

"Let me handle this, sir," Connell said quietly. "I can stay with her."

"You sure?" he asked, knowing how hard she found this, how much she hated the knock on the door.

Connell nodded.

"I'll be okay."

Baird offered Connell the ruined carton of apple juice. "You want this?"

"No, thank you," she said. She handed him her car keys. "But can you get Diana to the vet? It's the one on Ferry Road, down near the harbour."

He nodded, taking the keys. Connell crossed the kitchen, rounding the island and putting a hand on Melissa's shoulder. Baird watched for long enough to see her pull the other woman close, drawing her into a hug, then he made his way out of the house. The sun was fiercer than ever, but this time he was grateful for it. It burned off the worst of the misery from his skull, boiling away the grief that he felt every time he had to deliver the news of somebody's death. He stood there for a moment, his head to the sky, his eyes closed, the world on fire.

"This bloody job," he said.

"Excuse me?"

The voice was so close he almost screamed. Even when he opened his eyes he couldn't see who was there, because the low sun was gouging its fingers into his skull. He lifted a hand, peering through its shadow to see a man standing by the open gate. He was in his early thirties, slim and handsome, wearing jeans and a white shirt that had been unbuttoned to his chest. His face was streaked with sweat.

"Who are you?" both men asked together.

"I'm polis," said Baird, answering first. He held up his warrant card. "And you?"

The man seemed to think about it for a moment.

"Waitrose," he said.

"Aye? I dinnae see any cantaloups."

"Van's on the road," the man said, hooking a thumb over his shoulder. "Always like to ask before I bring it in."

"How'd you open the gate?"

"Mrs Stewart gave me the code," he said. "In case she's out."

Baird walked to the gate, ignoring the barks from Connell's Fiat as Diana ogled him through the steamed-up window. Sure enough, there was a van sitting on the side of the road, its engine running. It was green, 'Waitrose' written on the side.

"Everything alright?" said the man.

"No really," said Baird. "Can you come back later?"

The man looked past him, to the house, then nodded.

"Sure," he said. "I'll keep it fresh."

He walked back to his van, giving Baird a dark-eyed look through the passenger window before driving off.

"Waitrose," scoffed Baird as he made his way back to the car. He tried again to get the straw into the carton, but the bloody thing wouldn't go. He put the hole to his mouth instead, squirting the contents into his mouth. There wasn't much left, and it did nothing to quench his thirst.

He opened the door, only just managing to catch the little dog as she made a bid for freedom. She furiously licked the juice from his fingers, her eyes bulging. He lobbed the empty carton into the back, where it instantly vanished into the mess, then he planted Diana on the passenger seat.

"Stay put," he said. "Understand?"

She barked, and despite everything, Baird smiled.

"I'm gonna take you to the doctor now," he said.

She cocked her misshapen head, her underbite exposing those tiny yellow teeth.

"But I'm no sure any vet will be able to fix whatever's wrong with you."

She growled, and he laughed. He started the engine, pulling out his phone.

"Ma'am," he said when Briggs answered. "We're at the Brightwell place. We've spoken to his wife and she confirmed the tattoo."

"Bugger," said Briggs.

"Aye, a big bugger. Our headless deid man is Gregory Brightwell."

CHAPTER TEN

The road down to the harbour took Baird right by the house where Beau Steiner had lived, the flower-power killer from his last case. He drove past the dirt track with a scowl on his face, even though he knew that the place was deserted. Both Beau and his wife had received custodial sentences for their role in the death of Barny Curdy and at least twelve others. Everyone else had fled the commune in the days after, most grateful to still be alive.

Others not so much.

Only the sheep remained, running wild in the fields behind the house, tended by the neighbours. He could hear them through the car's open window, a chorus of wild bleats.

A minute or so later, he spotted the veterinary surgery, Harbour Animal Care. He was in the process of pulling into the car park when he spotted a car valet service on the other side of the road, attached to a small showroom. A couple of bored young lads sat in deckchairs, staring at their phones. He pulled up next to them, leaning out the window.

"Yous still open?"

One of the boys nodded, uncoiling his lanky frame from the chair. He had to hold up his tracksuit trousers with one hand as he walked over, rags hanging from his pockets. He assessed the Fiat as he approached, taking in the dents, and the dirt, and the inch-thick coating of bird shit on the roof.

"Big job, boss," he said.

"Aye, and you havnae seen the inside yet."

The kid angled his frame so he could see through the window. He recoiled instantly, his nose wrinkling like he'd been pepper sprayed. Diana planted her feet on Baird's leg, barking her head off. Baird lifted her onto his lap, running a hand down her back to calm her.

"You been living in here, big man?" the kid asked.

"Pal, I'm *dying* in here," he said. "Honestly, I glanced into the back just now and got typhoid."

The boy laughed.

"You ken that scene in *Star Wars* when they're in the trash compactor?" Baird went on. "This is worse, and I swear there's some kind of beastie in the back. I saw it moving."

The kid didn't know whether to believe him or not. He glanced at the dog, then back at Baird.

"Honestly, boss, I think it may be beyond saving," he said. "I can take it out back and torch it, if you like."

"Tempting," said Baird. He pulled out his wallet, finding three twenties inside. "But it's no mine. Will this do for a scrub doon and a hoover?"

The kid made the money disappear like he was a professional magician. He glanced back at his friend to make sure he hadn't seen, then he nodded.

"Might take a while."

"That's fine," said Baird. "I've got to go see a man aboot a dog."

The kid opened the door for him and he got out, clutching Diana to his chest.

"Sorry aboot all the pish on the seats," he said as he crossed the road. "It wasnae me."

The surgery was a bungalow set back from the road, the front garden a small car park devoid of any hint of greenery. He reached the door at the same time as a young woman in green overalls and a black hijab, who was so busy fumbling for her keys that she didn't notice him on the other side of the glass. When she finally looked up and saw him staring through the window, she actually screamed.

"Sorry!" he said, taking a step back. "I didnae mean to scare you."

The girl put one hand to her heart, holding her keys like a set of knuckle dusters. The look on her face was that of a rabbit about to be eaten by a wolf. Then she saw the dog in his arms and she seemed to relax a little.

"We're closed," she said.

Baird glanced at the sign on the door, on which a poodle and a tabby cat held the word *Open*.

"Clos*ing*," she said. "We're all done at five. There's an emergency vet in Lowestoft if you need urgent help."

She studied the dog again.

"I honestly can't tell if she's okay or not," she said.

"She looks like she's been through a mangle, but she's fine," said Baird. He jiggled the dog to his other side so he could pull out his warrant card. "I'm the one who needs help."

The woman opened the door, but she didn't move out of his way. Diana craned herself forwards, her tongue exploring the air as she tried to reach the girl.

"We found this wee thing at a crime scene," Baird said. "She's been oot in the woods for a while, I think."

"By herself?" asked the girl. She held her fingers in front of Diana's nose, earning a lick for her trouble, then scratched the back of her head. The dog must have enjoyed it, because she started dribbling. "Poor thing. I've never seen a dog with a face quite like this. Her *eyes*."

"I ken. If I had a pound for every time she looked me in the eye, I'd have fifty pence."

The girl didn't laugh.

"I need to find out who she belongs to, so we can get her home," said Baird. "Have you got one of those chip scanner things?"

"Of course," said the girl. She pulled out her phone, checking the time. "I can give you a few minutes, but any more than that and I'll miss my bus."

"A few minutes'll be grand," said Baird.

The girl opened her arms and Diana practically jumped into them. She carried her inside the building, cooing like a kid at Christmas. Baird closed the door behind him, turning the sign to *Closed* before following the girl across a small reception and through a door behind the desk. Diana seemed to realise what was happening, because she started growling, struggling in the girl's arms.

"What's your name?" Baird asked as they walked through the examination room and into a larger space behind.

"Noor," she replied.

"You been a vet long?"

"I'm not actually a vet," she said. "I just help out, clean up, do the phones and stuff. Lock up, obviously. But I've been here long enough to know what I'm doing."

She stopped beside a metal table, putting the dog down. She unclipped the glittery pink collar, taking a look before setting it aside. Then she nodded to a device that looked like a cross between a remote control and a Geiger counter.

"Grab that, will you? It's the big green button."

He picked up the scanner and turned it on. Diana barked at it, her face even wonkier than ever as she tried to make herself look big.

"Chips are usually in the back of the neck," she said. "Just wave it about a bit."

"Technical, I like it," said Baird.

He held the scanner over Diana's scrawny neck. It was bigger than the dog.

"Nothing?" asked Noor. "Here, swap."

Baird took Diana and Noor grabbed the scanner, sweeping it back and forth. The dog was growling so hard she was foaming at the mouth.

"Calm doon, Diana," said Baird. "She's no gonna eat you."

"Diana?" said Noor, putting the scanner back on the desk.

"No my choice," he said. "I'd have gone for Munter."

She still didn't laugh.

"No microchip. No tags on the collar?"

"No, just the D."

She took the dog's head and gently prised her mouth open, staring inside. Diana gargled, one eye locked on Baird as if imploring him for help.

"She's not in too bad shape. A little neglected, her teeth could do with a clean." She ran her hand down the dog's back. "Her fur's pretty matted. And she's obviously filthy."

"You've no had anyone asking aboot a missing chihuahua?"

"Not here," she said. "But we've got a database. I can check in the morning."

She pulled out her phone again.

"Look," said Baird. "If you could stay for a bit longer, check it oot, then I can get a polis car to take you home. It would really help us. And her."

Noor bit her lip for a moment, deep in thought. After a second or two she nodded.

"That will give my dad a heart attack," she said, smiling. "Me turning up in a police car."

"You're a legend," said Baird. "You need me to stay?"

"No," she said.

"*You* need me to stay?" Baird asked the dog.

Diana yipped.

"I'm taking that as a no," he said. "I've got some calls to make, but I'll be back in an hour, if that's enough time?"

"Sure."

Noor gave Diana a squeeze. The dog licked her chin, happy as Larry. So happy, in fact, that Baird felt a little put out as he walked back into the heat of the afternoon. The two lads across the road were swearing angrily as they wrenched armfuls of rubbish from Connell's car, so he slunk off down the road before they spotted him.

It was only a mile or so to the harbour from here. To his right, the sweeping meadow led inland like a green sea, the horizon impossibly flat. It was mirrored by the actual sea, which he caught in glimpses through the tall hedge. Even when he couldn't see it, he could smell it, the air heavy with salt, making him feel instantly homesick. He thought of his sister Elspeth back in Aberdeen. His granny lying in her bed at the care home, probably wondering where he'd gone.

He thought about Baggy the cat, pining for him.

Then he laughed, because Elspeth's house was a palace compared to his old flat, and unlike him, she wasn't too cheap to put the central heating on. The cat would be lying on a windowsill with a belly full of kippers.

After fifteen minutes, he spotted the caravan park that sat next to the town's harbour. It was busier than it had been when he'd come this way during his last case, a bunch of kids tearing about between the static caravans and earning scowls from the older folk, who sat on their balconies drinking mugs of tea. A few dogs barked at him, and he resisted the urge to bark back. It felt like a million years ago that Connell had driven him down here to the place where Curdy's body had been found.

It had been less than a month.

You wouldn't know a man had died here—two men, in fact, because they'd found Derek Kate a day later, drained of blood. Boats bobbed in the channel like playful ducklings, sailors and fishermen gathered in groups on the road. Their laughter carried through the warm air, all the way to the car park where the ice cream shack sat. Samara was framed in the hatch, serving a couple of teenagers, a great big smile on her face. Her curly hair was held in place by a Rosie the Riveter band, just like the last time he'd seen her. He wandered over.

"Let me guess," she said when she spotted him. She handed some change to one of the kids, and tucked a strand of hair into the colourful headband. "Connie's sent you for a tub of raspberry ripple?"

She checked her watch.

"Actually, it's dinner time. She'll want something with a little more substance. Pistachio? For the protein?"

Baird laughed, walking into the welcome shade of the canopy.

"I'm only after a coffee, Sam," he said.

"Milk and fourteen sugars?" she asked. "The way I always make it?"

"Just black," he said. "No sugar. Extra coffee."

She disappeared into the back.

"Connie's letting you out by yourself now, is she?" she called back.

"Aye, I've got my big boy shoes on. We're on a job. I had to take a dug to the vet up the road."

"A dog?" Sam said as she reappeared, a takeaway cup in her hand.

"Aye, we found it in the woods. Actually..."

He pulled out his phone, holding up a photo he'd taken of Diana. For an unfortunate looking dog, it was an even more unfortunate picture.

"My God," said Sam. "That's a dog? What happened to it?"

"I think that's what she's always looked like," said Baird, a little defensively. "You havnae seen it around here? Fur all matted. Dribbles everywhere. Smells like the gates of Hell have opened."

"Headcold Pauly turns up every now and again, and he matches that description pretty well," she said. "But he's not a dog."

"Sparkly pink collar?"

Sam shook her head.

"Sorry, never seen her before. Or smelled her. It has something to do with your case?"

"I have no idea," he said.

She passed him the coffee and he took a sip, instantly recoiling as it boiled into his mouth.

"Argh," he said, sucking a fuzzy tongue.

"It's hot," she told him.

"Did you make it in the bloody sun?"

"Here," she said, taking a sample spoon from the cup and extracting a dollop of vanilla from a tub in the open freezer. She offered it. "It'll help."

"I'm fine," he told her, although he definitely wasn't.

She wiggled the spoon like a mother with a reluctant child, and after a second or two he gave in. The ice cream was cheap, crystals of ice landing on his tongue, but the cold softened the pain.

"See," she said. "Trust Sam."

She gave him a smile that made his stomach wobble, and he had to turn away.

"Uh, cheers," he said, feeling the blush creep into his cheeks. "How much do I owe you?"

"How about dinner?" she asked, and he almost choked on his burnt tongue.

"*Dinner*?"

"Tea," she said. "Supper. I don't know what you call it up north. The evening meal. Food. Wine."

"Uh..." said Baird.

"Stimulating conversation," she said, the smile still on her face. "Just like you're giving me right now."

"Uh..."

"Think about it," she said, the smile wavering. "You can let me know anytime."

"Ach, it's no that, Sam," he said, blustering. "You're a sweet lassie, but, you know, I'm no gonna be here much longer. In England. I'm going home."

He flapped his spare arm like a wounded penguin.

"Sorry."

He took another sip of his coffee to hide his embarrassment, gargling in pain as it seared its way down his throat. This time, Sam didn't offer him any ice cream.

"Well, you know where I am," she said, fiddling with the spoons in the cup.

He nodded, trying to smile at her and grimacing instead.

"Sorry," he said again. "Thanks for the coffee."

He turned to go, then spun all the way in a circle.

"Listen, Sam, do you ken that actor fella who lives round here, Geoffrey Brightwell?"

"Gregory?" she said.

"Aye, him."

"Yeah, he sometimes brings his boat into the harbour. Always buys an ice cream, great tipper."

She frowned.

"I asked him out, now that I think about it, and he turned me down too. Why?"

"Because he's married, probably," he told her.

"No, why are you asking about him."

"You havnae seen him this week?"

"No," she said. "I don't think I've seen him since last summer. He okay?"

"What aboot Carl Denton?" he went on.

It was impossible to miss the way Sam's expression changed. Her body grew tense, like she was holding her breath, and she wrapped her arms around her chest. When she glanced past Baird into the car park, it was like she'd suddenly spotted a wolf.

"What?" he asked.

"Nothing," she said, an obvious lie. "Why are you asking about him?"

"Just curious," he said. "I met him this afternoon. Interesting man."

Sam nodded. She was a completely different woman to the one who'd welcomed him with a smile five minutes ago.

"What is it?" he said. "You can tell me."

"It's nothing," she managed. "It's fine. Just... just be careful, yeah? Whatever you think you know about Denton, it's worse."

A couple of people were wandering up from the harbour, but Sam turned the sign on the counter to Closed.

"Sorry," she shouted them. "I'll be back in the morning."

"Sam," said Baird. "Talk to me."

"Just be careful," she said again. She leaned over the counter and put her hand to his face, an unexpected touch that took every single word out of his head. "Nothing about him is what it seems."

She left her warm fingers against his cheek for what felt like forever, before reaching up and unhooking the shutter. It dropped into place with a clatter, a lock sliding shut.

Baird stared at the peeling paint, gripping the coffee cup like a kid holding onto a floatie in the pool.

Then, still speechless, he walked away.

CHAPTER ELEVEN

He drank his coffee by the water, a cool breeze rushing in off the sea and doing its best to cool his raging cheeks, calm his racing pulse. He could still feel Samara's hand, like she'd left an electric charge on his skin.

"Well," he said to himself, watching a blue boat chug its way up the channel. "That was unexpected."

About ten minutes after she'd closed up, Sam emerged from her shack, locking the door and running across the car park. He watched from a distance as she climbed into a blue Ford Fiesta, gunning it onto the road. Gravel spewed from the tyres as she accelerated, vanishing around the corner.

He pulled out his phone to call Connell, noticing that he had a missed call from a local number. He dialled it back, finishing his coffee and throwing the cup in a bin as he waited for it to connect.

"Hello," said a woman's voice. "Harbour Animal Care."

"Noor?" Baird asked. "I missed your call."

"Oh, yes, are you the policeman?"

"Aye."

"I just wanted to let you know your dog's ready. She's

fine, in pretty good health all things considered. No chip anywhere, but she's had surgery."

"Hold up," he told her. "Tell me in person. I'm ten minutes away."

"Can I still get a ride?"

"Aye, leave it with me."

He called Briggs, who didn't answer. He tried Connell again, and after six rings she picked up.

"Sir," she said, almost a whisper.

"Everything okay?"

"Not really. Melissa's in a bad way. How did you get on?"

"I'll catch you up in a bit. Any chance there's a PC free with a car?"

"Trouble?" Connell asked.

"No, I need to give somebody a lift."

"Oh, uh... right. Leave it with me. Where are you?"

"The vet's, by the harbour. The sooner the better."

He hung up and legged it along the road, arriving at the bungalow fifteen minutes later, out of breath and dripping with sweat. There was no sign of the lads who'd cleaned Connell's car, but most of the bird shit had gone from the roof and it definitely looked a little shinier.

The surgery door was locked, and he knocked. Noor appeared almost instantly. She was holding a little chihuahua, but Baird wasn't immediately sure if it was the same one. The clumps of tangled fur had been shaved away, the dreadlocks gone. She looked like she'd been washed and brushed, her nails clipped. When she growled at him to indicate how much she'd hated the entire experience, he saw that even her teeth were a little less yellow.

He probably should have mentioned that the dog was

technically evidence, but Noor looked so pleased with her work he didn't have the heart.

"Wow," he said, scratching Diana's head and earning a lick. "Who's this princess, and what have you done with the blobfish I came in with?"

Noor laughed, using her free hand to cover her mouth. Diana growled again, unimpressed. Even her sparkly pink collar had been polished, he noticed, the D gleaming.

"I just thought she needed a bit of TLC," said Noor. "And her breath won't knock you out now. Like I was saying on the phone, she's not chipped—there's not even a mark where she might have been chipped. But she's had surgery at some point."

She turned the dog over to expose her side, holding on tight as Diana tried to wriggle out of her grip. There was a long scar running up her ribs that he hadn't noticed beneath the filthy fur.

"I'm not a hundred per cent certain, but it looks like she's had a tumour removed. It's certainly not from being neutered. It's weird."

"Weird how?"

She turned the dog the right way up again.

"Well, this kind of surgery is expensive. Like, thousands. Most people would need insurance to cover it, yeah? But most insurance policies insist your dog is chipped. I think so, anyway. And if you care enough about your dog to save her life, you probably want her to be registered."

Noor shrugged.

"Anyway, there's no record here of a chihuahua having this kind of surgery. I can ask the doctors, though, when they come in tomorrow. They can check with other places in the area."

"That'll be grand," said Baird. "You dinnae fancy taking her home for the night, do you? She obviously likes you."

"I can't, sorry. My mum and dad don't allow dogs, you know? I can leave her here? She'll be perfectly safe."

Diana gulped, her eyes bulging like she'd understood. Baird thought about it for a second then shook his head. He held out his hands and Noor passed the dog to him. Diana stretched up, her body vibrating. She pushed her wet muzzle into his chin, furiously licking. He couldn't stop the laugh that bubbled up.

"I was only gone a minute, you daft sod," he said. "Behave yourself."

He heard an engine, and turned to see an IRV rolling up the street. PC Percy Albright was behind the wheel, still bright red. He pulled into the car park and leaned out of the open window.

"I'm not a bloody taxi service, you know," he grumbled.

"Oh," said Noor. "Sorry, I—"

"Ignore him," said Baird. "Trust me, he's no doing anything useful."

Noor locked up, and Baird escorted her to the IRV. He opened the back door and she dropped inside, giggling.

"Dad is going to *freak*," she said. "Can we put the siren on?"

"No," said Percy, at the exact same time that Baird said, "Aye, go for it."

Percy flicked the switch, the blues rolling.

"Thanks, Noor," Baird said as he closed the door. "Oh, and if he falls asleep on the way, just give him a poke."

Percy glared at him as he drove out of the car park, accelerating up the street. They vanished behind the hedge, and a couple of seconds later Baird heard the siren fire up.

He laughed, holding onto Diana as he crossed the road to the car wash.

"So," he said. "What's your secret, eh? Who's your ma and da?"

The dog answered with a growl, her body tensing as she stared across the empty lot. Baird stopped, his own hackles rising. There was no sign of the young men, or anyone else. The door to the little office was closed, and locked. Diana was still growling, her entire body thrumming like a bass speaker.

"What is it?" he asked her.

He made his way to the Fiat, peering through the open window to see the keys in the ignition. The car was spotless, all the rubbish cleared away and the seats hoovered. It actually smelled like a car again, rather than an elephant's urethra.

"Cheers," he called out, in case anyone was still here.

He opened the door, clambering inside and plonking Diana on the passenger seat.

"I guess you're coming with me," he told her. "Dinnae pish on the nice, clean seats, eh?"

He pulled out his phone, trying Briggs again. This time, she answered.

"My officers are not at your beck and call, Harrison," she said. "PC Albright isn't a chauffeur."

"No offence, ma'am," he said, "but all I've seen Percy do since I got here is eat, sleep and pick his nose. Sometimes all at once."

"Be that as it may, I'd rather you weren't running an Uber service with my IRVs. Any news?"

"No really," he said. "I spoke to the vet, the dug's no chipped but we might be able to trace the owners through an operation she had. Won't find oot until the morning, though. You spoken to Connell?"

"Yes. She's still with Melissa Stewart, and will be for the foreseeable. So I need you to do something else for me."

"Aye?"

"Aye," echoed Briggs. "The hospital just called. Our witness is awake."

THE LAST THING he wanted to do was return to the cesspool that was Ipswich town centre, but sadly, he didn't have a choice. He drove with the window down, the wind almost taking the Fiat's roof off on the faster stretches of the A12. The dog's face flapped in the breeze like a rubber mask, drool flying, but she seemed happy enough in the passenger seat.

She was less happy when he parked the car and got out.

"I'll no be long, quine," he said. "Sorry they cleared away all your floor snacks."

He closed the door, leaving the window open an inch or so. The hospital was a big one, and it took him a while to find the right ward. A couple of uniformed officers sat in the waiting area down the hall, both bored out of their skulls. Two young men and a girl occupied the other side of the room, all dressed in summer clothes and looking like they'd been scared half to death. One of the PCs pointed to a corridor, and Baird headed along it until he reached a door. He knocked gently before opening it. The room inside was so dark that he couldn't work out if there was anybody inside.

"Hello?" he said.

"What do you want?" came a terse reply, a man's voice.

Baird wondered if he had the wrong room, then he

blinked into the gloom and saw a young woman in the bed. A chair had been pulled up next to it and a man sat there, cloaked in shadow.

"Anyone mind if I fire up the lights?" asked Baird. "I cannae see a thing."

"I'd rather you didn't," said the man, but the girl in the bed shuffled under her covers, clearing her throat.

"I'm fine, Dad," she said, her voice thick, the words distorted. "You can switch them on. Just be warned, I'm not pretty."

Baird clicked the switches by the door, and one by one the lights flickered on. The young woman hadn't been exaggerating. Her head had been wrapped in clean, white bandages, but they did little to hide the swollen mess of her eye, the bruising around her cheek and her mouth. She looked like she'd been trampled by a herd of buffalo.

"Ouch," said Baird, walking over.

He gave the girl a sympathetic smile, then nodded to the man in the chair. The guy was probably in his early fifties, although his receding hairline and sunken eyes made him look like he was ready for his grave. His skinny frame was drowning in a white shirt and black trousers, and he pushed a pair of silver wireframe glasses up the bridge of his nose before speaking.

"Who are you?"

"My name's Harrison," he said, pulling out his ID. "Baird. I'm working with Suffolk Constabulary."

"You don't sound very *Suffolk* to me," said the man.

"Dad," muttered the girl in the bed, trying to adjust her position again.

"What? He doesn't. You found him yet, the man who did this?"

Baird perched on the edge of the bed, careful not to

squash the girl's legs. She really had taken a walloping. He'd seen drunks on Union Street with fewer bruises than her.

"Flora?" he asked.

She nodded, and seemed to instantly regret it. She put one hand to her bandaged face, flexing her jaw.

"And you're Mr Arbon? The father?"

The man bared his teeth in reply, sitting back in the chair.

"Charles," he said.

"First," said Baird. "I'm truly sorry this happened to you. We're doing everything we can to find out who did this. I want you to know that you're safe here, Flora. We've got officers outside, and they're no going anywhere."

"You think he's coming back?" said Charles. "To what? Finish the job?"

"No," said Baird. "I dinnae think that. But until we know why somebody would do this, we're no taking any chances. Flora, I ken it's hard to speak, but can you tell me why you were in the Benacre woods this morning?"

"She's already told you," said Charles. "One of you, anyway. She spoke to the police who found her."

"I'd like to hear it for myself," said Baird, looking at Flora. "Take your time."

The girl glanced at her dad, as if asking for permission. She opened her mouth and stretched her neck, her expression full of pain.

"It was stupid," she said. "This stupid thing we do. You've heard of *The Court of Avalonia*, the book?"

"I've no stopped hearing aboot it today," said Baird. "Havnae read it, though."

"You're not missing much," said Charles, and it was like his daughter had been struck again.

"It's just a bit of fun," she said. "The woman who writes the books lives around here, and those woods, they're like a kind of… I don't know what the word is. Like a pilgrimage."

"You were there with friends?" asked Baird.

She nodded as well as the thick bandages would allow.

"Kind of. I know some of them, but a few were there from the group."

"Group?"

Baird's back was aching from the angle he was sitting at, but he didn't want to move for fear of startling her. The girl had the nervous energy of an injured bird.

"It's this online thing, a fan club, really. You can sign up for it at the bookshop in town."

"How many of you were there?"

"I don't know. Me and these two guys, Lucas and Anders. And Darcey, I know them all from university. I'm sure they'll talk to you if you need them to. I have their details."

"I'm pretty sure I saw them ootside," said Baird. "One guy in a pair of shorts that borders on the obscene."

Flora's smile was genuine.

"That's Anders. They're still here?"

"Aye. So yous four, and how many other people?"

"About six, I think. In the woods. But I didn't really talk to them. They were already there when we arrived, and… and all this happened very quickly."

"You've never met these others before?"

"Online, yeah. But you don't really *meet* people online, do you? They could be anyone, I guess."

Baird pulled out his phone, opening the Notes app.

"Just gonna write some of this doon," he said. "Memory like a sieve."

"That's reassuring," said Charles, earning another hissed reprimand from his daughter.

"Okay, ten of you in the woods. Doing what, exactly?"

Even with the injuries, Baird could see Flora's face flush with anxiety.

"*I'm* not telling him," said Charles when she didn't speak.

"I heard something about tugging your pizzle?" Baird said.

To his surprise, this got a laugh out of the girl. She regretted it instantly, grimacing.

"It's *pizzle*," she said. "Not puzzle."

"That's what I said. Pizzle."

She stared at him.

"Pizzle," he said again, in as English an accent as he could muster. "Can you explain it for me, because what I'm imagining cannae be right."

Another laugh, this one obviously causing her a great deal of pain.

"It's a running joke in the book," she said, pulling one hand out of the duvet to touch her temple. "They have these, like, magic powers, and they can bring anything to life and ride on it. So they have... sticks, I guess? Pizzles, they call them, because when you have them between your legs they kind of look like..."

Charles raised his head to the ceiling and groaned.

"Three years of English at the UEA, and this is what we get for our money."

"Dad!" said Flora. "It's... I know it's not Shakespeare, it's a bit of fun. That's what books should be. Fun. They bring people together."

"Okay," said Baird. "So you all met in Benacre woods this morning, at aboot half past nine, right?"

She nodded.

"You're all together?"

"Yeah," she said.

"But you were found alone," said Baird. "What happened in between?"

Her face creased as she attempted to remember, her eyes wandering left and right like the answer was hiding in the room.

"I fell," she said. "I tripped and dropped my stick. And... well, in the book, that's a cardinal sin. You never drop your pizzle. You get punished if you do."

"Punished with a whack to the heid?" said Baird.

"No. God no. In the book they just kind of chase you a bit. It's like a hunt. They say they're going to kill you, but they don't really. So I dropped my stick and then everyone was running after me, and I went into the woods..."

"By yourself?" asked Baird when she tapered off.

"They were right behind me," she said. "At least, I thought they were. I just kept running, because the woods aren't big, it's not like you can get lost in them. And..."

She fell quiet again, silence pouring into the room. Even Charles held his tongue, glaring at his daughter the way no father should ever look at their child.

"I saw a man," she said after almost a full minute had passed. "I thought it was the Wild Man, from the book."

"Vy'Agare?" said Baird.

"Wait, you *have* read it?"

"I got the Cliff Notes. You thought it was Vy'Agare?"

"Yeah," she said. "He's this dark lord who's in love with Princess LeFreene. But he's vile, he's all tattered and thorny. Grim. But he loves her, and at one point he gives her this love potion that kind of makes her fall for him, but it doesn't work properly because the old ways don't let you use magic for—"

"But it wasnae the Wild Man," said Baird, who was confused enough without a summary of the book. "Tell me what you actually saw."

Flora swallowed, wincing again.

"I don't think it was real," she said. "The man. It looked like... I don't know, it just looked like some sort of Halloween thing. Blood and... and all these feathers. Arrows, I think. It didn't even have a head, so how can it have been real? People don't just..."

She looked at Baird as if waiting for him to tell her she was right, that it wasn't real. And as much as he wished he could, he didn't.

"Oh," she said, and her eyes filled with tears. "That was a person?"

"I'm really sorry," he told her, resting a hand on top of the duvet where her arm lay. "I ken it's no what you want to hear. I cannae imagine how awful it must be. But I dinnae think it's a coincidence that you were attacked when you found the body. Do you remember anything else?"

She shook her head, but she spoke anyway.

"I heard something," she said. "Some kind of animal, growling. And I saw it moving in the woods. This huge wolf thing."

"You saw it?" asked Baird, thinking of Diana.

"I mean, kind of. Not really. But you could tell it was big. It... I don't know if that's what hit me, I can't remember. It's all..."

She waved her hand around her head.

"It's all just black, like it's been deleted. I don't even remember waking up in the woods, I just... There's just here. That's the first thing I remember. Being in bed. I'm sorry."

"You have absolutely no reason to be sorry, Flora," said Baird. "You're sure this thing you heard was a dug? Could it have been somebody pretending to be a dug? A man?"

The idea of it was enough to fill her face with fear. She didn't answer, but she didn't need to. Baird pushed himself off the bed, one hand on his lower back to relieve the pain.

"Think hard. You're sure you didnae see the person who did this to you? A glimpse? A voice?"

The young woman stared at the top of her duvet for a moment, a tear breaking free and rolling down her cheek.

"I didn't see anything, but he did speak."

"He?" said Baird. "You're sure it was a man?"

"I'm not sure about anything. I don't know what's real and what's not. I could have dreamed it. But I thought he said he'd been waiting for me."

"Waiting for you?" said Baird. "In the woods?"

She shrugged, not meeting his eye.

"That's all he said."

"That's good, Flora," said Baird. "Is there anything else? A feeling, even. Or a smell."

"A smell?" she said, and Baird wasn't sure if it was a question or not. "Maybe. I..."

She sniffed the air, like she was smelling it now.

"I remember something sweet. Something... I can't think. It was like shower gel, you know? Or soap. Something like that."

Baird nodded, making a note of it all on his phone.

"That's braw," he said. "Thank you, Flora. I hope you start to feel better soon. If you remember anything else, get one of the polis outside to call me. Aye? Disnae matter how small it is. You call me."

The girl nodded, stretching a hand towards her father. He studied it like an old maid would look at a cockroach, making no effort to take it. Baird opened the door before he said something he regretted, stepping into the corridor. Flora's voice followed him, a soft croak he almost didn't catch.

"It was lemons. That's what I smelled. I'm sure of it. Lemons."

CHAPTER TWELVE

THE THREE OTHER YOUNG PEOPLE WERE STILL SITTING in the hospital waiting area when Baird walked out of Flora Arbon's room. One of the two lads, the shorter, uglier, sweatier one, jumped to his feet as soon as he saw him. He was wearing shorts and a white T-shirt that showed off every bulge. He had his hands clenched together like he was praying, and his round face was etched with concern.

"Are you with the police?" he asked.

"Aye," said Baird. "You the three who went into the woods with Flora this morning?"

The young man nodded, a wisp of limp hair falling over his face.

"We've already told you everything we know," he said.

"Aye, but we're no aliens. We dinnae all share the same collective intelligence. What's your name?"

"Lucas."

"You got another name to go along with that?"

"Bude," said Lucas, and he spelled it out like a nursery teacher, counting off the letters on his fingers. "B-U-D-E."

"You're Anders, then," said Baird, looking at the other

man—whose shorts seemed to have shrunk even further in the time he was in the room—then the woman. "And Darcey."

They all nodded, and he waited.

"He's Yarl," said Darcey. "I'm Birch."

She was wearing a pink dress that would have been better suited to a wedding, the satin pocked with dirty smudges and pieces of twig and leaf. Beneath the frilly hem was a pair of black boots with thick metal soles. They must have weighed a tonne.

"Is Flora okay?" asked Lucas. "I keep asking, and nobody will tell us anything."

"She's awake," said Baird. "She's going to be fine."

They took a collective sigh of relief. Lucas crashed into his chair, chewing on his knuckles. Baird sat opposite them, pulling out his phone and finding the camera app.

"Any of yous mind if I take a photo? I've got a memory like a fishing net full of holes."

"All fishing nets have holes," said Darcey. "That's literally how they work."

Baird paused for long enough to understand she was right, then he took a couple of photos of the trio. He opened the Notes app.

"Right, give me the highlights, starting from when you got to the woods."

They looked at each other, as if they were about to start singing. It was the short guy who spoke, leaning forward in his chair with his elbows on his bare knees.

"I drove," he said. "I picked everyone up and we went to Benacre woods. Parked on the lane and walked up, because my car can't handle the potholes."

"You picked Flora up from home? In Southwold. After nine, aye?"

Lucas nodded, scratching his head. He'd used some kind of wax in his hair, but he hadn't rubbed it in properly, a greasy clump right over his ear. *Greasy Clump* would have been a good nickname for him, Baird thought, because it described the boy in so many different ways. He looked, as his granny might have said, like he'd been dookin' for apples in a chip pan.

"Huh?" he said, when he realised he'd missed what the kid had said next.

"I said I picked Anders and Darcey up together. From Halesworth. They're, you know, a thing."

Anders confirmed it with a nod. Darcey didn't seem as keen to admit it, although Baird wasn't sure why because the other lad was handsome enough to be a catalogue model.

"So you got to the woods, and then what?" he asked.

"We rode our pizzles to meet the others," said Lucas, and he did a little jiggle in his chair like he was riding one now. "But Flora fell over."

"She didn't just fall over," said Darcey. "She went completely arse over tit. I mean, it was some *Chuckle Brothers* shit. *You've Been Framed*, whatever. A full flip, pizzle stick in the crotch, face in the dirt, legs akimbo. You couldn't have fallen over like that if you'd tried."

Anders had to cover a smile with his hand as he remembered it.

"Funny, was it?" Baird asked him, unamused. The man's face returned to stone.

"You kind of had to be there," said Darcey, shrugging.

"I didn't think she was *that* bothered," said Lucas. "I thought she'd see the joke, because the first rule of ride your pizzle is—"

"Dinnae drop your pizzle," said Baird. "Aye, I ken."

"You've read it?" said Darcey.

"I have not. So she does a prat fall, she gets upset, and she legs it into the woods?"

Lucas nodded.

"And you chased her?"

"Yeah," he said. "Like in the book. You should read it."

"I'm no gonna read it. Who's doing the chasing?"

"Everyone," said Lucas. "It's part of the whole thing."

"You're all running together?"

"No," said Lucas. "We split up, because we didn't know where she'd gone. It's dark in the woods, even in the day. We thought she was playing, that she was acting it out."

"You're all on your own, then?" said Baird, looking at the others.

"Kind of," said Darcey. "I mean, we could all still see each other, a bit, and we were all making noise. Whooping and shit."

Baird wrote 'whooping and shit' in his notes, although he wasn't sure why.

"Who found her?" he asked.

"I did," said Lucas, wiping his damp lips. "Well, me and Darcey arrived pretty much at the same time."

Darcey nodded, her face glum.

"She was on the ground, and I thought she was playing," said Lucas. "So I go to pounce on her—"

"Pounce on her?" said Baird. "Like a cat?"

"No, like one of the pizzle guards. In the book. If you just read it then—"

"No."

"Well, I just ran to her, and then I saw..." He faltered, his eyes widening like he was watching it all in a movie. "There was blood on her head, and I thought it was too dark to actually be blood. It looked black, like oil. I thought she'd brought it with her, a prop or something. But there was some on her face as well, which is how I knew it was real. And she wasn't moving, and then..."

He swallowed, looking at Darcey. She stared back, both of them reliving the horror.

"And then?" prompted Baird.

"We saw the man," said Lucas.

"Hang on," said Baird. "What man? The man tied to the tree?"

"No," said Lucas. "He wasn't tied to anything, he was running away, into the bushes, and he—"

"Hang on," Baird said again. "Slow doon. Describe him."

"I didn't really get a good look," Lucas said, leaning back in his chair. "Because he was legging it. Right, Darcey?"

She didn't look sure.

"Darcey?" said Baird.

"I saw something," she said. "Some*one*, yeah. He was gone before I really got there. But I saw him moving in the trees."

"You're sure it was a man?"

"He was big," said Lucas, before Darcey could answer. "Could have been a woman, I guess. A big one. But he was moving fast, too. Like he was fit. You don't get many big, fit women. They're mostly chunky wobblers."

"Hair? Clothes?" said Baird, doing his best to ignore the comment.

"Both, I think," said Lucas, thinking hard.

"I mean what was he wearing?"

"Oh... black?" said Lucas, like he was asking the question. He turned to the young woman again. "Black?"

"Yeah, maybe," she said. "Honestly, I was so scared I kind of switched off. I just wanted to help Flora, so I called the ambulance and sat with her. The guy didn't come back, that's the main thing."

"Okay," said Baird, making a note. "How long was it between Flora running into the woods and you finding her?"

"It wasn't long," said Darcey. "Like, ten minutes? Less?"

"About that," said Lucas. "I don't know, exactly. But we got there together, and we saw Flora, and the man who was running away, and the thing on the tree."

"The thing on the tree," said Baird. "The dead man?"

Darcey actually laughed.

"It wasn't a dead man," she said. "It was some Halloween prank."

"In Spring?"

"Like, from last year or something," she said. "Or some *Court of Avalonia* fan decided to make a shrine to the Wild Man. I don't know. It can't have been a dead man, it didn't even have a head."

"Right you are," said Baird, who didn't have the heart to tell them otherwise. He turned to Anders. "You're being awfie quiet, pal."

"What do you want me to say?" he said, his voice heavy with an accent. Norwegian, he thought. Or Danish.

"When did you show up?"

"When I heard the screaming," he said.

"Aye? Who was screaming?"

Baird looked at Darcey, but it was Lucas who lifted a hand.

"That was me," he said. "It wasn't really a scream. I was trying to let people know that something had happened to Flora."

"It was a scream," said Anders.

"Yeah, it was definitely a scream," said Darcey. "A Fay Wray special."

Lucas flapped his arms in silent protest.

"You went to help?" Baird asked Anders.

"Of course," he said. "By the time I found them there were already a few people. I couldn't do much to help."

"You didnae see the man in black? Or anything else?"

"No," he said. "I went to the road to wait for the ambulance."

Baird nodded, writing it all down.

"Any of yous see a dug?"

"What?" said Darcey.

"A dug," he said. "*Dog*. Wee yappy chihuahua with a face like a skelped arse."

They looked at each other.

"Nobody in the group brought a dug?"

"No," said Lucas. "There was no dog."

Baird slipped his phone back into his pocket and pushed himself out of the chair.

"Oh, and did anyone smell lemons?"

They stared at him like he was a madman.

"Braw," he said, walking off. "Well, dinnae leave toon, I may need to speak with you again."

CHAPTER THIRTEEN

BAIRD RELAYED EVERYTHING HE'D LEARNED AT THE hospital to Briggs as he walked back to the car. Diana was standing on the driver's seat, her face smooshed against the steamy window. She started barking as soon as she saw him.

"Aye, I missed you too," he told her, gently pushing her out of the way as he climbed in.

She tried to jump onto the passenger seat and failed spectacularly, flopping into the footwell with what might have been a bark or a fart. She bounced back quickly enough, staring at him like he'd pushed her.

"It's no my fault you've got wet noodles for legs."

He drove out of the car park, juggling the myriad balls of the case as he made his way back onto the A12. At around half eleven yesterday evening, Gregory Brightwell had driven out of the hotel—if Headcold Pauly hadn't dreamed it, of course. He'd arrived in Benacre woods a little while later, where somebody had tied him to a tree, shot him with twelve arrows, then cut off his head.

Or vice versa.

And there he'd hung until the next morning, when a bunch of kids playing tug the pizzle had discovered him.

"You couldnae make it up," he told the dog, who was up on her back legs and too busy staring out of the window to reply.

The girl who'd found Brightwell had been attacked when she'd stumbled across the body—smacked around the back of the head by a mystery assailant. The witnesses, Darcey, Anders, and Greasy Clump, had spotted a big man dressed in black legging it through the bushes. It might have been the killer, it might not. But whoever it had been hadn't bothered to call the police when he'd spotted a headless dead man tied to a tree—which put him squarely on the guilty list.

"And then there's you," Baird said as he overtook a lorry, the Fiat's engine whining. "Mystery dug, mooching aboot the crime scene and embracing your right to silence."

He swerved back into the slow lane, traffic thundering past him. The day was giving itself to the evening, the sky darkening. His stomach growled, and he cursed himself for not picking up a piece from the canteen before heading out of the hospital. There weren't even any of Connell's floor snacks he could grab, thanks to the fellas at the car wash. He eyeballed the dog, and she finally looked over her shoulder at him.

"Ach, dinnae worry," he said. "There's no enough meat on you to make it worthwhile."

He parked his thoughts, concentrating on the drive. It seemed to take forever to climb the map, forty minutes passing before he spotted the signs for Southwold. He turned off onto the dusty B-road, instinctively knowing he was heading east, towards the sea. It was barely wide enough for two cars here, but fortunately the Fiat didn't really count as a whole one, and there wasn't much in the way of oncoming traffic.

In fact, the only other vehicle in sight was the white van that had followed him off the A12. It rode his rear end, filling his rear-view mirror. Even though the day was still bright enough, it had its headlights on. Maybe even its full beams.

"Jog on, you numpty," he said, hitting the brakes for a second just to let them know he was pissed off.

The van kept coming, dangerously close. The driver was a dark shape in the windscreen, hunched over the wheel. They were both doing fifty, and Connell's Fiat was made of tin foil and glue. It wouldn't last five seconds if the van hit it.

"Back off," Baird yelled.

He tapped the brakes again but the van was too close. He had no choice but to speed up, the tight turns trying to ambush him. There was nowhere to pull over, the narrow road lined with tall hedges and old trees.

"You are in so much trouble," he said, wondering if he should stick his warrant card out of the window. He didn't dare take his sweaty hands off the wheel. "Get off my arse you bawheided walloper!"

He hammered the horn, but the noise it made was little more than a dusty breath. Diana was barking her head off, foaming at the mouth as she picked up on his panic.

"You're alright," he told her. "Just hang on."

They turned a corner—too fast—and he spotted a track up ahead, leading into a field. He hit the brakes for as long as he dared, the van practically humping him now. He turned hard, the Fiat's wheels screeching as it swerved. He was going to pull over and let the van pass, then he was going to follow it wherever it was going and batter the driver into the middle of next week.

"So be warned, you—"

The van's engine roared, and it slammed into the back of the Fiat. The impact was hard enough to lift the little car's rear end off the ground, Baird's head cracking off the wheel. He choked out a cry, grappling with the car as it started to spin. The van was still there, shunting him towards the side of the road, the shriek of shearing metal enough to make his ears bleed.

He took his foot off the brake, slamming it onto the accelerator and twisting the wheel to the side. The car turned sharply, and for a second the van looked like it was going to push it over—the Fiat up on two wheels, the tyres smoking. Baird grabbed Diana by the collar as momentum hurled her towards the dashboard.

"Jesus suffering fuck!" he yelled, dumping the dog into his lap.

The car thumped down, spinning like a Catherine wheel. The van filled the front windscreen now, the driver still a smudge of darkness. It thumped into the front of the Fiat, Baird's head cracking off the wheel again. The windscreen shattered, a storm of sound blasting inside.

"You arse cramp!"

He stamped on the clutch, ripping the gear stick into reverse and flooring it. The car tore free, the bumper clattering onto the dirt track. He twisted around so he could see out the rear window, the Fiat whining as he steered up the track, the dog whining even louder as he gripped it between his thighs. The van was accelerating towards him again, flattening the fallen bumper, gaining ground too quickly.

He turned the wheel hard, trying to change gear at the same time. It didn't work, the Fiat reversing into the field.

Corn stalks battered the windows, not tall enough to hide him. He hit the brake, his heart doing a hornpipe in his chest. The bonnet was smoking, Connell's car on its last legs. He wondered whether he should get out now and make a run for the trees. But it was too late. The van was turning off the track, coming for him again. He still couldn't see the driver, but whoever sat there had a perfect view of him through the broken windscreen.

"Get tae fuck!" he yelled at them, lifting a middle finger for a second before using the same hand to wrestle the gear stick into first.

He hit the accelerator, trundling back towards the road. The car bounced on the hard ridges of the field, something else falling off it with a thud and a clang. Baird's head rang off the ceiling, the dog trampolining in his lap.

"Come on," he told the Fiat. "Dinnae give up on me noo."

He glanced in the mirror, the van closing in fast. It was struggling too, rocking wildly as it picked up speed. Baird thumped back onto the track, the tyres skidding. He tried to slow down as he reached the turn, but nothing happened when he drove his foot onto the brake pedal.

"Shite!" he wailed, wrenching the wheel.

The Fiat skidded onto the road, almost colliding with another car that was barrelling around the corner. Something popped behind him, and for a second he thought it was a gunshot. Then the car started vibrating and he realised a tyre had gone—maybe more than one. He kicked at the brake again, and the pedal snapped off.

"Ya wee fud!"

The Fiat was getting faster, the entire thing vibrating like a broken washing machine. Another car passed him, the driver wide-eyed. Baird glanced into the mirror, expecting to see the van picking up the chase again. But it sat at the junction between the road and the track, the driver watching him go behind the tinted window.

He turned the corner as best he could, the speedometer hitting forty and still climbing.

"Would you just stop!" he screamed.

He spotted another track up ahead and he veered into it. The car just about took off as it thumped over a ditch, the back window shattering this time. Baird grabbed the handbrake.

"Come on, you bampot!"

He wrenched it so hard he thought it was going to snap off too. The wheels locked, the car jolting and bumping and finally skidding to a halt.

Baird sat there, his heart a foaming mess inside his chest, his head screaming like broken machinery. His entire body felt numb, and he had to look at every limb in turn to make sure it was still attached. Diana sat in his lap, her tail so firmly between her legs it was poking her in the chin. Her eyes were big and wet and googling all over the place. He gently put a hand on her back, and she gave his fingers a reassuring lick.

"You alright?" he asked her.

He heard an engine, his heart imploding wetly as he craned around in his seat. It was just a car, driving past on the road. Nothing else followed. Still, he was a sitting duck here. He tried to open his door, but it was jammed. He scooted over to the passenger seat, pulling the handle. The door fell off completely, landing in the dirt. He clambered over it, clinging onto Diana as he made his way across the field to the nearest hedgerow. More cars zoomed past, and every time they did he felt a stab of panic in his gut.

But there was no sign of the van.

"Aye, you better run," he muttered as he moved behind a tree, his feet sinking into the soft ground. He pushed his forehead to the rough bark for a second, thanking every force in the universe for keeping him safe.

Then he pulled out his phone, and called Briggs.

THE FIRST IRV arrived nearly fifteen minutes later, Connell practically hanging out of the window. Baird could hear her cry of distress from halfway across the field, where he sat on a grassy verge throwing sticks for the dog. The police car struggled for half a dozen yards before the driver gave up. Connell's door opened and she flew out, flapping across the ridged ground like a panicked emu.

"Bertram Pickle!" she howled. "No!"

The car was a wreck. Two of the tyres on one side had blown, making it slump like a drunk. The front and back windscreens were shattered, the panelling dented, both bumpers gone. One door still lay where it had fallen. Smoke rose from the bonnet, further darkening the evening sky.

"He's dead!"

Baird stood up, lobbing another twig for the dog. Diana seemed to have forgotten all about the ordeal, her tail wagging as she scuttled over the dirt. Baird couldn't keep track of who tripped over their own feet more, the dog or the DC.

"Connie," he shouted, meeting her by the car. Everything ached, especially his head. His brain felt like it had been put through a mincer.

Connell stood beside her little Fiat, her hands in her hair. Her tears caught the sun, and when she looked at him over the roof he could see genuine distress in her expression.

"Why?" she sobbed.

Before Baird could answer, a Range Rover grumbled through the gap in the hedge. It moved over the rough ground with ease, steering around the IRV and parking in front of the Fiat. The driver was almost too short to be seen over the wheel, but Baird knew whose car it was. Sure enough, DCI Briggs opened the door and dropped down. She looked at Baird, then at the car, then at the dog, as if trying to work out which one to shout at first.

The answer was kind of inevitable.

"You'd better have a damned good explanation for this, Harrison," she said, walking to Connell's side. "We got a 999 call from somebody saying you were playing Dodgems with a van in the middle of a public road."

"That's no exactly what happened," he said, trying to massage the ache from his temples.

"He's dead," Connell said again, genuine heartbreak in her voice.

Briggs put a hand on Connell's shoulder, squeezing. Diana had wandered over to them, sniffing Briggs' shoes and then planting her feet on Connell's shins. If Baird didn't know better, he'd have thought the dog was making sure she was okay.

"First things first," Briggs said, looking at Baird. "Are you hurt?"

Baird patted himself down again.

"I mean, I'm battered," he said. "Black and blue. But I'm no *hurt* hurt. Thanks in no small part to your car, Connie. Bertie was tougher than he looked."

He frowned.

"Although it was a wee bit disappointing when the airbags didnae go off."

"Was this an accident?" Briggs asked.

"No, ma'am," said Baird, wishing he had a chair. The bones in his legs felt like they were dissolving like Parma violets in Coke. "It wasnae. The van followed me off the A12. It waited until the road was empty and then it ran right into the back of me. Forced me into a field. It would have flattened me if it'd had a chance. It was sheer luck we managed to get away."

"We?" said Briggs, and Baird nodded to the dog, who was now cradled in Connell's arms.

"Did you see who was driving?" said the DCI.

"Nut," he said, picturing the silhouette hunched over the wheel. Their face had been invisible, but their posture had told Baird everything—whatever had happened, it had happened with intent. "Sun was in the windae, or it was tinted."

"Plates?"

Baird shook his head.

"But they were trying to hit me, nae question."

"Why?" said Briggs.

He sucked in a breath, his ribs throbbing.

"I mean, it was a pretty obnoxious car," he said.

Nobody laughed. Briggs waited.

"I dinnae ken," he said. "But there's a good chance the van followed me all the way from Ipswich. I wouldnae've noticed it on the main road. Maybe they were at the hospital. Maybe they thought I'd found something out from Flora, or one of the others. The kids said they saw somebody in the woods."

"A man running into the bushes," said Briggs. "I heard. That's what they told the Uniforms when they were first interviewed."

"Aye, a big fella, black clothes."

He shook his head, thinking.

"That van might have been tailing me for even longer," he said. "Could have been on us since Gregory Brightwell's place. Or from Denton's. Which reminds me, I can think of one big fella who likes to wear black."

"I'm not going there," said Briggs. "Not yet. We'll need a lot more than *big fella, black clothes.* The Superintendent's shoe is still lodged squarely in my colon after your impetuous behaviour in the last case. Is that clear?"

"Clearer than I'd like it to be," said Baird. "Listen, if they tried to kill me after talking to the kids, there's a chance they'll go after Flora and her friends."

Briggs nodded, and she was about to speak when there was an almighty crunch from the Fiat. An airbag had detonated from the steering wheel, filling the interior with white powder.

"Oh, right, there it is," said Baird. "Super."

"I've put more Uniforms in the hospital," Briggs went on. "And I'll make sure the three friends are escorted back to their homes. The other kids who were in the woods all have alibis for Friday night, and didn't see a thing on Saturday. They don't seem mixed up in this at all."

Connell had put the dog down in order to rest both hands on the roof of the fallen Fiat. If Baird had owned a bugle, he'd be playing Taps.

"If you can believe it," he told her, "I'd just had him cleaned. Hoovered, polished, the works. Cost me sixty quid."

Connell sniffed, stroking the flaking paint.

"I'm no joking, Connie. Your wee car saved my life. Saved both our lives, even if the airbags were late to the party."

"I want you to get checked out, Harrison," said Briggs.

"I'm fine, ma'am. Honest."

"You're a long way from fine. Get checked. Now. Boone will take you, and your four-legged friend."

Baird nodded, patting his legs until Diana scampered over. He picked her up, sloping towards the IRV. He stopped halfway, looking back. The sun had almost vanished, and it had set fire to the horizon on its way out. The world was burning, turning Connell and Briggs into silhouettes.

"I cannae say who was driving the van, ma'am," he said, stroking the dog's head. "But I ken one thing for sure."

The DCI looked at him, waiting.

"Nobody tries to take you oot like that unless you're getting close to the truth."

CHAPTER FOURTEEN

THE JUNCTION WITH THE A12 HAD BEEN CLOSED OFF for the forensic team, so PC Boone went east instead, heading towards Southwold. It was just as well, because before he could take the long way round to Ipswich, Baird leaned over from the back seat and told him not to bother.

"I'm alright, honest," he said. "Where I'm from that wouldnae even count as a collision. That's just traffic."

He asked to be taken home, but as they were approaching the little seaside town he decided against it. He directed the IRV north instead, getting Boone to drop him off on the road outside the Sheltered Oaks Retirement Village. He plopped Diana on the long driveway, letting her sniff her way along the row of neatly trimmed bushes. Halfway there she hunched over, trembling and gurning as she went to the toilet.

"You gonna clean that up?" he asked her.

He patted his pockets, as if by some miracle a poop bag had appeared, but the shite was the size of a chocolate raisin, so he opted to leave it. He picked her up and walked to the main doors.

And there he stopped, the way he always did, like there was a glass wall between him and the home.

Even though he'd been here again half a dozen times since that first meeting—half a dozen awkward conversations with his father, half a dozen trips down the nightmare alley that was memory lane—he still felt like he was marching to war. After twenty-four years, the old man was a stranger. A man who wore his dad's skin like a mask, who spoke of Baird's childhood, his sister, his mum, as if he was reciting a script. Every time he walked up to these doors, he thought about turning around again, leaving the county, leaving the *country*, heading home—a home he'd forged for himself piece by piece without any help from Douglas Bawjaws Baird.

And every time, he walked right in.

"You're a diddy, Harrison," he told himself.

The care home was a sauna, the heat oppressive. When Baird saw the little man behind the reception desk, his groan filled the entire room.

"Well, if it isnae Bev the Beaver Botherer," he said as he walked over.

Bev snapped his head around like he'd heard the fire alarm go off. He glared at Baird over the top of his computer monitor, the way he always did, and Baird fired a smug grin in his direction—the way *he* always did.

"Do they never let you go home, pal?" he asked. "Or do you live here with the other old folk?"

"I do not live here," said Bev. "And for your information, I am not old. I'm thirty-two."

"*Thirty-two*?" said Baird, genuinely shocked. "In tortoise years?"

"No, in human years."

"I think you're confused," said Baird. "I think you were *born* in thirty-two. How can you be younger than I am?"

He shifted the dog to his other arm to relieve the ache in his ribs. Bev finally noticed her, his lip curling up in disgust.

"There are no animals allowed inside the home," he said. "Please take your... *thing* outside."

"It's no an animal," he said. "It's a puppet. I brought it to cheer up the residents."

Diana looked up at him with one eye, the other one pointing in the approximate direction of Bev. There was a string of drool hanging from her lips halfway to the floor. He gave the dog a gentle squeeze and she barked.

"That is not a puppet," said Bev, although he didn't look sure.

"Aye, it is. Do you think they make dogs this ugly in real-life? My hand's up its arse right now. Look."

He squeezed again, and this time the dog sneezed, the drool cartwheeling through the air.

"It can do all kinds of things. Da loves puppets. I thought it might bring him oot of his funk."

"If you want me to call security, Mr Baird," said Bev. "You're going the right way about it."

Baird lifted Diana, doing his best to speak without moving his lips.

"Ah dinnae be such a wet blanket, Beverley. I'm no a dug, I'm a puppet. And why do you need security? I thought you were a mean old Viking."

Something pinged on the computer, and Bev glanced down. Baird took his chance, bolting for the stairs.

"Oi!" Bev roared. "It's not even visiting hours!"

Baird ran up the steps, getting through the first set of fire doors before setting the chihuahua down on the carpeted floor. They walked the rest of the way together, arriving at Douglas Baird's room to find the door open. The TV was blaring, as usual, the canned laughter and abrasive music from a game show of some kind. Baird stopped for a moment, seeing the back of the chair where his father sat, a balding head, a skinny arm, crooked fingers tapping out a beat in time to the TV. Once again, he felt the utter impossibility of it, of being here with this man.

He knocked, following the dog into the heat of the room, into the aroma of soap and aftershave that transported him right back to childhood, to when he'd stand next to him at the bathroom sink with bubbles on his face, pretending to be a grown man. The force of the memory after so long took his breath away.

He cleared his throat, knocked again.

"Da. It's me."

Still nothing, and he wondered if Dougie was asleep, or if he'd slipped away in the night—a thought that conjured feelings of both grief and relief.

Then he rounded the chair and saw that he was awake, his glassy eyes fixed on the screen. His mouth hung open, his tongue probing at dry lips and yellow teeth. He wore tracksuit trousers and an old Rangers football shirt, his feet bare. He seemed even smaller now than he had the last time Baird had visited, as if he was slowly decomposing in the humid room.

"Da," Baird said again.

This time, the other man glanced up. Their eyes met, and Baird felt like he'd been kicked in the gut—that same explosive mix of emotions that he couldn't make any sense of, that turned him into a little boy again. Dougie nodded once, the way you would at the postman, then he turned back to his show.

"Back again, then," he said, just a trace of his accent left.

"Aye," said Baird. "Though I have no idea why."

The dog was heading back into the corridor, and Baird didn't blame it. The room was like a furnace. He pushed the door closed before she could escape, and cranked open the stubborn window. Not that it made much of a difference, the air outside seemed reluctant to enter. Nothing wanted to be inside this room, it seemed. He put a hand to the cast iron radiator and instantly pulled it away again, his skin just about sizzling.

"Christ," he said. "Is this place powered by lava?"

But there was no way to turn it off, the valve painted shut.

Baird took off his jacket, slinging it on the back of the spare chair before sitting down. Diana trotted over, nuzzling his ankles, but he didn't pick her up. He just watched his old man, wondering again what had gone so wrong, what had happened to turn the fearless giant of his childhood into this sickly specimen. What had happened to that booming laugh, to the songs he'd belted out in the car, to the jokes he'd told?

What had happened.

Or *who*.

"Da," he said. "I've no got long."

The man still didn't acknowledge him, so Baird groaned his way over to the TV and switched it off. The silence in the room felt suffocating. The entire building may as well have been empty—the entire *world* may as well have been empty—just the two of them left, father and son.

"I was watching that," said Dougie.

"No you weren't," said Baird, returning to his chair. "I said I've no got long. I just wanted to swing by."

"Why?"

Baird laughed, although there was no humour in it. Dougie looked over, studying his suit.

"What happened to you, then?"

"Got into a fight with Bev doonstairs," he said. "He looks worse."

Dougie nodded.

"You got kids?" he asked.

"*Kids*?" said Baird, the question so out of left field it took him a moment to figure out how to answer it. "I've been here six times, Da, you think I'd have mentioned them?"

"That's a no, then? You a poofta?"

"*What*?" he said.

"Gay," said Dougie. "Don't give a shit if you are. Pooftas can still have kids."

"Jesus Christ," said Baird, sitting back in the chair. "You ken why I dinnae have kids? It's because I'm too scared that being a useless bampot might be genetic. If I did to my wee'uns what you did to yours, I'd jump off a bridge."

"You weren't exactly wee, Harry. You were practically a grown fucking man."

"I was twelve, Da."

Dougie shrugged, staring at the TV like there was still something playing.

"You checked him out, yet?" he asked after a moment.

"Who?"

"Who do you think? Kett."

"Nut," said Baird, although that was a lie. The wall of his living room had become a tribute to the man, a mosaic of photographs and dozens of newspaper articles. Whatever you said about Robert Kett, he'd been busy. "And I did the maths, Da. He's forty-seven. He would have been in his early twenties when you left us. How the hell would a kid that age be responsible for anything?"

Dougie sniffed, turning his small eyes to Baird.

"Weren't just him, was it? He was just part of it, but he's the one who fucked me over. He's the one who burned me."

Diana scratched at the door, trying to escape. Baird loosened his tie, feeling like he was being hanged by it.

"You're making a lot of noise, Da, but you're no saying anything," he said. "You either tell me what happened, or you let me go. Because there's no much of me that disnae believe you're full of shite."

"Exactly," he said. "That's why I can't just tell you. You won't believe me. Fucking Kath didn't believe—"

"The next time I hear my mother's name in your mouth, it better no sound like that," said Baird.

"Well she didn't," Dougie went on, pouting like a child. "Said I was a liar. Said I was full of shit, that if I was innocent then I should have gone to the police. But they *were* the police. I couldn't do a fucking thing, Harry. And you won't believe me if I tell you, you have to see it for yourself."

"I didnae bring my time machine with me," said Baird. "How'm I gonna see it?"

Dougie picked at the arm of his chair, scratching the worn fabric.

"I weren't a bad guy," he said. "All this started cos I was trying to be the good guy, you understand? I was trying to make something of myself, for you and Elspy and your ma. That's the whole reason I went down there."

Baird settled back, wishing he had a bucket of popcorn for what he knew was going to be a feature-length parade of bullshit.

"I wanted to make some money. I weren't even doing anything illegal, not properly. Nobody was getting hurt. I had a mate in the city, this Geordie, but I could trust him. He had a good thing going, running numbers south of the river. No harm in that, right? Nobody gets hurt. And I tried doing it the right way, Harry, you know I did. All those weeks on the rigs, you remember them?"

Baird shook his head.

"I was gone a long fucking time before I actually left, you know what I mean? Worked myself to the bone for you. This was going to be different. Couple of years in the smoke, work my way up, make enough to sort out a proper life for you and your sister."

He cleared his throat, struggling to draw in enough breath to carry on. He was gripping the chair now like he was on a roller coaster, like he was afraid he might end up upside down, or on the floor, or flying out the window.

The night is young, thought Baird.

"It was going to be different," he said again. "The fella who ran the lines, he was known as Big Bird, because his name was Swann. Wasn't a player or anything, but he kicked up to a couple of real pricks. A man called Nigel Topper. Mad Dog, they called him."

"Big Bird and Mad Dog?" said Baird. "Is this a true story or an episode of *Sesame Street*?"

"Mad Dog," Dougie said. "If you ask me, that was an insult to dogs. Proper prick. Him and his son, Tommy Topper. And you know who *they* kicked up to, don't you?"

"Aye," said Baird, who could see where it was going. "The polis."

"Was different back then," said Dougie.

"Da, you pished off in 2001," said Baird. "It's no exactly the wild Seventies. It wasnae even the last millennium."

"You couldn't do anything without putting a big chunk in their suit pockets," the old man went on. "But if you did, they'd let you do anything you wanted. Anything, Harry. Whole city was a madhouse."

He coughed again, wheezing in a breath.

"You alright?" Baird asked.

"No," Dougie shot back. "It's what I'm telling you, innit? I'm not fucking alright. See, I don't even know what happened. I was working for Big Bird Swann, but I was helping the police out as well. That's what I mean, about doing the right thing. I was helping the coppers, getting information to them."

"A CI?" said Baird, leaning forward.

"I was a snitch," he said. "Undercover, whatever you want to call it. I wanted these guys off the streets as much as they did. Especially Topper and his little shit smear of a son. Proper psycho, was Nigel. Still is, I think, even though he's a cripple now."

"And the money helped, I take it?"

"It didn't hurt," said Dougie. "But that's not why I did it. I weren't a bad man, I keep telling you. I'd never have fucking killed him, no matter how much they were offering."

"Hang on," said Baird, holding up a hand. His heart was doing a polka behind his aching ribs. "Back up. Killed who?"

"Tommy fucking Topper," said Dougie, as if it was the most obvious thing in the world. "Nigel's son. He got himself shot one night. Him and Big Bird both, dumped in the Thames. Thing is, I knew it was going to happen, yeah? The Toppers were getting too big for their breeches, and I heard this foreign lot was after 'em. Algerian. Or Albanian. I can't remember. Wanted a coup. I told my contact at the police that Tommy was going to get himself plugged, and he said he was going to stop it. Told me to tell Tommy and Nigel he wanted to meet them both, give them an opportunity to get out. So I set it up."

He was getting agitated, and he sucked in another lungful of air, coughing hard.

"Take it easy," said Baird.

"I'll fucking take it easy when I'm done, mate. You listening to me? You hearing it? This cop told me to tell Mad Dog and his lad to meet him that night, up by the docks. Nigel didn't go, but Tommy did, and he took Big Bird with him. They turned up, and they both got plugged. *They* did it."

"The *polis*?" said Baird. "Hang on."

But Dougie was steamrolling.

"He was a nasty cunt, that copper. John Cooper. Had a pack of little shits working for him, all plods. He's the one who told me what to do. Said Nigel and Tommy both trusted me, and if I arranged the meet, I'd be safe. Lying prick. Tommy dies, Nigel loses his fucking mind. Couple of days after Tommy floats back up near Gallion's Reach, I get a knock on me door. One of Coop's men, this arrogant prick in uniform. Pushed into my flat like he owned the place, made me sit down like a... like a child. You know what he said to me? Said I was going to get the heat for Tommy's murder. Said I was the chief suspect, and they had enough on me to put me away for the rest of my life—which wouldn't be long, in Belmarsh. He made that very fucking clear. And that was only if Nigel didn't get to me first, when the news got out that I was the one who shot his lad."

"He didn't arrest you?" asked Baird.

"No. He said he was going to give me a choice. Take the heat and end up in prison, face up to Mad Dog and end up in the river. Or disappear."

There was a hurricane blowing inside Baird's head as he tried to make sense of what his father was saying.

"That sounds like bullshit, Da. Why would they let you walk away from that if they had enough to put you away?"

"So I wouldn't blab," spat Dougie. "That's all they cared about, upsetting the apple cart. Rocking the boat. Whatever you want to call it. Tommy was dead, Nigel was out of his mind with grief, he was done. Coop had his head firmly up the arsehole of the foreign pricks who happily waltzed in and took over everything from Lewisham to fucking Hackney. I was a loose end, and I was lucky, because they could have dumped me in the river too. Would've been easier for them."

"You were a CI," said Baird. "An informant. There would have been paperwork to prove you were trying to do the right thing."

Dougie's face peeled open into a ghoul's smile, something right out of a horror movie.

"There was," he said. "Coop's prick officer brought it all with him. He set fire to it right in front of me, burned the lot in my own fucking sink. And he told me, that prick; he looked me right in the eye and said if I was in the city in the morning I was a dead man. Said if I was in the country in the morning I was a dead man. Said if I went back north, I was dead."

He leaned over and poked a finger into Baird's chest, hard.

"Said if I ever spoke to Kath or my kids again, then it wouldn't just be me who was buried in a shallow grave. It would be you lot, too."

"Get lost," said Baird, wafting his father's words away with both hands. "You expect me to believe that?"

"Exactly," said his father. "You won't believe it until you see it for yourself. That kid who came to my house? His name was Robert Kett. He's the reason I didn't come home, Harry. He's the one who ruined everything. You know something else? He's the fuck who shot Tommy Topper. I'll put money on it. Nobody but me knows that. Not even Nigel knows. Kett did it. You think he'd be out there walking around if Nigel knew?"

It was Baird who felt like he was on a roller coaster now, and he pushed himself out of the chair, bracing a hand on the wall so he wouldn't keel over.

"You sound insane, Da."

"Yeah? Well why don't you go ask Coop what happened? Oh, yeah, you can't. He's dead. Hung himself in prison a few weeks after he and Kett had a scuffle. What about the other copper who hung around with them? Barry Benson. Everyone called him Bingo. Where's he?"

"Dead," said Baird, who recognised the name from one of the articles.

"Murdered the same night as the man who took Kett's wife. Kett probably killed both of 'em. You only have to look, Harry. Look at the trail of shit he's left behind, and ask yourself why do all that unless he's burying something, something big. He came up under Cooper and those others, he was poisoned from the start. A bad fucking kid when he showed up at my door, and a bad fucking man now."

There was no air in the room, and Baird staggered to the door. He opened it, tripping over the dog and practically falling into the corridor.

"You want the truth, Harry, you just have to find Kett."

He didn't have any words to reply with. He just kept walking, the dog trotting by his side, his da's voice chasing him.

"You just have to ask him."

There must have been a bad look on his face, because

not even Bev tried to stop him as he marched across the lobby. He let the dog out first, then he stumbled into the night, ready to scream his grief at the dark sky, ready to pound the earth with his fury.

Finding that all he could do was cry.

CHAPTER FIFTEEN

Sunday

It felt like five minutes later that the sound of his alarm woke him.

Baird opened his eyes, seeing nothing but darkness. When he tried to get a breath in, he found he couldn't. He gargled in panic, putting his hands to his face to discover a lump of soft, hairy flesh clamped there. He sat up so fast that whatever it was went flying, landing on the duvet with a bark.

The dug, he remembered as his heart started to settle. When he'd shut her out of the room last night, she'd sat by the door making a noise like an accordion in a cement mixer. After about seven minutes he'd ended up bringing her to bed with him.

"Christ, Di," he said, flexing his aching neck. "I'm trying to help you, and you're trying to finish me off."

The alarm stopped, then immediately started again.

Without the chihuahua's damp arsehole plastered to his eyeballs, he saw that it was morning, light pouring through the cracks in the curtains and forming puddles on the carpet. He also noticed that it wasn't his alarm at all, it was a call. Connell's name was on the screen.

"Alright," he said when he answered it. He licked his lips, plucking a hair from his tongue. His mouth tasted of fish even though he couldn't remember eating any. "What's happening?"

"Well, Bertram Pickle is well and truly dead," she said. "They won't even try to fix him."

It took him a second or two to realise she was talking about her car.

"I'm sorry, Connie. He didn't deserve that." He shuffled out of the bed, heading for the bathroom. "Is that why you called me at the crack of dawn?"

"It's after seven," she said. "And no. I'm calling because Briggs wants us in HQ ASAP."

"There's a break?" he asked as he fired up the shower. Diana followed him in, watching his every move.

"The opposite, I think," said Connell. "No breaks. No leads. No clues. Nothing."

"You're no exactly selling it to me, pal," he said. "But I'll be there in a jiffy."

HE LEFT the dog in his kitchen with a dish of water and a plate of pre-cooked chicken, giving her strict instructions not to trash the place. It was a seven-minute walk from his flat to HQ, and he strolled along the seafront, trying not to look at the horizon where the sun was already doing its best to blaze a hole in his skull. The wind helped diffuse the situation, a cool breeze that tousled the waves and wrapped him in the sweet, saltwater smell of home. The gulls rode it like kids on their bikes, calling to each other as they dived and wheeled against the blue. There were already people on the pier, the hollow sound of running feet and the laughter of kids following him up the hill.

There were worse places in the world, he thought, although he'd never say it out loud.

He was the last to arrive at HQ, the smell of coffee filling the little building as he walked through the door. Briggs was in the kitchen, and he half expected to see her brewing up an instant coffee with out-of-date Nescafe. He was pleasantly surprised to see a brand-new machine on the counter.

"Crivens," he said. "Am I dreaming?"

"We figured if you're staying with us, we'd better start making proper coffee," said Briggs as the machine hissed and puffed.

"The jury's still oot on me staying, ma'am, but this cannae hurt."

She passed him the cup and they walked into the makeshift Incident Room together. Connell was already there, nursing a hot chocolate in a mug the size of her head. There was an enormous mound of cream on the top, and a not insignificant blob on the end of her nose.

"Please tell me that's no breakfast, Connie."

"I will certainly tell you that, sir," she said.

DI Henry Crump sat next to her, finishing off a bacon sandwich that was apparently so good he couldn't take his eyes off it. His beard was thick with grease.

"Any more of them going?" Baird asked him, remembering that he hadn't eaten dinner.

"They're from the seafront, sir," said Connell. "I can run out and get you one?"

"No you can't," Briggs shouted from the kitchen. "If he'd wanted breakfast, he would have eaten it at breakfast time."

"Alright, *Mother*," he muttered beneath his breath.

He sat down at the table, studying the wall of evidence. Gregory Brightwell took centre stage in three photographs. In the first, he grinned at the camera from a magazine shoot, his face alive with confidence. The second was a close-up of his arse, and that godawful handprint tattoo.

In the third, he hung headless from the tree in Benacre woods, his body bristling with arrows.

On the right-hand side of the wall was a mugshot of a mad-eyed Carl Denton that had to have been taken a few years ago, his gold teeth gleaming. On the left was a pyramid of pizzle kids, photographed at the scene. Flora was at the top, then Darcey and the lads, and underneath them the six others who had met them in the woods.

There were two new additions since yesterday. The first was a blurry photograph of a white van, captured by a traffic camera on the Ipswich road. The driver was a little clearer here, but it was immediately obvious why Baird hadn't been able to identify him. He was wearing a black hat, the lower part of his face covered by a mask or a scarf.

The second addition was a poster, and this was infinitely more interesting. The image showed a gangly teenage boy wearing an orange vest and a red headband. The photo had obviously been taken at the exact moment a large ball had made contact with his head, his face smooshed, his eyes screwed shut, and a wad of spit exploding from his lips. The text beneath the picture read:

The East Anglian Constabularies' Annual Dodgeball Competition. Sign up now!

"What is that?" he asked. "Dodgeball?"

"Yes," said Briggs, as she walked in, a cup of tea in each hand. She sat down next to Baird. "It's a godawful indecency that happens every year. Unfortunately, the Superintendent wants us to put together a team. He's desperate to beat the savages from up north."

Baird lifted an eyebrow, and she answered him before he could ask the question.

"Norfolk," she said. "I don't suppose you're a sporting man, Baird?"

"I'm no a runner, sorry," he said.

"You don't have to run. You just have to not fall over, and not get hit."

"To be honest, I've been failing at all those things since I got here," he said, rubbing his neck. "I'll pass."

"Good," said Briggs. "I'll add you to the list."

"Of people who are *no* playing, aye?"

She didn't answer, nodding to the photograph of the van.

"That was taken yesterday evening, on the A12 four miles north of Ipswich," said Briggs. "Your car, Connell, is right in front. We're still trying to access footage from the hospital car park, but you were right, Baird, they followed you all the way to the B1387 and took their shot when the road was quiet."

"No plates," said Baird.

"No," said Briggs. "We know it's a VW Crafter, a first generation, but we're not hopeful about getting anything else from it."

"How's that?"

"Because the driver took it to Wenhaston at some point

in the night and torched it. The fire service managed to put out the blaze, but the van's a shell. VIN numbers have been scratched off. It's a dead end, unless we can trace it back to where it started following you and get lucky with some cameras."

Baird took a sip of his coffee but it was far too hot. He settled for inhaling the steam, trying to get his caffeine hit through his nose.

"Do we know any more about what they were trying to achieve?" said Connell, fingering cream into her mouth.

"Use a spoon, Connie, for heaven's sake," said Briggs. "No, we're none the wiser. But as you alluded to last night, Baird, it seems somebody is trying to stop us from finding out the truth. If the driver assumed you had discovered something from Flora and her friends in the hospital, then it makes sense he'd try to keep you from sharing it."

"The kids okay?" he asked. "Nobody came after them?"

"No," said Briggs. "But it doesn't mean it won't happen."

"What aboot the woman from Denton's?" he asked. "The purple-haired loon who flew oot the windae. Any news on her?"

"Not yet," said Briggs. "Denton's has a policy of not using cameras, unless it's to record staff, so we're unlikely to find out unless she tries to enter the room again. We're still waiting on that warrant, not that it will do us much good. It was definitely a woman you saw, not our man in black?"

Baird closed his eyes, picturing her face as best he could. His stomach flipped as he remembered stepping out over the balcony.

"Aye, it was a woman," he said. "She was wearing black. Might be the same person."

"Well, whoever it is, I think you're right. The individual

the kids saw in the woods is the same individual who killed Gregory Brightwell. They're panicking, trying to cover their tracks."

"I was thinking aboot that," said Baird, trying his coffee again and burning his lips. "Covering your tracks would be a whole lot easier if you didnae cut a man's heid off and tie him to a tree, right? This guy could have buried Greg in a shallow grave and the kids would have ridden their pizzles right over him."

"Indeed," said Briggs.

"So he didnae want to cover his tracks. He wanted the world to see what he'd done. This wasnae just a murder, it was a... I dinnae ken, a ritual or something."

"That's exactly what I think," said Connell.

She reached beneath the table, pulling a notebook from her bag. When she put it down on the table she nudged her mug with her forearm, frothy hot chocolate sloshing over the side. Baird could hear Briggs' eyes rolling in their sockets.

"Whoops, sorry. I'll get that in a second. I did some research last night. Couldn't sleep, because of the awful thing that happened to my car."

"I'd just like to point out that it happened to me n'all," said Baird. "A real human being, with feelings."

"I kept asking myself why somebody would do that to another man," she went on, ignoring him. "Tying him up like that, butchering him. It's barbaric. But it's symbolic, too, right? We spoke about it yesterday, Edmund's death."

"Noel Edmonds?" Baird said, struggling to remember.

"No, *Saint* Edmund. That's what I was looking into last night. So King Edmund was this king, obviously. He ruled East Anglia about a thousand years ago. When the Vikings invaded, he was captured. They tied him to a tree and shot him with arrows, and then they cut off his head and threw it into the forest."

"Which reminds me," said Baird. "Any sign of the heid?"

Briggs shook her head, and Connell continued.

"This is a copycat killing, it has to be. The doubly weird thing is that in the legend, when Edmund's followers found the head, it was being guarded by a wolf. And we found Diana at the crime scene."

"She's aboot as far from a wolf as Henry is from being a detective," said Baird, glancing at Crump. The DI was too engrossed in his sandwich wrapper to notice. "But it's hard to deny the coincidence."

"So I asked myself, why would somebody murder a man in the same way as a king from all those years ago," said Connell. "Turns out, Edmund was made a saint because of *why* he died. Not the arrows and stuff, but the reason. He refused to denounce his Christianity. That's why the Vikings killed him."

Connell paused for long enough to take a giant swig of her hot chocolate, swiping the back of her hand over her mouth.

"Of course, that's just the church's side of the story. The truth is the Vikings killed pretty much everyone, and they would have made a show of executing him because he was the king. But I think the answer's in there somewhere. Oh, I forgot, I asked a local history guy if he could help us. I think he's going to put some stuff together, bring it up later today. But I'm thinking either Greg was unalived because of his religious beliefs, or because somebody saw him as a king who was getting in the way."

"Did he have religious beliefs?" asked Baird, struggling to keep up with Connell's sugar-fuelled, rapid-fire delivery.

"Doesn't everyone?" said Crump, who had managed to extract every last globule of fat from the wrapper. He stared at it like he could summon another one through the sheer power of prayer.

"No, not all of us worship at the greasy shrine of the bacon gods, Henry," said Baird. "I'm no religious."

"I don't think he was either," said Connell. "I spent quite a bit of time with Melissa yesterday, Greg's wife. She told me about their wedding, it was at the registry office in Ipswich, before either of them made it big. They don't go to church. Greg didn't seem to have any religious orientation at all."

"So there's nothing for him to denounce," said Briggs, polishing off her first cup of tea and picking up the second.

"No, but that's not all I found. Edmund was supposed to be this amazing guy. Kind, fair, benevolent. He was the perfect king. Greg had the same reputation. His wife told me everyone loved him, people went out of their way to help him out. He was a devoted husband. A genuinely nice guy, even after the fame and the money. So, after Edmund died, there was this cult of people who kind of worshipped him, I guess."

"Where is this going, Connie?" asked Briggs.

Connell faltered, staring at her page of notes for a moment.

"Well, I don't know, exactly. I was just thinking people see movie stars as more than human. I couldn't get the king thing out of my mind. Greg's at the top of his game, isn't he? I was literally channel hopping last night and I saw him twice. Ever since the *Star Wars* thing he's been getting offers for everything. I checked his IMDb page and—"

"His what?" said Crump.

"His movie database page," Connell explained. "He's

got, like, four films about to come up, and two more in development. One of those is a Martin Scorsese thing, and this is where it gets interesting."

Everybody waited as Connell paused for dramatic tension.

"I went down a bit of a rabbit hole, with some celebrity stuff online. Everyone assumed the lead role of this film was going to go to Leonardo DiCaprio, right? Because he's Scorsese's darling. Then Greg goes and gets it. Snatches it right out from under Leo's feet."

She paused again, her eyes bright.

"So maybe that's why he was killed like this. Greg was a new king, and somebody wanted to take him out so he wouldn't get all the good roles."

Nobody replied. Baird took a deep breath, his ribs still aching.

"Connie, are you suggesting that Leonardo DiCaprio, the multi-millionaire, Oscar-winning Hollywood superstar, got on a plane, drove to the arse end of Suffolk, and beheaded Gregory Brightwell in the middle of the woods?"

"I mean, you'd never suspect him, would you?" she replied. "And I always thought Leo had a strange look about him. I mean, he's fifty something, but he still looks like a shifty little baby."

"I fear we may have strayed off on a tangent," said Briggs, rubbing her cushioned face. "For now, we're not going to consider Leonardo DiCaprio as a suspect."

Connell pouted, consoling herself with more hot chocolate.

"But you may be onto something," the DCI went on. "Did Melissa give you anything else? Did she mention any rivalries, any conflicts Gregory might have been having with other people in the industry?"

"No," Connell said, flicking to another page in her book. "Greg didn't share much with her, he kept most of his work stuff to himself. Oh, one thing she did mention was that he sometimes enjoyed a bit of weed."

"Aye?"

"Not much, usually after filming had wrapped, or if he was learning some lines."

"In the hotel, then? She say where he got it?"

"No. She said it hardly ever happened, and there was nothing stronger. According to her, he was very vanilla."

"You think there's any chance *she* did this?" asked Baird. "The wife? I mean, Greg must have been worth a few bob. That's a big incentive for murder, especially if your other half's a wee bit boring."

"I didn't get that sense at all," said Connell. "You saw her, sir. She was genuinely devastated."

"But she's an actor too, right?" he said.

"Kind of," said Connell. "*Coronation Street.*"

"That's where I know her from!" exclaimed Baird, snapping his fingers.

"I'm not sure she'd be able to put on a performance like that. I don't know. I guess anything is possible, but she's not exactly big, is she? She'd have needed to overpower him, tie him to the tree and shoot him full of arrows. And I'm no expert, but I bet it's hard work trying to cut somebody's head off."

She made a chopping motion, as if she was imagining it, then pulled a face.

"Urgh," she said. "It's horrible."

"There's another thing," said Baird. "Brightwell was in the woods in his dressing goon, nothing underneath. If he was there with somebody else, it must have been somebody he trusted. You dinnae go oot in the nud with just anyone."

"Unless he was coerced," said Briggs.

"Aye," Baird conceded.

"My gut is telling me it's not Melissa," said Connell.

"Is your gut telling you anything else?" asked Briggs.

"Only that it might be a little early for hot chocolate," she said, pushing her mug away. "Even for me. Oh, but there was one thing that was weird."

She studied her notes again.

"I remember thinking it when I was in their house, but it was such a little thing it fell out of my head."

There was a frisson of excitement that lasted all the way up to the end of Connell's next sentence.

"I spotted three copies of *The Court of Avalonia*."

Briggs groaned.

"Maybe DiCaprio used one to bludgeon Gregory to death," said Baird, his chair creaking as he sat back. "And Spielberg was his getaway driver."

"No, it's not that," said Connell. "One was a hardback first edition, from way back when the book first came out. I had a peek, and it's signed by Charlotte DeVere. Uh..."

She looked at her notes again.

"'To Greg, with love and adoration, CdV.' The date was last year."

"A signed book isn't exactly unusual," said Briggs.

"No, ma'am, I agree. But what *is* unusual is the copy I found in Brightwell's office. It was a newer one, and it was absolutely rammed full of Post-its. Hundreds of them, all different colours."

"He must really love that book," said Crump.

"I think it's more than that, sir," said Connell. "Greg was an actor, right? What do actors do when they get given a role from a novel?"

"Read it," said Baird, sitting forward again. "They're making a movie?"

"I couldn't find anything about it online," said Connell. "Nothing official, anyway, but there have been rumours for years."

"That's good thinking," Baird told her. "You said this Charlotte DeVere is local, aye?"

"As far as we know," said Briggs. "She's incredibly secretive, and she writes under a pseudonym. But she's spoken about Suffolk and Southwold in interviews, as both her home and the place which inspired her to write the novel."

"That's a connection," said Baird. "More than one. DeVere, or whatever her real name is, got the inspiration for her book from the Benacre woods. At some point last year she meets Gregory Brightwell, or speaks to him. Whatever happened, it's enough of a connection for her to give him a signed copy of the book. Then, a year later, Greg turns up dead in those very same woods, *sans* his heid."

He polished off his coffee, standing up.

"If we want to find oot what happened to Greg, then we need to speak with Charlotte DeVere."

"I'll find you the address from her publisher," said Briggs. She reached into her pocket and pulled out a plastic key fob. "You can take the Rover."

CHAPTER SIXTEEN

"Oh cripes," said Connell. "This is a bit scary, isn't it?"

She was driving Briggs' Range Rover, perched on the edge of the seat and struggling to see over the wheel. The car was a beast, easily the size of a tank and probably more expensive. It was an Autobiography model, and almost brand new, the interior made up of hand-stitched leather that was soft enough to have come from a baby's arse. Every time the young DC stood on the pedal it made a noise like a plane taking off, accelerating effortlessly.

"Aye, it's got a wee bit more punch than your Fiat," said Baird, clinging onto the strap over the door as they lurched and growled up the road. "Gentle touches. You're no Fred Flintstone, you dinnae need to put your foot through the floor."

She hit the pedal again, almost colliding with the car in front. Baird was sweating, and that was partly to do with the fact that Connell had managed to fire up the heating. The air that was spewing out of the vents was practically volcanic.

"Are you sure you don't want to drive, sir?"

"Aye, maybe I should," he told her, fiddling with the various dials and switches to try to bring the temperature down.

He'd only offered her the wheel to help take her mind off what had happened to Bertie, but Connell's driving was giving them both flashbacks to the previous evening. She pulled over, opening her door and falling out—*literally*—squawking as she missed her step and vanished from sight.

"You alright, Con?"

She appeared at his door, brushing herself down. He got out, letting her hop in.

"Why does anyone need a car this big?" she said, sinking into the passenger seat.

"They dinnae," Baird replied once he'd got behind the wheel. "They're overcompensating."

The engine was still running, and he pulled away from the curb. The big car purred as he picked up speed, and as much as he tried, he couldn't keep the grin from his face.

"I'll tell you something," he said. "If I'd been driving this yesterday, I wouldnae have had any trouble."

Connell's face fell.

"Sorry," he said. "It's nothing personal. It was just a car."

"It wasn't just a car, sir," she said. "I mean, it was, but it was *my* car. First thing I bought when I joined the Service."

"I get that," said Baird, reaching the end of the road and waiting for the traffic to clear. "Did the same thing myself, up in Aberdeen. First paycheque, picked up a second-hand BMW 7-Series from a dealer doon the road."

"A 7-Series?" said Connell. "How much do they pay you up there?"

He laughed.

"Well, turned out it wasnae a seven, it was a four. But I know nothing aboot cars, so I didnae realise until I showed up at work the next day and everybody pointed it oot. Was too embarrassed to take it back, claimed I'd bought a four deliberately. Still got it, if you can believe it, though she's no been oot my granny's garage for a while."

"You get attached," said Connell. "They're part of the family, and hard to say goodbye to. You know you can just go, sir."

He looked at the solid line of traffic on the road he wanted to join, then at her.

"You're in a Range Rover. Different rules."

"Good point."

He pulled out in front of a slow-moving car, ignoring the blare of its horn.

"I'm beginning to see why the boss likes it," he said as they picked up speed.

"Bertram Pickle *was* family," said Connell, watching the world go by outside her window. "Mum didn't leave me much, when she died. But there was a bit. I used it to buy the car, and I picked one I knew she'd like. She was mad about green things."

"It was yellow," said Baird.

"He was *green*. Pickle green. Mum would have laughed herself silly seeing me drive up in that." She shrugged, studying her nails. They'd been chewed to pieces, Baird saw. "That's why I loved him, because every time I got in, I heard her laugh."

"Och, Connie, I had no idea," he said, the guilt washing through him. "There really wasnae anything I could do. It was either the car, or me and the dug."

"I know, sir," she said, wiping away a tear. "And I

couldn't have lived with myself if anything had happened to the dog."

He gave her a reproachful look that she didn't catch.

"It's the next left," she said. "It should be up here somewhere."

The road was narrowing, the hedges on either side growing so high that they met overhead. It was like driving through a tunnel, the emerald light full of sparkling dust and sweeping shadow. Connell was rapt, her hands and her face pressed to the window.

"I had no idea this place was even here," she said. "This is just like the Avenue of Plough Hill, in the book!"

Baird drove out of the vegetation to find himself, inexplicably, at the top of a hill. Laid out in front of him was a tapestry that bordered on heavenly, sweeping meadows cuddling up to cosy woodlands, all drenched in sunlight. The only building in sight was a grand stone manor house which sat in the middle of the parkland to the left of the road. It was ancient, its big windows and square jaw giving away its Georgian heritage. Most of the house was covered in a blanket of ivy, as if it had just woken.

"Oh! My! God!" said Connell. "It's the Court! Of Avalonia!"

She stared at him as if she wanted him to share her excitement.

"Just like in the book!"

"Right," he said, managing a lacklustre fist pump. "So we've got the right place, then."

He turned off the road, driving the Range Rover through an open gate and along a winding track lined with perfectly manicured bushes.

"In the book these are all animals," said Connell, her head jerking from side to side as she took it all in. "But they're alive, and they can move. And there are guards everywhere on their pizzles. And oh! Oh! Look, there's the Old Tower of Poot."

She was pointing to a wooden pole that stood beside the house.

"Fairly sure that's for the telephone line," he said, looking at the wire that ran from the pole into the house.

"I can't believe I'm here," said Connell, unbuckling even though he hadn't stopped the car yet. "I can't believe I'm going to meet Charlotte DeVere. Do you think she'll have a book she can sign for me? They're almost impossible to get, sir, because she never does signings, not public ones. You can get one too!"

"Nope," he said, pulling up at the front of the house.

They got out, the sound of their doors closing the loudest thing in the still, warm air. The windows were dark, no sign that anybody was here. Baird made his way over the gravel drive to the enormous oak door, spotting a rope hanging from the lintel. He gave it a tug, hearing a bell ring deep inside. Connell grunted, fidgeting on the step like a child about to meet Santa.

"The bell!" she said. "The bell!"

"As much as I hate to ruin your day, Quasimodo," said Baird, "we're here because of the dead fella in the woods."

That did the job. Connell's excitement slid off her face, her body slumping.

"Oh, yeah," she said.

There was a clatter from inside, then the sound of footsteps. A key turned, followed by a bolt, and another bolt, then a second key. The door creaked open, and a man peeked out of it. It was the very definition of a face that only a mother could love. The wide nose seemed to have been stuck on with glue. The eyes were far too close together, sheltering under a monobrow like two eggs beneath an umbrella. The beard was scraggly at best. If it had been a nest, it would have been crafted by pigeons. His head was far too big for his body, and wisps of greying hair battled each other over the scabbed, flaking scalp.

"Ogre," squeaked Connell.

"What?" barked the man.

He was taller than Baird, dressed in a pristine black suit and a blue waistcoat. His bowtie was as tight as a noose, the skin bulging around the collar of his white shirt.

"You're no Charlotte, I take it," said Baird, pulling out his warrant card and opening it. The man snatched it out of his hands, squinting at arm's length. "I'm DI Baird, this is DC Connell. Is Ms DeVere in?"

"The Lady is not to be disturbed," said the man, handing back the warrant card. "I'm afraid you will need to return at another time, and with an appointment."

He retreated into the house, but Baird got a shoe over the threshold as he closed the the door. The bloody thing weighed a tonne, his toes screaming.

"Yeow! Listen, pal, we're no fans looking for an autograph."

"Although we wouldn't say no," said Connell behind him.

"We're polis, which means you can't shut the door in our faces. Charlotte's in, aye? We'd like to speak with her."

The butler, because Baird had no doubt that's what he was, paused for a moment, eyeballing Baird like he meant to pick him up and carry him off the premises—something he probably wouldn't have found hard, given the size of him. After a second or two he stood back, opening the door again to reveal a long, dark corridor.

"I will talk with the Lady," he said. "If she feels well

enough, she will grant your request. Please wait in the drawing room."

"Cheers," said Baird. "What's your name?"

The man showed them to a door, and walked away without an answer. Connell had already entered, and Baird followed her. The heavy curtains were still drawn, a single, dusty lamp struggling beneath the weight of the gloom. Two sofas and four armchairs filled the space like a dentist's waiting room. The walls were panelled and papered, a chandelier hanging from the high ceiling.

"Immo Dium," whispered Connell.

"Excuse me?"

"The butler. There's one in the book, called Immo Dium. He's an ogre. He's a little loose—"

"With a name like that, I'm no surprised," said Baird.

"—in his morals, but he works in the Court, for the Princess. He betrays her in the second book. He kidnaps her and takes her to the Wild Man of the Woods. He looks just like him!"

"Aye?" said Baird, who couldn't have cared less.

"Yes. You've got to read it, sir."

"I absolutely do not have to do that."

He peeked into the walnut-panelled corridor. It seemed to stretch forever, as if the house was as deep as it was wide. There wasn't a single sound here, no ticking clocks, no barking dogs. The entire place might have been frozen in time.

"You notice anything aboot our butler?" he asked.

"Big fella, black clothes," said Connell.

"Aye. Big fella, black clothes. This might be our man, so stay sharp. No gushing, no telling her majesty how excited you are to be here, or what a huge fan you are. Aye?"

"Of course, sir," she said. "Should we call for backup, just in case?"

There was no time. The clack of the butler's shoes rose up as he appeared from another door, gliding towards them like some kind of arse-faced apparition.

"Her Ladyship will see you," he said. "On two conditions. The first is that nothing you learn here may be shared beyond these walls. Lady DeVere has been unwell these last few months, and does not wish for anyone to know of her illness."

"Fine," said Baird. "Nobody needs to ken. What's the second thing?"

"Her ailment has unfortunately left her with, ah, some facial disfigurement."

"Oh," said Connell. "That's so sad."

"She does not wish for anyone to see her at this point. She will talk with you, but only from behind a curtain."

"She can hide in the broom closet for all I care," said Baird, growing impatient. "Where is she?"

The butler studied him for a moment, something murderous in his expression, then he turned and walked away.

"Follow me."

CHAPTER SEVENTEEN

The DeVere residence wasn't a house, it was a labyrinth.

The nameless butler led Baird and Connell through a door and up a wide, creaking staircase before guiding them along a smaller corridor and down a second set of stairs. The curtains were all drawn, the hallways illuminated by flickering bulbs that carried no warmth and very little light. It was so dusty that Baird felt his eyes burning, and Connell must have sneezed a hundred times before they finally stopped outside another door.

"Remember, nothing of this may be spoken outside of these walls," said the butler. "The consequences are unimaginable."

He turned the handle and pushed the door open, revealing a dark room.

"You may enter," he said.

Baird didn't want to enter. He had a sudden image of walking through the door and being attacked by the ogre who'd brought them here. The guy was a proper unit, easily capable of overpowering him and Connell. If this was their killer, then how long would it take him to grab his bow and arrow? How long would it take him to saw off their heads?

"Listen," he said, and then he stopped, because Connell was already walking through the door.

"Hello?" she said. "Ms DeVere? I can't tell you how excited I am to be here."

The butler studied him over the tip of his bulbous nose, waiting.

"Ach, it's nothing," said Baird, patting his pocket to make sure his phone was there. "Just dinnae shut the door, alright?"

And dinnae decapitate me, he added silently.

He set off after Connell, feeling his way into the gloom. There wasn't a single light on, and he shuffled slowly in case Charlotte had a thing for coffee tables as well.

"Anyone in here?" he said. "Can we turn on a light?"

There was a crunch from deeper in the room, then an orchestra of springs. Somebody cleared their throat and spoke in a dry whisper.

"There's a lamp in the corner."

Baird had no idea which corner she meant, but he got lucky. He clicked on a standing lamp to see that he was in a bedroom, an enormous four-poster filling the far side. Thick net curtains hung from the frame, concealing the woman who lay there, but he could hear the squeak of the mattress as she moved.

"I do apologise," said the voice, still nothing but a scratchy whisper. "I'm too ashamed to show my face."

"It's absolutely fine, Ms DeVere," said Connell, giddy with excitement. "We just want you to be comfortable. My name is Constance Connell, I'm a police officer. I'm also a huge fan. Like, your *biggest* fan. I've read *The Court of Avalonia* a hundred times."

She giggled nervously.

"Go team Gavé Escon!"

Baird cleared his throat to get her attention, then shot her a warning look.

"Sorry to bother you, Ms DeVere," he said. "This won't take long. Do you ken a man called Gregory Brightwell? The actor?"

It might have been his imagination, but he thought he heard the woman on the other side of the curtain hawk up a throatful of spit.

"I do not," she said.

"You've never met him?"

"No."

"You've never signed a book for him?" Baird persisted.

"I don't know," came her reply. "I sign hundreds of books. I sign books for everyone who asks for them."

"Can I get a signed book?" asked Connell.

"No," Baird answered for her. "Ms DeVere, we found a copy of your book in Gregory's possession that was signed to him, quite affectionately. The date was from last year. Do you remember meeting him?"

"Fine, I remember," she said. "Hard to forget a wanker like that."

Connell gasped like she'd heard the Queen swear.

"You didnae like him?"

"Well, at first I did. He's charming, isn't he? Gift of the gab. I thought he was marvellous. As you must know, I don't do *public* signings, but he had a meeting with my publisher and weasled my phone number out of them. We spoke a few times. He told me how much he loved my writing, my world. He told me it was the best book he'd ever read. He told me he wanted to make it even bigger."

"He wanted to make a film," said Connell. "Didn't he?"

"He promised me it would be a thing of remarkable beauty," Charlotte replied, moving in the bed again. "He knew I wasn't interested in the money. God knows the books make me enough. But he said it would be a work of art, a testament to my genius."

She laughed bitterly, and it turned quickly into a hacking cough.

"Can we get you some water?" Connell asked.

"That's Cockhead's job," she said. "Useless bastard. Where is he?"

"Cockhead?" said Baird. "The butler?"

He glanced back, but either the man had walked off or he was listening to them from out of sight.

"Good name," he added. "Suits him."

There was another snort of laughter, this time genuine.

"So Gregory Brightwell bought the rights to the book?" asked Baird.

"No. He tried, but I wouldn't sell. I didn't believe a word that came out of those plump, soft, perfectly formed lips."

"This was last year?"

"December. And about a week after I told him where to stick it, I got a letter from him, hand delivered to my own house. A letter with a very clear threat."

"Can you tell us what it said?"

"I cannot," she said. "I will carry that secret to my grave."

"Your grave, or somebody else's?" asked Baird. "Because Gregory Brightwell was found dead yesterday morning, in the woods outside of Southwold."

There wasn't a peep from the bed.

"Somebody killed him, Ms DeVere. On Friday night."

Still nothing. If it wasn't for the absence of squeals from the mattress springs and the fact there was nowhere to go, Baird would have assumed the woman had legged it.

"Did you hear me?" he asked.

"Yes," came the croaked reply. "And I think I'd like you to leave now."

"But it's just starting to get interesting," said Baird. "Can you tell me where you were on Friday night, Ms De Vere. Around midnight. And, probably more importantly, where your butler was."

The bed made a noise like an accordion as she moved in it.

"I was exaggerating," she said, her voice starting to break as if speaking was a struggle. "I never actually had it out for Greg. I just hated how everything was so bloody easy for him. I detest people like that, the ones who are born with a silver spoon twixt their teeth. Do you know how easy it is to get what you want in life when you look like Gregory Brightwell?"

"Sadly not," said Baird.

"Women fall over themselves to be with you. Men will do anything just to *be* you, they will mount you on a pedestal in the hope that some of your light radiates upon them. The thing I despised about Greg was how he thought he was the architect of his own fortune, that he'd somehow earned his fame, his riches. He didn't earn them, he was handed everything by good genes and good parents. It fell in his fucking lap."

Charlotte was shouting now, and her voice had dropped into a solid bass. She cleared her throat, speaking once again in a whisper.

"He was a wanker, but he didn't deserve to die. And I didn't kill him. How could I? I'm bedridden."

"Aye, but your butler's fine," said Baird.

"Cockhead wouldn't know how to kill a chicken if it ran straight into the blade of his cleaver," she said. "He's bloody useless. You're barking up the wrong tree, Detective."

He wondered how much of 'barking' and 'tree' was coincidence, given what had happened in the woods.

"Still," he said. "I need to hear where you both were on Friday night."

"Here," came the reply, a distinctly deeper voice. It was followed by another series of coughs, then the higher voice of the woman. It was almost like there were two people hiding in the bed. "Please, my strength is waning. If you have any more questions, pose them to my solicitor."

Again, the last few words changed pitch, like a kid whose balls had decided to drop midway through a school assembly. Baird walked to the bed, trying to make sense of the shapes through the curtains.

"Stay away," Charlotte hissed. "It's contagious."

He glanced past the bed, to the wall. Like the rest of the house, it was panelled, but he thought he saw a crack in the panelling by the headboard, as if it had come loose.

Or as if there was a door there.

"Connell," he said, "go find the butler, will you?"

"He's busy," said Charlotte.

"Aye, I'll bet. Busy playing silly buggers. You in there too, Cockhead?"

He grabbed the nearest curtain and yanked it, hard enough to rip the entire thing away from the frame. Past the cloud of dust that erupted from the ancient fabric, he saw a single figure in the shadowy interior of the bed, crouched on the mattress. With his bald head and his furious face, it was immediately apparent who it was.

"Get oot, pal," said Baird. "I'm no messing around."

He scanned the mounds of blankets, trying to find Charlotte DeVere. But the butler was alone in there.

"You've fucking ruined it!" the man roared. "You've fucking ruined it!"

He propelled himself off the bed, his shoulder connecting with Baird's arm and spinning him backwards. Baird landed on his arse, and for a second the giant butler stood over him, his bunched fists the size of melons.

"Oi!" yelled Connell. "Get away from him!"

The butler bolted, crashing through the loose panel in the wall and slamming it behind him. There was the distinct sound of a bolt being drawn.

"Sir, are you okay?" Connell asked, offering Baird a hand. He took it, struggling back to his feet. His body was throbbing from top to toe as his injuries from the car crash reawakened, but the landing had been soft enough.

"I'm fine," he said, a little winded. "Can you get him? I'm no a runner."

Connell staggered to the bed, dragging the blankets off the mattress and piling them on the floor.

"Ms DeVere?" she said. "Are you in there?"

The answer was a resounding no.

"Where did she go?" Connell asked. "What did he do with her?"

Baird reached the panel, giving it a shunt. It barely wobbled.

"You see a way of opening this?"

Connell was searching the blankets on the floor now. She ducked onto her hands and knees to look under the bed. Baird lost his patience, driving his foot into the side of the panel. The wood was solid and he danced back, the pain burning up his spine.

"You jobbie-flavoured walloper!" he roared.

He was about to try again when he heard a thump from overhead, dust raining down from the dark wooden beams.

"He's gone up," he said, heading for the door. "Come on, Connie."

"She must be here somewhere, sir," Connell replied, still crawling. "People don't just disappear."

Baird abandoned her, making his way into the corridor. He ran to the next room, which was empty, and took the corridor that branched off after that. At the end of it was the staircase they'd come down on the way here. If there was a passage inside the walls, it had to lead this way.

"Oi!" he yelled as he climbed the stairs, no idea if the butler could hear him. "If you make me chase you all over this hoose, I'm gonna..."

He was too knackered to think of a decent threat. He grabbed the banister as he doubled back, hauling himself up to the first floor. He stopped on the narrow landing, his heart fizzing, his pulse making so much noise he couldn't hear anything past it.

"Where are you?"

He was answered by creaking footsteps, coming from nearby. He set off again, the soft floor singing beneath his feet like the building was going to collapse. He was halfway along the corridor when a door opened right in front of him and the butler walked out. He had a suitcase in his hands, and he was so intent on trying to lock the clasp that he didn't notice he wasn't alone until it was too late.

"Found you," said Baird, and he gave the suitcase a mighty shove.

The butler's leg gave way, and he folded beneath the weight of his case, gargling a cry of pain as he hit the floor. Baird didn't give him the chance to get up. He dropped onto the case, pinning it against the man's stomach. He'd never heard a more perfect 'oof' than the one that came out of the butler's mouth.

"The more you move, the worse this gets," said Baird, bouncing on the case. "I can ride this all night, just like a pizzle stick."

The man gargled again, his tongue sticking out. Baird couldn't figure out what he was saying, so he took a little of his weight off the suitcase.

"Alright," said the butler. "You win. I'm done."

"Braw," said Baird. "What's your name?"

"See for yourself," the man said, flailing at the case like it was attacking him. "It's in there."

Baird sucked in a breath, bellowing.

"Connell! I'm upstairs!"

He stood, staying tense in case the butler made a run for it. But the man wasn't lying, he looked beat. He lay on his back, staring at the ceiling, his tongue probing his lips. Baird pushed the suitcase to the floor and opened it.

Whatever he'd been expecting to find, this wasn't it.

The case was full of women's clothes; colourful dresses scrunched into wrinkled bundles, a padded bra, a pair of enormous dungarees, and right at the bottom, at least three cheap nylon wigs of different colours.

"Well, I'm officially confused," said Baird, scratching his head.

He rummaged gingerly in the case, unloading a couple of laptops and six hard drives. He had to wade through several boxes of medication before finding what he was looking for. The passport was an old EU one with a burgundy cover, and when he opened it he saw the butler's glowering face on the information page.

"Bruce Fishbourne," he said, reading the name. "That's marginally better than Cockheid, I suppose."

The date of birth put him at fifty-one years of age, and the address listed was this one. Baird flicked through the pages, finding a handful of stamps from various countries.

"Right," he said. "What did you do with Charlotte DeVere?"

"What do you mean what did I do with her?" said Bruce.

"I mean we were talking to her just now, in the bed, and then she vanished."

The man shook his head with obvious disgust.

"Are you actually a detective?" he asked. "Because this is pretty detectable."

"Help me oot," said Baird. "I ran up a lot of stairs, there's no a lot of blood in my heid. I'm gonna ask again, and then..."

He tailed off, looking at the clothes, at the wigs.

"Finally," said Bruce, seeing the truth of it dawn on Baird's face. "Took you bloody long enough."

There was a furious creaking as Connell made her way up the steps. He could hear her panting from halfway down the corridor.

"Too... many... stairs," she said, her cheeks bright red.

"Too many breakfast cocoas, more like," muttered Baird.

"What did you do with Ms DeVere," Connell said, pointing a finger at the butler. "If you've hurt her, I'll lock you up and throw away the key."

"Listen, Connie," said Baird. "I've got some bad news."

"He killed her?" she asked, horrified.

"No. He *invented* her. There is no Charlotte DeVere, is there, Bruce? There never was."

Connell gasped, slapping both hands to her mouth loud enough for it to sound like a gunshot.

"What?" she mumbled through her fingers. "That's *worse*!"

"It's really no," said Baird. "You want to tell me where you were on Friday night, Bruce? Around midnight?"

"I was in Avalonia," he said. "Flying through the azure skies, dreaming of better worlds."

"Were you, aye?"

Baird toed one of the laptops.

"You need a password for these?" he asked.

"Of course. My life's work is on there."

"*Her* life's work," said Connell.

Bruce laughed quietly, still staring at the ceiling.

"My life," he said. "They can't take it away. They're still my books."

"No they're not," said Connell, deep in her denial. "They're *hers*."

"'Alas, my dear Captain Gavé Escon, my tranquil gaze doth yonder fall upon your bosom,'" said Bruce in the same whispered falsetto they'd heard from the bed. "'I love thee with all the birdwing beats of my heart!'"

"No you don't!" Connell said, utterly miserable.

"Gregory Brightwell knew your secret?" asked Baird.

Bruce nodded.

"He found out. I still don't know how."

"You were prepared to attack a couple of polis officers to keep this hidden," said Baird. "What were you willing to do to anybody else?"

Bruce sneered.

"Nothing," he said. "I didn't touch him."

"He tried to force your hand, so you killed him before he could share your secret. Am I getting warmer?"

This time, the butler didn't answer, but there was something in his expression, a flicker of panic.

"Well, I guess there's only one thing left to do," said Baird, leaning over the other man. "Bruce Fishbourne, you are under arrest for assaulting a police officer, and for the murder of Gregory Brightwell."

CHAPTER EIGHTEEN

They searched the house just as soon as Bruce Fishbourne had been taken away in an IRV.

It was an impossible job, partly because the property was so enormous—at least nineteen bedrooms and half as many reception rooms, plus assorted bathrooms, two kitchens and enough cupboards to play an infinite game of hide and seek—and partly because every other door they came across was locked.

It seemed a little harsh to use a pry bar in such a beautiful house, so Baird asked Connell to call a locksmith. They waited downstairs, wandering between the grand living spaces and marvelling at the antiques Bruce Fishbourne had managed to collect. He hadn't just done okay with *The Court of Avalonia*, it seemed, he'd made an absolute fortune.

"I still can't believe it," said Connell. "I've read her books—"

"*His* books."

"For the last decade. I read the first *Court* novel in my first year of high school. It was my awakening."

She looked genuinely distressed as she opened a door, staring into a toilet that stank of bleach.

"I honestly thought Charlotte DeVere was some kind of sage, a muse. This woman looked into my soul and saw exactly what I needed to hear. I thought she was speaking to me, nobody else. You know? She was my soulmate."

"He," said Baird, trying another door to find it locked. "Your soulmate's a fifty-one-year-old bald fella with terrible breath and a nose like a squashed potato. Did you no wonder why she never appeared in public?"

"I thought she was shy, you know? Some people don't like showing their faces. I just don't understand how I'm supposed to process it. First Bertie, and now this. What's next?"

Baird felt a sudden wash of sympathy for the young officer. He put his hand on her shoulder, giving her a gentle squeeze.

"Go home, Connie," he said. "Chances are, we just nabbed the bastard who killed Greg. Go home, let me do this."

"You really think it's him, sir?" she asked.

"I think he's got the three Ms," said Baird. "Motive's the good one. Greg found oot his true identity. He threatened to reveal it, so Bruce went to extreme measures to keep him quiet."

"It's like you said, though," said Connell. "Why not just bury him on the grounds here? The garden's huge, we'd never find him. Why go to the trouble of cutting off his head and shooting him with all those arrows."

"Ach, he's a writer," said Baird, waving her words away. "They're all loony-eyed dobbers who spend half their lives hallucinating violent deaths for their characters and half greeting because they never make any money. They're insane, every last one of them."

She accepted his argument with a nod.

"But why would Greg meet Bruce in his dressing gown?"

"One thing at a time, pal."

"So we've got motive," she said as they walked to the next door.

"Aye, the first M. Then we've got means. Did Bruce have the right equipment to kill a man?"

"He's big," said Connell. "He got you on the floor without any difficulty."

"He wrong-footed me," Baird said, a little defensively. "If I was ready for it, he'd have bounced right off."

"And he's fast," said Connell. "If he hadn't stopped for his suitcase, he'd have left you in his dust."

"I keep telling you, I'm no a runner."

He tried the handle of the next door and it opened. He had to switch the light on before understanding that it was a library, wooden cases lining the walls and every single shelf stuffed with books. There were other things in here too, including a suit of armour holding a sword. It didn't look like a replica.

"Christ," said Baird. "He's got a bloody claymore right there. He could have taken Greg's heid off with that."

"Or that, sir," said Connell, pointing to a medieval battle axe that was mounted above one of the bookcases. She swivelled her arm to another sword on a shelf, this one a curved Samurai blade in a colourful scabbard. "And definitely that."

There were half a dozen other things in here that would have done the job, and Baird ushered Connell out of the room.

"Let's let forensics deal with these," he said. "So, we've got motive, means, and..."

He paused, trying to think of the other word.

"Opportunity, sir," said Connell.

"Nut, I dinnae think that's it," he said, wracking his brain. "It starts with an M, I'm sure of it. The three Ms. Mmmmm..."

He hummed his way to the end of the corridor, but it still wouldn't come.

"Och, we'll call it opportunity for now," he said. "Until I remember the right word."

Connell huffed like an annoyed parent.

"Did Bruce have the opportunity to kill Greg?" Baird asked. "He lives here alone. Nobody would have seen him come or go."

"Benacre is less than five miles away," said Connell. "He'd have been there in minutes."

"Aye, that's right, and he might have told Greg to meet him there. He might have said he was ready to sign the movie deal."

Connell pulled a face.

"I mean, maybe," she said. "But if some guy who I knew didn't like me called me to say he wanted to sign a deal, but could we do it at midnight in the middle of the woods, I'd probably say no. Especially in my dressing gown."

"Aye, but Benacre's where the whole thing started," said Baird. "It's where she... sorry, *he*, came up with the whole *Court of Avalonia* thing. It's symbolic."

"I guess," said Connell.

"And if Bruce was finally willing to sign, then Greg would have come straight oot from the hotel. It's only doon the road, he might no have bothered with clothes. Actors are as weird as writers."

"We need to check Greg's phone records, sir, and Bruce's, see if they were in touch. But that's definitely opportunity. He ticks all three boxes."

"It's no opportunity," said Baird, shaking his head. "Moment? It's something like that. A meaningful moment. But no that, exactly."

"A meaningful moment, sir?" said Connell.

"I said *no* that. But something like it. What other words start with M?"

Connell shrugged, down in the dumps again.

"Look, if you dinnae want to go home, at least go and take a break," said Baird. "We cannae do much until the smithy gets here anyway."

"Are you sure?"

"Aye. Keep an eye oot for him. I'll keep going."

She gave him a grateful smile before heading into the labyrinthine interior of the house. Baird whipped out his phone, Googling 'motive, means and the other M' only to be presented with the word opportunity listed over and over again.

"Bastard," he grumbled, scrolling down the entire page before giving up on the search.

He spent the next twenty minutes trying a few more doors before giving up on this search too, heading the same way Connell had gone. There were a few rooms along the back of the house, mostly cramped servants' quarters and a bunch more cupboards. He opened one and found himself face to face with a forest of mops.

"*Mop*portunity," he said, looking around to see if there was anybody there to appreciate his joke.

He found Connell in the kitchen, sitting by a huge window that overlooked the garden. She was eating something from a bowl, the smell of strawberry almost overpowering.

"Tell me you didnae raid his freezer," he said as he walked over. Sure enough, her bowl was full of ice cream.

"Well he's not going to need it, is he, sir,?" she said, pulling the bowl close as if worried Baird might take it away. "I didn't have any breakfast."

"You had a literal gallon of hot chocolate," he said. "Look, Connell, I know I've said it before, and it's none of my business, but—"

"You've said it before," she said.

"But—"

"And it's none of your business," she finished. "*Sir.*"

He lifted his hands in surrender.

"It's your liver, pal," he said. "Listen, that reminds me. I stopped off for a coffee at Sam's place yesterday. I got a weird vibe from her."

A smile landed on Connell's lips, but only for a second.

"It's because she likes you," she said. "A *lot.*"

"Aye, I picked up on that when she asked me oot for dinner."

Connell dropped her spoon into her bowl, her eyes wide.

"Spill it, sir. What did you say?"

"Ach, it's no gonna happen," he said. "I've already got a wee lady at home."

"*What?*" said the DC, slamming both hands on the table.

"Called Diana," he said.

Connell looked at him blankly.

"The *dug,*" he explained. "But that's no what I was getting at. I was talking to Sam aboot the case, and I mentioned Carl Denton. Her reaction... she looked like she'd seen a ghost, Connie. What's that aboot?"

Connell sat back, picking up the spoon again and resting it against her lips.

"I'm not really in a position to speak for her, sir. And I don't know the whole truth. But Sam's got a pretty... turbulent past."

Baird perched against the table, waiting.

"She used to work for Carl," Connell went on.

"At the hotel?" he asked.

"This was before the hotel. She's never really told me what she did. Before Carl went straight, he used to provide certain, uh, services. Mainly for Ma Keeble and her clients. Girls and drugs."

"And now he's running a million-pound club for celebrities?" said Baird, the anger burning up from deep inside. "Living the good life. How?"

"Because we could never pin anything on him," said Connell. "I told you before, he does everything through proxies. There's never any evidence, just hearsay and rumour. And nobody is brave enough to talk."

"Bastard," said Baird, getting up. "How're these arseholes in every town, every city?"

"Carl's out of it now, sir," said Connell. "As far as we know, he's straight."

"Aye, I've heard that before."

He walked to the window to try to cool his rage. They were at the side of the house here, the angle not quite right for the driveway that led in from the main road. There were plenty of outbuildings, though, including a line of old, brick stables on the other side of a wide courtyard. A barn peeked over the top of them like it didn't want to be found.

"It'll take all year to search this place," he said. "And the chances of Bruce having left anything are next to zero. That's the other thing about writers, they're all anally retentive. Everything's planned to the last detail. If there was evidence here, it's long gone."

"I hope not," said a voice from outside.

Baird and Connell turned to see DCI Briggs enter the kitchen, pulling a line of PCs behind her like a mother duck with her ducklings. She walked over, bracing her hands on her hips.

"This is certainly a turn-up for the books," she said. "Charlotte DeVere's a work of fiction?"

"Yes," said Connell, dropping her spoon into her bowl. "She never existed. The whole thing was a lie."

"I had my suspicions when I read the books," said Briggs. "Not many female writers would describe a woman's chest as, and I quote, 'a plump, puckered bounty of heaving earthly plunder.' What do we know about Bruce Fishbourne?"

"No much, ma'am," Baird started. "He's fifty-one, this is—"

"Connell, please tell me you aren't eating our prime suspect's raspberry ripple," Briggs interrupted.

"I *could* tell you that," she said. "And it's strawberry, ma'am."

Briggs sighed, rubbing her face.

"We're waiting on the smithy," said Baird.

"No need," Briggs told him, pulling a little leather pouch from her handbag. "I'm here. Where do you want me to start?"

"There's a big room at the front," said Connell. "Right by the door. In the books, that room is where the magic stems from. I'm guessing that's her office."

She sighed.

"*His* office."

They made their way back through the house, stopping outside a double door in the front hall—just opposite the waiting area. Briggs struggled onto her knees, removing a couple of picks from her pouch. In less than ten seconds, she'd picked the lock.

"I'm impressed," said Baird, helping her up.

He took the lead, flicking on the light switches to reveal a large room full of the same assortment of antiques and bookcases. A presidential desk sat on the left, by the window, and he made his way over to it, tugging apart the heavy curtains as he went. Dust poured out of them, choking him.

"These havnae been open in years," he said. "This guy really didnae want anyone to see him."

"I wish nobody had," said Connell. "I'd rather live with a happy lie than a devastating truth."

The desk was littered with crap. There was no other word for it. Chocolate wrappers and empty drink cans were strewn everywhere, and a little stack of medication boxes sat in the corner. There were a few copies of the Avalonia books lying about, and when Baird opened the cover of one he saw that it had been signed, the date from a couple of days ago.

"'To Gloria, with love and adoration,'" he read. "Isn't that what he wrote in Greg's?"

He tried another book and saw the same message beneath a different name, then he turned to the medicine.

"This guy had everything wrong with him," he said. "Look at this. Indigestion tablets, pain meds, asthma inhalers, creams for itchy skin, dandruff, eczema. Diarrhoea *and* constipation, no idea how it's possible to have both. Look, you've got half the cast of the books here."

Connell stomped over, looking at the names on the boxes.

"Gavé Escon, Immo Dium, Ven Tolin, oh God," she said.

"Dinnae forget the Viagra," added Baird, nodding to a stash of little blue pills. "Here's your Wild Man of the... *wood*. He obviously just glanced this way every time he needed a new name."

Connell groaned, utterly miserable. She turned away, then pointed to the floor.

"Dog," she said.

A couple of silver bowls sat by the desk, one empty, the other half-full of water.

"You think Diana belongs to Bruce?" said Baird.

"He's been feeding something, sir."

"He's been hunting something too," said Briggs from the other side of the room. She was standing in the corner, looking at something that had been shoved into the gap beside a filing cabinet. Baird had to walk over before he could figure out what it was.

"Crossbow," he said. "An old one."

"And black arrows," said Briggs, straightening up. "I think you made the right call. Bruce looks like our man."

"Aye, that's what I think," said Baird. "Motive, means, and a meaningful moment."

Briggs looked at him like he'd gone mad.

"Let's go see what he has to say for himself."

CHAPTER NINETEEN

They swung by Baird's flat on the way through Southwold, so that he could check up on the chihuahua. Diana welcomed him with a bark, doing a tap-dance on the kitchen floor. As soon as he sat down, she sprang onto his lap, drool spattering everywhere.

"You been making yourself at home, quine?" he asked, running a hand down her back, feeling the bobbles of her spine. She nuzzled his chin, her cold nose making him laugh.

"Aye, I missed you too. Hey, you don't happen to belong to a fella named Bruce, do you?"

The dog cocked her head as she tried to understand him.

"Big fella, terrible face, bald heid, although he sometimes wears wigs?"

She barked an answer, and he shrugged.

"In English?"

The dog started to pad in circles on his lap, ready to settle down, and he plonked her on the floor next to the pillow he'd given her.

"I'm sorry, I've got to heid oot again."

She whined a protest, one tiny foot raised like she was waiting for a treat.

"I'll no be long. I promise. Just snuggle up, make a tea, do the crossword."

He unclipped the glittery pink collar to make her more comfortable, slinging it onto the table. She sat on her haunches and yawned so hard she almost fell over.

"Exactly, you're knackered," he said. "I'll be right back."

He topped up her water, even though the bowl was big enough for her to swim in, and slung some more chicken down. It broke his heart to close the door, and the first thing he did when he got back into Brigg's Range Rover was ask a question.

"Can she no come with us, ma'am? She's basically polis."

"She's a dog, Harrison," said the DCI, craning over the wheel as she thundered towards the A12. "And a pretty useless one at that."

"Wee bit harsh," he muttered, looking to Connell for support. The DC was staring out the window, lost in her own thoughts.

"Speaking of which," Briggs went on, "the *real* dogs have arrived at Benacre. If the head's there, they'll find it."

"Here's hoping," said Baird.

With Briggs behind the wheel, it only took twenty minutes to get to Lowestoft police station. Bruce Fishbourne had already been processed, and he was waiting for them when Baird walked into the little interview room. He seemed even bigger and uglier than he had in the house, and the scowl he wore didn't make him any prettier. Baird recognised the woman sitting next to him as one of the duty solicitors, and there was no denying the blush in her cheeks.

"Alright, Bruce," said Baird, sitting down on the other side of the table. "Long time no see."

He pulled out the chair so Connell could sit next to him. She started the camera and made the introductions, during which Bruce didn't once break eye contact with Baird. He was an intimidating fella for sure, although not in the same way as Carl Denton, who looked like he could eat you for breakfast. Bruce's anger simmered at a lower temperature. He looked still on the surface, but there was a lot of rising heat.

"You sizing me up for one of your books, pal?" Baird said. "I'd make a good captain of the guard, I reckon. Handsome, witty, and I always get my guy."

He frowned.

"By which I mean catch the criminals, no find a nice husband."

Bruce leaned over the table to make himself as big as possible, but it was his solicitor who spoke.

"My client is here to address the false allegations you have made against him. Not to talk about his wonderful books."

She gave Bruce a sideways look, like she couldn't believe she was here.

"Aye, we'll get to them," said Baird. "You didnae want to answer this before, but I'm gonna try again. Where were you on Friday night, anytime from eight in the evening to aboot ten yesterday morning?"

"I was writing," said Bruce.

"All night?"

"I'm nocturnal," he said. "Always have been."

"Like a badger," said Baird. "In other words, you can often be found scuttling aboot in the woods after dark. Is that what you were doing on Friday? In Benacre?"

"He just said he was writing," said the solicitor.

"He didnae say where, though," said Baird. "You use a laptop, aye? As far as I remember, you can take them anywhere. Why were you with Gregory Brightwell?"

"I wasn't," said Bruce.

"But you had a good reason to meet him, aye? You told us yourself, Greg threatened you. He told you he was going to reveal your secret to the world. I'd say that was a pretty decent motive to kill him."

Bruce leaned back, folding his arms over his flabby chest.

"I didn't meet him. I didn't kill him."

"But you do admit you have a good reason to kill him."

"Don't answer that," said the solicitor. "What we like to see in these interviews, Detective, as you well know, is a shred of proof."

"Alright," said Baird. "Gregory was tied to a tree on Friday night, where he was shot with twelve arrows. After that, the killer cut his heid off."

There was no mistaking the look of shock on both faces on the other side of the table. The solicitor put her hand to her mouth.

"This is *the* Gregory Brightwell," she asked. "From the TV?"

"Aye," said Baird. "We've no found his heid yet."

The solicitor picked up some paperwork, but she wasn't really looking at it. She glanced at Bruce again, but there was a nervousness in her expression now.

"Do you happen to own any weapons, Bruce?" said Baird.

"No," he grunted. "Of course not."

"You dinnae have a room full of swords and axes?"

"They're replicas," he said, licking his dry lips. "They're not real."

"And what aboot the crossbow in your office?"

"The fuck?" Bruce said. "How did you... you've got no right to go in there, it was locked."

"You wrote it yourself," said Connell. "In the second book. 'Justice is the key that opens all doors.'"

"Not my fucking doors," said Bruce, turning his ire to his solicitor. "They can't bloody do that, can they?"

"This is murder, Bruce," said Baird. "We can do anything we like."

"That's not quite true," said the brief, frowning.

"Does it work? The crossbow?"

"No," said Bruce, squirming in his seat. "I mean, I don't know. I haven't tried it. It's 200 years old, for fuck's sake, it's an antique. For show."

"Did you show it to Greg?" said Baird.

"I never saw Greg!" he whined. "The man's a wanker, I told you. He tried to fuck me over but he wasn't clever enough. That was the end of it. I didn't sign his stupid deal. I called his bluff, told him if he wanted to tell everyone about me then he'd get lynched. Cancelled. You know how many people have read my books? Millions. Two of them are right here in this room. You'll read them too, when all this is done."

"No, I won't."

"Greg was a scheming prick, but he wasn't stupid. He knew if he came out with the truth then everyone would hate him. Nobody wants to look at the author photo of their favourite book and see this, do they?"

He gestured to his face, and there were no arguments.

"They want to see Charlotte DeVere. Somebody magical, somebody beautiful, somebody perfect. The queen of romance, the lady of lust. Somebody they'd want to roll around naked with, the boys *and* the girls. You think anyone wants to roll around naked with me?"

He looked at Connell when he said this, and she flinched so hard her knees cracked into the bottom of the table.

"Exactly," said Bruce, and there was a hitch in his voice. "You know, I tried for years to get *The Court of Avalonia* published. I sent it to fourteen editors, all the big houses. They all read it, they loved it, then they met me."

His big hands flew into the air.

"And suddenly they weren't interested any more. It wasn't until I had a meeting with Harper Collins that somebody said maybe it would work if I wasn't the author, if I ghost wrote it for somebody else. They wanted some celebrity to do it, and I told them to fuck off. But it gave me the idea for Charlotte. There was no looking back. I sent it to Penguin next, with a photo of some random AI woman I found online, and that was that. Six figure deal for the first book. Sunday Times bestseller, New York Times bestseller, Amazon bestseller. A true global sensation. I stated in my contract that I didn't do publicity. I didn't do editorial meetings. I didn't do launch parties with canapés and champagne and shit. All I did was write."

He jabbed a finger at Connell as if he held her personally responsible.

"But they're *my* fucking books, not hers."

"That's a big secret to keep, Mr Fishbourne," said Connell. "You've sacrificed a lot. You live in the dark in case people take photos through the windows, don't you? You pretend to be Charlotte DeVere's butler. This isn't just a gimmick, it's your life."

"Something you'd want to protect at all costs," Baird

added. "I can see the anger, pal. And I've seen your temper, it put me on my arse. You're no a stranger to violence."

Bruce slammed his fist onto the table with a sound like a cannon going off, making everyone in the room flinch. Even Baird felt his heart do a barrel roll.

"I'm not fucking violent, you cunt!" he roared.

"Oh, fine, sorry, my mistake," said Baird. "No sure where I got that impression from."

It looked, for a second, like Bruce might throw himself over the table. But his solicitor put her hand on his arm, calming him.

"This is just like when Gavé Escon was on trial," she said. "In Book 4. They did everything they could to bait him, but he never flinched. Be more like Gavé Escon, Bruce."

"Aye, it'll help with your indigestion too," Baird added. "Do you have anyone at all who can verify you were at home on Friday night?"

"Actually, I do," said Bruce, which took Baird by surprise. "I live alone, but I share my writing hours with a couple of other authors, both of whom prefer to write under the cover of darkness."

"They were at your place?"

"We communicate on WhatsApp," he said. "I chat to them all night, most nights."

"That disnae help much, pal," said Baird.

"There is a log of our conversation. You can see that I was in regular contact with them on Friday night, until the early hours of Saturday morning. Have a look for yourself. We call ourselves the..." He paused, licking his lips again. "The Super Special Chums."

Nobody spoke. The solicitor glanced at her notes again, increasingly desperate.

"We'll check," said Baird. "If nothing else, all those messages will pinpoint your location."

"I keep my location services turned off," said Bruce. "For obvious reasons."

"Aye, but you cannae change what towers the messages ping off, can you?"

A frown creased the man's forehead, and he glanced at his solicitor as if to ask whether that was true.

"You may have made this much easier for us," said Baird. "So here's what's gonna happen. You're gonna enjoy a wee holiday right here in Lowestoft's cheeriest B&B. We're gonna check your crossbow to see if it works, and to see if the arrows match the twelve that we found in Gregory Brightwell. We're gonna look through your phone and your computers to see if you've been in touch with him. Then we'll be back."

He stood up.

"Interview terminated," he said, switching off the camera. "Come on, Connell."

They'd made it out of the door before Bruce called to them from the room.

"Everything you find on the computer is research," he said. "For the books. That's all it is, research."

"Aye? What am I going to find? Instructions on how to tie a man to a tree? A guide to beheading?"

"Uh, no," said Bruce, tugging at his collar. "It's more... all the boobies."

Baird shook his head.

"The queen of romance indeed," he said, and he slammed the door behind him.

BRIGGS WAS WAITING for them in Lowestoft's Major Investigation Team office, and she had a look on her face like she'd just sat on a pin.

"Anything?" she asked.

"He's giving off all the right energy, ma'am," said Baird. "Violent, aggressive, obstructive. He denied the weapons, and meeting Brightwell, and his only defence was a couple of writers on WhatsApp."

"His phone and his computers are being checked now," said Briggs. "It's a pretty poor alibi."

Baird nodded, staring at the wall and running through the interview in his head.

"What?" asked Briggs.

"I'm no sure, ma'am. I was saying to Connie earlier, that writers are fairly meticulous. They plan everything, and they dinnae leave loose ends."

"You've not read many Charlotte DeVere books, have you?" said Briggs. "Every end is a loose one, and that's not a euphemism."

"DeVere always said she was a pantser," said Connell. "I mean *he*, damn it. *He's* a pantser."

"A panther?" said Baird.

"No, *pantser*. He doesn't plot, he just flies by the seat of his pants. He makes it up as he goes."

"What does that have to do with anything?" said Briggs.

"Well, no writer worth his salt would have the main suspect waiting for the police inside his own hoose, right next to all the weapons he used to kill his victim. It disnae make any sense."

"You said it yourself, sir," said Connell. "They're all loopy-headed weirdos."

"Loony-eyed dobbers, is what I said," corrected Baird. "If this is him, and those are the weapons he used to kill

Greg, and he left them there for us to find, then either he's so convinced we'd never find him he didnae bother to clean up, or he's just insane."

"Or he left those weapons as a distraction," said Connell. "And he hid the real ones."

"Aye, maybe," said Baird. "I'm no sure what to think. I can go back in, have another crack at him?"

"Later," said Briggs. "I need you in the woods. The dogs struck gold."

"You've found the heid?" said Baird.

"Oh yes. We've found the head."

CHAPTER TWENTY

BENACRE WOODS FELT DIFFERENT, SOMEHOW, EVEN though it was only twenty-four hours or so since he'd last been here. The trees seemed to stand a little closer together, their canopies hunkered into a protective scrum. When Baird stepped out of the sun into the shade, a broken branch scratched its bony finger along his cheek hard enough to make him yelp. A warning, if ever he'd had one.

The woodland wanted to keep its secrets hidden.

"Tough shite," he said as he ploughed on.

"What was that, sir?" said Connell, treading on his heels.

"Nothing. You remember where it was?"

"That way," she said, pointing past his left shoulder.

He'd taken a few more difficult steps through the thick undergrowth when a shout hailed to them from the *other* direction. Baird squinted past the crooked trunks to see a PC in a yellow jacket, waving to them. He shot Connell a look, but she was directing all her energy into not tripping over in the brambles.

"Alright?" he called out when they were a little closer. "I hear you've found the heid?"

"The what, sir?" said the PC, holding up a branch so Baird could duck under it. He did the same for Connell, who staggered through.

"The heid," said Baird. "*Head.* Jesus, it's no like I'm speaking Gaelic. Where is it?"

The PC led them on, past the oak where Gregory Brightwell's body had hung. The clearing was masked off by a ream of police tape which drooped unenthusiastically in the unnaturally warm air. Poor Greg had been removed, but there were still a handful of arrows in the tree, and the ground below had been churned into crimson mud. That blank circle of a face was still there, scratched into the bark. It seemed to watch Baird as he walked, and the goosebumps rose up on his arms, the hair standing to attention on the back of his neck.

"This is giving me the heebie-jeebies," he said.

"Me too, sir," said Connell. "But hearing you say heebie-jeebies makes me feel a little better."

They were approaching a crowd ahead. A perimeter of uniformed police, complete with dogs, stood around an inner circle made up of Declan Bundy and some of his forensic technicians, all dressed in white overalls like they were off to a hen party. Fred was there too, the ancient pathologist fiddling awkwardly with his bowtie. Everybody was staring at the ground, but Baird was too far away to see what they were looking at.

"Afternoon," he called out.

Declan rolled up the sleeve of his overalls to check his watch.

"It's still morning," he said.

"It cannae be," said Baird, checking his own watch to

see that it had only just gone half past eleven. "Christ. Time stops when you're having an awfie day, eh? Is that the heid?"

"That is the head," said Declan. "*Heed* is what I recommend you take, because the ground is treacherous."

By the time he'd made sense of the rubbish coming out of the young man's mouth, Baird had tripped on a branch and almost turned his ankle in a divot. He staggered into the group, a PC taking his arm to stop him falling any further. It was just as well, because right in front of him was a small, circular hole in the dirt, maybe three feet across and two deep, and nestled in the cavity was a filthy cardboard box. The lid was closed, but it was the perfect size to hold a human head.

A smell hung in the air, deeply unpleasant.

"You've had a peek?" he asked.

"We have," said Fred, his expression heavy with sadness. "The head is inside."

"It's Gregory Brightwell?"

"Or somebody who looks just like him."

Baird turned to the dog handlers. There were three of them, each with an animal at his feet. Two were German shepherds who looked like they'd been doing steroids at the gym, the third was a dainty wee cocker spaniel who stared happily at him, her tongue lolling out of her mouth.

"Who found him?" he asked.

The handler with the spaniel lifted his hand, and the dog sprang up, ready for action.

"Me, sir," said the man. "Betty picked up the trail from the tree, came straight here. Took a while to find the exact place, the scent has been masked."

"Masked?" said Baird. He sniffed the air, close to

gagging. The smell was atrocious, but it wasn't just a dead person stench. There was something else.

"Have a look," said Declan. "See if you can tell."

He held out a metal ruler.

"Can you no do it?" asked Baird.

Declan didn't reply, and after a second or two Baird snatched the ruler from him, using it to lift the top of the cardboard box.

"Hello, Greg," he said.

Gregory Brightwell stared up at him, his eyes wide open and covered with a translucent film. His tongue was thrust out so far it looked like he'd been using it to try to dig himself out of the hole. His hair was caked with dirt, his skin the colour of a bruised apple and streaked with brown smudges. Fortunately, Baird couldn't see the neck past the sides of the box, but there was no doubt that Greg now ended just below the chin.

The smell rolled out of the box, hitting him like a mallet to the face. He recoiled, his free hand clamping his nose shut.

"I'm gonna boak," he said.

"You wouldn't be the first," Fred replied, looking at the uniformed officers. "It's not pleasant."

"What am I smelling?" said Baird. "That's shite, right?"

"Dog excrement," said Declan. "A lot of it. It's been rubbed all over his face and hair, and the box is lined with it."

"It's a good way of concealing something," said the handler. "Dogs are attracted to most smells, but they'll stay away from poop."

"That's true enough," said Fred. "We used to have a labrador that never stopped digging. Destroyed our back garden. Our trainer told us to bury its faeces in the soil, and we did. It never dug there again."

He sighed.

"Ended up excavating half of my neighbour's garden instead, but that's an unpleasant saga for another day."

"So whoever buried the heid kent what they were doing," said Baird. "They didnae want us to find it."

"That's weird," said Connell, who was doing her best to look anywhere other than inside the box. "Why kill a man with all that ceremony, and leave his body in the open like that, then bury his head?"

"Something to do with Edward's legend, maybe?" said Baird.

"Edmund, sir. And in the story, they found the head lying on the ground, guarded by a wolf. It wasn't buried."

"There are hundreds of versions of the death of Saint Edmund," said Fred. "All a little different. Nobody knows the truth, of course."

"But our killer was interested enough in the story to do this to Greg," said Baird. "They're trying to tell us something, I just cannae see it."

"Well, the contents of the box might help," said Declan.

"The heid?"

"Yes, but that's not all that's in there."

"The shite?"

"No," said the young man, losing his patience. "There are items in the box. Use your eyes."

Baird leaned over again, still pinching his nose. It was hard to see anything other than the severed head, but sure enough there was something wedged between the dead man's cheeks and the sides of the box.

"What is that?" he said, craning forward. The loose dirt

slid out from under his foot, raining into the hole, and he almost lost himself to gravity. "A cat? It looks like a cat."

"A real one?" said Connell, horrified.

"Nut, an ornament of some kind. Dec, can you get it oot?"

The young man bristled at the shortening of his name.

"It might be better to wait until we get the head out," he said.

"It won't make any difference to me," said Fred. "Go for it."

Declan pulled a set of tongs from his bag, then a stainless-steel tray. He passed the tray to Fred and got down on his knees beside the open box. It took him a few tries to work the object out with the tongs, and he delicately placed it on the tray. Everybody crowded in to get a better view. It looked, to Baird, like a small china figurine of a white cat, sitting up straight, one paw to its mouth. Its ear had broken off.

"One small figurine of a white cat," said Declan, his nasal voice burrowing beneath Baird's skin. "Porcelain, maybe eight centimetres tall. The cat appears to be sitting and possibly grooming its face. One ear has broken off."

"Thanks for describing what we can all see," muttered Baird. "Anything on its arse?"

Declan used the tongs to lift the cat. There was a small hole for the mould, but there was nothing inside, and nothing written there.

"What else?" said Baird.

Declan rummaged inside the box again, pulling out another little ceramic figure. This one was smaller, and painted green. It looked like a tortoise.

"One small, porcelain—"

"Tortoise," said Baird.

"Tortoise, about five centimetres long, painted—"

"Green, we can all see it, what else?"

"Green," Declan went on, speaking like the announcer at the train station and obviously enjoying himself immensely. "And brown, for the shell. I think it's perhaps an Indian star tortoise, although the detail on the pattern makes it hard to tell. There is..."

He turned it over.

"Nothing," said Baird. "There's nothing. What else?"

"Nothing on the bottom."

The young man deposited the tortoise next to the cat and dived back in. What he pulled out next was another animal. It looked like a bunny with a little pink nose, one ear up and one ear down. The body was chipped and cracked.

"One brown, ceramic bunny rabbit," said Declan. "One ear raised, the other floppy. It has sustained some damage, as if it has been repeatedly dropped, or perhaps attacked with a hammer."

"Both of which, incidentally, are about to happen to you," said Baird. "What else?"

"The nose is pink. It's approximately eight centimetres in height."

He placed the animal on the tray, and went back for the next one. Baird resisted the urge to boot him into the hole, turning to Connell instead. He didn't need to ask the question.

"I have no idea, sir," she said. "I don't remember there being any animals or anything in the legends, other than the wolf.

Declan had added a ceramic bird of some kind to the tray, but Baird continued to tune him out.

"They mean something," he said. "Did you see any china figures at Fishbourne's place?"

Connell shook her head.

"There's no animals in the books? Tortoises and stuff?"

"No, sir. There are eagles, because you need to put an eagle feather in your pizzle stick to make it work."

"Is that an eagle, son?" Baird asked Declan.

"If you'd been listening to me, you'd already know it's a lapwing," he replied. "Made of porcelain, approximately seven centimetres—"

"Lapwings?" Baird asked Connell.

"No," she said. "There's nothing like that. I think Greg might have done an animal film, a Doctor Doolittle thing, years ago, before he made it big. Maybe that has something to do with it? Somebody might be angry about it?"

She shrugged.

"Angry that he was talking to the beasties," said Baird. "I'll add it to the list. Next to Leonardo DiCaprio."

He sucked in a deep breath for as long as it took him to remember the smell of dog shite.

"You see anything interesting with the heid?" he asked Fred, once again cutting Declan off mid-sentence.

"I'm going to take it to my laboratory now," he replied. "I shall be able to tell you everything you need to know by the end of the day."

Baird nodded. The smell, and the fact that Gregory Brightwell's severed head was still staring at him, was making him feel dizzy. He was sweating buckets, and he took off his jacket, pressing it to his face in case he suddenly projectile vomited over the crime scene.

"If either of you find anything interesting, holler," he told them.

"Why?" said Declan, holding a hedgehog figurine in his tongs. "Where are you going?"

"For a walk," he said.

CHAPTER TWENTY-ONE

"I just can't see it, you know," said Connell as they traipsed through the woods. They were heading back towards the road, the trees thinning. Sunlight gathered between the trunks, as if welcoming Baird and Connell back from the depths of darkness, ushering them out of the tangled branches and into the golden day.

Baird emerged with his hand over his eyes, gurning and groaning his way into the insufferable heat.

"See what?" he said. "I cannae see bloody anything thanks to that bloody bampot in the sky."

"The sun, sir?"

"Aye, the sun. What are *you* talking aboot, Connie?"

"The animals, sir," she said. "The ones in the box. I just can't see Bruce Fishbourne handling those delicate little figurines. Using an axe to chop off Greg's head, yes. Tying him to a tree, yes. The crossbow, yes. But something about the animals makes me..."

She shrugged.

"It just feels wrong," she finished. "I can't explain it any better than that."

"Aye, me too. I thought maybe it was a split personality thing, you ken? Like, he's been Charlotte DeVere for so long he takes on her attributes for real. Some days he's Bruce, the axe-wielding ogre, some days he's Charlotte, the china figurine hoarder."

"So *Bruce* Bruce does the killing, *Charlotte* Bruce adds the animals to the box?" said Connell, uncertain.

"Aye, when *you* say it, it sounds daft. I cannae think of any reason why anyone would do it. *Any* of it. It's almost as if they were giving Greg something to go away with, to take to the next world."

"Like the Egyptians," said Connell. "That makes sense. The figurines are a gift."

They made their way along the track, kicking up a storm of dust that floated over the field.

"Actually, sir, that *does* make sense," she went on. "We're assuming somebody killed Greg because they didn't like him, or because they were angry, or jealous, or because they wanted to get him out of the way, right?"

"Aye, they're usually the reasons people do the whole murder thing."

"That's not every reason, though. People kill for love all the time."

They'd reached the top of the hill, the land sweeping down into a vista of green. Past that was the sea, fast asleep in the sun. Baird stopped for breath, enjoying the tickle of the breeze on his sweaty face.

"What if somebody killed Greg because they loved him," Connell went on. "They loved him so much they wanted to... I don't know, *keep* him. Make him theirs forever."

Baird thought about it for a moment, nodding.

"It happens," he said. "We had a case not so long ago.

Young lassie, still at school. Wanted to leave her boyfriend and he didnae want to lose her, so he picked her up one day and drove her up to Tyrebagger woods. Put a Tesco bag over her heid and suffocated her."

"God, sir, that's awful," said Connell.

"Tried to off himself as well but he chickened oot. Told us he wanted to keep her forever, and that was the only way he kent how to do it. Wee shit's now doing life at Grampian, but it's still life. He won."

He had to turn away from the sun because the combination of the heat and the light and his anger was making him feel like a lit fuse.

"With any luck, somebody'll do the same thing to him," he said.

"We can't say that, sir," said Connell. "We can *think* it, we just can't say it."

"Aye," he said, walking down the other side of the hill. He tried to punt a stone and missed, jarring his knee. "But that's good thinking. People idolise movie stars, put them on pedestals."

"The gods of the silver screen," said Connell.

"Somebody gets obsessed with Greg, they want to be with him. He turns them doon, or disnae even notice them. The only thing left is to chop off his heid and shoot him with arrows."

"And leave him with a handful of animals, for company," said Connell. "Maybe that's why they buried the head? They knew the body would be taken away, but they were planning to come back for the rest of him?"

"They covered it in dog shite, Connie, there's no way they were coming back for that."

He stopped by Briggs' Range Rover, purging the stench of the woods from his nose and replacing it with the saltwater smell of the sea. Now that they weren't crunching on the gravel track, he could hear the water, a soft lullaby that made him yawn. It went on for so long that his ears popped, his eyes watering, and when he finished he saw Connell staring at him like he'd had some kind of medical episode.

"It was just a yawn, Connie," he said.

"No, sir," she said, peering over his shoulder, as alert as a cat that's seen a mouse. "Behind you."

He spun around, seeing the road, which was boxed in by vegetation.

"What?" he said. "The hedge?"

"*In* the hedge, sir! A woman!"

He only saw her when she moved, a flash of purple that vanished into the tangled foliage.

Purple.

"It's the woman from the hotel," said Connell. "I'm sure of it."

"Can you get her?" he said. "I'm no much of a... Oh, forget it."

He took a breath and yelled.

"Hey! Come back here, right noo!"

She didn't, of course.

Baird dumped his jacket and jogged for the A12, skidding to a halt as a truck barrelled past at fifty miles an hour, choking the air with dust and fumes. When the coast was clear, he crossed the road and threw himself into the hedge on the other side. It did *not* want him there, rejecting his advances with finger-like twigs in his eyes and mouth. By the time he'd plopped out the other side, about ten years later, every exposed part of him was burning.

"Awa' and boil yer fud," he said, jogging onto a wide, open parkland dotted with trees. The woman was halfway across it, her arms and legs pumping, her hair impossibly bright in the sun. She really was a ninja.

Baird started off again, a stitch already forming in his ribs. He'd only taken a few steps when he heard Connell shouting from his side. She was running through a gap in the hedge, struggling to keep up.

"There's nothing over there except the beach," she yelled. "There's nowhere for her to go."

The woman seemed to know it, angling off to the right and heading for a strip of woodland.

"Oi!" Baird yelled. "We're polis!"

If anything, it seemed to make her run quicker. Baird put his head down, chuffing like a runaway donkey as he galloped across the meadow. He wished he'd had a couple of constables with him, but he didn't dare get his phone out because it would only slow him down.

The woman vanished into the trees, fifty yards ahead. If it had been anybody else, he might have left it at that. But he was still so angry about the fact he'd had to follow her down the drainpipe of Denton's hotel that he pushed through the pain.

He crashed into the trees ten seconds later. They were far enough apart for the woman to be immediately visible, her purple hair flashing like a beacon.

"Would you just stop!" he pleaded.

He limped on, dead wood cracking beneath his feet. The woods weren't big, and he crossed them in no time. What he saw when he emerged from the other side, though, was far worse.

"Oh for Pete's sake," he muttered.

There was a huge body of water ahead, stretching from left to right as far as he could see. It was maybe a hundred yards from here to the far bank, and the purple-haired woman was a good way across thanks to a little red rowing boat.

"Are you kidding me?" he yelled, his voice carrying. "Dinnae think I'll no swim!"

He wasn't going to swim, but she didn't need to know that. He pulled out his phone, calling Briggs. When she answered, it was her voicemail.

"Aye, I'll leave a message, *ma'am,*" he said after the tone. "Answer the phone! We're chasing the woman who got away from us at Denton's place yesterday. She's—"

There was a noise like an angry yeti emerging from its cave, and Baird turned to see Connell explode from the bushes. She lurched towards him, carrying half the forest in her hair.

"She's on a boat," he said into the phone. "I dinnae think we can catch her. There are Uniforms in the woods, see if they can get to her before she vanishes again."

"We're in Benacre Park," Connell shouted. "The lake, it leads down to Lock's Lane."

Baird ended the call so the message would send, then he turned back to the water. The woman was struggling, because she didn't have an oar. She was using her hands to sweep herself through the water, the boat floating in clumsy circles.

There was still a chance.

"How good a swimmer are you, Connie?"

"I float quite well," she said. "But we might not need to swim, sir."

She pointed to a wall of rushes that grew up along the side of the lake, and Baird was surprised to see a monstrous swan staring back at them, its long neck craning upwards and taller than he was. It was such an unexpected sight that he flinched.

"The hell is *that*?" he asked, getting ready to batter it if it showed any sign of aggression.

Connell was already running towards it, wading into the shallow water and grabbing the swan's neck like she was going to wring it. For a second, Baird wondered if he was dreaming, or if he'd collapsed due to exhaustion and sun stroke. Then Connell pulled the swan free of the reeds and he saw what it was.

"A pedalo?" he said.

"Yes," said Connell.

"Where the hell did it come from?"

"I have no idea," she said, clambering in. The swan rocked wildly, and she had to hold on hard so as not to fall. She collapsed into the seat, causing a small tidal wave to wash up on the shore. "Hurry up!"

"Help ma boab," he muttered as he ran to the lake.

Connell shifted up a little and he grabbed the swan's head, climbing in. The interior was full of freezing water, soaking his shoes and his socks in an instant. It rocked alarmingly, and he dropped into the seat before he fell out. That was wet too, his arse drookit.

"Now what?" he said, trying to look past the swan's enormous wings to see where the woman was.

"We pedalo, sir!" said Connell, putting her feet on one of the two sets of metal pedals and pushing hard. They were covered in rust, turning jerkily, something frothing beneath the water. "Come on."

"Alright, alright," said Baird, trying to get his feet on his set of pedals. "Stop a minute, will you, we have to work together."

She wasn't listening, her legs pounding, kicking up a wash of brackish water from the floor that soaked him in seconds. He planted his shoes on the pedals and kicked hard, already exhausted. The pedalo was slowly reversing, wobbling like a spinning top.

"How do we turn around?" asked Connell.

"I dinnae ken, he's your swan."

He tried turning his pedals the other way, and gradually the pedalo began to spin. The lake drifted into sight, as did another pedalo lost in the reeds and, past that, a second rowing boat—this one with its oars.

"For the love of... did you no think aboot grabbing the boat, Connie?"

"The pedalo..." she panted. "Is faster."

The woman was two thirds of the way across the lake, but losing strength. She glanced back, a glimpse of her face. Baird pointed a finger at her to let her know they were on their way, but he wasn't sure how intimidating he looked in the giant swan. He moved his legs as fast as they would go, the pedals jamming and lurching and screeching and resisting every rotation. They were going about half a mile an hour, and drifting back towards the bank where they'd started.

"Faster!" he barked. "We have to pedal at the same speed or we'll go in circles."

"Can't you..." said Connell, beet red, "go slower?"

The swan wasn't just pootling along, it was filling up. Water was pouring into the base through one of the many cracks, up to their shins now and making the pedalling harder than ever. He reached down and scooped a little up, throwing it out.

"Oh no!" said Connell. "Are we sinking?"

She collected some water in her own hands, and in her panic scooshed it right in his face. She'd done it twice more before he screamed at her to stop.

"It's going right back in the swan," he said. "Throw it that way!"

It was no use, the water was nearly at the top of the seating compartment now, more gushing over the edges as they sank into the lake.

"We're going doon, Connie," said Baird. "I hope you weren't lying when you said you could float."

He pulled his phone from his pocket, drying it as best he could on his shirt. Then he called Briggs again. This time she answered.

"Harrison? What's going on? Have you got her?"

"No, ma'am," he said.

The woman had reached the far bank and was scrabbling out of her boat. She glanced back, and although it was a little too far for him to see the expression on her face, it looked like she was doubled over with laughter.

"We've lost her," he said. "And we're in a bit of trouble. We're in the middle of a lake and our swan is sinking."

"Swan?" exclaimed Briggs.

"It'll take too long to explain, ma'am. Send the PCs. And maybe a rescue helicopter. Aye?"

"Harrison, I have no idea what you're saying," said Briggs. "I—"

Connell was still trying to scoop handfuls of water out of the pedalo, and her flailing arms smacked him right in the hand. His phone sailed out of his wet grip, landing with a plop in the lake. For a few seconds, they both stared at the rippling water.

"Right," said Baird with a heavy sigh.

The swan was bubbling as it disappeared into the water. Baird had the sudden urge to stand up and salute, as if he was the captain of the Titanic. It was probably better to just disappear beneath the waves than try to live this down.

"We're going to drown!" said Connell. "What do we do, sir? What do we—"

The swan clunked into the lakebed, settling in the mulch—just its head and the tops of its wings poking from the surface.

"Oh," said Connell. "It's not as deep as I thought it was."

Baird stepped out of the pedalo, waist deep in freezing water. He kicked his shoe about a bit, looking for his phone, but it was a lost cause. There was no sign of the woman now, she'd vanished into the bushes that led back to the road. Baird wondered if she'd taken a photograph first. He could picture it on the front page of whatever awful local paper serviced this part of the world.

Coppers Come a Cropper in a Giant Swan.

The only plus side was that he could hear sirens riding on the wind.

"You think she'll send the helicopter, sir?" said Connell.

"Aye, Connie. I'm sure she will."

He started wading back the way they'd floated. Connell squealed as she stumbled out of the pedalo, the water almost reaching her chest. She held her phone aloft, and when it rang a few seconds later, she answered it.

"Yes, ma'am... We had an incident, ma'am, but we're alive... Yes, ma'am, a big swan... No ma'am, it fell in the lake... I'll tell him."

She hung up, splashing faster to catch up to him.

"The bad news is there's no helicopter," she said.

"Shame," said Baird. "What's the good news?"

"Uniforms caught the purple-haired woman, sir. She's on the road."

CHAPTER TWENTY-TWO

They made their way back to the road in silence —aside from the slosh of their clothes and the squeak of their shoes, that was. Baird felt utterly miserable. He wasn't quite as wet as he had been on the last case, when he and Arnold Mutton had gone for a swim in the harbour. But the lake was stagnant water, and it reeked like Nessie's arse crack.

The shame of the whole episode didn't help either.

Sure enough, a congregation of uniformed officers stood in the field on the side of the busy A12. The purple-haired woman sat in the middle of them, her legs pulled up and her face buried in her knees. She'd been cuffed, which was a relief. She'd already scooted down a building, outrun him twice, and rowed across a lake with nothing but her bare hands. Baird half expected her next trick to be sprouting wings and flying off.

They waited for the traffic to break, then hopped up the verge on the other side.

"What on earth happened to you two?" said one of the PCs. It was Percy Albright, and the smile on his face was just asking to be rubbed off with a starchy rag. "Go for a swim?"

"Aye. We went for a swim. Keep up the smart remarks and you will be too."

Baird turned to the woman.

"*You...*"

He said it loud enough to wake her from her stupor. She was older than Baird had first thought, maybe somewhere in her late thirties. As well as the purple hair, which was soaking wet, she had a dozen or so piercings in her ears, the metalwork glinting in the sun. Faded tattoos peeked out of the collar and sleeves of her sodden black top and the ankles of her matching tracksuit trousers. She flinched, her terrified expression softening what Baird had been about to say into what actually came out of his mouth.

"... have got some explaining to do. What the hell were you thinking, bolting like that? *Twice.* I nearly died chasing you down the back wall of the hotel."

"And we nearly drowned just now," said Connell, standing by his side. She was shivering hard despite the heat. "They were going to send out a *helicopter*."

The woman opened her mouth, but nothing came out. Baird walked a little closer, so she could see the expression on his face. He wasn't in the mood for any nonsense.

"I'm only gonna give you one chance, before I arrest you," he said, speaking over the traffic that whipped by. "One chance. What's going on?"

"I'm sorry," the woman said. She tried to hold up her hands but the cuffs snapped tight, making her grimace in pain. Water dripped from her purple hair. "I didn't want anything bad to happen, I didn't want anyone to get hurt. I just... I panicked."

She adjusted her position, trying to get comfortable in the dirt.

"Help her up," said Baird, and a couple of the PCs did as he asked. She stood there, hunched and afraid, looking back and forth between Baird and Connell. "What's your name?"

She glanced at the PCs, as if they might offer her some protection or guidance. Baird snapped his fingers, although they were still wet, so the sound they made barely carried.

"Talk to me, no them. What's your name?"

"Karen," she said, and when Baird spun his hand around, she kept going, "Kirby."

"Right, good. Karen, can you please tell me what the hell you're doing."

"Just..." she started, shrugging. Her accent was from the southwest somewhere. "You know, just..."

She faltered, looking to the sky for answers.

"Just loitering around the scene of a serious crime," said Baird. "Running from the police. Wandering aboot the hotel rooms of dead men."

It was like he'd physically struck her. Karen recoiled, backing into the arms of an officer.

"He's *dead*?" she said, shaking her head. "He's actually dead? Don't say that. Don't say it, please."

"I didnae say anyone was dead," said Baird, trying to remember if he had or not. "I just mean—"

"No," said Karen, clamping her hands to her heart. "I knew it. I knew it. I *felt* it. Greg, right? Gregory Brightwell?"

She looked at him with such intensity that he didn't see how he could hide the truth.

"Aye," he said. "Greg."

She doubled up, making a noise like she might vomit.

And just when Baird was about to try to comfort her, she sprang back up again, as violently as a switchblade.

"How?" she said. "Did somebody do this to him?"

"I cannae say, because we dinnae ken, no for sure. And I'm no answering any more of your questions until you answer mine. What's your relationship with Greg?"

She looked to the sky again, making a noise like a broken engine.

"You related?" asked Baird. "A friend? More than a friend?"

"No," she said. "None of those. I... Look, I didn't actually know him."

"No? You're pretty emotional for somebody who disnae know him."

"I *did* know him," she said, contradicting herself. "Like everyone knew him. Only I knew him better than everyone. And he knew me too. I'm a fan. His biggest fan."

Baird frowned, seeing the same expression of confusion on Connell's face.

"A fan?" he said.

"I've got proof," she told him. "In my pocket."

"Anything else in your pockets, hen? Anything sharp?"

"No, of course not," she said. "Well, my keys. And a pen. And maybe a scalpel, now I come to think of it. But no, nothing that will hurt anyone."

Baird nodded to an officer, who pushed a gloved hand into the pocket of Karen's trousers. The first thing she pulled out was a craft knife, the blade retracted.

"It's for photographs," Karen said, grimacing as a truck thundered past just feet away. "I meant my wallet."

The PC pulled it out and brought it over. It looked like it belonged to a teenage boy, Greg's face beneath the *Star Wars* logo. Baird opened the Velcro flap, checking the woman's driving licence to make sure she'd been telling the truth. It had expired two years ago.

"You know this is oot of date," he told her.

"They don't go out of date," she said.

"Och, well that's okay then," he said. "It's proof of your ID, but why does it make you a fan?"

"Not that, the cards, in the money bit."

He rummaged in the wallet, pulling out a small, glossy photograph. In it, Karen lay in a bed next to Greg, the sheets pulled up to their necks, both of them grinning.

"You dinnae ken him, then?" said Baird, holding it up.

"Oh God," said Karen. "I forgot... no, that's not real. It's Photoshop, honest. Just look closely, you'll see the joins."

Baird peered at it, finding the crude lines where Greg's face had been pasted onto the original photo.

"Right," he said, putting it back. "That's no creepy at all."

He found a little collection of business cards in the same compartment. They were bright pink, and scratchy with glitter. On one side was a grinning photograph of Gregory Brightwell, dressed like he was in a Jane Austen adaptation. He had his shirt open, his chest shaved, the bulge in his tight trousers like he was stashing his lunch there. The look he was giving the camera was so sultry Baird was worried the card might spontaneously combust.

He turned it over, reading the text.

"Karen Kirby, President and CEO of the Official Gregory Brightwell Fan Club."

There was a phone number and a website underneath, and, right at the bottom, a line of text that read: **Not actually official*.

"So yeah," said Karen. "That's me."

"This official, unofficial club, what does it do?" asked Baird.

"We just celebrate Greg," she said. "All his movies, his TV stuff. We all love him, this is our way of showing it. We've got quite big, since the *Star Wars* thing. Nearly 300 members."

Her face fell.

"What am I supposed to tell them?"

"Absolutely nothing," said Baird. "None of this leaves your mouth, understood? If you announce his death it will blow up our chances of finding Greg's killer. Speaking of which, where were you on Friday night? Eight until eight, but especially around midnight."

"Wait," she said. "You think *I* could have done this?"

"Listen, Karen, I saw you shimmy doon a drainpipe like Catwoman. You broke the hundred metre sprint record crossing that field. You're practically a superhero."

"No, that's not what I mean. I *loved* Greg, I couldn't have hurt him."

"It's funny. Me and Connell here were just having that exact conversation. How love makes people do the stupidest things. So answer the question. Friday night. You. Where?"

She shuffled her trainers in the dry dirt.

"I mean, I was here, kind of," she said.

"Here, as in the exact place where Greg was killed?"

"No. I mean... Look, I know this is going to sound weird, but I sort of follow him around. If he's got a job on or something. On set. You know. Like those storm chasers who drop everything to find tornadoes. I do the same thing. Only I find... Greg."

Baird rubbed his temples, his head banging from the sun —and probably from some kind of brain-rotting lake plague too. He could just about feel the bacteria crawling over his wet skin.

"How did you ken he was here?" asked Baird. "In the woods. You followed him?"

"Kind of," she said. "Not on Friday night, I was asleep. But... Look, it's probably easier if I show you."

"How?" asked Baird.

"My van's just around the corner. I've got logs, records, spreadsheets. Photos, too. I can show it all to you, if you think it will help."

"Will it get me oot the sun?" he asked.

"Well, yeah," said Karen. "We'll be inside."

Baird nodded, and Karen started walking. She was struggling in the cuffs, but Baird didn't want to risk losing her a third time. Besides, the PC accompanied her, holding her arm so she wouldn't trip on the rough terrain of the field.

"It's just a couple of minutes away," she said. "I drove by yesterday, saw the police cars. I thought it was a movie at first, that you were all filming something. Got dead excited, because I always said Greg would make an amazing TV detective. Parked in a track just up there and walked over the field. Was hoping to get a shot for the newsletter, you know?"

"It's a good job you didnae," said Baird, thinking of the headless body strapped to the tree.

"Took a few photos of the cars and the police, but then it all started to feel a bit too real, you know? There's usually cameras, food vans, all the set stuff. And the crew, obviously. There was none of that, and I got worried something bad had happened."

"So you went looking for Greg at Denton's?" asked Baird.

"Right," she said. "I know he stays there. One of the

girls who works in the kitchen is in the fan club, she always gives me a bell if he shows up. She called me on Wednesday and I came straight down."

"From where?" said Baird. "Where's home?"

Karen sniffed, looking at her feet.

"It's just been a bit of a weird year," she said. "Me and Phil are going through a hard time."

"Your husband?"

"I mean, yeah, I guess he still is. But the old divorcaroony is on the horizon. He's already handed me the papers, says it's my fault, says I wasn't paying him enough attention, and that I was in love with another man."

"I dinnae think he was wrong," said Baird.

"I know, but it's not like I was sleeping with Greg," said Karen, angry now. "I only spoke to him twice in ten years, and we said about three words between us. It's not an affair, is it, if you never have any bloody interaction with them? Now if I was rolling about in the sack with Greg every afternoon, all naked and stuff, all hot and sweaty and..." She swallowed hard. "Then I could understand him being pissed off. But is that sort of thing possible? No! And believe me, I've tried."

She was getting flustered in the heat, and she shook the PC's hand away.

"So fuck Phil and his big house and his saggy arse. I like my van, and it means I'm not tied to anywhere. Get to go wherever I please, get to follow Greg all over the country. Not that I can even do that any more, because he's bloody *dead*."

She stopped walking, hanging her head and releasing a choked sob. It didn't matter, because Baird caught a glimpse of a campervan up ahead, parked a little way down a gravel path with its nose to the road. He trudged over to it, Connell right behind him.

"What do you make of her?" he asked quietly.

"Nuts," came her reply.

"Aye."

He tried the door, which was locked, then he made his way around the van. It was an old Transit that had been converted, and it didn't look like a professional job. One of the tyres was the spare, which looked like it was hanging onto life with a wing and a prayer. Through the windscreen he saw that the dash was covered in so many pieces of plastic tat that it was a wonder anyone could see out of it. The back doors, which were also locked, boasted a collage of bumper stickers.

"'If my husband was as nice as my van, maybe I'd ride him more,'" he said, reading one aloud. Then another: "'If this van's rocking, then I finally caught up to Greg Brightwell!' I can see why Phil was having doubts."

By the time he'd done a full circuit of the van, Karen had caught up. She fished her keys from her pocket and unlocked the side door, then she stopped, fidgeting nervously.

"Actually, can I just go in and grab what I need?" she asked. "There's not much room in there, and it's probably better we do this outside."

"If I didnae know better, I'd think you were hiding something," said Baird, walking to the door. She stood in front of it, barring the way.

"No. I mean yeah, but it's not what you think. Honest."

He gave her a look and she stepped aside, grunting with frustration.

"Just don't look in the bed, okay? That's private."

"I'll no look in the bed," he said.

He climbed the step, the van wobbling as he ducked through the door. There were thick net curtains on the windows, and it took a moment for his eyes to adjust to the dark. When they did, he wasn't sure whether to laugh or scream.

Every single wall in the van was covered with photographs of Greg. Some had obviously been cut out of newspapers and magazines, and most had been there a long time, their colours faded and their corners peeling. Others were proper printed photos, showing Greg on set and at conventions. Mounted on the wall above the sink was an open wooden cabinet, the kind that usually held ancient reliquaries. This one displayed an A4-sized photograph of Karen standing next to Greg in front of a *Star Wars* backdrop. She was grabbing his waist with both arms, the look on her face positively euphoric. Greg looked a little alarmed. The shrine was packed with souvenirs and trinkets: tickets, brochures, merchandise from various movies.

There was a little porcelain figurine there, too, of a field mouse clinging onto an ear of wheat.

"Just don't look in the bed," said Karen from the door.

"Och, aye, thanks for reminding me," he said, making his way to the bed. It was a single bunk tucked beneath the window, the covers pulled up over the pillows. There was a distinctive, human-sized lump beneath the duvet.

Baird tensed.

"You on your own in here, Karen?" he asked.

"Yes," she said, far too quickly. He spoke to the bed.

"Because if there's anybody else in the van, they're about to get my wet shoe up their arse."

The lump didn't move. He grabbed the covers and pulled them off, jumping back when he saw the man who lay there.

"Shite on a bike," he said.

It was Gregory Brightwell, and he grinned up at Baird from the bed like he was inviting him to jump in for a roll around. It was so dark in the caravan that it took him all of three seconds to understand that it *wasn't* Greg. It wasn't even a man. It was some kind of stuffed effigy made up of pillowcases and dressed in pyjamas. The head was a cushion onto which a photograph of Greg's face had been taped.

"What in the name of..." he said, his heart still clattering.

Outside, Karen groaned.

"You looked in the bed, didn't you?"

"Aye, I looked in the bed. Can you come in here, please."

She joined him in the caravan, obviously mortified. Connell was right behind her, her eyes boggling when she saw the man in the bed.

"Oh," said Connell.

"Oh is right," replied Baird. "I'd ask you to explain, but I'm too scared of what I'll hear."

"It's not bloody illegal," said Karen

She pushed past him and dragged the covers back over Greg's face. As she did so, the head detached, falling onto the floor with a dull thud. Baird felt the blood drain from his face as he remembered the head in the box—the *real* head. He had to look away, suddenly dizzy.

"Bloody hell," said the woman, picking it up and cradling it like a baby. "Sorry, Greggy."

It was all getting a bit much, but there were now two people between Baird and the way out. He took a couple of deep breaths to fend off the claustrophobia.

"Just gets lonely out here," said Karen, rocking the head back and forth. "We're not doing anything wrong."

"We?" said Connell. Karen held up the head.

"Yeah, *we*. Me and Greg."

Connell shared a look with Baird.

"Leaving aside the... whatever this is," said Baird, gesturing at the bed and then turning his hand to the shrine. "Can you tell me aboot this. The wee moose. Where did you get it?"

"Moose?" she asked.

"Mouse," translated Connell.

Karen clutched the cushion head to her chest, the cuffs rattling. She seemed to be doing a fair bit of squirming.

"Nowhere," she said. "It's just something that reminds me of Greg. He did that film, the animal one, where he could talk to them. He had the pet mouse who lived in his... his trousers. That just makes me think of him. That's all this stuff is, it just reminds me of my Greg. Look..."

She took a moment to find her words.

"I know you probably think I'm insane."

"Never crossed my mind," said Baird.

"But Greg is special. He's... you don't find men like him very often. Not just the way he looks." She held up the cushion to show off his face. "Although God knows that helps. It's... he's a nice guy. He's kind, he listens to you. Even though I've only met him those two times, and there were queues and time limits, I could see how good he was. He took the time to listen to me. His wife says it all the time, how lucky she is, how sweet Greg is to her. *Everybody* says it. He's a good man. He's a *saint*."

Baird met Connell's eyes again.

"I love him. And it might not be the sort of love other people have, but it's still love."

She was crying now, and she used the cushion to wipe her face.

"I'll always love him."

"Look, Karen, I'm gonna need you to come and have a talk with us, okay? At the polis station. We're gonna ask you a few more questions."

"Why?" she snapped, still clinging onto that severed head. "I haven't done anything wrong. I invited you in here, didn't I? I offered to help. I want to catch whoever did this to my Greggy. I haven't done anything illegal."

"You mentioned you had something that would help us," he said, speaking as calmly as he could.

"Oh, yeah, right," said Karen, sitting on the edge of the bed and running her hand along Greg's face. "I can show you exactly where Greg was before he was killed."

"How?"

She looked up, sniffing.

"Because I put a tracker on his car."

CHAPTER TWENTY-THREE

THE TRACKER ON GREGORY BRIGHTWELL'S CAR WAS connected to Karen Kirby's laptop, and as the signal in the little van was spotty at best, Baird opted to take it back to Southwold HQ. Karen, meanwhile, was driven up to Lowestoft Police Station for further questioning.

He wasn't sure it would help her case that she'd insisted on taking her Greggy sex pillow with her.

"What do you think, sir?" asked Connell from the back of the IRV as they accelerated down the A12. "Bit weird, right?"

"A bit weird?" he said, leaning over from the passenger seat. His trousers had dried a little, but he was still soggy, and he could feel the pond creatures breeding in his various nooks and crannies. "Connie, she was off her heid. An utter nutter, as my granny would say."

"No, I mean the situation," she said. "The dead Greg thing with the detachable head."

"Aye, that was a wee bit too close to reality for me. Did you see the wee moose figurine over the sink? It was just like the ones we found with Greg's heid."

"And she called him a saint," said Connell.

"One coincidence is a coincidence. Three is the universe trying to tell us something."

"She's obviously fit, sir. Strong enough to climb down the wall, and paddle across the lake, and get away from you."

"I'm no a runner," he said in his defence.

"I wouldn't fancy my chances against her," Connell went on. "She said she knew Greg, she admitted to stalking him, following him around the country. He knew her, because of the fan club, so maybe if she called him and asked to meet, he said yes."

"In his dressing goon?"

Connell didn't answer. Baird faced front as they drove into Southwold. The PC at the wheel had to slow right down to avoid hitting the crowds of weekend tourists that overspilled the pavements.

"He could have been in Benacre for a different reason," said Baird. "Maybe he was doing some research for his movie. He was staying doon the road, aye? It was the middle of the night. Maybe he couldnae sleep, drove over to the woods for some inspiration. It's no like he would have expected to bump into anybody at that time of night. Karen tracks him there. She follows him in, does the deed, cuts off his heid and plops it in a box with some more creepy wee animals. Job's a good'un. Buy why?"

"It's like we were saying, she was obsessed with him, she wanted to... I don't know, possess him. So she kills him. Maybe she was going to go back for the head, like we said. She doesn't look like the kind of person who's bothered by a little dog poop. Maybe she was going to attach his real head to her creepy snuggle doll."

The PC threw a concerned look in the mirror.

"And you saw what she was wearing, sir," said Connell.

"Aye. Big *lassie*, black clothes."

They were still struggling to move past the throng of people, so Baird reached over and flicked on the siren. The couple of old dears who were idling down the road almost shed their skin as they tumbled back onto the pavement. The constable picked up speed, heading for the beach.

"Well, whatever Karen's secret is, Briggs will get it oot of her," said Baird. "Between her and Bruce Fishbourne, we must have the right person."

The IRV pulled up outside HQ and Baird clambered out, opening the back door for Connell. They were halfway up the stairs to the little fisherman's cottage when the blare of a horn filled the street.

Baird turned to see a small, white van parked along the road, the passenger door opening. The balding man who was getting out was obviously struggling, partly because he was shaped like a barrel, and partly because he was holding a mountain of files. He was wearing a blue shirt tucked into dark jeans, and he pushed his glasses up his nose as he leaned into the van. He was shouting so loudly Baird could hear him up the hill.

"No, Ron, I don't know how long I'm going to be. Do you know how long you're going to be with my mother, eh?"

He slammed the door hard enough to rock the van before waddling up the road towards them.

"Oh!" exclaimed Connell, who had just noticed him. "I can't believe he's actually here."

"Dinnae tell me it's another local celebrity," said Baird.

"Kind of."

She waited for the man to reach the gate.

"Sir, this is the legendary Norman Balls. Norman, this is DI Harrison Baird."

Balls tripped up the steps, almost dropping his load as he stretched out a sweaty hand for Baird to shake. There was something about his face that made it impossible to guess how old he was, somewhere between nine and sixty.

"It'll be a pleasure to meet me," said Balls, giving Baird's hand a dozen pumps. "Shall we go inside? This weather is disgusting, and Ron doesn't even have air conditioning in his stupid van."

"Does Ron want to come in?" said Connell, offering a wave to the man in the van.

"No, he does not," said Balls. "He deserves to wait right there, in the insufferable heat, with plenty of time to think about the consequences of dating my mother."

Baird had no idea what to say to that, so he pushed open the door and walked into the relative chill of HQ. The cool air found his wet clothes immediately, a shiver ripping through him.

"What happened to you two?" asked Balls. "You're both green."

"Just wait in there for a second, will you?" Baird replied, pointing to the Incident Room. "Try no to look at any of the confidential stuff on the walls."

"You don't have to worry about me," said Balls, strutting into the room like he owned the place. "I'm an officially deputised officer of the Norfolk Constabulary."

"He's not," said Connell as she walked into the kitchen. She dropped Karen's laptop on the counter. "But it's better to let him believe it."

"Remind me who he is," said Baird, who had met so many weirdos since arriving in Southwold that he could no longer tell them apart.

"Norman Balls. Self-proclaimed expert on East Anglian

legends and folklore. He's got this blog thing, a website. *Balls Knows it Alls.*"

"And does he?" asked Baird, filling the kettle. "Ken it all?"

"You wouldn't think it, to look at him, but he's actually been pretty helpful to NorCon. He's basically attached to the Extreme Crime Task Force up there, even if they'd never admit it."

Baird was halfway to reaching for a mug, but he pulled his hand back. It had felt colder in here than outside, but it suddenly felt icy.

"Extreme Crime? That's Robbie Kett's unit, right?"

"Yeah," said Connell. "They've had some gnarly cases these last few years."

"Worse than a heidless man?"

"Much," she said. "If Balls can help them, maybe he can help us too. I'll come in with you, he's always fun to chat to."

"Actually, Connie, can you get into Karen's computer?" Baird said, remembering the mugs and putting them on the counter. "I'll talk to Balls."

She looked a little disappointed, but she nodded.

"Just stroke his ego a bit," she said as he left the kitchen. "And he'll tell you anything."

Baird walked into the dining room, shutting the door behind him. Balls practically had his nose pressed up against the wall as he studied the photograph of Greg's body tied to the tree. There were more documents fixed to the wall, Baird saw, including a photograph of the figurines from the cardboard box, arranged on a steel surface. There were eleven of them, all animals.

"Now this is extremely interesting," the strange little man said, adjusting his glasses. "If I was recreating the death of St Edmund, I would have posed it exactly like this. See the arrows? Perfectly spread over his body. And the head, removed with some ferocity."

"We already ken that," said Baird, leaning against the table.

"The clothes are wrong," Balls went on. "Edmund would have been in his royal attire, or possibly battle garments. They didn't have cotton dressing gowns in the ninth century."

"They didnae?" said Baird, gasping. "Hang on, let me write this doon."

Balls was oblivious to his sarcasm, or he just didn't care.

"That tells me something, Detective," he said. "Something important."

"Which is?" Baird said, when he didn't continue.

"Whomever your killer is, they went out of their way to end this man's life in the same manner as Edmund's execution. Yes?"

"Aye, it looks that way."

"They tied him up, they shot him with at least..."

"Twelve," said Baird when he saw the man counting.

"Twelve arrows. Then they removed his head. They took their time. This must have taken the better part of an hour, maybe longer. Where is the head?"

"They put it in a box and buried it," said Baird.

"Longer, then. This was a ceremony. The killer was putting on a performance, even if it was just to himself."

"And?" said Baird.

"The details were important to him. Authenticity was important. So why did he leave the victim in his dressing gown? Why not change his attire to something more traditional, or perhaps strip him naked entirely? Why neglect this essential detail?"

"Maybe they didnae have the right costume to hand?" said Baird.

"And yet they had a bow or a crossbow. They had arrows. They had a tool of some kind for the decapitation. Why would they bring all that and not a change of clothes for their sacrificial victim?"

"You're saying it *wasnae* important to them?" Baird asked. "That the whole Edmund thing is, what? A distraction?"

"A classic bit of misdirection," said Balls. "Designed to muddy the waters, pollute the investigation. I've studied enough of these cases to tell the genuine historical obsessives from the ones who couldn't care less. Let me ask you, how much time have you wasted finding out information about Saint Edmund?"

"Well, I'm sitting here talking to you," said Baird.

There was a knock at the door and it opened, Connell peeking through.

"Room for a little one?" she asked, carrying three mugs of tea over to the table. "Have you solved it yet, Norman?"

"Aye, we can all go home," said Baird. "Connie, can you give us a wee minute?"

She seemed reluctant to leave, so he stared at her until she got the message.

"I'll be in the kitchen, then," she said as she trudged out. "By myself."

She closed the door, and Baird turned his attention back to Balls.

"I hear you work for Norfolk Constabulary," he said. "For Kett's unit?"

Balls sat down in the nearest chair, steepling his fingers and peering over them.

"I do," he said. "Not only am I a member of the Task Force, but Robbie is my very best friend."

"Right," said Baird. "You ken him well, then?"

"Better than anyone. Better than his co-workers, and his wife, and his children."

Baird sat down opposite Balls, so close that their knees were almost touching. He leaned in and spoke quietly.

"Tell me aboot him," he said. "What's he like?"

Balls sat back in his chair as if trying to escape Baird's sudden intensity.

"Why?" he squeaked.

"Because I'm asking. What's he like?"

"Uh..." said Balls, struggling. "I'm not sure I understand the question."

"Then let me rephrase it. You ken him better than anyone. Is he bent?"

"Bent?" said Balls. "You mean *corrupt*?"

"Aye."

"No," said Balls, but there was something in his expression that said otherwise, in the way he looked anywhere except at Baird.

"He breaks the rules. Aye?"

"The rules?" said Balls. "Yes, I suppose he does. *Regularly*, now that I think about it."

"He hurts people?" Baird pressed.

"No," said Balls, growing increasingly flustered. "Unless you're talking about the Pig Man. The hammer thing? Or his old superintendent, Bingo Benson? Or the Monk guy who burned in the fire? Or that kid by the beach? Or the police officers who lost their lives last year during the Cold Iron thing? It wasn't *all* Robbie's fault."

Baird was too stunned to reply.

"Or do you mean Hollenbeck?" said Balls. "All those

people who died? It's not what it looks like. Sometimes, when you're dealing with real evil, people die. Bad people. Good people too. But he's not a bad man. He's a *good* man, he's a good policeman. He's my best friend."

Balls swallowed, his lips flapping. He was desperately trying to position his legs so they wouldn't brush up against Baird's knees, but because of the angle of the chairs he couldn't easily get up.

"I'm not sure I should be talking about any of this," he said.

"Aye, you should. Last question: do you ken anything aboot his time in London, when he was with the Met?"

"No," said Balls.

"He went rogue doon there too, aye? That whole Otley brothers case when the wee lad was kidnapped, people died then. You ever heard aboot the gangs that used to run numbers south of the Thames? Tommy Topper, shot and dumped in the river? Nigel Topper, aye? What about—"

He stopped short of mentioning his father's name.

"And John Cooper, all those bent polis? You ken anything aboot them?"

Balls shook his head, his jowls wobbling.

"Robbie does what needs to be done," he said, finding some of his bluster again. "Whatever it takes. The end justifies the means. You must understand that."

"Aye," said Baird, finally sitting back. "I do."

There was a moment of awkward silence, the room feeling like it was underwater. Baird picked up his tea, even though it was far too hot.

"You were saying, Norman," he said. "Aboot the dressing goon."

"Right, yes," said Balls, patting his stack of papers. "I

made notes, it's all here. I should probably go, with Ron outside and everything."

He jumped out of his chair, knocking it over behind him. He edged towards the door, a nervous grin plastered to his round face.

"Good luck, with the case and everything."

"Cheers," Baird replied, watching him go.

Balls opened the door, reversing into the corridor like Baird was a wild dog he didn't want to turn his back on.

"And Norman," Baird called after him. "It disnae leave this building, aye? You dinnae tell anyone what we talked aboot in here. Ever."

For some reason, Balls saluted him. Then, just like that, he was gone.

CHAPTER TWENTY-FOUR

BAIRD WAS RAGING; SO ANGRY THAT HE DIDN'T EVEN let Connell know he was leaving HQ.

He stormed out of the front door and down the steps, turning right so he wouldn't have to talk to Balls as the strange little man clambered into his van. He didn't know where he was going, only that he needed to go somewhere. If he stayed here then something in his brain was going to overheat. He was going to go into meltdown, and he didn't know what would happen next.

The conversation with Balls had hit him like a hammer, and he knew why. Up until now, there had always been a chance that his father was full of shite, that the story he'd given Baird was just that: a story. In a way, it would have been preferable. Dougie Baird would have stayed Dougie Baird, the useless fanny who'd up and left his wife and his kids twenty-four years ago, who'd vanished into thin air for no better reason than he was a crappy husband and a worse parent. Baird was used to that anger. It was old, and familiar. It had become a comfort over the years, because it was easy to hate one man, even if that man was his da.

Everything had become infinitely more complex the night he'd walked into Dougie's room, three weeks ago.

And now, after what he'd heard from Balls, there was every chance his father was telling the truth. He'd no had a choice. He'd only run away from everything he loved—his wife, his own children—because somebody had forced him to.

Because *Robert Kett* had forced him to.

There were too many slow-moving people on the pavement, and he didn't want to smack any of them in the back of the head, so he crossed the road and took the stairs down to the beach. Even with his feet in the sand and the water next to him he couldn't calm down. Everything felt different. It felt *worse*. How many times had he wished his own da dead because he'd left them. Too many to count, but he remembered them all, the endless horrors he'd inflicted on Dougie in his mind's eye.

And now he wasn't sure he'd deserved any of them.

He didn't know what to do with all those open wounds, the ones that had never been allowed to heal. He couldn't see Dougie as his enemy any more, he couldn't hate him. But he couldn't stop the hate. It was like a fuse burning down, one he couldn't quench or extinguish. The fury was going to explode, it was inevitable. He'd had a nuclear arsenal pointed at his da for all these years, and now he needed to aim it at somebody else.

And he knew exactly who.

He stopped, picking up a stone from the beach and trying to crush it in his palm.

"Bastard," he said.

He lobbed it out to sea with a guttural roar, then doubled up as the pain tore through his ribs—the injuries from yesterday reigniting.

"Ooh ya bun," he grunted.

He had to calm down. There was no use getting riled up, not until he knew for sure. And there was only one way of doing that, one way of finding the truth.

He does whatever it takes, Balls had said.

Baird needed to do the same.

He needed to speak to Kett face to face.

He started walking again, struggling on the soft sand. Everything ached, his blood boiling and his ribs singing and his head full of broken glass.

"You never should have come to England, you daft sod," he told himself. "Nothing good ever happens in England."

He didn't know where he was. He'd never walked this far down the beach. He'd left the town behind, the sand giving way to wisps of seagrass, and past that the endless meadow that swept towards the horizon. It could have been the end of the world here, and he half wished it was. No awful murders to solve. No bastard criminals to catch. No family shite to deal with.

Just sweet oblivion.

He patted his pockets, ready to call Connell, then he remembered his phone was at the bottom of a lake. He didn't fancy walking all the way back along the beach so he kept going, spotting a cluster of buildings up ahead that could only be the harbour. It was a proper slog to get back onto the road, but ten minutes later he staggered into the car park looking like a man who'd washed up from a shipwreck. The sand had stuck to his damp trousers. It had filled his shoes. His shirt had come untucked from the effort of the walk. The sweat was rolling off him as he shambled across the tarmac.

"You having a bad day, Harrison?"

He looked up to see Samara standing at the open back

door of her ice cream shack, one hand to her face to shield her eyes from the sun. She was holding a flattened cardboard box in the other, and she dumped it into a bin.

"What makes you say that?" he asked, walking over. "The fact I look like I was eaten by a walrus and then regurgitated on the beach?"

She laughed, and it was a good sound. It threw a little water on the fire, calming him.

"You want to come in? Get a drink? Maybe a 99, to cheer you up?"

He thought about it for a moment, then nodded.

"Aye, that might be nice. If you're no busy?"

She retreated into the shack, holding the door open for him. It was bigger than it looked in here, although most of the space was crammed with boxes and humming freezers. There was a small kitchen area by the door that led to the serving hatch, a stack of mugs by the sink. A velvet sofa sat against the left-hand wall, beneath the only window, a paperback book resting there with its spine broken.

"Och, no you too," he said when he realised it was a copy of one of the *Avalonia* books.

"Never book shame a girl," said Sam. "It's a more complex story than you'd think."

He laughed quietly.

"Believe me, I'm well aware how complex it is."

"You want to sit down?" she said, gesturing to the sofa. "I'll fix you up a coffee."

"I'd better no sit," he said, hovering awkwardly by the door. "You'll never get the sand oot. But I'll take the coffee. Just black."

She walked to the sink, pulling a cardboard takeaway mug from a box and dumping a teaspoon of instant coffee into it. She filled it from the hot water boiler.

"Are you sure you don't want some milk and sugar? I thought only psychopaths drank black coffee."

"That fits," he said. "Honestly, after the day I've had, I'm close to losing it."

"You can tell me about it," she said, fitting a lid on the cup and carrying it over.

"Actually, I cannae," he said as he took it from her. "It's the job."

She gave him that look again, the same one from yesterday, and he felt like he was going over the top of a roller coaster. He took a sip from his drink to try to distract himself and recoiled, gasping.

"It's hot!" Sam said, throwing her hands in the air, exasperated. "You literally just saw me pour it. Are you okay?"

"I'm fine," he croaked. "I've got to stop doing that."

Sam filled another cup with cold water from the tap, handing it to him.

"Next time you come I'm getting you a Ribena. In a sippy cup."

He downed the water, suddenly realising how thirsty he was. She took the cup from him, holding it in both hands.

"Better?" she asked.

"Aye. Sorry. Got a lot on my mind."

"That makes two of us," she said, chewing on something. She perched on the sofa, her elbows on her knees. "I'm sorry about yesterday, running off like that."

"You dinnae have to apol—"

"No, I do," she said. "It was rude. And odd. But there's a reason."

He thought about telling her again not to bother, but she deserved more than that. He stood there, waiting for her to find the words.

"I, uh, didn't always sell ice cream," she said, studying

the cup in her hands. "Back in the day, I used to work for Ma Keeble."

Baird nodded, even though she wasn't looking at him.

"Everyone around here worked for Ma, or one of the Keeble boys," she said. "Well, not everyone, but a lot of folk. Easy money, and they were good to you, if you behaved yourself. Don't judge me."

She met his eye, caught in a spear of honey-coloured light from the window. He felt his heart flutter again, his legs wobbly.

"I know you're a copper, Harrison, and you probably think I'm an arsehole or something, but I'm not. You have no idea what I was running from, and Ma gave me a place to hide, some money for myself, some self-respect. She looked after me, and she never put any pressure on. I... I didn't do anything awful, not in the grand scheme of things."

She looked like she was waiting for a reply, but before Baird could open his mouth she was off again.

"I got out, after a few years. Paid off the Keeble debt, saved enough to buy this place, and my flat. Happy days. Ma was a tyrant, but she never came after me for anything else, never tried to talk me into coming back. A deal was a deal, with her."

She placed the cup on the floor and took a deep breath, like she was building up to something.

"I got out because for the last year or so she had me working for... for Carl."

And here, again, she looked past Baird like she was expecting to see the bogeyman walk through the door.

"You've met him. You know what he's like. There's something about him... he's a hard man to say no to, and even when you do..."

She curled even further into herself, almost bent double.

"This is ten years ago, near enough," she said. "I was in my twenties, and... well, I didn't look like I do now, put it that way. I started off doing deliveries for him, pushing Ma's product around his club, selling to his clients. Christ, what you must think of me, eh?"

"I'm no thinking anything, Sam," he told her. "I'm just listening."

"The trouble is," she went on, speaking to the floor. "You end up slinging your gear at parties, and it gets pretty wild. And before you know it, you're being asked for all kinds of things. I'm not... I'm not just talking about the drugs. You're being asked to sell *all kinds of things*."

She groaned. He didn't know whether to approach her or give her space, and in the end, he stayed exactly where he was.

"Carl never endorsed it, but he never stopped it, not even when it got proper dark. And he always took his cut." She sniffed again. He couldn't tell if she was crying. "I went to Ma about it, when it got bad. Not just bad for me, but for all the girls."

"Aye?" he said, just a whisper.

"She said she'd stop it, but she never did. She never stopped anything when they were kicking the top right back up the hill. And Ma was Ma, but even she was scared of Carl. Scared of who he worked for back in the States."

Baird's anger, which had died into a quiet ember, was starting to burn back.

"I don't know why I'm telling you this, Harrison. I don't make a habit of it. Connie knows. Some of it, at least. Just feels like the kind of thing we should get out of the way, you know? And... I trust you, I think?"

She didn't seem sure, even when she looked up at him.

"It's all in the past, believe me. Been years now, and I've never looked back. Never spoken to Carl again, he's never asked me for anything either. He probably wouldn't even recognise me if I showed up at his hotel. Truth is, everyone says he's straight, going out of his way to make up for all the shit he did, and I've got nothing to prove he hasn't."

Sam sat up, wiping the tears from her cheeks.

"But he shows up in my nightmares most nights, and every time I hear his name I still want to run."

Baird put down the coffee on the nearest box and opened his arms to her. Sam stifled another sob with her hand.

"Are you sure?" she asked. "I'm a soggy mess."

"Aye, me too. Come here."

She folded herself into him, her arms around his waist, her head on his shoulder. He gripped her as tight as he dared, holding on even though the pain flared in his ribs. They clung to each other like that for a small eternity, and only parted when there was a shout from outside.

"Hello? Is anyone in there?"

Sam pulled free, her eyes bloodshot but bright. She wiped the snot from her nose, laughing nervously.

"I must look a right state," she said.

"That makes two of us, hen. At least you dinnae have pond weed in your crotch."

She hesitated for a moment, then she leaned up and planted a kiss on his cheek. It was as gentle as a butterfly, but it felt like she'd floored him with an uppercut.

"That's for being kind," she said.

She walked to the door, looking back.

"Please don't tell anyone what I just said, yeah? I've

been off Carl's radar for years, I don't ever want to be on it again."

"I'll no say a thing," he told her. "I promise."

She smiled, and walked out of sight. He listened to her talking to whoever was outside, her cheery voice betraying none of the emotion he'd just heard. She could hide her anger well.

He, on the other hand, could not.

He grabbed his coffee and made his way out the back door into the sun. The rage was bubbling again, a rancid stew of bile that made his stomach ache. He thought about his da, about the man who'd done so much damage to his life.

He couldn't do anything about Kett, not yet.

But there was somebody else who deserved his fury.

CHAPTER TWENTY-FIVE

He pulled up outside Denton's half an hour later, paying for the taxi with a sodden ten-pound note. The driver studied him in the rear-view mirror, shaking his head.

"Friendly warning, mate, not sure they'll let you in looking like that."

"Like what?" said Baird, studying the hotel through the window.

"Like something Shrek shat out the morning after curry night."

Baird gave him a hard stare as he climbed out of the taxi. He was buzzing, his body electric with anticipation as he made his way across the gravel car park towards the main doors. There was no sign of Headcold Pauly, or anyone else for that matter. It was only when he entered the lobby that he caught his first glimpse of life behind the reception desk. It was the same woman who'd been there yesterday, Tracey, her nametag emblazoned on her red waistcoat. She looked up with a smile that only lasted a couple of seconds.

"Can I help you?" she said, looking at his damp suit and his murderous expression.

"Aye, you can help me," he said. "You remember me?"

"Yes," she said, uncertain. "Police, right? I didn't recognise you without the dog."

She checked the floor, warily.

"Is she here? The dog?"

"Where's Carl?" he asked, ignoring her question.

Tracey looked behind her, to the little office. Then she turned to her computer, and finally back to Baird.

"He's not available," she said.

"I didnae ask if he was available, Tracey, I asked where he was."

A door on the far side of the room opened, and two more members of staff appeared: a man and a woman, both wearing the same awful waistcoats. The guy was carrying a tray of drinks, and he glanced at Baird before heading for the private dining room where Denton had hosted them yesterday. The woman joined Tracey behind the desk. She was in her late twenties, and her nametag said Bethany.

"Everything okay?" she asked, her tone less than friendly.

"He's asking for Carl," said Tracey, speaking softly. "Is he here?"

"I can call down," said Bethany. "Can I ask what it's about?"

"He'll ken what it's aboot," said Baird. "Call doon? He's in the sex dungeon?"

To his surprise, Bethany laughed.

"Uh, no," she said, one hand on the phone. "No, I don't think he's—"

Baird walked past the desk, ignoring the protests from the two women. He ducked into the office, heading for the door opposite. It was closed, but when he turned the handle it squeaked open to reveal a narrow flight of stairs leading down.

"You're not allowed in there," said Bethany, following him into the office. Tracey was right behind her, speaking on the phone. "I'll call the police."

"I am the polis," he said. "Call whoever you want."

The walls of the stairwell were painted red, and dozens of framed pictures had been mounted above the handrail—all showing half-naked people lying on sandy beaches, or standing beneath tropical showers, their eyes full of lust. Even before Baird got to the bottom he could hear music, a soft lullaby that would have been better suited to a lift, or for when you were on hold on the phone. The air smelled sweet, the scent unmistakeable.

Lemons.

There was a door at the foot of the stairs and he pushed through it, finding himself in another corridor. The walls here were exposed brick, the ceiling vaulted. Electric candles flickered in recesses, and the same awful music blasted out of hidden speakers. He could hear something else, too. Something that sounded like a woman crying out in pain, the wrenching sobs almost unbearable.

The corridor had four doors, and he opened the first to reveal a small room with dark walls and a low ceiling. A woman sat on a bed, wearing nothing but her underwear, and she screamed when she saw Baird.

"Dinnae panic," he said. "I'm polis. Carl doon here?"

The woman nodded, pointing to the wall on her right. She was terrified, folding into herself.

"Next room?" he said, and she nodded again. "Stay here."

He jogged back into the corridor, seeing Bethany at the bottom of the stairs.

"You can't be down here!" she shouted. "Carl!"

Baird reached the next door, hearing the same cry of distress from inside. He turned the handle, but this door was locked. He took a step back, bracing himself.

"Don't!" yelled Bethany, seeing what he was about to do.

He drove his shoe into the wood, right beneath the handle. It was a solid kick and a flimsy lock, and it opened explosively, crashing against the wall.

Baird stormed in, seeing a bigger room this time. The air was thick with the same smell of lemons, strong enough to make his eyes water. But he could still see the three women who sat on chairs in the middle of the space, all screaming. Carl Denton stood behind one of them, dressed all in black, his hands on her neck like he was choking the life out of her. He stared at Baird in shock, his gold teeth glinting.

"Get the fuck away fae them," Baird said, striding across the room. "Right now."

The women scattered in fear, knocking over their chairs as they bolted, all shrieking. The girl Denton was holding tore free of his grip, falling to the floor.

"Run," he told them. "Get oot of here!"

"The fuck is this?" roared Denton. He squared up as Baird approached, seeming to swell to twice the size of an ordinary man. "Get out!"

"No until they're safe," said Baird, feeding on his anger, feeling it fuel him. "No until you learn you can't always get away with it."

"With what, you freak?"

Baird kept moving, closing the distance between them. Denton rolled up his sleeves, revealing forearms bursting with veins.

"You want it, then fucking bring it," he said, settling into a boxer's pose.

There wasn't a hope in hell of beating the man in a fair fight, Baird knew. As he walked past the chairs where the women had been sitting, he picked one up. It was metal, and it weighed more than he'd been expecting, every muscle in his torso protesting. He hefted it over his shoulder, then swung it like a baseball bat.

Denton weaved out of the way as though he was made of rubber, the weight of the chair spinning Baird in a circle. He staggered, trying to find his balance.

"Last chance, you prick," said Denton. "Or I'll knock your fucking head off."

"Aye, and I wouldnae be the first to lose my heid, eh?"

He swung the chair back again, and this time the bigger man caught it in an iron grip. He pulled it free, tossing it across the room like it was a child's toy.

"You're mad," he said.

"You'd better believe it," Baird replied.

There was a scream from the door and Denton glanced up. Baird took advantage of the distraction, throwing his fist into the meat of the big man's chin as hard as he could. Denton's head rocked back with a gunshot pop, and he stumbled away, gargling with pain. Baird moved in with another punch, this time an uppercut to his gut. It was like hitting a bag of cement, the pain clawing up his arm and into his aching ribs.

"Ya bastard," he said, shaking out his hand before making a fist again. "Would you just get on the floor."

Denton wasn't going down. The big man was insane with rage, his eyes boiling in his head like blood blisters. He stretched out both arms like a grizzly bear, loosing a roar that could have brought the building down.

Then he charged.

"Oh shite," said Baird, spinning around and legging it.

He'd almost reached the door when he felt Denton's trunk-like arms wrap around his waist. He was hoiked off the ground like he was a chicken, his legs kicking the air as he struggled to free himself. Denton squeezed and he felt his injured ribs pop, the pain like somebody had lit a fire inside him. He couldn't even get a breath in to shout with.

"You think you're a hard man?" came a growl, right in Baird's ear. "You're a fucking mosquito."

Denton twisted his body, and suddenly Baird was airborne. He crashed through a chair and hit the floor, sliding into the wall. By the time he'd rolled himself onto his back, the big man was coming for him again.

"Just say when you've had enough," said Denton.

"Aye, you too pal," Baird croaked.

He tried to kick himself backwards, but there was a wall behind him. Denton grabbed his ankles, reeling him in. With a grunt, he hefted Baird off the ground again, holding him upside down with apparently superhuman strength. Baird planted one hand on the floor, trying to grab the man's legs with his other.

"Give up," said Denton.

"You give up, you radge wee shite!"

He could just about see Bethany in the door, waving somebody down the corridor.

"This way, he's in here! Hurry!"

The rush of blood to his head was making it hard to see, but he thought it was a uniformed copper that ran into the room. Baird wasn't sure if he felt relief or disappointment.

"Oi! Put him down!" the PC said.

"With pleasure," said Denton.

"Wait!" yelped Baird.

The grip on his ankles loosened and he dropped hard, his head crunching into the floor and his body following. He lay there for a moment, trying to work out if there was any part of him that wasn't broken.

"Are you okay?" said the PC. "Sir?"

Baird rolled onto his back, sparks detonating against the ceiling. Denton had retreated, Bethany and Tracey and one of the women he'd found in the room now crowding around the door. The PC crouched beside him, concerned.

"Sir? What's going on?"

"What does it look like?" he said. "I'm saving them. From the sex dungeon."

Incredibly, Denton started laughing, the sound of rolling thunder.

"The sex dungeon?" he said. "Now I know you're mad."

And Baird would have replied, if the flashing lights hadn't turned into pulses of darkness—a wave of quiet night which swept him peacefully into unconsciousness.

IT WAS the pain that woke him, the pain and the sound of an argument.

He peeled open his eyes, which took far more effort than it usually did. He couldn't work out where he was: a small, dark room, a narrow bed, flickering candlelight and a door that led into a blood-red corridor. There was a smell of lemons in the air.

Sex dungeon, he reminded himself.

There were four other people in the room. One was Carl Denton, who sat in a chair in the corner, his hands cuffed. Bethany, the woman from reception, stood next to him, one hand on his shoulder. Facing them was the tall PC who'd arrived just as Baird had been about to kick Denton's arse, and DCI Briggs.

"That's beside the point," Briggs was saying. "You can't just beat up a police officer."

"He was defending himself," said Bethany. "That guy is insane! He charged in and started punching Carl in the face. What was he supposed to do? We've got half a dozen witnesses who'll say he started it. He was like an animal."

"I can assure you," said Briggs, "that is *not* what happened. Baird is a consummate professional, and I know he will give a very different version of events."

Bethany glanced over, seeing that Baird's eyes were open.

"Well why don't you ask him, then?" she said. "He's awake."

Everyone turned to Baird as he gingerly sat up on the bed. He felt like somebody had taken a sledgehammer to his ribs.

"Finally," said Briggs. "Can you talk, Harrison? There's an ambulance on the way."

"Aye, ma'am," he said, his voice hoarse. "I'm fine, honest. How long was I oot?"

"About fifteen minutes," said Denton. "Sorry about that."

"Nothing to be sorry for, pal. Barely even felt it."

He shook his head to clear the fog, the room spinning.

"Harrison, I know you'll be able to set things straight," said Briggs. "What are you doing here?"

"Sex dungeon," he said, trying to summon up the strength for more words.

"Sex dungeon?" said the DCI.

"Sex dungeon," said Denton, laughing. "I have no idea where he's got that idea from. This is a spa retreat."

"It's no a retreat, Carl," said Baird. "It's where you bring your girls, aye? The ones you're putting to work in the hotel. This is where you keep them, break them doon, force them to sell themselves. See, I ken about your past. Call it what you like, but bad things are happening here."

DCI Briggs sighed, scratching her head.

"Believe me, ma'am," Baird went on. "When I came doon there was a woman being held right here, on this bed, stripped almost naked."

"She was waiting for a massage," said Bethany. "Deep tissue, with Andre."

"Likely story," said Baird.

"You're literally sitting on a massage table."

He glanced down at the bed, seeing the face hole, suddenly smelling the fragrant oil. He was starting to feel a little uncomfortable.

"She looked terrified," he said.

"She looked terrified because you came charging through the door," said Bethany. "Anyone would be terrified. Look at you."

He glanced at his clothes, which were still damp and filthy. His roll about on the floor hadn't helped either.

"What about next door then?" he said. "Three women were locked in there. *Locked.* Carl had his hands around one of their throats. He was threatening them."

"I was helping them," said Denton, adjusting his enormous frame in the chair. "We lock the door during sessions to stop people walking in. Or breaking in, in your case. These are vulnerable women. They come here to talk, to share their stories, to find connection."

"And they need a hand on their neck to do that, do they?"

"I was reassuring Deb, that's all. A gentle, human touch

to centre her, loosening the knots in her shoulders. She's out there, you can ask her."

"Bullshit."

"Baird," said Briggs, a warning.

"Ach, he's talking oot his arse, ma'am. Everybody kens he used to sell girls for the Keebles. People dinnae change. Eh, Carl? How many lives did you ruin? How many of those poor women still live with the horror of what you put them through?"

"*Baird,*" Briggs said again. Two strikes.

Denton held up both hands, the cuffs cutting into the bulk of his forearms.

"He's right, Ruth," he said, like Briggs was his best friend. "I'm not gonna deny it. I've never denied it. Everyone here knows what I did, what I used to be. And I feel the shame of that every single day."

Baird blew a raspberry.

"But people *do* change, Harrison," Denton went on. "People change every day. *I* changed. This place is part of my penance, a way of giving back. It's a safe place for women, and men, who've been through the shit, like I have. It's a place to recover from old wounds. And believe me, I know this personally, those old wounds are the hardest ones to heal."

Briggs put a hand to her face like she was holding a cigarette, exhaling a long sigh through her fingers.

"Baird, can you at least tell me you have a tranche of indisputable evidence to back up your raid?"

"It was more of a hunch, ma'am," he said, feeling the blood rush to his cheeks. "I admit, I might have been a wee bit hasty. I probably shouldnae've burst in and duffed up Denton."

"I hear he had you by the ankles," said Briggs.

"Yep," said the tall PC. "Was holding him up like a piñata."

"It was intentional!" protested Baird. "I knew exactly what I was doing. If your man hadn't run through the door I would have got oot of it, piece of pish."

Nobody seemed impressed.

"It was an even fight," said Denton, massaging his jaw. "You've got a hell of a right hook on you."

"Aye, well..." Baird didn't know what to say, falling into an awkward silence.

"This is a complete and utter mess," said Briggs, slapping her hands to her sides. "Carl, I'm going to have to open an investigation. I'm sorry. And Baird..."

She didn't finish, but the look she gave him was all he needed.

"Look," said Denton, heaving his bulk out of the chair, filling the room like a storm cloud. "If it helps, I have no interest in pressing charges. Way I look at it, if I *was* doing some evil shit, you'd want somebody like this guy to come and fuck it up. If these girls were in trouble, he'd have gotten them out."

It was an unexpectedly generous account from the big man.

"I know it's not exactly standard policing, but we need cops like him. People who get shit done. You British love the rules too much, I've always said it. You tie your own hands together. But I've got nothing to hide, not any more. I'm clean, I'm straight, and I really do want to help. You can talk to anyone in the club, staff and guests. They'll all tell you the same thing. Carl Denton is one of the good guys."

He looked at Baird.

"So no hard feelings, okay buddy?"

"That will do for me," said Briggs. "Uncuff him, Paul. Baird, can you walk?"

"I can walk!" he said, watching the PC take Denton's cuffs off. "Ask *him* if *he* can walk."

He hopped off the massage table, teetering like a drunk.

"Lead the way, ma'am."

She did, Baird shuffling after her and the PC bringing up the rear, just in case he decided to take a swing at Denton on the way out the door. The big man watched him go, a look of genuine sympathy on his face—a face which, Baird noticed with some small satisfaction, was a little swollen around the jawline.

They climbed the basement stairs, passing half a dozen more police officers on their way through the lobby. Briggs didn't say a word until they were outside in the car park, surrounded by IRVs. There, she squared up to Baird, looking ten foot tall even though she was a head and a half smaller than he was.

"That was unacceptable, Harrison," she said. "I am livid. Of all the stupid, arrogant, irresponsible things to do. Picking fights with Carl Denton. Do you have any idea who he is? He used to box in the US army, for heaven's sake, before he joined ranks with the Chicago Mob. You're lucky we're not scraping you off the bottom of his shoe, and doubly lucky that Paul was down the road to put an end to it."

"I was winning!" he proclaimed. "Another five minutes and he'd have been on the floor greeting like a bairn."

She gave him a look that made his cheeks burn again.

"I had to cut short my interview with Karen Kirby for this," she said. "It's extremely unprofessional."

"Aye, ma'am," he said. "I dinnae ken what came over me. I..."

He couldn't tell her about Samara, of course, about the fury he'd felt when she'd told him her story. And he couldn't tell her about Kett, either.

It didn't leave him with much of an excuse.

"It's just men like him, they do nothing but damage," he said. "I've seen it before, so many times. They carve a path through life, raping, using, killing, destroying. And they're untouchable. He never got caught, but everybody knows he did it. You think he's changed?"

"It's not up to me to say whether he's changed or not," said Briggs. "The fact is, he hasn't done anything that we can prove. Not then, not now."

"So he gets away with it? It disnae even matter if he's straight now. He still gets to walk away from all the shite he did back then?"

Briggs sighed.

"As much as I hate it, it's the job. And it's *your* job, too. You have to decide what kind of police officer you're going to be, Harrison. What kind of *man*. Somebody ruled by his anger, or somebody in control of it. What you did in there, it makes you as bad as them. Do you understand that?"

Another IRV was coming down the driveway, making its way towards them. Its flashing blue lights left imprints in Baird's vision.

"Do you understand?"

"Aye, ma'am," he said.

"Carl Denton is off limits," said Briggs. "You got lucky this time, but that could change at the drop of a hat. We leave him well alone, we do not harass him in any way, we do not accuse him of anything. Nobody in the Suffolk Constabulary will so much as think his name for the foreseeable future. Is that clear?"

"Crystal," he said.

The IRV pulled up next to them and the passenger door opened, Connell practically rolling out. She was holding the laptop they'd taken from Karen Kirby, and she looked positively frazzled.

"Ma'am, is Carl Denton still here?" she said.

"Yes, Connie," Briggs answered with a sigh. "I was just saying, he's off—"

"He killed Greg Brightwell," she said, holding up the laptop. "He's our murderer. I've got proof."

CHAPTER TWENTY-SIX

The three of them sat shoulder to shoulder in the back of the IRV, with Connell in the middle—like sardines, slowly roasting in the infernal heat. Connell perched Karen Kirby's laptop on her knees while she unlocked it, her sweaty fingers struggling to register on the trackpad. Baird and Briggs leaned in as much as the space would allow.

"I can't believe you picked a fight with Carl Denton, sir," Connell said as she worked. "He's like a truck."

"*I'm* a truck," said Baird. "I would've had him if—"

"If you hadn't been upside down," said Briggs, crushed up against the door. "Yes, we all know. Now focus, Connell, tell us what you found."

The laptop came to life, the background image—Gregory Brightwell, of course, reclining on a bed with his shirt open—almost obscured by hundreds of icons.

"I've connected it to my phone's data," said Connell. "The signal's a little iffy. Bear with me."

She double-clicked the tracker app and a map of the local area appeared on screen, covered in colourful lines.

"Okay, so Karen has had a tracker on Gregory Brightwell's car for three years now. God knows how she managed to keep it hidden for so long."

"It's longer," said Briggs. "When I interviewed her, she admitted she's used several of them. She's been keeping tabs on him since 2007."

"Creepy," said Baird. "You get anything else out of her, ma'am?"

"A lot of snot, tears and nonsense," Briggs replied.

"That can wait," said Connell. She clicked a box with a date on it, and all but one of the lines vanished. "I want to show you this first. This is Wednesday, right? Greg drives from his house to Denton's hotel at four-ish."

"That's what Carl told us," said Baird.

"Right. The car doesn't move again until Friday, hang on."

She clicked another box and the lines on the map changed. Baird leaned in, and so did Briggs, Connell letting out a strangled cry as she was squashed between them.

"That's the hotel," said Baird, jabbing the screen. "And that's Benacre woods. What time was this?"

"That's the weird thing, sir," she said. "There are lots of them. His car made five journeys from the club to the woods and back again, all between 11:48 on Friday night to 3:12 on Saturday morning. I thought it was a glitch at first, but it's not."

"Why would he make the journey five times?" asked Briggs.

"That's if he's the one behind the wheel," said Baird. "Some of those journeys could be our killer."

"Right," said Connell. "The tracker doesn't show who's driving. But this is proof that Greg's car went to the woods, and that's not the best thing."

She pointed to the screen, running her finger up the line of the A12 then tapping.

"This is the track where Karen parked her van," she said. "Did she mention anything about her security system, ma'am?"

"No," said Briggs. "Like I said, she was doing a lot of sobbing and not much talking. The word 'hysterical' is grossly overused, especially with women, but in this case, the glove fits."

"Well, get a load of this."

She closed the tracking app and double clicked another icon on the messy desktop. This time a blurry video feed appeared, the image so pixellated that Baird couldn't make out what it was.

"Signal's iffy," said Connell. "It'll pick up in a bit."

It did, the image clearing slightly to reveal a country lane with high verges, and past that a field brimming with crops. A single figure stood in the middle of the shot, wearing a constable's uniform. He was currently in the middle of mining his nose with a finger.

"Goodness gracious," said Briggs. "Who is that? And why is he trying to self-lobotomise?"

"That's Percy," said Connell.

"I told you," said Baird. "The man eats, sleeps, and picks his nose."

Albright pulled something out of his nostril, studying it for a moment before wiping his finger on his uniform.

"Oh for the love of... is this live?"

"Yes, ma'am. The camera's on the dash of Karen's van. It's filming 24/7."

On screen, Albright rammed his hand down the back of his trousers, scratching an itch.

"It's like watching the chimps at the zoo," said Briggs. "Get rid of him, Connie."

"Permanently," added Baird.

Connell clicked on a thumbnail and the image changed. It was night now, the empty lane picked out in shades of emerald green. Baird couldn't quite see the A12, because of the high verges.

"I went through the feed," said Connell. "Found all the times that Greg's car drove past."

"You can see it?" said Briggs.

"Well, that's the problem," she said. "Look. This is at 23:59."

She pressed play, and everyone crowded in again.

"Can't... breathe..." she gasped.

On screen, a lorry passed by, the cab visible over the wall of crops. About a minute later, the feed brightened as a car drove down the road, the light fading almost instantly.

"You cannae see it," said Baird.

"No. Greg's car's too low, the view's blocked."

"Super useful," he added.

"Just wait," said Connell. "There's a bit of traffic overnight, but not much. It's quiet. I checked, and a car drives past Karen's van at the exact time the tracker puts Greg here. That's him. But look at this..."

She clicked on another thumbnail and Baird read the date stamp.

"Quarter past midnight on Saturday morning," he said. "Sixteen minutes after Greg."

"Watch, sir."

They waited, barely breathing. The screen started to brighten, and suddenly a car roared past—this one tall enough to be seen over the top of the verge. It was gone before Baird could make any sense of it.

"Rewind that," said Briggs.

"I don't need to," Connell told her, clicking on another icon on the desktop. This time it was a screenshot of the exact moment the car came into sight on the dashcam feed.

It wasn't a car at all, it was an SUV.

"A Range Rover," said Briggs. "I can't make out the driver."

It was too dark to see anything through the tinted windows. Connell closed the image and loaded up another one. This time, the Range Rover was facing the other way, and the window was open.

"Holy shit," said Baird.

They leaned in together, compressing Connell so tightly that he heard something pop in the young officer's back.

"Ow," she said.

It was hard to make out the driver in any detail, but there was more than enough to go on: the square head, the turtleneck jumper, the thick arm resting out the open window, and the glint of golden jewellery.

"Denton," said Baird. He checked the date stamp. "Thirty-six minutes after he drove by the first time."

"That's enough time to kill a man," said Briggs. "Especially if he'd already done the groundwork."

"There's something else," said Baird. "Flora Arbon told us that when she was attacked in the woods, she smelled lemons. That basement reeked of them. Did you smell it?"

"I did," said Briggs. "There was a diffuser in the therapy room."

"He'd have carried that smell with him," said Connell. "I bought one for my flat. Used it once and stank of bubblegum for weeks."

"He's got means," said Baird. "He's a big fella, easily strong enough to overpower Gregory Brightwell."

"And you, sir," said Connell.

"Nope, just Greg. Pulling a bow and arrow would be no trouble, and I bet he swings an axe like an executioner. And this, right here, is Mopportunity."

"Did you just say *Mop*portunity?" asked Briggs.

"Aye, the three Ms. The only one we're missing is motive."

Briggs opened her door, relieving the crush.

"Then let's go ask him," she said.

FOR THE SECOND time in half an hour, Carl Denton sat in his own hotel wearing a set of handcuffs.

Now, though, he didn't look so calm.

They were inside the private room where he had first entertained them, half a dozen PCs clustered around the chair where the big man sat. They looked nervous, and it wasn't hard to understand why. Denton was giving off the same aura of violence that he had when Baird had attacked him—wild-eyed and dangerous.

He was giving off a hell of a stench as well, the sharp reek of citrus filling the room.

He had been formally arrested, and the plan was to take him up to Lowestoft police station. But they were waiting for a riot van. Baird was pretty sure the big man could peel off the roof off an IRV like a tin of beans.

"Of course, you don't have to answer any questions without your solicitor," said Briggs, who sat opposite him. "But it might help your case if you start talking. Let me ask you again, where were you on Friday night, around midnight?"

Denton didn't answer, doing his best to stare her out. Briggs wasn't impressed, not breaking eye contact once.

"What kind of car do you drive, Carl? Something grand, right? I love my Rover but it's far too big for me. You, though, must fit quite comfortably in yours."

Still nothing, other than an arrogant flash of gold teeth.

"So be it," she said. "It's easy enough for us to check. We're going to pull the CCTV you have over the front desk as well, and in the staff quarters."

She turned to Baird and Connell.

"Connie, search his quarters."

Baird nodded, one hand to his aching side.

"And Harrison, get in that bloody ambulance."

"I'm fine," he said, heading for the door. "It's a victory pain."

"I don't think you are fine, sir," said Connell once they were out in the lobby. "I think you might have broken a rib."

"I've no broken a rib," he told her. "It's just a stitch."

"From all the standing still you've been doing?"

He waved her away, heading for the reception desk. The same two women, Bethany and Tracey, stood behind it, as well as a third member of staff—a young man who was trying to deal with a line of flustered customers.

"Alright," wheezed Baird as he limped up.

Both women glared at him.

"We're going to need access to Denton's rooms," said Connell. "I'm assuming you know where they are."

The women glanced at each other.

"I don't think we can do that," said Tracey.

"Aye, you can," said Baird. "Your boss has been arrested on a murder charge, so we can do whatever we want."

"Murder?" said Bethany. "That's insane. You can't just throw accusations at him because he beat you up."

"He didnae beat me up," said Baird. "It was a draw. And it's nothing to do with that."

"You police are all the same," Bethany went on. "Little men who take out their impotence on everyone else. It's all about power, isn't it? Carl's ten times the man you are, so you have to take him down."

"That's a bit harsh," said Baird. "I'm no that wee."

"I didn't mean—"

"Or impotent," he added. "Just throwing that oot there."

Bethany looked at him like he was a cockroach that had crawled out of her shoe.

"Can you just get the keys, please," said Connell. "We don't want to have to arrest you too."

Bethany's expression was one of shock. She looked to Tracey for some backup, but the other girl wouldn't meet her eye.

"Fine," she hissed through gritted teeth. "Trace, would you escort them to the room. I'll sort the keys."

The crowd at the desk was getting bigger, everyone demanding to know why there were so many police on site. Bethany vanished into the office at the back, while Tracey headed across the lobby.

"Sorry about Beth," she said as she led the way up the grand staircase, which creaked beneath them like a drunk on an organ. "She's not got anything against you, honest. Carl's done good by her, is all."

"How so?" asked Baird.

"She used to go to his group," Tracey explained, heading along the landing and through a heavy fire door. "Downstairs."

"The sex dungeon," said Baird.

"It's really not. It's nothing like that. It's a good place, it's helped a lot of people. A few of us got jobs here because of the retreat."

She cast her eyes back at Baird.

"I hope he can keep it open. It'll be devastating if it has to close."

She reached another door, using her staff key card to open it.

"Does Carl live in the hotel?" Baird asked.

"Yeah," said Tracey, escorting them down an identical panelled corridor, lined with gloomy oil paintings. "He owns a place in Ipswich, I think, but he's always around. He's got a suite just down here."

"Was he here on Friday?"

"Uh..."

She looked at him apologetically.

"I don't know. Sorry."

"What about you, Tracey? You happen to be working on Friday night?"

"Yeah. I don't usually do Fridays and I don't do nights, but Ruby's off and she asked me to cover. I got to see Greg, which is always exciting."

Her voice hitched when she said Greg's name, and Baird wondered if the rumours of the star's death had reached the hotel.

"You saw him on Friday night?"

She shook her head.

"Not for want of trying," she said, a little bashful. "I saw him on his way to dinner, though. Bottled it before I could ask for a selfie."

"Do you ken how well Greg and Carl know each other? Did they ever have any disagreements? Arguments? Anything like that?"

They'd reached a door, this one bigger than the others they'd passed. Tracey stopped outside it, fidgeting.

"Shouldn't I have, like, a lawyer or something?"

"You're not in any trouble," said Connell. "This is just between us."

Tracey looked back along the corridor to make sure they were alone.

"I probably shouldn't say this, and you can't tell anyone it came from me, okay? But I don't think they always got on."

"Aye?"

"It's just hearsay. You know what these places are like, all the gossip, especially when you get folk like Greg here. Hollywood people. Never seen anything myself, but I heard it from a few of the staff, that they don't get on."

"You ken why?"

A door crunched deeper in the hotel, somebody walking this way. Tracey shook her head.

"Talk, Tracey. Now."

"Something to do with money," she said, flustered. "That's all I know. Greg's gorgeous, the nicest guy. Everyone loves him, but he doesn't live in the real world, you know? He never pays for anything, including his room."

"Never?"

"I don't know, it's just what people say. He keeps showing up, every month, sometimes every week. But he's like all the celebrities, isn't he? They're richer than the bloody king but they think they deserve everything for free. Carl keeps asking him to pay his bill, but he won't. That's all I know."

She was speaking quickly now, the footsteps getting closer.

"Look, is he alright, Greg? Everyone keeps asking about him, everyone is saying stuff. Has something happened?"

"Can you do me a favour?" said Baird, ignoring the question. "Can you ask around the staff, see if you can find out more?"

"No, I—"

She clamped her mouth shut as the door at the end of the corridor opened. Bethany strode through, eyeing them suspiciously as she walked up. She stared at Tracey.

"Disaster," she said. Tracey hung her head, staring at the floor. "What's going on?"

"Nothing," said Baird. "But you're right, this is a disaster. Is that the key?"

It was, but she didn't seem keen on giving it to him. She clamped it to her chest.

"You'd better be sure about this," she said. "Carl doesn't let anyone in here, ever."

"I'm sure."

She held the card to the lock, which beeped softly. The heavy door opened into an enormous living room. Light streamed through the two giant windows, revealing a plush sofa and two armchairs, all pointing towards a TV the size of a garage door. The décor was that of a 1920s brothel, all patterned wallpaper and feathered lamps and sheepskin rugs and vintage modesty screens. About a dozen bushy plants completed the look, too green to be anything other than fake. The space stank of cigar smoke and carpet cleaner.

And lemons, of course.

There were three doors leading out of the room, and they split up to investigate them, Bethany and Tracey watching like they were on a movie set. Baird opened the first door to reveal a cramped, windowless kitchen area that looked like it had never been used. He tried the next one which led into a toilet.

"Bedroom, sir," said Connell from the other side of the room, and he joined her there.

If the living room was sumptuous, the bedroom was something else. The four-poster bed was big enough to fit a football team in, the silk sheets immaculate. Expensive artwork hung from the patterned walls, more plants basking by the window. There was an empty glass and a book on the brass nightstand, and Baird wandered over.

"We should all be feminists," he said, reading the title. "You think he was trying a wee bit too hard?"

There were two more doors in here, and Connell was emerging from the first.

"Bathroom, sir," she said. "It's bigger than my flat."

She tried the handle of the next door along.

"Locked," she said.

Baird tried it too, ignoring the look she gave him.

"Still locked," he said. "Bethany, can you get in here?"

She walked through the door with a face like a bulldog chewing bees.

"That key work for this one n'all?"

She pressed the card to the reader without a word, the lock disengaging. The door opened into an office, a desk by the window and six massive filing cabinets next to it. There were shelves everywhere, groaning beneath the weight of various books and other items.

One of these items in particular caught Baird's eye, and he nodded to it.

"Would you look at that, Connie."

It was a black, compound hunting bow, resting on a shelf between two stacks of books. It was fitted with a sophisticated handle, various hooks and weights making it look like something Batman would own. The string was taut, and there was even a targeting reticle like you'd find on a rifle.

"Nobody's missing anything with this," he said.

"No arrows, though," said Connell, searching the room.

"Because they're all in Greg. It's been cleaned."

The metal body of the bow was polished to within an inch of its life, not a speck of dirt on it—in perfect contrast to everything else on the cluttered, dusty shelf.

Baird could feel himself getting excited, the pieces finally clicking together in a way they hadn't with Karen Kirby or Bruce Fishbourne.

And it got better, too.

"Look at the desk, sir," said Connell.

He did, seeing a mountain of paperwork, more books, a tray of cigars.

And right in the middle of the wide, walnut surface, a little porcelain figurine of a dancing bear.

"It's him," said Connell, beaming. "Carl's our killer. He has to be."

"Aye, Connie, you're right. Let's go tell the boss."

CHAPTER TWENTY-SEVEN

Half an hour later, Carl Denton was escorted into the back of a police van and driven away from his hotel.

Baird wasn't there to gloat about it. DCI Briggs had forced him into an ambulance as soon as he'd limped down from Denton's quarters, telling him even if he didn't think he needed to go to hospital now, he would when she was done with him. He lay on the stretcher in the back while a paramedic prodded him in the ribs.

"Yeow!" he said, feeling like she'd knifed him. "Can you stop?"

"It hurts, then?" she asked.

"It's a bit tender," he said, feeling like he was about to pass out.

"What about here?"

She tried another spot, the pain even worse.

"Gerroff!" he said, a wave of sickness passing through him as he tried to squirm out of the way. "I'm no a bloody piñata, and it disnae hurt."

"Is it worse when you breathe?"

She tried again and he almost screamed. He wondered

if Briggs had slipped the woman a twenty pound note to make him suffer.

"I think you may have cracked a rib," the paramedic said, sitting back. "You're going to need an X-ray, at the very least."

"I've no got time," he said. "Can you just give me a paracetamol and send me on my way?"

She didn't dignify the question with an answer, leaving an awkward silence as they drove to Ipswich hospital. Baird would have filled it with his phone, but even if it wasn't in the lake he would have struggled to hold it. The truth was he was aching something rotten, his entire left side on fire. He'd caught a glimpse of his ribs when the paramedic had pulled up his shirt, and his skin looked like a bowl of his granny's plum pudding. He wasn't sure if it had happened during the incident with the van, or in the tussle with Fishbourne, or when he'd definitely won the fight against Carl Denton—maybe all three—but he wasn't in a good state.

An hour or so later, he was standing in the X-ray room while two doctors and a nurse ummed and ahhed over a monitor. He was in more pain than ever, partly because he was shirtless and trying to suck in his gut, partly because nobody had given him any pills yet.

"What's the verdict, doc?" he asked. "Am I pregnant?"

"Yep," said the doctor. "Twins."

"Braw."

"And I've got more good news for you. There's no broken rib."

He barely had time to celebrate before she continued.

"But there's a serious bruise to your chest wall, and that's no joke."

"Aye, I'm no laughing. Am I free to go?"

"It's up to you," said the doctor. "I'd recommend a few

hours in a bed here to make sure the injury doesn't complicate, but seeing how you're a policeman, and allergic to good care and rest, I imagine you'll be straight out chasing bad guys and running marathons."

"I'm no a runner."

Baird stretched gently. The pain was awful, but knowing nothing was broken helped take the edge off it. The nurse had left the room, and she walked back in as he was putting his shirt on, handing him a paper capsule and a plastic cup of water.

"Paracetamol and ibuprofen," she said.

"I'll pretend it's morphine and single malt," he said, knocking back the tablets and downing the water. "Cheers."

He headed out, trying to get his bearings. It was as he was following the signs to the car park that he realised he was close to the ward where Flora Arbon was being treated, and he took a detour. Other than the PC who sat in the waiting area, bored out his skull, there was nobody else here, and no sign of Flora's three friends.

"Alright?" Baird asked the constable. "Any news?"

"No, sir," said the young officer, getting out of his chair and arching his back. "Been quiet."

"Quiet is good," he said, heading for the door.

"You haven't got a couple of quid for the coffee machine, have you, sir?" the PC asked. "I'm gasping."

Baird pulled out his wallet, finding his last soggy five-pound note.

"What's your name?"

"James."

Baird handed the money over.

"All I've got, James, but knock yourself oot."

A nurse buzzed him through the door into the ward, and he wandered aimlessly around it as he tried to remember which room was Flora's. When he found it, he saw the door was closed, the room dark. She was probably asleep, but he peeked through the window anyway, struggling to make sense of the shifting shadows. All he could see was the curtain, drawn around the bed.

He pushed the handle as quietly as he could, easing the door open. He could hear somebody breathing deeply, and he hesitated, not wanting to wake her. But he thought he could see the glow of a mobile phone.

"Flora?" he whispered. "You awake?"

The breathing fell quiet, the soft light snapping off. Baird entered the room, pulling the curtain aside to see Flora in the bed, stirring. A man stood next to her, and Baird thought at first that it was her father. Then his eyes grew used to the gloom and he saw that it was Lucas Bude, the greasy pizzle rider. He was staring at Baird like he was expecting to see the man in black from the woods.

"You scared me," he said, putting a hand to his heart. "Why are you creeping around like that?"

Flora sat up, her eyes blinking, her face twisted into a look of panic like she'd just woken from a nightmare. She looked at Baird, then snapped her head around to see Lucas.

"Where's Dad?" she asked.

"He popped home," said Lucas. He pulled Flora's blankets up from where they'd rucked by her waist, fussing with her pillow. "He looked exhausted. I said I'd watch you until he got back. He won't be long."

She nodded, trying to get comfortable in the bed. She put a hand to her bandaged head, wincing.

"I don't feel so good," she said. "Can you get somebody?"

"Aye," said Baird.

He leaned out the door, hollering.

"Can we get someone in Flora's room, please."

He returned to the bed.

"You're alright," he said, sitting on the edge of the bed where he had the day before. "Have you got a phone? I'll call your da."

She shook her head, although he wasn't sure if she was saying she didn't, or if she was too confused to answer the question. He turned to Lucas instead.

"Give me yours," he said.

Lucas put his hand to his pocket, then pulled it back.

"No," he said. "Sorry."

Baird clicked his fingers.

"Now, son. You ken the number, Flora?"

She nodded, but Lucas was shaking his head.

"It's dead," he said. "I haven't had time to charge it."

"You sure aboot that? Because I saw a phone when I came in the room."

"I don't think you did," said Lucas.

An older man in scrubs bustled into the room, flicking on the lights. Everybody squinted, Flora covering her face with her arm. Lucas' cheeks were blazing like he had hot coals beneath his skin. Baird stood back to let the nurse in.

"Sorry," said the guy. "How are you doing, Flora?"

"Not good," she said. "I feel sick."

"I'll be outside," said Baird, heading for the door. "Lucas, come on."

"I can stay," said the young man. "In case she needs me."

"She disnae need you."

He ushered the young man through, closing the door behind them. Lucas was halfway down the corridor, scuttling around the corner like a bug making a break for the darkness beneath the fridge. By the time Baird caught up to him, he was at the ward door.

"Lucas," he said.

The kid turned back, struggling with the button to release the lock.

"I've got to go," he said. "Loo break."

"Here," said Baird, pointing to the floor in front of him. "Now."

Lucas shuffled over like he was five years old. He looked greasier than ever, everything about him giving off the sweaty vibe of bad chicken.

"You ken, Lucas, my granny had a word for a certain kind of man," said Baird. "Well, three, actually. Sticky wee jobbies. Can you guess what a sticky wee jobbie is?"

The boy shook his head, not meeting Baird's eye.

"It's pretty simple, really. Granny said they were shitty men who liked to touch things, and they left sticky wee fingerprints everywhere. Like the bits of shite you get stuck to the toilet bowl. Impossible to get off."

"I don't really—"

"Aye, you do," said Baird. "You may be a sticky wee jobbie, Lucas, but you're no stupid. And neither am I. Give me your phone."

"No," he said, taking a step back. "You're not allowed to see my phone."

"You learn that from law school, or from Netflix? Phone." He clicked his fingers.

"Are you arresting me?" said Lucas. "Because unless you arrest me—"

Baird leaned past the boy and hit the button, pulling open the door. The PC was sitting by the vending machine, sipping coffee.

"James, pal, you busy?"

The PC set down his cup and walked over. Baird was happy to see he had a Taser.

"See him, Lucas? See that wee yellow thing on his chest? You ken what that is?"

Lucas nodded.

"You a good shot, James?"

The PC nodded.

"I'm no," said Baird. "I used one once and I accidentally shot a man in the bollocks. It wasnae my fault, to be honest, he had enormous bollocks. Impossible to miss. Have you got enormous bollocks, Lucas?"

"Uh..." said the young man, shaking his head.

"Well, nae bother. The point is, I've had a bad day. The worst day. I'm just aboot at the end of my tether. So what's gonna happen if you dinnae hand over your phone is I'm gonna borrow James' Taser and shoot you with it. Will I hit you in the bollocks?"

He shrugged.

"I'll try not to, but I'm no gonna promise anything. So, Lucas, what's it gonna be? Your phone, or a deep fried bawbag?"

Lucas looked to James, as if the PC might save him. James, to his credit, simply popped the stud on the holster.

"Fine," said the kid, redder than ever. "But you have to remember that I'm a victim too. I had to see that thing in the woods, and for all I knew I was going to get attacked too. You lot care all about women, but you forget that men can suffer as well."

"Oh, I'm suffering right noo, believe me," said Baird.

Lucas handed over his phone, which was so oily that Baird almost dropped it. The image on the screen was a scantily dressed cartoon woman with breasts bigger than her head, and there was plenty of charge.

"Code," he said when Lucas didn't offer it.

"I can't remem—"

James pulled the Taser halfway out of the holster.

"Fine! 6-9-6-9-6-9."

Baird gave him a look that told him exactly what he thought about that. He typed in the digits and the phone opened exactly where it had been when he'd walked into Flora's room.

The camera app.

"It looks bad," Lucas stuttered. "But I was taking photos for the doctors, so they can see if she's recovering, see where the issues are. I'm going to medical school myself, one day."

Baird opened the photos, bracing himself for what he knew he was going to find. Sure enough, there was Flora fast asleep in her hospital bed, her nightgown pulled up to her thighs—then pulled down to her waist.

"Medical photos," said Lucas, who looked like he was about to spontaneously combust. "That's all they are."

Baird scrolled through the folder, finding dozens of images, all shot when Flora was asleep.

"And I didn't even take them," said the boy. "You can't prove it."

"That's no your horrible buttery face, then?" said Baird, holding up a selfie that Lucas had taken. He was lying in bed with Flora, her unconscious head pressed against his shoulder, her arm around his chest.

"It's not actually illegal to photograph people, anyway," said Lucas, obnoxiously confident. "You can't do anything."

What Baird felt like doing was making the young man eat his phone, but he needed it. He kept scrolling back, finding a few photographs of Lucas and Darcie and Anders in the waiting area, then some from the woods yesterday when the police had arrived.

"Give me my phone," said Lucas, and he tried to snatch it from Baird's hand.

"Ach, pack it in, you wiggy fud," said Baird. "Lucas, you're under arrest for intent to cause harm. You dinnae have to say anything, but it may harm your defence if you do not say, when questioned, anything you later rely on in court. Anything you do say may be given in evidence. James, call a car and get somebody to take this donkey bollock oot of here."

"What?" said Lucas, with genuine outrage. "This is bullshit, I haven't done anything wrong. She was asleep when I found her, for fuck's sake, why would she even care what I was doing?"

For a second, Baird almost went for the Taser. James must have seen the fury on his face, because he practically folded the boy in two, snapping cuffs around his wrists. He hauled him away with a hand around his neck, Lucas' whimpers echoing back down the corridor long after he'd vanished from sight.

Baird returned his attention to the phone, his hand trembling as he flicked backwards through Lucas' perverted slideshow. He stopped when he saw Flora again, fast asleep —not in a hospital bed this time, but lying in the dirt of Benacre woods. Her hair was caked in blood, a gash on her temple. The strap of her dress had been pulled away from her shoulder, her bra visible. He moved to the previous photo, another shot but this time up her dress, her skin filthy.

There were fifteen photos of her, all from different angles, all indecent. Lucas had obviously moved her around, too, because in the first few she was on her stomach, in the later ones on her back. Fifteen photos, all from different angles, all different poses. How long had that taken him? Surely ten minutes, maybe more.

He checked the boy's call records. He hadn't dialled 999 at all.

Baird found Darcey's number and called it. It rang a handful of times before she answered.

"Look, Luke, I told you, I really—"

"It's no Lucas, Darcey. This is DI Baird, the policeman. We met yesterday."

"Oh, right," said Darcey. "Has something happened? Is Flora okay?"

"She's fine," he said. "But I should probably tell you that your pal Lucas is under arrest for being a pervy wee shite."

Darcey didn't reply, which was damning in itself.

"Listen, when I spoke to you yesterday, you said you and Lucas found Flora at the same time after she was attacked," he said. "Was that true?"

"Yeah," she said. He heard her walking, then the sound of a door clicking shut. When she spoke again her voice sounded different, like she was inside a bathroom. "Kind of. When I saw Flora she was on the ground, and Lucas was there. He must have arrived right before me, because he was out of breath, all flustered and everything."

"Jesus," muttered Baird.

"He said he'd just got there. Said he didn't know what to do. He looked scared. I think he asked me to go to the road and get help, I can't remember."

"Was Flora face up when you found her, or face down?"

"Uh... up. The wound was on the front of her head, she must have hit it when she fell. She's okay, though?"

"She's alright," said Baird. "One more question. You

said you saw a man in black running away from you, right? Through the trees."

Darcey sniffed.

"Think back, you definitely saw him?"

"Kind of," she said again. "I saw *something*. There was somebody out there, because I heard them. Branches cracking, you know? But I didn't really see anything. It was Lucas who saw him. He told me it was a man, he said he was wearing black. He seemed scared."

"So as far as you ken, there was no man in black?"

"There could have been. Like I said, I just wanted to help Flora. I'm sorry, you kind of... everything goes weird when something like this happens, doesn't it? Tunnel vision. I don't remember."

"Dinnae worry, that's really helpful. Thanks, Darcey."

He went to hang up, then heard her voice again.

"You really arrested him?"

"Aye."

She sniffed again.

"Good. Throw away the key."

"With pleasure."

He hung up, returning to the Photos app and cycling through those fifteen photos of Flora on the ground. They looked more like crime scene photos than anything, because of the way the young woman was lying, because of the blood and the filth, and he wondered how sick in the head you had to be to get off on them—especially as there was a headless dead man hanging from the tree somewhere nearby.

The thought was so disturbing that he almost missed it.

The fourth photo had been taken at a lower angle than the others, the camera almost at ground level and aimed up Flora's dress. For some reason, the focus was off, the young woman blurry. In contrast, the trees and bushes on the other side of the clearing were perfectly sharp.

There was a shape in the leaves, something that didn't belong there. At first, Baird wondered if it was Gregory Brightwell, hanging from his tree, but the location was wrong—Greg had met his end *behind* where Lucas was standing when he'd taken the shot. This looked like somebody running away, a flash of white as somebody bolted through the woods.

"It's no a big fella wearing black, that's for sure," he told himself.

He slid the sticky phone into his pocket, using the dispenser to skoosh a plum-sized ball of hand sanitiser into his palm as he made his way out the door.

CHAPTER TWENTY-EIGHT

He hailed a taxi outside the hospital, asking the driver to take him up to Lowestoft so he could join the others at the police station. He spent the first ten minutes of the journey staring nervously out the back window, waiting to be rear ended by an angry van. But the roads were quiet, the going good.

He spotted the signs for Southwold as they thundered up the A12, and it was only there that he remembered the little dog that he'd imprisoned in his kitchen. He'd lost all sense of time, and when he checked his watch he was surprised to see that it was already late afternoon. He told the driver to take the turn.

Twenty minutes later, he unlocked his front door and trudged up the steps, oofing with every step thanks to the fact that the painkillers weren't doing their job at all.

"Alright, Diana," he called ahead of him, so she wouldn't worry. "It's only me."

He opened the kitchen door, reeling at the stench of dog shite. He covered his nose, seeing a mound of poop on the floor that looked bigger than the dog. Diana sat beneath the chair by the window, growling.

"Could you no have slung that in the bin?" he asked her. "Some house guest you're turning oot to be."

He sidestepped the mess, easing himself into the chair and lifting the dog into his lap. She kept growling for another few seconds, then uncoiled like a spring, her back end twerking as she tried to jump up and lick his mouth.

"Och, I missed you too," he said, the laughter hurting his ribs. He patted her tiny head, scratching her ears, then her belly when she flopped upside down. "I'm sorry it took me so long, hen."

He plopped Diana on the floor and heaved himself up. He refilled her water bowl, even though it didn't look like she'd touched it, then opened the fridge. There was no more chicken there, so he opened a packet of Cheesy Wotsits and tossed a handful on the floor.

"Dinnae tell anyone you've been eating these."

She snoofled herself into a cheesy delirium while he cleaned up the shite, almost boaking.

"Although it cannae be any worse than what you've already been eating, you absolute minger."

By the time he'd finished, so had she. She stared at him as he made his way to the door, her expression almost enough to bring tears to his eyes.

"I ken, quine, but I cannae just show up to work with a goblin in my pocket."

Diana cocked her head, whining.

"What am I supposed to tell Briggs? That I felt sorry for you?"

She cocked her head the other way, lifting one paw.

"Och fine," he said. "Come on."

She scampered over to him, and he clipped her pink

collar around her neck, carrying her down to the waiting taxi.

"The hell is that?" said the driver when he saw what was under Baird's arm. "A gerbil?"

"Aye," he said. "And she's nae fuss."

That wasn't strictly true. Diana was either snarling at the driver or barking out the window for the entire journey to Lowestoft police station, and she left her funky smell behind her when they got out. She calmed down a little inside police HQ, but only because Baird put her down and let her sniff her way around the empty chairs in the waiting area.

"Briggs aboot?" he asked, and the receptionist buzzed him through.

He found the DCI in the small kitchen, chatting to DC Connell. Connell had a face like a skelped arse, but she cheered up when she spotted Diana.

"Oh hello!" she said, dropping onto her knees and scratching the dog's ears. "I missed you, my little cutsie wootsie, my little dumpy-wumpy, my little squidgie-widgie!"

"I missed you too, Connie," said Baird.

"Did you have to bring the dog, Harrison?" said Briggs with a sigh. "We're about to interview Denton, for heaven's sake."

"She can be bad cop," said Baird. "She's quite intimidating, when she wants to be. She left a crap the size of a koala on my kitchen floor. Where are we with Carl?"

"Much the same as when you left us," she said. "He's denying everything. No broken rib, I take it?"

"Nut, barely even a scratch," he said, pulling the phone from his pocket. "Carl's a wimp. But get this, I ran into Lucas Bude in the hospital, the kid who found Flora's body.

The sticky wee jobbie was taking photies of her while she was bleeding to death, up the skirt and down the dress and everything."

"Ew," said Connell.

"Ew disnae even come close. I dinnae think he was satisfied with just taking photies. He's here, somewhere, wearing cuffs. But he took this in Benacre."

He unlocked Lucas' phone, holding it for Briggs to see.

"Look at that, in the trees. Somebody running away, wearing white. I think he made up the whole big fella in black clothes because he wanted to distract us from the fact he was molesting Flora. I dinnae think he saw anybody. But there *was* someone there."

"Could it be Carl?"

"I mean, it could be anyone, to be fair," said Baird, trying to make sense of the picture.

"Well, we've got Denton dead to rights," Briggs said, picking a file from the table. "There's plenty in here to convince a jury, as you'll see in a minute. You said it yourself, Baird, men like him do nothing but damage. He never got punished for what he did in the past, let's make this time different. Who's coming in?"

"I'll look after the dog," said Connell, who had returned to squidging Diana's face.

"I wouldnae miss it," said Baird.

CARL DENTON LOOKED as comfortable in the interview room as he had in his hotel. He sat on the far side of the desk, his feet on the table, his chair on two legs and looking like it was about to give up on life. He had his cuffed hands behind his head like he was relaxing by the pool. The only hint that he wasn't as calm as he looked was the way his swollen jaw bulged, his teeth gritted.

That and the fact he shot daggers at Baird as soon as he walked through the door.

Sitting next to Denton, and looking much more tense, was a woman in her early fifties. She wore an immaculate black trouser suit, her bleached hair scraped back so tightly that it might have been painted on. She had a notebook open in front of her, a pen clutched tightly in one hand.

"About time," said Denton in that purring accent. "We were getting lonely in here."

"Well the good news, Carl, is that where you're going, there are plenty of people to talk to," said Baird, waiting for Briggs to take her seat, the file of documents still in her hand. "In fact, it's hard to get away from all the company. Feet off the table, pal."

Denton didn't budge. It still gave Baird more than a little pleasure to see that the man's dark skin was mottled around the chin.

"I'm no gonna ask again. Feet off the table or you'll be on the floor."

Denton must have counted to ten inside his head before he dropped his expensive shoes to the ground, his chair righting. He put his elbows on the table instead, the biceps bulging beneath his black shirt. He made a show of cracking the swollen mess of his knuckles.

Briggs started the recorder, making the introductions.

"I'm going to keep this short and sweet," she went on. "Sweet for us, that is. Not for you. Where were you on Friday night, Carl, around midnight?"

"I already told you," the big man said, leaning further across the desk and taking a long breath, like he was trying to suck the air from the room. "Away, on business."

Briggs opened the file and pulled out a photograph. It was the dashcam image from Karen Kirby's van.

"That's not your big head, then?"

Denton didn't even glance at it.

"It's impossible to identify that driver," said the solicitor. "It could be anyone."

"Not anyone," said Briggs. "And not everyone drives a red Range Rover. This was taken just after midnight on Friday night, Saturday morning. It's the A12, about thirty seconds from Benacre woods. You are aware, of course, that this is where Gregory Brightwell was murdered."

"Found dead," said the brief, flicking through her notes. "We don't know it was murder yet, do we?"

"I mean, no for sure," said Baird. "There's a wee chance he shot himself with twelve arrows and then chopped his own heid off."

The woman stared at him like she couldn't comprehend what he'd said.

"It was murder," said Briggs. "And you were right there."

"Wasn't me," said Denton. "I wasn't in the hotel at all. I was away. On business. If somebody drove my car, I wasn't aware of it."

Briggs was prepared for this. She slapped another printed photograph on the desk. Baird had to angle his head to make sense of it. It was a shot from the security camera over the hotel reception desk, Denton coming out of the office, dwarfing the other members of staff. The time stamp was 20:54.

"That's you, isn't it?"

"Whoever he is, he's handsome," said Denton. "It don't prove nothing."

"We've gone through all of the footage from the hotel,

Carl," Briggs went on. "Every single member of staff working that night is seen behind this desk. You're the only one who goes missing after this shot. Later that night, you took your Range Rover and you drove to Benacre. Thirty-six minutes after that, you drove back down the same road."

She showed him the second dashcam photo to prove it. Denton was much clearer here, to the point that not even the solicitor questioned it. She glanced at her client, then back at Briggs.

"Circumstantial," she said. "He could have been going anywhere."

"Yes, he could have. So where *were* you going, Carl?"

Denton shrugged.

"None of your beeswax," he said. "Business, like I said. Prove that I killed him, or let me go."

"Okay," said Briggs. "We gained access to your accommodations inside the club. Shall I list everything we found that is relevant to this case? Because there's quite a bit."

Denton was looking less sure of himself by the second. Baird sat back in his chair, lacing his hands behind his head, loving every second of it. He had to resist every urge to put his feet on the table.

"One, and probably the most important: you own a bow, Carl, don't you? A 1.3 metre aluminium compound bow designed for hunting. Not an easy weapon to use, you require a great deal of strength. But there's a handy fibre optic sight to help you hit the target."

"It's not mine," said Denton.

"Well, it's funny, that," Briggs went on, looking like she was having quite a good time too. "Because we searched your desk and found the receipt for it, from two years ago. You're good at keeping records, Carl, I'll give you that."

"Doesn't prove anything," he said.

"Our forensic team analysed the arrows we found in Brightwell's body. They fit your bow."

"Most arrows would," he said.

A smile glanced across Briggs' face, crinkling her cheeks —gone in a flash.

"Granted, but it seems these arrows actually came with your bow. The website that sells these weapons provide the bow and the arrows in the same kit. Twenty-four carbon arrows with real feathers, twelve broadhead arrows tips."

"You were telling the truth, then," said Baird. "You *are* a big game hunter."

Denton gave him the same mad-eyed glare he had at the hotel. The solicitor sat back in her chair, heaving a sigh.

"Circumstantial," she said. "How many of these bows were sold in the last two years? Hundreds, I'm sure. I trust you're giving those other owners as hard a time as you are my client."

"Well, if their phone records showed us the same thing your client's did, we would be."

"What?" said Denton, looking at his solicitor. "What are they talking about? They don't have shit."

"Actually, we do," said Briggs. "Normally it would take us a while to access them, but you were kind enough to leave your laptop on your desk."

"You can't fucking touch my—"

"Actually, we can," said Briggs. "As everything is linked these days, your phone records were right there. You received a call from Brightwell's phone at 23:13 on Friday evening. It lasted just under a minute. Yes?"

"No," said Denton. "I don't remember."

"What did he want?"

"He didn't fucking call me."

"Did he ask to meet?" said Briggs, relentless.

Denton looked at the solicitor again, but she seemed reluctant to throw herself between them.

"I didn't speak with him. Ask me again, Ruth, and we're going to have a fucking problem."

"What about this, then?" said Briggs, finding another photograph. This one was of the little porcelain bear that had sat on Denton's desk.

"What's this?" said the solicitor.

Everyone, including her, turned to Denton for an answer.

"It's a bear," he said. "Fuzzy thing, eats honey. What else do you want to know?"

"Where did it come from?"

"The woods?" he said. "Who fucking cares?"

"It's sitting on your desk, pride of place," said Briggs. "Why?"

Denton put his cuffed hands to his face, his fingers probing the swollen bruise. He was thinking hard about how to answer, but not hard enough, because he didn't speak.

"Let me put this in context for you," said Briggs. "You're aware that Gregory Brightwell's head was removed after he was killed? With brute force. My pathologist tells me it took just two strikes. It was packed inside a cardboard box and buried in the dirt on the other side of the woods. Also inside the box were a number of porcelain figurines, eleven of them in total, all depicting an animal of some kind."

"Circum—"

"Yes, circumstantial," said Briggs, before the solicitor could finish. "While also *substantial*. Alone, these things might not mean much, but together they are damning. We're not even done yet, Carl."

"We're no?" said Baird, practically giddy with delight.

"There is a van registered to Denton's club, is there not?" said Briggs. "A VW Crafter from 2016. White."

Baird looked at her, and she gave him a tight smile.

"Where is it?"

"I don't know," said Denton, staring at the ceiling like he was examining the hangman's noose.

"Because a van that matches this description was used to try to run one of my officers off the road yesterday evening, a few hours after he'd been to your club."

Denton lowered his eyes to Baird.

"You," he said.

"Aye."

"Shame they didn't finish the job."

"For Christ's sake, Carl," said the solicitor. "He didn't mean that."

Everything in Denton's demeanour said he absolutely did.

"What did you do yesterday, after we left the hotel?" said Baird.

"Fumigated," he replied, grinning at his own joke. "I never left, ask anyone."

"We will," said Briggs. "And while we're on the subject, can you tell me where you were yesterday morning, at nine-thirty?"

"What?" said Denton. "Fuck does that have to do with anything?"

"Answer the question."

"At the hotel," he said with a meaty shrug. "Ask anyone."

"Greg owed you money, didn't he?" said Baird, changing tack. "A lot of money. Did that piss you off?"

"The fuck are you talking about?" said Denton.

"He never paid for anything. How much did that come to, over the years? Thousands, right?"

"You're talking shit, you Scottish dick."

"Rhyming won't get you oot of this, Carl," said Baird. "Did he owe you for other stuff, too? Because Greg used to enjoy a bit of a puff, aye? Once a movie had wrapped. A wee celebration. Did he no pay you for that, either?"

"Greg was a fucking wet blanket," said Denton. "Wouldn't put a foot out of line. He never asked for anything illegal, and I certainly didn't supply it."

"There is no proof that my client in any way deals drugs," said the solicitor.

"Except for the fact that everyone knows it," Baird went on.

"*Proof*," she said.

"I think we have more than enough to be getting on with," said Briggs. "You are going to be charged with murder, Carl, that's inevitable. If you'd like to say anything, now's your chance."

Denton leaned over the table again, fixing Baird with a scrotum-shrinking stare.

"Just that you're barking up the wrong tree," he said, turning his glare to Briggs. "Like a couple of weak, cockless bitches."

Baird stood up, his chair scraping.

"Save that one for your female empowerment group, eh?" he said. "We're done."

CHAPTER TWENTY-NINE

Carl Denton had left such a bad taste in Baird's mouth that getting out of the room wasn't enough. He and Briggs collected DC Connell and Diana the dog from the kitchen and headed outside, allowing the fresh air and evening light to carry them east towards the sea. Connell had attached a phone charging cable to the dog's pink collar, using it as a lead as they trundled through Lowestoft's twisty streets.

"What do you reckon, ma'am?" Baird asked, taking a deep breath of salt-scented air. "Guilty?"

Briggs reached into her pocket and pulled out a packet of cigarettes. She lit one, offering the packet to Baird.

"I'm carcinogenic enough, thanks," he said.

"There's a lot pointing to Denton," said the DCI, exhaling smoke. "But he'd have to be supremely arrogant to assume we'd never find everything he left for us in his quarters."

"Supremely arrogant fits," said Connell from behind them. She gave Diana a gentle tug on the lead to coax her on. "I'm not sure I've ever met anyone so full of himself."

"But to leave the bow and the figurine in his office, his laptop open?"

"He destroyed the van," said Baird. "Maybe he was planning on getting rid of the rest of it too?"

It didn't sound massively convincing. Denton was a bastard, sure, but he wasn't a fool.

"And why would Carl kill Greg like that?" he went on. "So the man owed him some money? Hell, I've loaned Crump about fifty quid for chips since I got here, but I'm no planning on decapitating him."

"Decapitating," said Connell, imitating his accent.

"What, Connie?" asked Briggs.

"Oh, nothing, sorry. Just sounds nice. Everything is musical when you say it in Scottish."

"Aye, a musical decapitation, just what the doctor ordered. Seriously, though, Denton disnae have links to the county, he's no gonna be interested in the myth of King Edward or whatever his name was. Why go to all that trouble to kill a man?"

"Maybe he shot him first," said Connell. "With the arrow. Carl gets a call from Greg, asking for something. I don't know what, but it's enough to make him drive out to Benacre to meet him. He takes his bow, just in case. They argue, fight maybe, and Carl shoots him."

She stopped to let Diana have a sniff of a piss-drenched dandelion.

"But then he panics, because it's not exactly a common weapon. So he sets up the whole Saint Edmund thing to cover his tracks. He ties the body to a tree, shoots him a bunch more times, then cuts off his head, for... I don't know."

"Shits and giggles," said Baird.

"Because it makes it look like a religious killing, or a cult thing," said Briggs, taking a long drag on the cigarette. "It's a diversion."

"Right. That way, we don't come knocking at his door."

"The only problem with that, Connie," said Baird, "is that we *did* come knocking at his door, because Greg had a key card, for a *door*, in Denton's hotel. If he was trying to point people away from himself, why leave his bloody name there?"

"Oh," said Connell, frowning. "Right."

"And something else is bothering me," said Baird.

They'd reached the seafront, and it couldn't have been more different to Southwold. Enormous warehouses had gathered like corrugated iron giants, so rusted and neglected that they might have sat there since the war. The only thing they guarded was a wasteland, weed-strewn concrete yards and ranks of sickly bushes that were penned in by miles of wire fencing. Baird couldn't even see the water, because there was a concrete embankment in the way, one that stretched all the way down the coast from one industrial eyesore to the next.

"The figurines," he said, stopping by the embankment, listening to the sea as it tried to find a way onto the land. "I mean, Carl Denton? Why would that sausage-fingered troglodyte collect dainty wee china figures? And why throw them in a box with Greg's heid? And why leave just one on his desk for anybody to find? And why no deny that it was his when we asked him aboot it? I mean, he could have said somebody else left it there, or he'd never seen it before, but he clearly knew what it was, and he as much as admitted he owned it. *Why*?"

He said the last word so loud that Diana stopped what she was doing and glanced up at him with her slightly less googly eye.

"Exactly," he told the dog. "It makes no sense."

She didn't have an answer for him, and neither did anyone else.

"Where do we stand on our other suspects, ma'am?" asked Connell.

Briggs took another puff, holding it for a few seconds before exhaling. She had a halo of smoke that made her look like a rosy-faced cherub.

"We haven't given up on them, but we've hit a couple of snags. Bruce Fishbourne's alibi checks out. He was alone, but he was talking to his super special chums all night on a message board. It's hosted on his PC, which means he wouldn't have had access from a phone, or even a laptop. IT are trying to figure out if there's a way. The other problem is there's a neighbour down the road with a Ring camera on her front door. We've been through it, and there's no sign of Fishbourne's car on Friday night or Saturday morning. He also took delivery from an Amazon van at nine-twenty yesterday morning, ruling him out of the Flora Arbon attack."

"He could have walked to Benacre from his place on Friday," said Baird.

"Indeed he could. We haven't ruled him out. And of every motive, his is the strongest. Greg threatened to reveal his secret, he used Bruce's entire life as a ransom."

"What about Karen Kirby?"

"The interview didn't give us much else," said Briggs. "She's obsessed with Greg, to the point of concern. She was literally a hundred yards from Benacre woods when he was killed, but she claims she was asleep in her van all night."

"And let's no forget she had a creepy Greg sex doll in her bed, with a removable heid."

"Quite," said Briggs. "There are two things in Karen's

favour. One, she has a solid alibi for Saturday morning as well. Two, she's losing hair at an alarming rate. Alopecia. It's all over her camper. Forensics haven't found any at the crime scene."

She took another drag from her cigarette.

"On that note, they have found various samples of non-purple hair," she said. "From several different people."

"It's a popular place to visit," said Connell. "A bit of a sacred site for fans of Charlotte DeVere. I see folk in the woods every week when I drive past."

"And there were ten of them riding their pizzles there on Saturday morning," added Baird.

"Quite," said Briggs. "It doesn't help us."

The longing to see the water was too much, and Baird struggled up the steep embankment to the footpath at the top. A wall of rocks had been dumped below to act as a defence, the sea hissing with fury as it boiled over them. The spectre of evening had gathered at the horizon, advancing west and pushing the light from the sky. It brought a breeze with it, cool and welcome, but it was a small mercy: for a reason he couldn't quite put his finger on, he was dreading the night.

He turned to the others.

"This is a disaster," he said.

Diana cocked her head, then she pulled free of Connell with more force than the DC had expected. The chihuahua started to scrabble up the embankment, but her little legs couldn't cope with the gradient, and after a few seconds she slipped back to where she'd started.

"It's alright," Baird told her. "I'm coming."

He clattered down the slope, going too fast and almost losing his feet. Connell caught him at the bottom before he started doing roly-polies.

"Cheers," he said, nursing his bruised ribs. "Probably shouldnae've done that."

"What now, ma'am?" asked Connell as she took Diana's lead.

"I'm going in for round two with Carl Denton," she said. "See if I can get anything else out of him."

"He's an angry man," said Baird. "As much as he tries to hide it. Rile him up and something will crack. But be careful, otherwise it will be your heid."

"I can handle Carl," she said. "I need you two back at his hotel. We should take advantage of the fact he's not there and grill the staff. Somebody must have seen him leave on Friday night, and I'll bet they can shed a little more light on his relationship with Greg as well."

"I'm no sure they'll talk to us, ma'am," said Baird. "Whatever Denton's doing there, they seem pretty loyal to him."

"Well, we can but try," she said, crushing the cigarette beneath her heel. "Just don't lose any more fights, Harrison."

"I WAS WINNING!"

Baird was still protesting the outcome of his fight with Carl Denton thirty minutes later as they drove the DCI's Range Rover into Southwold. The evening had caught up to them, the town bathed in twilight, every light twinkling. The streets were quiet, but the pub courtyards bustled, the sound of laughter filling the cooling air.

"You were upside down, sir," said Connell, sitting up straight so she could see over the wheel.

"Being upside doon and being a winner aren't mutually

exclusive, Connie." He petted the chihuahua on his lap but she didn't notice, too busy staring out of the window. "Where are you going?"

"We haven't eaten all day, sir. Are you not hungry?"

He was famished, now that she'd mentioned it. The last thing he'd had was a slice of toast heading out of his flat that morning, and a bit of the chicken he'd stolen from the dog. He'd gone past hunger a few hours ago, his stomach a knotted fist of disapproval whose angry cramps had been lost in the pain from his ribs.

"Aye," he said. "I could eat. What have you got in..."

She answered his question before he could finish it, parking the enormous car outside an ice cream parlour called Mary's. There was a grating sound as she scuffed the rims on the kerb.

"Urk," she said, pulling a face. "Do you think she'll notice?"

"Only if she's no gone blind. Look, Connell, there's a chip shop right up the street. How aboot a fish supper before your pudding?"

"Ice cream helps me think," she said, opening the door and falling out again.

Baird clambered down, shutting Diana in the car and following Connell to the shop.

"It's protein, sir," she said. "Calcium, all the good fats. And this place does a saffron pistachio that is to die for."

"Aye, well at the rate you're going..." he said, but she'd already walked inside.

He wandered down the street to the chippy, grunting in frustration when he realised it was closed.

"Pudding it is, then," he said.

But by the time he'd doubled back, Connell was

standing outside the parlour with an ice cream the size of her head, and the Closed sign hung from the door.

"That was quick, sir," she said, looking at his empty hands. "You must have been hungry."

"Aye," he said, looking enviously at her meal. "Give us a lick, Connie."

"No!" she said, pulling it out of his reach. "You had your chance."

He grumbled his way into the driver's seat of the Range Rover, fending off an attack by the little chihuahua as he waited for Connell to climb in. She was struggling with the sheer size of her dessert, ice cream dripping from the cone faster than she could collect it with her tongue.

"Oh poop," she said, wiping the leather seat with her sleeve and doing nothing but smear it around.

"The dug'll fix it," he said as Diana burrowed herself into the chair, her tongue moving faster than a hummingbird's wings.

Baird took off, making the journey to Denton's in less than five minutes. He drove down the long driveway, fairy lights in the hedges giving the sweeping gardens an unearthly feel. Beyond them, the woods were pitch black, a strip of shadow darker than the sky—as if a giant wave was foaming across the land, ready to wash it all clean.

He pulled into the car park, focussing so hard on steering the boat-sized monstrosity past the brick pillars that he almost hit the man who was loitering in the middle of the road. He slammed on the brakes so hard that Connell face-planted in her saffron pistachio.

"Oh drat!" she said, using the back of her hand to wipe it away.

Headcold Pauly stood in front of them, caught in the

headlights like a rabbit with myxomatosis, his face twisted into a grimace of terror.

"What the hell are you doing?" he yelled. "You almost squashed me!"

Baird rolled down the window.

"Aye, I'll try harder next time."

"What?" said the man as he walked around. "Oh, it's you."

He stood on his tiptoes to see inside, wiping his hand over his permanently leaking nose. Baird couldn't work out whose face had more gunk on it, his or Connell's. Behind Pauly, the car park was almost empty, a handful of smaller cars alongside a single IRV and a couple of forensic vans.

"Alright, Connie?" asked Pauly. "Back again. Nice wheels, they can't be his, can they?"

"Why can it no be mine?" said Baird, revving the engine.

"Why. Can. It. No be?" echoed Pauly, screwing up his face. "Why does he speak like Yoda?"

"I'd rather speak like him than look like him," he said, nodding to the coating of yellowy-green snot on Pauly's top lip.

"You done with Carl yet?" Pauly asked Connell. "All hell's broken loose in there, nobody knows what to do. Most of the guests have fucked off."

"He's not going to be back for a while," she told him, frantically trying to stop her ice cream from melting. The dog was in the footwell with its mouth open, like a drunk beneath a dripping beer tap. "We need to go inside. Can you park it for us?"

"Only if that twat gets out," said Pauly. "I'm not sitting on his lap."

Baird obliged, swinging open his door hard enough to send Pauly scuttling back.

"You almost hit me!" he squeaked again.

"Aye, you're faster than you look," he said, collecting the dog on his way out. "Dinnae scratch it."

"Dinnae scratch it," parroted Pauly in a falsetto as he climbed behind the wheel. "You're lucky you caught me, I'm just heading off. Hardly anyone about."

"Who's in charge with Carl gone?" Connell asked.

"Beth," he said. "And Ryan. But they're both losing their heads."

"Well, that's definitely the theme of the weekend," said Baird, holding the shivering dog to his chest. "Let's see if we can make things worse."

CHAPTER THIRTY

Headcold Pauly hadn't been lying, Denton's was dead.

The young PC standing outside the front door didn't help, his arm resting on his Taser as he watched the exodus of people from the hotel. It was the tall constable who'd stopped Baird from decking Carl earlier, although he couldn't remember his name.

"Any trouble?" Baird asked him, clutching Diana to his chest.

"Not yet, sir," he said, opening the door for them. "Although you're back now, so..."

Baird didn't stop to ask the PC what he meant, walking inside. Connell did her best to polish off her ice cream, but it was too much even for her. She plopped it sheepishly in the planter outside before following Baird in, scrubbing her hands together to get rid of the evidence.

A member of staff greeted them inside the stifling heat of the hotel lobby, a woman in her early thirties who had to push a curtain of curly hair out of her eyes in order to see them. She smiled apologetically at Baird and Connell, lifting a clipboard like she might be about to whack them with it. The badge on her red waistcoat read Marie.

"I'm *so* sorry," she said, glancing at the dog for a second as if making sure it was actually a dog. "We've had a bit of a snafu tonight. We did try to get in touch with everyone. We may not be able to honour your booking. Can I take your names?"

"DI Baird and DC Connell," he said.

Marie studied her clipboard for a few seconds before Baird put her out of her misery.

"We're with the polis. You've kicked everybody oot?"

"Yeah," she said, the clipboard slapping against her leg. "Most people wanted to leave, with all the police and everything. We've put them up across the town, in the Swan. A couple over in Henham. I have no idea what's going on, to be honest."

She looked over her shoulder, then leaned in. Diana licked the air between them as she struggled to peel herself out of Baird's arms.

"Is it true? Did Carl really do *that*? To *Greg*?" asked Marie.

"We dinnae ken what happened, yet," said Baird. "Were you here on Friday night?"

"Yeah," she said. "But I didn't see much. Carl keeps us pretty busy, and he seemed extra angry that night."

"Aye?"

"You what?" said Marie.

"*Aye*," he said. "I was asking what you meant by angry."

She seemed confused, but she answered anyway.

"Not angry, maybe. Stressed. He was supposed to be going away for the weekend, so we were all a bit shocked when he turned up."

"He say what he was doing?"

"No," said Marie. "He just came in late, grabbed some stuff, then left."

"When?"

The young woman shrugged.

"Sorry, it's too hard to keep track of time on the night shift."

Connell pushed past them both, heading for the reception desk. It was mobbed with half a dozen people, their angry voices carrying. A single member of staff stood there, but she was on the phone.

"You ever see Carl and Greg together?" asked Baird. "Ever see them arguing, anything like that?"

"I don't want to say," she told him. "It doesn't seem fair to Carl, speaking behind his back."

"But?" said Baird when she didn't continue.

"Like, Carl had a bit of a beef with everyone. It's just who he was. He's an okay guy and all. Like, fair. But you don't ever want to see him angry. He's a boxer, or used to be. He beat up some policeman today, apparently, down in the basement."

"I heard the policeman kicked his arse," said Baird. "But carry on."

"That's it, really," said Marie. "He's a big guy, and he's fine most of the time, but..."

"But not all the time," said Baird, remembering Denton's wild eyes, the murderous look on his face as he'd chased Baird around the therapy room. "You've seen him lose his temper?"

Marie nodded.

"We all have. He wants this place to be perfect. And if it isn't, he lets us know. It's fair enough, I guess. It's his."

"You ever seen him fighting? Physically?"

She took a long breath, everything about her expression

telling him how uncomfortable she was. When she answered, she spoke to the dog, offering Diana a finger to sniff.

"Never seen it. But everyone talks about it. If people don't pay their bill, he'll happily throw them out the door. We get some proper arseholes staying here sometimes. Rich people often are, you know? He's not afraid of any of them."

"He ever had to step in to defend any of you?" Baird asked.

She laughed.

"From guests? No. God no. The guests are royalty, he'd pick them over us any day of the week. It's the first thing you learn when you start here. We're replaceable. They're not, as long as they pay their bill."

She looked past Baird into the empty car park.

"I'd probably better..."

"You never said if you've seen Carl and Greg arguing."

"No, I've never seen it. But Greg was one of the ones who never paid for anything. And I mean anything. Carl was always moaning about him, threatening to..."

"To what?" said Baird.

Marie shook her head.

"He wouldn't actually do it, though. He'd never, like, *properly* hurt somebody."

The door to the private dining area opened and a couple of staff members walked out in their garish uniforms, looking just as flustered as Marie. She turned to watch them so sharply she might have broken her neck, only breathing again when they'd trotted out of sight.

"Sorry," she said. "Everything's a little tense."

"Last question, Marie," said Baird, shifting the dog to his other arm. "Then we'll leave you in peace. You ever speak to Greg while he was staying here?"

She nodded, her face opening up.

"Yeah, all the time. He was a lovely guy. Didn't deserve any of this. He had a wife, didn't he?"

Baird nodded.

"Poor thing," she said.

"Aye," he told her.

He started to walk off, and Marie touched his arm.

"No dogs," she said. "I'm really sorry. You can leave her out there?"

"She's no a dog, Marie," he told her. "She's my pal."

He caught up with Connell by the reception desk. She'd pushed to the front of the queue, much to the irritation of everybody else. The collection of people there had grown, all of them standing with their suitcases and yelling at the poor lassie behind the desk—who was still on the phone.

"Hey!" said Baird. "She's no a bloody robot, give her a break."

If they'd heard him, they couldn't have cared less, fighting each other like a mob of corgis over a packet of ham. Connell sighed, walking around the back and standing beside the woman. She slammed both fists on the desk with enough strength that every single person flinched—including Baird.

"Right," said the young DC, reading the woman's tag. "As you can plainly see, with your eyes, Alison here is on the phone. You'll know when she's ready to speak to you, because she'll be speaking to you. Form a line, and wait quietly. Okay?"

Connell said it with such unexpected authority that Baird found himself standing in the same queue as everybody else. The woman on the phone, Alison, hung up, throwing Connell an appreciative smile.

"Can we grab a master key?" Connell asked.

"Sure," she answered. "Beth said to give you whatever you need."

She primed a key card and handed it over. Connell walked out from behind the desk, giving the waiting guests a hard stare before heading across the room.

"Nicely done," said Baird, following her.

"I didn't think I had it in me, sir," she said, stifling a giggle. "If there's one thing I hate, though, it's entitled people being rude to employees."

She held up the card.

"Where shall we start?"

"Upstairs," he told her. "Let's see how forensics are getting on."

They made their way to the first floor. The dog was protesting so much in Baird's arms that he plonked her down on the landing, holding onto the temporary lead to stop her bolting. He couldn't quite remember the way to Denton's quarters, but fortunately Connell got them halfway, and from there they followed the screech of somebody who sounded exactly like Tina Turner belting out a tune. It turned out to be Declan, who was on his hands and knees in the middle of the suite's living room, picking something out of the carpet with a pair of tweezers.

"So now, I see through your eyes, all I can give you is love," he quavered.

"Ooh, that's a Spice Girls song," said Connell. "*Mama*. One of my favourites."

Declan didn't react, presumably because of the enormous headphones he was wearing over the hood of his overalls. Baird handed the lead to Connell and walked over to him, giving him a gentle prod in the arse with his boot. The young man's song became a gargled scream as he rolled onto his back. He lay there, like a turtle, staring at

Baird through the narrow slit left between his hood and his mask.

"What?" he grunted, pulling off his headphones. "You almost made me void my bowels."

"Sorry," said Baird. "I thought you were Sporty Spice."

He offered a hand but Declan ignored it, bouncing back to his feet like a white-suited ninja. He spun in a circle, finding his tweezers and collecting them from the carpet.

"Anything new?" said Baird.

"As it happens, yes," said Declan, pulling down his mask. "Several, all of which have been reported to Detective Chief Inspector Briggs. I had one of my team take a cursory look at the accounts on Denton's laptop. Brightwell's bill is huge, in the tens of thousands. He hasn't paid for a thing since 2019."

"Why would Carl keep letting him stay?" asked Connell from the door.

"Good for the hotel's reputation," said Baird. "Having a celebrity like Greg."

"He was losing his patience, though," said Declan. "There was an email on the laptop where Denton made it perfectly clear to Brightwell what would happen if he continued his refusal to pay. Have a guess when it was written."

"Monday?" said Baird.

"No."

"Tuesday?"

Declan shook his head.

"Just tell me. Wednesday? Thursday?"

"No, and no," said the young man.

"Have you ever been kicked really hard in the bawbag, Dec?" Baird asked.

"Friday," said the young technician. "At six."

"That's just hours before Denton drove to the woods," said Connell. "Have you got it?"

"The laptop has just been taken in," said Declan. "You'll need to ask Briggs. The porcelain bear has several good prints on it. I'll run them as soon as I'm back in the lab. It seems to have been bought from an antique shop in Belgrade that specialises in collectible figurines, I can't seem to find this exact bear anywhere other than their website. I also spotted a couple of the other pieces in their catalogue, animals that were discovered inside the box with Gregory's head parts."

"Belgrade?" said Baird.

"Yes. Belgrade. The capital city of Serbia, which is a country in Eastern Europe between—"

Baird shut him up with a look.

"You've given them a call?"

"I have," said the young man. "They're closed on Sundays. I'll try again in the morning, as soon as I have time. As you may have noticed, I'm on my own. I've had to split my team between the woods, Bruce Fishbourne's house, Karen Kirby's van, and here."

"Well, if there's anything we can do to help..." said Baird.

"Actually, there is—"

"Then dinnae bother asking, because we're up against it too."

Declan's glare was so full of fury that Baird almost felt bad.

"Then maybe I won't tell you about the chapel," Declan said, looking infuriatingly smug.

"What chapel?" asked Baird.

Declan pretended to zip his mouth shut, throwing away the key.

"What chapel?" said Baird, taking a step towards him and holding up the card they'd got from reception. "And bear in mind you dinnae want me shoving this master key into your gob to unlock it, aye?"

"It's outside," spluttered Declan. "Round the back, past the courtyard. You'll never guess which saint it's devoted to?"

"Edward?" said Baird.

"He means Edmund," said Connell from the door.

Declan nodded, placing the tweezers inside his bag.

"Go check out the stained glass. I would take you, but I'm done here. If I don't get to the lab in the next thirty minutes, I'll be working until dawn."

"Cheers," said Baird, heading across the room. Connell watched him approach, Diana straining at her lead to get to him. "I'm no sure if any of this makes it better or worse for Carl."

"Worse, sir," said Connell. "Definitely worse."

CHAPTER THIRTY-ONE

THE HOTEL SEEMED TO HAVE GROWN EVEN IN THE short time they'd been in Denton's quarters, and it was partly for this reason that Baird ended up completely lost. He led Connell in what he thought was the direction of the main staircase, only to find himself around the back of the building.

"Did you mean to come this way, sir?" asked Connell as they trudged down the deserted corridors.

"Aye," he said, and left it at that.

He found a way down eventually, tucked behind a door with a fire escape sign that needed the master key to open. The stairwell must have been a newer addition to the old house, the steps concrete and the windowless walls roughly plastered. He picked up the dog and they dropped back to ground level, landing in an industrial corridor that was part of the staff area.

It was a stark contrast to the cosy warmth and rose-tinted décor of the hotel itself, everything whitewashed and decorated with propaganda posters that looked like they belonged in the Imperial War Museum. In most of them,

Carl Denton's angry face glowered out, various lines of text printed underneath.

"'Cleanliness is next to Carl-iness,'" read Baird. "'Carl's First Commandment: guests are always right.' Christ, he thinks he's the Messiah."

"But he's a very naughty boy," said Connell, staring at another poster. "'Loose mugs sink clubs.'"

"Catchy."

"What do you think he's asking them to stay quiet about?" she asked.

"Whatever happens in Denton's, stays in Denton's," he answered.

They passed through another fire door into a shorter stretch of corridor, equally featureless. Baird could hear voices raised in what might have been an argument, and he could smell food—something mouth-wateringly good. The dog was pulling on her lead, her claws skittering and scratching on the smooth floor.

"Easy, Di," he said quietly. "Whatever it is, I'm sure you'll get some."

There was an open door ahead, a blade of light slicing out of it. It was the kitchen, he saw when he peeked inside, a forest of stainless-steel equipment from wall to wall. Six people in staff uniforms leaned against the counters in the middle of the large room. One of them was Tracey, who seemed to be crying. Bethany was consoling her, as well as a man in his early twenties. Another guy stood at the industrial grill, dressed in an apron and turning sizzling burgers with a spatula.

They were all completely oblivious to Baird and Connell until Diana pulled hard enough to snap the charging cable. The dog face-planted, picked herself up, then torpedoed across the room towards the group, yapping her head off. All eyes turned to her, and then to the door where Baird stood.

"Sorry," he said, entering the kitchen.

The chihuahua was in a frenzy of excitement, jumping around the staff like a pinball as she looked for treats. She kept bouncing off people's legs and landing on her back, squirming on the floor as she tried to right herself. She was drooling so much she was leaving puddles.

At least, Baird *hoped* the puddles were drool.

"She's a bit broken, but she's friendly enough," he said. "And hungry."

That made two of them, the smell of the burgers making *him* drool as well.

"Is this your supper?" he asked, wiping a sleeve over his lips.

Bethany scooped the dog off the floor, handing her to Tracey. Diana proceeded to lick the woman's lips like she was part sausage, almost bringing a smile to her tear-swollen face.

"There are no dogs allowed in here," said Bethany, walking to the head of the group. "As you know."

"We're still no a hundred per cent sure she is a dug," he told her. "I'm fairly certain somebody stuck some googly eyes to a baked potato."

"I'll take her outside," said Tracey, heading for the door.

"No need," said Baird. "She's fine."

Tracey looked at Bethany, as if asking for permission.

"She can wait in the cloakroom," said Bethany. "It's perfectly safe there, and out of the way."

Tracey started walking again.

"If I didnae ken any better, I'd think you were trying to steal my dug." Baird clicked his fingers. "She's with me, and she's fine."

Tracey hesitated for a moment longer, then carried Diana back over. Baird took her, clamping her protectively to his chest. The dog fought him, trying to get to the burgers.

"You dinnae need to worry," he told Tracey. "Carl's no here, so you'll no get told off."

"Where is he?" said another of the women. "When's he coming back?"

"Your guess is as good as mine," he said. "Maybe no for a long time."

Tracey let out another quiet sob, using her free hand to scrub away more tears.

"It's not fair," she said.

Bethany fired a warning look in her direction.

"Do you need something?" Bethany asked when she turned back to Baird.

"Any burgers going?" he said, glancing at the grill. His stomach was so empty it felt close to cramping. "I've no eaten all day."

"No," said Bethany without a second of hesitation.

"Right," he said. "It's just, there are, like, a dozen of them on the grill, and there's only six of—"

"No," Bethany said again.

"Braw. Well, since there's so many of you here, you mind if we ask you a couple of questions?"

"Look," said Bethany. "None of us knows anything, and we've already told every other police officer who's been here today, several times, the little we do know. None of us saw Carl after about nine on Friday night. None of us saw Greg leave, although those of us on nights heard his car, just before midnight. Nobody knows why Carl would..." She swallowed, and it looked painful. "Why he would hurt somebody like that, especially Greg. Greg was the nicest guy in the world."

There was a murmur of agreement from the others.

"Let me ask you this, then," said Baird. "Do any of you think Carl did it?"

"You can't ask us that," said Bethany. "Don't answer him."

"We're not trying to trick you," said Connell, stepping in. "We're just trying to understand what happened to him. You say Greg was a nice guy? He died a terrible death. The kind of death nobody deserves. Help us find the truth, for his sake."

Baird had never seen such a blatant 'go to hell' in anyone's expression as he did in Bethany's. But behind her, one of the women slowly lifted her hand.

"I think he could have done it," she said.

Bethany spun around, hissing another warning. But Tracey lifted her hand too, sniffing.

"Stop it," said Bethany. "He's not here to defend himself. He didn't do it. He *wouldn't*."

Two more members of staff lifted their hands, and Bethany grunted in frustration.

"You're not allowed to do this," she said.

"You're right," said Connell. "I'm sorry. We'll go."

"But can one of you show us the chapel?" said Baird.

Bethany grunted again, scooping up a metal ring of keys from the counter before marching towards the door.

"Save me a burger," she called back.

"Aye, me too," Baird said, chancing it. "Onions and a splash of sauce'll be grand. Maybe some cheese if you're melting it on. Is there any mustard?"

"You sure you don't want me to look after her?" said Tracey, staring at the dog in his arms. "While you're outside? She's lovely."

"Lovely's no the word I'd use," he replied as the

chihuahua gurned up at him, one eyeball bulging towards the ceiling. There was a fresh trail of drool on his jacket already, but when the little dog lunged for his chin he found himself smiling again. For some reason, he didn't want to part with her, and he tickled her neck beneath her collar.

"It's fine," he said. "She's nae trouble."

Tracey must have liked the dog too, because she puffed out a sigh of disappointment. Baird set off, catching up with Bethany and Connell in the corridor outside. Bethany shunted a fire door open with her hip, leading them into a floodlit courtyard. Brick outbuildings crowded around it like they were nosing in on the drama, dark windows watching intently. The night had fully settled now, chasing the last of the warmth from the air, carrying cool currents from the sea.

"Why do you need to see the chapel?" asked Bethany.

"Because I've got absolutely bugger all else to do," Baird told her, struggling to hold the dog as she tried to catapult herself out of his arms. As much as he was starting to love her, he was looking forward to not having to wrestle her everywhere he went.

"We heard it was dedicated to Saint Edmund," said Connell.

"I have no idea," Bethany replied, trotting so quickly across the courtyard that Baird had to jog to keep up. Their footsteps echoed between the buildings, making it sound like there were dozens of people in pursuit. It gave him the shivers, and he had to glance back to make sure he was only imagining it.

"Does anybody use it?" Connell went on. "The chapel?"

"No," she said, then she groaned out a sigh. "Well, Carl does, occasionally."

"He's religious?" asked Baird.

"No. I don't know. I don't think so, because he's been renovating the place, he wants to turn it into a guest suite."

They rounded a corner, heading down a path that was lit by dozens of fairy lights in the bushes. Baird could just about see the outline of the chapel up ahead, hulking in the shadows like a bulldog. As they closed in, a security light clicked on and he saw it was smaller than he'd anticipated, maybe five metres from one side to the other. It was an octagonal building made of crumbling brick, a squat tower jutting up from its front wall and large leaded windows framing the oversized door. The glass was dark, no sign of colour.

Bethany sorted through her keys, taking her time.

"I know what it looks like," she said, speaking so quietly that Baird had to close the distance between them in order to make out her words. "I know what *he* looks like. Carl. You see a man like that, you see his past, and you think he's guilty. You don't give him a fair shot. But he's not a bad person. He's helped a lot of us."

She found the key she needed and inserted it into the lock. It turned with a sound like a cannon firing. She had to use her whole body to push the heavy door open, slapping the wall until she found the switches.

"He helped *me*," she said, stepping inside. "Whatever he's done, whatever he might have... whatever happened to Greg, that has to count for something, right?"

Baird entered the chapel, the temperature in here about ten degrees lower than it was outside. He moved into the middle of the room, edging around the cramped pews. Pigeons flapped in the rafters, celebrating the arrival of unexpected guests with a rain of feathers and a splat of bird shit. It seemed like the perfect welcome party for this sad little ruin.

Only the windows still held a hint of their former glory. From outside, they'd revealed none of their art, but thanks to the security light they blazed with colour. There were only two of them, four feet wide and maybe twice as tall. In the first, a bearded man sat on a chair while a woman washed his feet, using her hair, by the look of things. He seemed like he was thoroughly enjoying himself.

The same couldn't be said for the man in the second window.

This guy was tied to a tree, his body full of arrows, his mouth screaming and his eyes alive with pain.

"That looks familiar," Baird said to Connell.

"He's still got his head, sir," she replied.

"You say Carl was renovating?" asked Baird, looking at the miserable interior, the cracked walls and the rubble-strewn floor. "He didnae get very far."

"He did those," said Bethany, nodding to the windows.

"These are new?"

She nodded.

"How new?"

"Last year," she said. "He wanted to repair the originals but they were too far gone, so he had these commissioned by a local glass smith."

"Wait," said Baird. The dog was getting too annoying, so he dropped her to the ground. She ran to the nearest crust of bird shit, licking it like she was Connell with an ice cream. "These designs, they were based on what was here before? St Edward there—"

"Edmund," said Connell.

"Aye, him, and that long-haired fella."

"That would be Jesus, sir."

"Right. They were in the original windaes?"

"I don't think so," said Bethany. "The old windows had

a bunch of men in them, I don't know who they were. Priests, or popes. Carl said he wanted something different."

"Did he say why he picked these designs?"

She shook her head.

"You know the story behind that one?" asked Connell, nodding to the first window.

"Aye," said Baird, who didn't have a clue. "But remind me."

"That's Jesus in the Pharisee's house, I think. Mary Magdalen washed his feet with her tears, and then dried them with her hair."

"Well I hope he asked for his money back," said Baird.

"She was a sinful woman, sir," Connell went on. "A sex worker. Jesus forgave her for her sins."

"Why would Carl pick an image like that?" he asked, studying the window. The answer seemed obvious, but it was Connell who spoke it.

"Maybe he thinks of himself as Jesus," she said. "Forgiving the sins of the women who used to work for him."

"That's pretty rank," said Baird. He thought of Samara, her terror as she remembered her time with Denton, and a shudder ripped through him that had nothing to do with the cold air or the festering surroundings. "Given he was the one who was pimping them oot."

"It probably doesn't mean that," said Bethany, who looked just as disturbed as he did. She folded her arms tightly over her chest, the keys jingling.

"You say Carl was the only one who used this place?" Baird asked.

"He just said he found it relaxing here," said Bethany. "Inspirational."

"Well, he was inspired, for sure."

He reached for his phone to take a photo, before remembering he didn't have it.

"Grab a photie, Connell," he said.

He kicked his way through the detritus, opening the only other door in the building to find a cupboard that was home to nothing except a million spiders.

"Nope," he said, closing it.

There was nothing else to see.

"You done?" said Bethany. "I should get back."

"Aye," said Baird, studying the windows for a moment more—that awful image of Saint Edmund being executed in the forest—before heading for the door. "We're done."

CHAPTER THIRTY-TWO

Even though Denton's hotel was haemorrhaging guests, the rooms mostly empty, every single light in the house was switched on. From outside, in the dark, the amber glow of the building made it look like there was a fire raging within—as if, now that its master had been taken away, the building had decided to burn itself to the ground in protest.

Or relief.

Bethany led the way, crossing the courtyard in silence. She'd unlocked the back door of the hotel and was halfway through before Baird's voice stopped her.

"What's in these?" he asked, looking at the jumble of outbuildings that surrounded the yard.

"Nothing," she said, looking back. "Supplies."

"Can we take a quick peek, while we're here?"

Bethany glanced at her watch.

"I literally showed you lot earlier. I've got so much to do tonight, can we just go?"

"Aye, we can go," said Baird, who was getting a little irritated by the woman's attitude. "Just as soon as you open these doors."

Bethany sorted through her keys, still grumbling. Baird leaned in towards Connell, handing her the dog.

"I'll do this," he told her, speaking quietly. "You go talk to the folk in the kitchen. They might open up a wee bit if Bethany's no there."

"Good idea, sir," she said.

"Where's she going?" asked Bethany as she watched Connell head through the back door into the main building.

"To check on my burger," said Baird. "Where do we start?"

Bethany opened the door of the closest outbuilding, a single-storey brick and flint structure whose roof was close to collapsing. She gestured inside for Baird to take a look, and he did, finding a few spare dining chairs and tables, as well as half a dozen swallow's nests in the rafters. There wasn't much in the next one, either, or in the stables on the other side of the courtyard.

"Happy?" said Bethany.

"Christ no," he said. "I'm never happy."

There was, by his reckoning, only one outbuilding left. It was the smallest of them, barely an outhouse, wedged between its bigger neighbours and almost invisible. The sign on the door read: *Equipment.*

"What's in there?" he said, nodding to it.

"Equipment?" said Bethany. "I don't know. There's no key for that door."

She held up the metal ring as if it was some kind of proof.

"No key for the building that says *Equipment*?"

"No. I don't know, Carl probably has one."

He made his way over to it anyway, trying the handle.

"Any objections to me getting it open the old-fashioned way?" he asked, taking a couple of steps back.

"What do you mean?" said Bethany. "Yes! I absolutely object!"

"Noted."

He drove his foot into the lock, the detonation of pain inside his ribs enough to make him feel like a grenade had gone off.

"Ya bastard," he wheezed, doubling over. "Shouldnae've done that."

The door had come out of its frame a little, but it still wouldn't open.

"There's nothing in there," said Bethany, squeezing herself between him and the building before he could get another kick in. "It's old, and it leaks. We haven't used it in years. Look, can we do this in the morning? I really need to get inside."

Before he could answer, Connell trotted into the courtyard. She still had the dog in her arms, and she was struggling with her phone.

"Call, sir," she said. "It's for you."

"It's no Briggs, is it?" he said. "Because if it is, I'm oot."

"It's not. It's somebody called Noor."

"Och, aye, the vet," he said, taking the phone when she offered it. "I'll bring it in."

Connell returned to the hotel, and Baird lifted the phone to his ear.

"Noor? How's things?"

"Hello?" said a voice, thick with static. "Can you hear me?"

"Aye, I can hear you. Everything okay?"

"Yes," she said. "Thanks for the ride, yesterday. As predicted, my father just about keeled over."

Baird laughed.

"You're welcome," he told her. "That's what police cars are for. You've got something for me?"

"Yeah," she said, and he heard the rustle of paper. "I've been doing some detective work, looking into your chihuahua. Is she okay?"

"I mean, 'okay' might be stretching it, but she seems healthy."

"Did you work out who her owner is?"

"Nut," he said. "No luck there."

"Well, I might have found something," she said. "Possibly. I don't know if it will help you or not. You remember I was saying Diana had undergone surgery at some point?"

"Aye," said Baird.

Bethany stood by the door to the little outbuilding, staring at Baird like he was responsible for every ill in the world and holding the keys in both hands like she was practising wringing his neck. In the glare of the security light, her waistcoat looked the colour of blood.

"I called around all the vets in the area, and I got lucky," Noor went on. "There's a place called the Three Rivers, on the other side of Ipswich. They said, and this is their words, not mine, they had a bug-eyed, bum-faced chihuahua with breath like death and flaky skin come to them a year or so ago."

"The description certainly fits."

"Somebody brought it in off the street, said they found it in a bin. It had a severe gastrointestinal disorder that had been untreated for years, wouldn't have had long left if it didn't have an operation, but there was nobody willing to pay for it. Anyway, one of the vets felt sorry for her and did it for free. Fixed her."

"What happened to her after that?" asked Baird.

"The vet put her up for adoption, said a nice family took her in. Local. I've got the details here, hang on."

He heard a rustling of paper.

"Henry Barker," she said. "That's an appropriate name, for sure. They're in Ipswich, do you want their address."

"Can you text it to this phone?" asked Baird.

"Sure. I'm not sure how helpful it will be, though. Ben, the vet, he said the family were only taking her temporarily. Fostering her. He checked the information on her chip and it's still theirs, but they told him the dog isn't with them any more."

"Wait, I thought you said she wasnae chipped?"

"Oh, right, I did. Because she isn't. Ben said if it's the same dog you found, he didn't chip her because of her skin condition, but they did give her a chip. They put it in her collar."

"Her collar?" said Baird. "The pink one?"

Bethany was still staring at him, her jaw bulging with furious impatience.

"I don't know," said Noor. "Sorry. Oh, and I found out her name. Dizzy."

"Dizzy?" said Baird. "I guess she is always spinning in circles."

"No, Ben said she was a nightmare from the moment she came in until the moment she left, and not just because she almost died. Dizzy is short for Disaster. That's what he called her."

"It fits. This is all really helpful, Noor. Thank you."

"You're welcome," she said. "It was fun, being a detective."

"Well, if you ever fancy a change of career, you'd fit right in with the polis," he said. "Cheers."

He hung up, pocketing Connell's phone.

"What was that about?" asked Bethany.

"Nothing," he said.

"You found the owner of that dog?"

"Aye, maybe. But more importantly, what are we going to do about this door?"

Bethany stared at the star-flecked sky, blowing a stream of breath into the cool air. She seemed to have resigned herself to his demands.

"I'll see if I can find the key," she said. "I'll meet you in the kitchen. But don't fuck with my team, okay? They've been through enough."

Baird muttered his thanks, crossing the courtyard to the open back door. Compared to outside, the hotel was roasting, all the radiators blasting out heat. He had to loosen his tie as he followed the corridor back around, and he would have lost his way if the heavenly smell of cooking meat hadn't lured him towards the kitchens.

He walked in to see that the huddle of staff had grown, nine of them now. Two were serving up the burgers, a couple already eating. Connell sat on a worktop, a bowl in one hand, a spoon in the other, and a smear of dark ice cream on her top lip that made her look like she had a little Charlie Chaplain moustache.

"They offered," she said before he could comment. "It's rude to say no, and it's liquorice flavour!"

"Aye, Adolf, I can see that," he said, handing her back the phone.

He turned to the other people in the room, some of whom were watching him like they were trying to figure out what he was doing there. A couple were staring at their phones. He couldn't see the dog anywhere, or Tracey, for that matter.

"Where's Diana?" he asked. "Or Disaster, as she's actually called."

"Disaster?" mumbled Connell, her lips wrapped around the spoon.

"Long story. Where is she?"

"Oh," said Connell, looking around. "She was right here. Tracey had her, she was treating her to some hamburger. I..."

"Got distracted," said Baird, heading across the room. "Aye, Connie. Ice cream, it's your Kryptonite."

He pushed into the throng of workers, trying not to get distracted himself as he passed the grills. His stomach felt like a clenched fist, the hunger pangs coming thick and hard and shortening the fuse of his impatience.

"Anyone seen Tracey?" he asked. "Or the wee dug?"

Nobody answered. Nobody even spoke. They nibbled on their burgers and checked their phones like he was a ghost.

"Hey," he said, clicking his fingers. "Tracey. Where is she?"

A grumbling of ignorance, nobody committing to an actual word.

"Last chance," he said, mad with frustration. "Or I fetch the PC by the door, and we do this the hard way."

"She went through there," said the woman called Marie that they'd met earlier, nodding to one of two doors on the far side of the room. "The dog needed a poo."

"Trust me, after what that dug did on my kitchen floor today, she won't need to shit until Christmas."

He started towards the door, only for another member of staff to ambush him from the side. It was the young man in the apron who'd been cooking, a spatula in one hand and an empty plate in the other. His name badge said Ryan. He was sweating hard, and grinning like a Punch puppet.

"You want a burger before you go?" he asked. "We've got some spare."

"Aye, thanks," he said. "Serve it up, I'll be back in a second."

"There won't be any left in a second," Ryan said, jiggling the plate. "Come on, mate."

Baird ignored him, pushing through the door into another stark length of hallway. This was part of the house proper, the ceilings high, the walls flaking, and the floorboards worn from centuries of use. The air was thick with the smell of damp and dust, catching in the back of his throat. Several oak doors stood open, leading into smaller rooms that were being used for storage. Only one was closed, and he might have walked right past it if he hadn't heard a familiar yapping from inside.

He opened it, finding himself inside what had to be a staff changing room. The space in the middle was packed to bursting with slatted wooden benches, and full-size metal lockers lined every wall. Tracey stood beside one of them, the door open as she rummaged furiously inside. Diana was by her feet, barking at her.

The dog wasn't wearing her collar.

"Everything alright?" asked Baird.

Tracey spun around like she'd been shot, one hand to her chest.

"Jesus *Christ*," she said, her eyes so wide they looked like they were about to roll out of their sockets. "What are you doing in here?"

Diana started running over to Baird, then turned around and went back to Tracey. She sat on her haunches, one paw raised like she was expecting a treat, squeaking out another high-pitched bark.

"I thought she needed a dump?" said Baird, looking around the room. There was a door on the other side of it, leading into a tiled space that might have been a bathroom. "Dinnae tell me she can use an actual toilet."

"No," said Tracey, forcing out a laugh. "She went. Outside. I was just coming back. Needed to get something."

She shut the locker door, picking up a padlock from the bench. Baird walked around the edge of the cluttered room, cornering her. This time, Diana came to investigate, sniffing his shoes, her tail drumming from side to side.

"What have you done with her collar, Tracey?" he asked.

"Nothing," she said, fumbling with the padlock. "It was too tight, it was hurting her. I took it off."

"You could fit a wedding ring around her scrawny neck and it wouldnae be too tight," he said. "What's going on, Tracey?"

He chanced it.

"You worried we might find oot she's your dug?"

Her laughter was bordering on hysterical, her eyes still on the padlock.

"I don't think you should be talking to me like this," she said. "I don't think you're allowed to be in here with me, alone. You could do anything, and nobody would believe me."

She finally looked up, a lunatic defiance in her red-flecked eyes.

"Or maybe they *would* believe me," she said.

The message was loud and clear, and he took a couple of steps back, giving her space.

"She's your dug, right? You got him off Henry Barker."

"So what if she is?" said Tracey.

"You want to tell me what she was doing in Benacre woods yesterday morning?"

Tracey shrugged, her eyes wild.

"I ken there's a chip in her collar," said Baird. "Is that what you're worried aboot?"

Tracey's smile wasn't all there, like something in her face had broken. She stared at Baird, then her eyes slid to the door behind him. He glanced back to find Marie there, and Ryan, the guy who'd offered him a burger.

"What are you doing in there?" said Marie, entering the room.

"I'm just asking some questions," he said. "You're welcome to join us."

"You can't just trap her in a room," said Marie. "Leave her alone."

The man entered too, holding his spatula like a sword and the empty plate like a shield.

"Maybe we should all go back through," he said with a nervous laugh. He waggled the plate again. "Burgers!"

"Aye," said Baird. "Good plan. But I'm gonna need that collar back, Tracey."

"You can't," she said. "I threw it away. Outside. It's in the..."

She burst into tears like somebody had pressed a button, burying her face in her hands. Her long nails dug themselves into the skin of her face, gouging hard, like she meant to peel it off.

"Hey!" said Marie, pushing past Baird hard enough to shunt him against a locker. She gathered Tracey in her arms, pulling her close. The dog jumped up and down, barking as it tried to climb Tracey's leg. "This ends here. Just fuck off and leave us alone."

"Everything okay?" said a voice from the door, and Baird was relieved to see Connell standing there. She'd been in the liquorice ice cream again, although it was more of a goatee now.

"Listen, Connie, do me a favour," said Baird. "Go grab the PC from the front, eh? It's getting a wee bit heated in here."

"Sure," said Connell, who looked anything *but* sure.

She turned to go, but Tracey called out, stopping her in her tracks.

"Wait! You don't have to do that. I'm not hiding anything, I..."

Marie squeezed Tracey's arm, hard enough to make her wince.

"I'm *not* hiding anything," Tracey sobbed, ripping free of the other woman and screaming the words at her. "I didn't do anything wrong!"

She ripped open the locker door, pulling out the pink glittery collar and throwing it to the floor.

"There," she said to Baird. "Just take it, I don't care."

"*Trace*," said Marie, more than a hint of a warning there.

"What?" she said. "He can have it. Maybe he *should* see?"

"I'm going to grab Paul," said Connell.

"Wait!" yelled Tracey, but the DC had gone. "Fuck's sake, this isn't right. I didn't do anything. I'm... I'm going to go. I need to go."

Tracey stepped over a bench, heading out the door.

"Trace!" Marie called out. She shot Baird a filthy glare before turning to the man with the spatula. "*Go*, Ryan."

"I dinnae think anyone should be going anywhere," said Baird, although Ryan had left the room before he'd finished the sentence. He turned to Marie. "What's going on? You covering for your pal? Because I can tell you now, the punishment for aiding and abetting a murderer isnae fun."

"Are you shitting me?" she said. "Tracey? A murderer? She has to have a bloody funeral for her fingernails every time she cuts them, because she feels bad. You've *got* the guy who killed Greg. It was Carl."

"You seem pretty sure aboot that," he said.

He walked towards the locker, but she blocked the way.

"You're not allowed to look in there."

"Aye? Who told you that? *Law and Order: Ipswich Division*? Move."

She licked her lips, thinking about it, and he gave her a look that he usually reserved for the crackheads in Tilly. She took a couple of shuffling steps back, shaking her head.

"I'm going to make sure you lose your job for this."

"Dinnae make promises you cannae keep."

Baird opened the locker door, checking the top shelf first to find a bundle of clothes, a couple of paperback books, and about fifty empty packets of paracetamol. Two creased white shirts and a pair of black trousers dangled on hangers, and beneath them was a massacre of old trainers. There was a shoebox down there as well, and he picked it up, sitting on a bench to give his aching ribs a break.

"Sir," came a voice from the door, and he turned to see that Connell was back, the tall PC by her side. He looked alert, one hand resting on his Taser. "Where do you need us?"

"Back in the kitchen," said Baird. "And see if you can find Tracey. Keep everyone in there, aye? Including this one."

"What?" said Marie, and she actually stamped her foot. "You can't..."

He gave her another look that clearly said he *could*, and she thumped her way to the door.

"Fucking hell!" she shouted as she went.

Drenched in the sudden silence, Baird let himself take a breath. Diana sat beside him, pining quietly as she sensed the tension in the air. He could feel the vibration of her body against his leg. He gave her head a scratch, her underbite jutting out in pleasure, her tongue like the emergency slide on a crashed plane.

"You're alright, quine."

He picked up the pink collar, running his fingers along the inside and finding a lump about the size of a grain of rice. It had been stitched in, the scar impossible to see against the filthy leather. Diana must have thought she was going for a walk, because she was up on her back legs scratching at his trousers.

"Why was she so worried about this?" Baird asked. The dog cocked her head as she tried to understand him. "There could be a million reasons you were in the woods, and a microchip's hardly proof of murder."

He checked the clasp, investigating the sparkly little D. It was glued in place, barely budging even when he picked at it with his nail. He tried the other side, scratching hard until, with a click, the D sprang open. It was like a locket, hinged on one side, but there were no photos in here.

There was just a SIM card, sparkling like gold in the bright light of the room.

"Hello," he said.

It was a standard sized SIM, and he knew without looking that it wouldn't fit in Connell's phone even if he still had it.

He set the collar to one side, prising the top off the shoebox and rummaging inside. There were more packs of paracetamol in here, as well as a box of citalopram—for depression, he remembered, because his sister had taken it for a while. There was a handful of change, a ring topped with a plastic bat that looked like it had come from a cracker, and a cotton facecloth that was wrapped around something the size of a chocolate bar. He pulled out the facecloth, laying it on the bench so that he could unwrap it.

Inside was a little porcelain figurine: a kitten, on its back, its legs in the air.

"Who are you, then?" he asked it.

Only the dog answered, barking loud enough to make his ears ring.

"Aye, Diana, I agree," he said, standing up. He slipped the collar into his pocket, and wrapped the kitten back in its facecloth. "Somebody's got some explaining to do."

CHAPTER THIRTY-THREE

By the time he got back to the kitchen, it was hotter than ever—in more ways than one.

With the grills on and the radiators blasting, the temperature was almost unbearable. It was like walking into a wall of heat, and he slipped off his jacket, slinging it on a countertop. He dropped the shoebox there too.

The tempers were heating up as well, the mob of staff members arguing with each other—and with Connell, who was doing her best to keep the peace. She'd managed to find Tracey, at least. The woman stood next to Tall Paul, the PC, looking like she wanted the ground to open up and swallow her. Her expression only changed when she spotted Diana trotting in behind Baird. She clapped her thighs until the dog ran over, then compressed her against her chest with such force the chihuahua's eyeballs almost popped.

The only person who wasn't here was Bethany.

"Alright!" yelled Baird, struggling to make himself heard over the raised voices. "That's enough, all of yous."

Nobody paid him any attention, so he smacked his hand

on the metal counter a few times, the sound like a church bell announcing a wedding.

Or maybe a funeral.

Gradually, the arguments dwindled into silence, and all eyes turned to him. He could see anger in every face. Fear, too.

"First things first," he said, seeing the empty grills, the plates in the sink. "Did anybody save me a burger?"

Nobody answered him.

"Braw," he muttered. "In that case, I'll have to settle for some answers. Normally I'd do this one person at a time, but it's late, I'm starving, and something tells me you'd all say the exact same thing. Am I right?"

They didn't look at each other, they just continued to stare at him. The heat was bad enough, but the tension in the room was worse. Baird felt like he was being cooked on one of the grills, and he loosened his tie a little more. He wondered if they should decamp to another room, but he didn't want to risk igniting a powder keg of movement. In here, at least, there weren't many places to hide.

Besides, PC Paul was a reassuringly tall presence, his hand still resting on his Taser, his eyes scanning the room in search of trouble.

"Alright then," said Baird.

He opened the shoebox, removing the pink collar. The D was still open, the SIM card visible inside.

"First question," he said, holding it up so everyone could take a look. "What am I gonna find when I put this in a phone?"

As expected, nobody said a thing. But he could almost see the current of panic that ran through the room, everybody bristling. He turned to Tracey.

"She's your dog, Tracey, aye? Why would you keep a secret SIM card in her collar?"

"It's nothing," said Tracey, her face pressed into the dog's back. "It's just a chip, in case she gets lost."

Baird shook his head.

"I found the microchip. This is something else. It's why you were so desperate to take her collar off, right? You've been trying to do it since we showed up yesterday, I just didnae see it. Whatever's on here, you dinnae want anyone to find it."

A thought entered his head, and he rubbed his chest—the injury he'd sustained in Connell's car when the van had tried to push him off the road. He'd assumed that whoever had been driving the VW Crafter had been trying to kill him, because he was too close to the truth.

But what if *he* hadn't been the target?

"You want to keep this hidden, at any cost," he said, looking at Tracey again. "You been driving the company van recently?"

"What?" she said, shaking her head.

"Yesterday afternoon, no long after I'd been here. Somebody tried to run me off the road. Me *and* the dug."

"No," said Tracey, horrified. "Nobody would do that."

"What aboot the rest of yous?" he said. "Because somebody took the van oot of Denton's garage, and me and Diana both almost died."

"It was Carl," said Marie, who had moved to the back of the crowd. "He's the only one who ever drove that thing."

"He's the only person who has access," said Ryan, the guy in the apron. "Nobody else is allowed anywhere near it."

"No even Bethany?" said Baird. "Mistress of the keys?"

There was still no sign of her, and he was starting to wonder if she'd bolted.

"Connie," said Baird. "Can you go find Bethany? Something tells me she kens more than she's letting on."

Connell nodded, heading for the door.

"And get some more bobbies oot here, aye?"

"You don't need to do that," said Marie. "We're cooperating, aren't we? We're giving you everything you want."

"Apart from the truth," he said as Connell left the kitchen, closing the door behind her. "And ma supper. We'll find oot, as soon as we can find a phone that fits it."

"I can do that, sir," said PC Paul.

He pulled a plastic brick out of his pocket, holding it up.

"That's a phone?" said Baird.

"Department issue. Nokias. They're indestructible. And they take older SIMs."

Baird handed the collar to him, and the constable peeled the SIM card out of its case.

"Come on," said Marie. "This is ridiculous, this has nothing to do with us."

"I need to go," said another of the women. "I've got to collect my kid."

"You can go in a second," said Baird.

He put the collar back in the box and picked up the facecloth, unwrapping it.

"Just as soon as somebody tells me what this is."

It was like he'd held up a knife, not a china figurine. A murmur of what felt like distress rippled across the room, followed by a groan from Tracey. She buried her face in the dog again, her words muffled.

"I'm sorry. I'm sorry, I couldn't."

"Fuck's sake," said Marie, putting both hands on top of her head. "Tracey!"

"You couldnae what?" asked Baird.

"Ignore her," said Marie, glaring at the other woman. "She's talking shit. Again. Aren't you?"

"Quiet," Baird told her. "Tracey, what could you no do?"

Some of the staff were starting to fidget, a current of quiet panic. A couple of the women were edging towards the door, Tall Paul too busy with the SIM card to notice.

"Dinnae even think aboot it," said Baird. "It's musical statues until we're done, and the prize for the losers is handcuffs and a ride in a polis car. Tracey, what's going on? What is this? Because I've seen these figurines before. A lot of them. One on Carl's desk, and the rest in a box in the woods where Gregory Brightwell was murdered. You ken what else was in the box?"

"No," said Marie. "How the hell could we know that?"

"It's nothing," said Tracey. "It was just a gift."

"Fuck's sake, Trace!" Marie yelled again. "Stop talking."

"A gift," said Baird, remembering what Connell had said when they'd found the box with Greg's head. They'd assumed somebody had given the figurines *to* Greg, a parting gift to the dead. But what if that hadn't been the only time they'd been offered as presents.

He thought about Karen Kirby's van, the shrine to Gregory Brightwell over the sink. The field mouse on its stalk of corn.

He thought about Carl Denton's bear, as well, claiming pride of place on his desk.

"Wait a minute," he said, trying to stop his thoughts from scrambling. "Who gave you the kitten, Tracey?"

"She bought it for herself," said Marie. "She—"

"I swear to God," said Baird. "Haud your wheesht."

The look Marie shot at him was dangerous.

"Or what?" she spat. "You're going to beat us into silence? Pummel us into the ground? Eh? It's what you lot do best."

"Polis?" he said.

"*Men*," she spat.

A murmur of anger from the crowd, the temperature rising another few degrees. Baird glanced at PC Paul, who was still trying to get the SIM into his phone.

"Answer the question, Tracey," said Baird. "Who gave you this? Because as far as I ken, these figurines all come from a shop in Serbia. You been there, recently?"

"Just tell him the truth, Trace," said Marie. "You've had that forever, since you were a kid, right? Just tell him."

Tracey must have been squeezing the dog like a stress toy, because Diana whined in pain. The woman lowered her to the floor and let her go, the tears rolling again. Baird was more than a little chuffed when the dog ran over to him, sheltering between his shoes.

"I'm sorry," Tracey sobbed, speaking to the dog. "I'm sorry, I'm sorry, Marie, I *can't*."

But she didn't need to. A picture was forming inside Baird's head: eleven porcelain figurines in a box, three more outside of it, and one person connected to all of them.

"Greg gave it to you, aye? He gave you this as a gift just like he gave one to Carl Denton, just like he gives one to his biggest fans at the conventions."

He surveyed the room, looking at every person in turn.

"Just like he gave one to all of yous, am I right?"

Marie scoffed, shaking her head.

"Why would a man like Gregory Brightwell give us a stupid animal statue? We didn't mean anything to him, we didn't even register on his radar. We're *staff*."

There was a soft bleep, followed by a quiet whoop from PC Paul.

"Got it, sir," he said. "I'm in."

Baird took the Nokia, studying the small screen. It had been so long since he'd used an older phone like this that he couldn't remember how to work it.

"Look," said one of the women. "I'm going to go, okay? I can't be late for my son."

"Wait," Baird told her.

She kept moving, heading for the exit on the left that led to the staff room. Baird nodded to the PC, who had to cross the room in a hurry to intercept her. He barred the way, his back against the door, his hand still resting on his Taser.

"You're not allowed to do this," said Marie, pacing at the back of the crowd like a caged tiger. "You can't keep us hostage here. He can't do this to us."

Baird ignored her, scrolling through the SIM's menu and selecting the option for recent calls. The list he found contained several mobile numbers as well as a few saved contacts made up of seemingly random letters. He pressed the number at the top, wondering if he'd hear the ring in the room. The call didn't connect, going straight to an anonymous voicemail. He tried the next one, but this did the same.

"Tracey, whose numbers are these?" he asked. "Because if you tell me now, it'll save me a lot of bother. And we're gonna find oot sooner or later."

"They're nobody," she said, still scrubbing away tears. "It doesn't mean anything."

"Let us out," said the woman who'd tried to leave. "I'm not fucking joking. I need to get to my son."

"Five minutes," he said, trying to diffuse the tension. "Give me five minutes and you can go."

He clicked back to the main menu, searching the text messages to see nothing at all. He dropped to the next item, contacts, and found the same cryptic letters he'd seen a second ago. The first read *AG-c-c-ni-s-np*. When Baird clicked on the name, he found another mobile number. He pressed call, and this time it rang.

"Yello," said a man's voice.

"*Yello* to you too," said Baird. "Who's this?"

The man ended the call.

"Rude," said Baird, and he tried the next contact. "AP," he read aloud. "M, C, Cr, I, S, P. What does it mean?"

He gave his audience a few seconds, then he called the number.

"I guess we'll ask them, then."

"Don't," said Tracey.

The phone rang, and rang, and just when he was about to give up, it connected.

"What?" said a woman's voice. "I'm at home."

A pause, a deep breath.

"Beth?" said the woman.

"Would you believe me if I said I was her?" asked Baird. "Dinnae hang up, this is the police."

He spoke the words to an empty line.

"Who was that, and why was she asking for Beth?" Baird said. He turned to Tracey. "This is Beth's SIM card?"

The young woman gave him nothing but tears, and nobody else was talking. He looked at the next contact.

"CH," he said. "E, K, I, NP. Shall we see what they have to say for themselves? Because I can do this all night."

He called the number, then ended it when something occurred to him. He scrolled down the list of contacts until he saw the one he was looking for.

"GB," he said. "E, C, M, K, H, I, D, NP. That's a lot of letters."

He looked up at the room, all eyes still on him.

"I think we can guess who GB stands for. What aboot the rest?"

"It's nothing," hissed Marie. "It's a stupid joke, it has nothing to do with you."

"Because I'll tell you what it looks like to me," he said, ignoring her. "When I was a wee'un, Ma would send us oot to the shops with a list. Me and my sister. But Ma was always too busy to write it oot in full, so Elspeth and I would look at this bloody list and see letters, nothing else. Just letters. E, M, F. Half the time we had no bloody idea what she was after, but we could usually guess. Eggs. Milk. Fags."

He frowned.

"She probably meant flour, thinking aboot it now. Nae wonder she was confused when we turned up with Benson and Hedges. But you get my point? GB. Gregory Brightwell. Aye? E, C, M, K. I'm thinking it disnae mean eggs, cheese, milk and..."

It took him a moment to think of anything.

"Kitchen roll?" he finished. "But this is a shopping list. Am I right?"

Tracey looked at Marie, her eyes bloodshot. The way Marie flinched was all the confirmation he needed.

"We ken Greg was into a bit of puff. M, marijuana? What about the rest? Cocaine? Ecstasy? Ketamine? Or kit?"

Marie tilted her head back and blew out a long sigh.

"His usuals?" said Baird. "Or maybe H is for heroin? Because I'm starting to get the impression Greg was a darker horse than he let on. What about the I? The D? NP? I'm struggling a little here. Icy dildos and some nose powder?"

Nobody was going to help him, that was for sure.

"You told me you're just staff," he said, speaking to Marie. "But that's no entirely true, is it? You were dealing, too. To the guests."

That ripple of distress passed across the room again, people starting to move.

"Stay where you are," said the PC by the door on the left.

"This has nothing to do with us," said Marie. "Carl made us do it."

"Shut up!" said Tracey.

"You shut up, you stupid bitch," Marie shot back. "This wouldn't have happened if you'd just—"

She caught herself, letting out a scream of frustration instead. She braced both hands on the counter, and for the first time Baird noticed the block of knives there. It hadn't escaped him how outnumbered he was.

"Alright," he said, sliding the Nokia into his pocket. "Here's what's gonna happen. Somebody put the kettle on, and let's calm doon with a cup of tea. We've got more polis on the way, and we're gonna question you all here, in the hotel, separately, and see if we can figure oot what's going on. Okay?"

"I can't wait," said the woman by the door. "I really have to go—"

"Oh give it up, Anne!" said Marie. "You don't even have a kid."

For a second, it looked like Anne was going to hurl herself at the other woman. Then the door on the right-hand-side of the room swung open slowly, the hinges creaking like something from a horror film. Connell appeared, shuffling into the kitchen like she'd crapped herself, her face twisted into a grimace.

"You alright, Connie?" said Baird. "The liquorice ice cream no agree with you?"

She didn't answer, and when she moved out of the way of the door it became immediately obvious why.

Bethany was right behind her, a large bow clenched in her left hand. An arrow had been nocked, the gleaming tip aimed at the back of Connell's head. The bow string was drawn as far as it would go, every muscle in Bethany's body tense as she held it in place.

"Och, shite," was all Baird could think to say.

CHAPTER THIRTY-FOUR

"ANYONE MOVES, AND THIS GOES IN HER FUCKING brain."

Bethany walked into the kitchen, holding the bow like a professional. She didn't look particularly strong, but she must have had muscles of steel to hold the string so steady. She wore a long, black quiver over her shoulder, a dozen more arrows inside it.

Connell moved a few paces in front of her, like she was on the way to her execution—which wasn't necessarily too far from the truth.

Everybody in the room was shouting at once, a rush of movement as people tried to find cover. Baird pushed himself away from the counter, almost treading on the dog between his legs. Bethany shot him a look.

"I'll do it," she said. "Stay fucking still."

PC Paul had taken a couple of steps away from the door, the Taser already out of its holster.

"Same goes for you, you twat," said Bethany, the point of the arrow a couple of feet from the back of Connell's skull, too close to miss. "Drop it."

Paul moved a little further, the Taser aimed like a gun. It would have been reassuring if he hadn't been standing on the other side of the room.

"It's no gonna reach, pal," said Baird. "So unless you're planning on throwing it, put it doon."

"Take it," said Bethany, speaking to Marie. "And his other shit."

Connell shuffled to the grill, stopping there and planting her hands on her head. She glanced at Baird, her face full of fear.

"I'm sorry, sir," she said.

"Shut up," Bethany told her.

"You've got nothing to apologise for," said Baird. "Just stay calm. This'll all be over in a minute. Bethany, can we have this conversation withoot the bow?"

"What do you think?" she said.

Marie yanked the Taser from Paul's hands, hurling it into the sink. She took his radio, too, dropping it on the counter. She tugged the baton from its holster, trying to figure out how to extend it.

"Now you," Bethany said to Baird. "Phone, on the floor."

He pulled the Nokia out of his pocket and dropped it. Diana sniffed it, nibbling on the case, oblivious to the violence in the room.

"They found the SIM," said Tracey.

Bethany didn't respond, positioning herself behind Connell. Her eyes were slits, her jaw clenched.

"Now what?" said Baird. "Are you gonna kill three polis officers, Bethany? Because I can tell you now, that's a really terrible idea."

"*So* terrible," added Connell.

"I said *shut up*!" said Bethany.

She was struggling to keep the wire taut, her arm trembling. She relaxed it a little, but not much. It wasn't a gun, but Baird had been close enough to Gregory Brightwell's body to see the damage the arrows had wrought, punching through his flesh and his organs, powerful enough to shatter bones. He wasn't planning on risking his life, or anyone else's.

"You had to keep pushing it," Bethany said to him. "*Why*? We gave you Carl on a fucking plate."

"They don't know anything, Beth," said Marie. "Not for sure. Just stop talking. We can still get out of this."

"They know," said Bethany. She turned her head to Tracey. "As soon as they got your stupid dog, it was all over."

"They found her cat, too," said Marie. "The figure. She kept it."

Bethany's expression was deranged with fury. She swung the bow towards Tracey, the string tensing again.

"Then you deserve this too," she said. "I knew you were too pathetic to go through with it."

"Wait," said Baird. "Dinnae do anything stupid."

"None of this is her fault, Beth," said Marie.

"Are you kidding me?" said Bethany. "This is *all* her fault. We were doing just fine until she fucked it up."

"It wasn't her fault!" screamed Marie. "He attacked her."

Tracey buried her face in her hands, shaking her head. Bethany looked like she'd been slapped, the tip of the arrow dropping a couple of inches. The anger in her expression had given way to something else, something that might have been grief.

"I know," she said quietly.

"It's not her fault, it's *his*," Marie went on. "Don't ever forget that."

"I know."

"Gregory Brightwell?" said Baird, hearing the hammer of his pulse in his voice. "He hurt you, Tracey?"

"He didn't," she sobbed. "It wasn't like that."

"Yeah," said Marie. "It was."

"What happened?" he asked. "Something to do with the drugs? You were all working together, supplying drugs to guests. Aye? Pills, cocaine, even a bit of kit. Anything they asked for, you lot could get your hands on. These are high-end clients, they're all minted. Was Carl behind it?"

"Yeah," said Marie, but the split-second pause before she answered told the whole truth.

"He didnae even ken, did he? You were doing this behind his back."

"He knew," said Bethany. "Carl did what Carl does best. Turned a blind eye at the same time as holding out his grubby hand."

"Beth," hissed Marie.

"It doesn't matter," said Bethany, swinging the pulled bow back towards Connell so urgently that Baird thought she was going to fire it. The DC screamed, dropping into a squat. "None of it fucking matters. Get up."

She said this to Connell, who jerked up like she was on strings.

"Sorry," said the terrified DC.

"So Carl let you work freelance in the hotel," said Baird. "And it wasnae just the drugs, was it?"

Nobody contradicted him, and he shook his head.

"I was right, it *is* a sex dungeon."

"It's not," said Marie.

"No? How many of you started working in the hotel

after you went to Carl's therapy rooms? How many of you used to do the work before you came here?"

He saw the answer in their faces.

"He was your pimp," said Baird.

"No," said Bethany. "He wasn't. He never forced us to do anything, never even encouraged us. He just took his cut, and..."

She tailed off.

"And gave you a safe place to work," said Connell. "Only it wasn't safe, was it?"

"Because of people like Greg, right?" said Baird. "Literally everyone I've spoken to here has told me the exact same thing, including half of you in this room. Greg was a nice guy. The kindest man in the world. Wouldnae hurt a fly. Farts rainbows. In fact, so many people were telling me that, it was starting to sound like a conspiracy. He wasnae nice, was he?"

Bethany made a noise like a hissing cat, and everyone else in the room copied her—a rush of noise that was so unexpected, so alien, so *loud*, that it made Baird feel like he'd been hurled into the North Sea in the middle of winter. It went on for close to ten seconds before cutting back to silence.

"He was the fucking devil," said Marie, wiping her mouth with the back of her hand. "He told the world he was a saint, but behind closed doors he was as evil as they come."

"Took whatever he wanted," said Bethany. "From anyone. Didn't matter if it was on offer or not. He took it, and he kept taking, and taking. Tracey."

Tracey wouldn't come out from behind her hands.

"Almila," said Bethany, looking at another woman. "Marie. Anne. Ryan. How many?"

Almost everyone in the room put up their hand.

"He took whatever he wanted," she said again. "Didn't matter if you were a man or a woman, didn't matter how old you were, if you were a *child*. He gobbled you down, like a monster. He ruined you. And Carl was supposed to stop him. Carl was supposed to keep us safe. But he didn't. Guests are always right. And we're just staff."

She hissed that same awful noise, the chorus filling the room as everyone joined in. It took all of Baird's self-control not to slap his hands to his ears.

"You don't get to do that," said Bethany when it had died out. "Not to us, not to anyone."

"Ever," said Marie.

"Ever," said a handful of others, as if this was a chant they had practised many times before.

Marie was holding the extended baton like she was planning on using it, like she was ready to cave Baird's head in. The other staff had grown tense as well, that same promise of collective violence he'd felt so many times on the job, back when he was in uniform, on crowded streets during protests, after football matches.

Before riots.

And just like that, the final piece of the puzzle clicked into place.

"So you killed him," said Baird. "All of yous."

Bethany smiled, and there was nothing friendly about it. The bow was pointing downwards now, the string relaxed, but the arrow was still nocked.

"Yeah," she said.

"Beth," barked Marie. "Don't."

"Twelve arrows," said Connell. "There were twelve of you. You all did it?"

"And twelve figurines," said Baird, looking at the shoebox. "If you count this one. Greg gave them to you. They were gifts."

"They were insults," said Beth. "He presented them to you when he thought he owned you, when he thought he'd broken you. Mice, kittens, sparrows, all the weakest animals. Because that's what he thought we were. Weak. Animals."

A hollow giggle spilled out of her lips.

"So we showed him we weren't weak," she said. "We showed him we weren't animals, that we couldn't be owned. We *showed* him."

"That explains Greg's car," said Baird. "The tracker. Five trips back and forth from here to the woods. You took turns."

Beth nodded, and so did a couple of the others.

"It took him so long to die," she said. "Hours. Yeah, we took turns, we took our time. He felt every single arrow before he slipped away."

"Then you cut off his heid. Why?"

"So nobody would have to see his grinning, sweating, screaming face hanging over them ever again," said Bethany. "Not in this life, or the next."

"Right," said one of the women who hadn't spoken yet. "Fuck Greg."

"Fuck Greg!" said another, and the rest of the room took up the mantra. The sound of it was terrifying, a clarion call of fury and vengeance that made Baird's skull feel like it was full of dynamite.

"Look," he said, yelling over the noise. "Let's calm doon a bit and—"

"Calm down?" said Bethany. "You really should know better than to tell a woman to calm down."

"Aye, I probably could have phrased it better," he said.

"But honestly, we can talk aboot this at the station, we can find a way to make it right."

"You and I both know there's only one way to make this right," said Bethany.

"By putting doon the bow?" he said, hopefully.

"No."

Bethany lifted her weapon, aiming across the room, pulling the wire with that same impressive strength.

And finally releasing it.

The arrow exploded from the bow, slicing across the kitchen in a fraction of a second and thumping into PC Paul's chest with a dull crack. He staggered back, his eyes wide with shock as he stared at the feathered shaft that jutted out of him.

"No!" screamed Connell.

Baird took a step towards Bethany, but she was already reaching for another arrow, nocking it into the bow with practised ease. He grabbed Connell's arm instead, dragging her towards the door to the changing room.

"Stop them!" screamed Bethany.

A wail of fury rose up from everyone in the room, a stampede of noise and movement as they charged. PC Paul was on his hands and knees, crawling into the maze of stainless-steel units and leaving a trail of blood behind him. Diana had vanished.

There was nothing Baird could do but run. He reached for the PC's radio as he passed it but he wasn't quick enough, an arrow thwacking into the wall inches from his head, a shrapnel of broken tiles hitting his skin.

"Christ!"

He wrenched open the door, shoving Connell through, almost falling over her as he followed. He shut it behind them, the head of another arrow splintering the wood and almost taking his eye out. He could still hear Bethany's shrill voice from inside the kitchen.

"The equipment room is open. Arm yourselves!"

Baird grabbed Connell and they clung to each other as they bolted, Bethany's laughter chasing them down the corridor.

"Let the hunt begin!"

CHAPTER THIRTY-FIVE

"Are you shitting me?"

Baird bolted along the corridor, past the changing room, Connell right behind him. Behind *her* was all the fury and fire of hell, a chorus of screams and shouts and laughter that chilled Baird to the bone.

He glanced back as he went, seeing the kitchen door open. Two of the women ran out, their faces wild as they started their pursuit.

"How is this happening *again*?" he said. "Three weeks ago we were being shot at with guns. Now arrows?"

"At least we're not on a boat, sir," Connell replied, pointing towards an open door on the right. "That way."

They ran through it together, wedging themselves in the frame for a second before popping out into a small office. Baird slammed the door shut, spotting a filing cabinet against the wall next to it.

"Here, Connie, help me."

They pushed the heavy cabinet together, managing to topple it against the door just as it started to open. The two women screamed like banshees on the other side, pounding on the wood as they tried to get in.

"There's nowhere to go!" taunted one, just a boiling eyeball through the crack.

"There's a door right there," Baird answered, spotting one on the other side of the room. The office was packed with shelves, filing cabinets, and two desks.

"The phone," he said, running to the nearest desk and picking up the receiver. "You still got yours, Connie?"

"Bethany took it," she replied, running to the other door. She opened it onto a dark corridor, the cool air rushing in. "I didn't have a chance to call for backup."

Baird dialled 999, trying to ignore the thunder of noise from outside.

"Poor Paul," said Connell, turning back to the room. "Do you think he's okay?"

"He had an arrow in his chest, Connie. I'm guessing okay isnae the word he'd be using. Bastards. They better no hurt my dug."

"Emergency," said the voice on the line. "What service do you require?"

"Police," said Baird. "We're at Denton's Hotel, near Southwold, multiple assailants armed with bows and arrows and—"

A soft click, the quiet replaced by static.

"Hello?"

He threw the receiver to the desk.

"They've cut the line. The bastards."

The hammering on the door fell quiet, a drum of footsteps fading into the building.

"Aye, you'd better run," he said, feeling a moment of relief before the sound of voices grew louder again. This time they drifted through the open door.

"They're coming around," he said. "Move, Connie."

He ran into the dark corridor, feeling his way along it, cracking his thigh on the corner of a table.

"You bastard," he grunted.

The shouts were closer, whoops of excitement that echoed back and forth through the dark. He heard the clatter of a handle, and a door opened behind them, a shaft of light puncturing the corridor like an arrow. Baird ducked as two women—he couldn't be sure if they were the same ones—burst through, both giggling like children. They doubled back towards the office.

"They've got to be in there," said one.

"Just be careful," said the other as they ran into the room. "Let Beth do it."

Baird kept moving, using the light to navigate down the corridor. There was another door at the end and he tried the handle, easing it open. Ahead was the private dining room where they'd sat with Carl Denton yesterday. It was empty, the tables steeped in shadow, the air perfectly still.

He crept inside, shutting the door behind him. Connell grabbed a chair, wedging the back under the handle.

"Good thinking," said Baird.

"Should we hide in here, sir?" whispered Connell.

"No chance. They ken the hotel, they'll find us eventually. We've got to get ootside."

Connell wrenched open the curtains, tugging the handles of the leaded windows.

"Nope," she said. "We can try the front door? It's right across the lobby."

They didn't exactly have much choice. The hotel was full of noise, so many shouts and howls he couldn't figure out where they were coming from. He crossed the room, Connell already at the far door. She gave him a look that was drenched in terror, waiting for him to nod before turning the handle.

The door creaked out an alarm as it opened, but there was nobody in the lobby to hear it. Baird set off, passing the empty reception desk and the wide staircase, running by the time he reached the big front door. He gave it a yank.

Locked.

"Bastard!" he said, turning to Connell. "They've—*shite*!"

Ryan was marching out of a door a dozen yards behind them, a huge bow in his hand. He lifted it, pulling back the string.

"Move!" Baird yelled, giving Connell a meaty shove.

She fell onto her backside, the arrow exploding from the bow and cutting through the air where her head had been. It hit the wall and rebounded, spinning to the ground.

"Bastard!" roared Baird, running towards him.

Ryan was reloading, but he was struggling. He nocked his arrow, lifted the bow, looking up just in time to see Baird's fist as it connected with his nose. His head rocked back with a wet crunch, a gout of blood erupting towards the ceiling. He staggered, and Baird kicked him as hard as he could between the legs.

"Bastard," he said, lunging for the man's bow.

An arrow *thwipped* past his ear, shattering a window. Two more women were approaching from the other side of the reception desk, one armed with a bow and reloading quickly.

"Stop fucking shooting at us!" Baird yelled at them, flapping his arms to emphasise his point.

It didn't work, the woman firing another arrow at them. This one went well wide, but she had plenty more.

"They're in the lobby!" she yelled as she fixed another arrow in place. "Hurry!"

Baird legged it, still holding the bow. Connell was back on her feet, and she met him at the foot of the grand staircase. Another arrow embedded itself in the handrail inches from where she held it—Bethany, this time, striding out of a door—and Connell screamed.

"Where are you going, little rabbits?" said Bethany through a smile.

Connell started climbing, panting like a knackered horse. Baird wasn't faring much better, his ribs singing a song of agony as he struggled on the stairs.

"I'm no sure how much longer I can go on," he said, the words barely audible.

They rounded the bend, making it onto the landing just as the three women started climbing below. Baird held the bow in his sweaty grip.

"You've got no arrows, sir," said Connell.

"I bloody know that, Connie!" he snapped back.

He lobbed it over the banister, the heavy bow soaring down the stairs and striking one of the women in the shoulder. She grunted, falling backwards. He didn't wait to see if she'd broken her neck, he just started moving again, slamming into the fire door that led to the rooms.

It didn't budge.

"Bastard," he said. "The master key, Connie. Where is it?"

"Bethany took it," she said.

Baird growled his frustration. The stairs were squeaking as more people climbed them, the hunt catching up.

"Greg," said Connell. "We had the key to his room. Have you still got it?"

Baird patted his pockets like he was trying to put out a

fire. He grabbed his wallet, pulling out the key card they'd found on Brightwell's body. He touched it to the sensor, and nothing happened.

"Give it a wipe," said Connell.

"I'll give you a bloody wipe," he muttered, scrubbing the card on his trousers.

"Found you!" said a voice from the top of the stairs.

Baird didn't look back. He pressed the card to the reader, and this time it beeped, the lock disengaging. Connell shouldered through it, and he followed, wincing as he heard the twang of a bowstring behind him, the thwack of the arrow hitting something. There was nothing to block the doors with, so they kept running, almost out of steam.

"If we... can get... into Greg's... room," said Connell, looking like she might pass out from the effort of talking. "We might..."

"Be able to lock the door," he finished for her. "Aye."

He couldn't think of a better plan, pushing through the pain in his ribs as they turned the corner into the back of the building. The second-floor staircase was right there.

"More bloody stairs," he said, grabbing the handrail and hauling himself up.

There was a suit of armour at the top and he gave it a kick, sending it crashing down the steps just as somebody appeared at the bottom. It was Bethany, the bow still gripped in her hand. She looked insane.

"There's nowhere to go," she shouted, struggling to clamber over the scattered pieces of armour. "I'll burn this fucking place to the ground before I let you leave."

"You could have told me that before you made me climb all these stairs," he called back, retreating along the narrow corridor. "What's your plan? You kill us, you all go away. For life."

"Nobody will know," she shouted. "We'll bury you both here, in the grounds. We'll tell everyone you left, that you eloped together."

"Ew," said Connell.

"*Ew*?" said Baird, looking at her. "What do you mean, ew?"

"Sorry, sir, I..." She shook her head like she was trying to dislodge something. "We should go."

Connell ran around a bend in the corridor, and he jogged after her as fast as his aching body would let him. She stopped outside a door, her hands on her hips as she struggled to pull in a breath.

"Penguin," he said, looking at the bird decal on the numberplate. "Well done."

He held the card to the reader, doing his best to ignore the sound of Bethany crashing through plate armour on the stairs. It bleeped, and he let out a long, painful breath of relief. Connell opened the door and they tumbled into Greg's room together, slamming it behind them. It was pitch black in here, and when Baird reached for the security bolt he couldn't find it—because he'd kicked the door in yesterday, he remembered.

He set off across the room, looking for the coffee table and finding it with his shin.

"Oof, you bastard!" he hissed, grateful for the dark because he was close to greeting. "Connell, help me."

The table weighed a tonne, but they managed to drag it across to the door, wedging it there. They stepped back together, Connell's shoulder pressing against his arm.

"They're going to find us, sir," she said. "What do we do?"

"I have no idea," he replied. "Might as well hit the minibar and go oot with a bang."

"Out," echoed Connell. "Wait, the *window*, the balcony."

Baird grinned at her, even though he knew she wouldn't see it in the dark.

"I could kiss you, Connie."

"Ew."

He crossed the room, catching his other shin on the second coffee table and almost screaming. He felt for the catch and flicked it, pulling open the large window. The cool wind rushed in to greet him, sucking the air from his lungs, making him feel like he was already falling. He gripped the frame so hard he thought he might pull it out of the wall.

"You okay, sir?" said Connell.

"Och, I'm braw," he said, fuming. "Never been better. Come on, before that dobby bawbag finds us."

It was too late. There was a bleep from the card reader and the door started to open, crunching into the coffee table.

"I know you're in there," said Bethany.

"It's no us," Baird called back, speaking in a quavering falsetto. He reached out, finding Connell's arm and steering her towards the window. "It's the ghost of Gregory Brightwell, and I'm very, very angry."

There was a rattle from the door, then a crunch as Bethany kicked it. The coffee table must have shifted, because a little more light poured in from the corridor.

"There's nowhere to go, you prick," she said. "Just come out and finish this."

"No thank you," he said, still speaking like a ghost.

Connell had made it out onto the balcony, clawing at Baird's face and his clothes in her panic.

"Enough," he said, slapping her arms away. "You're gonna have to jump."

"I can't," grunted Connell. "It's too high."

"I meant onto the next balcony, no over the edge."

"But I'm scared."

"It's a good thing it's dark, then," he said, glancing back as Bethany continued to kick at the door, inching it open. "You cannae see the ground. *Go*!"

He climbed onto the balcony beside her, barely enough room for the both of them. Bethany had managed to open the door far enough to squeeze in, and she slapped at the switches, the lights blazing on. She spotted them through the window, her face peeling open into a wicked grin.

"Found you," she said, lifting the bow.

"Move!" roared Baird.

Bethany drew the string, taking a step towards them and tripping on the coffee table. She tumbled over it with a gargled scream, loosing the arrow as she fell. It sliced past Baird's cheek, thrumming into the quiet night.

"Fuck!" she screamed, picking herself up. "They're here! Here!"

"No for long," said Baird.

Connell had managed to climb onto the stone balustrade, but she'd frozen there. Baird gave her a gentle prod with his fingertips and she made the jump with a chicken-like squawk, landing on the next balcony along.

"You shoved me!" she said, her wide eyes the brightest thing in the night.

"It was more of a nudge."

Baird clambered onto the handrail, taking as deep a breath as his lungs would let him before launching himself across the void. He crashed into Connell on the other side, her arms wrapping around his waist as she struggled for balance.

"No time for cuddles, pal," he said.

"Ew."

"Would you stop bloody saying that! Move."

She climbed onto the next balustrade, her clothes fluttering in a sudden gust of wind. She screamed again as she made the jump, and he heard the scuff of her feet as she landed.

He was about to follow her when Bethany appeared behind him, stepping through Greg's window onto the first balcony.

"You're making this too easy," she said, nocking an arrow into the bow.

"Well close your eyes," he told her. "It'll be more of a challenge."

He jumped, landing on the last balcony next to Connell.

"Where now, sir?"

"Doon the drain," he told her. "And quick."

Bethany aimed her bow. She was drenched in light from Greg's room, but Baird and Connell were under the cover of darkness. She fired, a gunshot crack as the arrow hit the wall a foot or so from his head, cartwheeling into the night.

"Like fish in a barrel," said Bethany, reloading.

"Hurry, Connie," said Baird.

"The railing's going to collapse," she said.

"At least Greg put up a fight," said Bethany. "He didn't run. Do you know how many times we had to shoot him before he finally dropped?"

Connell screamed again as she slipped over the edge of the crumbling balustrade. For a terrible second, Baird thought she'd fallen. Then he heard her scrabbling against the wall, the drainpipe creaking.

"I can't do this, sir," she said.

"Och, well come back up then," he said. "We can just stand here and get—"

Bethany's bow twanged, and this time something thumped into the meat of his shoulder—as hard as a punch. The impact shunted him into the handrail, and he felt the loose stone give, mortar raining to the ground below.

"Wank biscuits!" he bellowed, slapping a hand to the wound. There was no arrow, but it had torn through his flesh, blood pouring onto his fingers, as hot as spilled tea. "Stop fucking shooting at me, you bastard shitgibbon!"

He didn't wait for a reply—or another arrow. He grabbed the crumbling balustrade and straddled it, feeling the loose stone start to give. He reached for the drainpipe, stretching too far, gravity reaching up and yanking him off the balcony.

He grabbed at anything he could, finding the cast iron pipe at the last second. The pain blazed from his injured shoulder into his neck, too startling for him to remember how to scream. Blood dripped down his side, pattering to the ground below, surely too much of it. He gripped the pipe, sliding uncontrollably until his arse hit something beneath him.

"Stop, sir!" said Connell, her voice muffled. "You're on my face."

"Then *move*!" he yelled, the agony making the night flash neon bright. "Doon!"

He heard her panting, heard the rustle of ivy as she fought her way through it. He followed, his shoes slipping on the bricks, his fingers struggling to hold on. The ground was a black void a million miles beneath him. He felt like he was going to vomit, but he swallowed it down for Connell's sake.

There was a thump overhead as Bethany made the jump to the second balcony.

"Where are you?" she said in the singsong voice of a child playing hide and seek.

"Beth?" came another voice.

"They're climbing down," Bethany shouted. "Get everyone in the garden, they'll be sitting ducks."

They would be. The staff could take potshots at them at their leisure from down there—as easy to hit as Gregory in his tree. Baird upped his speed, trying to make any sense of the inky darkness below. They had to be halfway down by now, surely.

Another crunch as Bethany leaped to the last balcony. He looked up, seeing a deeper shadow against the night. Then he screwed his eyes shut as a light blazed on.

"Hello," said Bethany, holding her phone over the edge, the torch on. She rested it on the balustrade like a spotlight while she nocked another arrow in her bow.

Baird kept moving, one hand over the other, his feet scuffing their way through the ivy. He wondered if he was too high to jump—the ground was soft enough. But they'd only just passed the windows of the first floor.

Overhead, he heard the creak of the bow as Bethany pulled the string.

He looked up, seeing her leaning against the stone handrail as she tried to find the right angle. Dust floated down, blinding him.

"I wouldnae do that," he shouted.

"Kill?" she said. "Why? I'm quite good at it."

Her body tensed, her breath locked in her chest, her eye meeting his—as cold a look as he'd ever seen.

The balustrade cracked, the old stone splitting under

Bethany's weight. An enormous chunk of it broke free, crunching off the wall and almost taking Baird with it. Bethany teetered on the edge, perfectly silent as she struggled to keep her balance.

In the end, it was the weight of the bow that pulled her over.

She fell, plummeting past Baird without so much as a scream, hitting the ground with a wet thump.

"I meant I wouldnae lean on the railing," he said.

"Sir!" said Connell, and he thought he was sitting on her head again until she carried on. "Over there!"

He couldn't see where she was pointing, but when he looked up he spotted blue lights in the dark. He could hear sirens too, he realised, over the hammer blows of his heart and the roar of the pain.

Below, a door crunched, footsteps pealing out.

"Beth?" shouted somebody. "Where are they?"

"We're up here," he shouted, as loud as his injuries would let him. "And Beth's doon there, that wee puddle of broken bones. And do you hear that?"

Silence, other than the approaching sirens.

"Shit," said a woman after a second or two. "We've got to go."

"Aye," Baird called out. "Sounds like a plan."

He heard them running, then the crunch of a door. The lights were brightening the horizon, like a blue dawn. They were close enough that he could hear the growl of the engines.

"Keep going, Connie," he said.

"I don't think I can, sir," she told him. "I think I'm going to wait here."

"Right," he said, locking his hands in place. "You do you, pal. I'm absolutely fine."

He closed his eyes, resting his head against the cool pipe, feeling another wash of nausea roll over him.

"Absolutely fine."

CHAPTER THIRTY-SIX

"You look like a couple of bloody monkeys!"

DCI Briggs stood on the back lawn of Denton's hotel, framed in the headlights of the half a dozen IRVs, two ambulances and single Range Rover that had been parked there. Uniformed officers bustled around her, two of them carrying a ladder which didn't look like it was going to be tall enough to reach the place where Connell had glued herself to the drainpipe.

They'd only been clinging to the back wall of the hotel for a little over ten minutes, but it felt like it had been hours. Baird's body was as numb as a block of coal—except for his shoulder, which felt like a block of coal that was *on fire*.

The other thing framed in the blazing LEDs, like an actor on stage caught in the spotlights, was Bethany. She lay in the soft dirt next to the section of handrail that had given way, a perfect streak of bright red blood splashed across the grass that bordered the flowerbed. It was thanks to this soft dirt, though, that she wasn't dead. She groaned at the sky, her legs kicking weakly, her hands grasping at the flowers as if she was still trying to reach the bow that lay there. A couple of paramedics knelt beside her, speaking quietly. Their shadows stretched up the wall like they were giants.

There was no sign of any of the other members of staff who had chased them, but Baird could hear shouts from inside the hotel as they were rounded up by the tactical team. They'd already found PC Tall Paul, who—thanks to another miracle, and a first aid kit he'd discovered in the kitchen—was also still alive.

There had been no sign of the little chihuahua.

"Like a couple of annoying bloody orangutangs who do everything they can to make my life miserable," Briggs went on. "What on earth is going on, Baird?"

"What's going on, ma'am, is I got shot in the shoulder, and I'm about four seconds away from losing my grip on this drainpipe, or spewing my guts over Connell. Possibly both."

"Please don't throw up on me, sir," said Connell from her nest of ivy four feet or so beneath him.

"I mean with the case," said Briggs, looking at Bethany. "This woman killed Gregory Brightwell?"

"Aye," said Baird, trying to adjust his weight to stop his hands from cramping. "But she didnae do it on her own."

"They all helped her," said Connell. "The hotel staff. There were twelve of them, I think."

"Twelve?" said Briggs.

"Watch yourself, ma'am," said one of the constables holding the ladder.

Briggs stood to the side as they rested it against the wall, one PC bracing the bottom while the other started to climb. It was bigger than it had looked, the top rung level with Connell's head.

"Easy, Connie," said the PC. "I'll help you over."

"They were all here tonight?" asked Briggs. "Twelve of them?"

"Aye," said Baird. "The night shift."

Connell stepped onto the ladder, which wobbled alarmingly as she made her way down. Baird felt a rush of relief when he saw her land on solid ground—partly because she was safe, and partly because he could start moving again. He didn't bother with the ladder, sliding down the drainpipe like a wet jobbie before plopping back to earth. His legs were too tired to hold him, so he stayed on his backside in the dirt, leaning against the wall and trying to unlock the joints of his frozen fingers.

"They had some kind of cabal," said Connell. She was shivering uncontrollably as a paramedic wrapped a foil blanket around her shoulders. "A club. I don't know what it was. They were selling drugs to the guests. And maybe... other things, too."

"Other things?" said Briggs.

"Services," said Baird.

"Oh," said the DCI. "I see."

Another paramedic ducked down beside Baird, gently probing his shoulder with a gloved finger. He winced, the numbness slowly giving way to a body-wide agony that made him feel like he'd been dropped in a vat of boiling water.

"What happened to you?" the paramedic asked.

"That lunatic bawcramp happened to me," he told her, nodding to Bethany.

"I mean what sort of injury?"

"I was shot," he told her.

"Yeesh," said the woman, helping him peel off his jacket. "With a gun?"

"An arrow."

"I'm not sure that counts as being shot," she said. "You got lucky."

"Aye, I feel it. Lucky Baird, the Charmed Bloody Leprechaun. That should be my nickname."

He *had* been lucky, he knew. Lucky that Bethany hadn't decided to shoot him first instead of Paul, lucky that he'd escaped the kitchen, lucky that he'd been able to hide inside the hotel, lucky that Denton's staff hadn't been better shots, lucky that backup had arrived before everyone had started taking potshots at him from the back lawn.

Lucky that he'd had Connell with him.

He glanced at her now to see that she was looking back at him, her body trembling.

"You alright, quine?" he asked her.

She nodded, but he could see the fear that was still etched in her young face, the growing horror of what had happened—and what *might* have happened. She pulled the foil blanket tighter around her neck, her teeth chattering.

"Keep going," said Briggs, lighting a cigarette and earning a reproachful glare from the paramedics. "Twelve members of staff, dealing narcotics for Carl Denton?"

"I dinnae ken," said Baird. "No officially. I think he kent what they were doing, and he was taking a cut, but they were working for themselves."

"It's what he always does," said Connell. "He lets them be self-employed, so he has plausible deniability if they're caught."

"So why did they kill Brightwell?" asked Briggs, exhaling an enormous cloud of smoke. "Nobody had a bad word to say about him. Was it something to do with him not paying his bills? Because I've known a lot of dealers in my years, and I've never seen any of them kill a man the way he was killed. Brightwell's death was personal."

"Aye," said Baird. "It was. Behind closed doors, Brightwell was a monster. I think he attacked more than one member of staff."

"Attacked how?" said Briggs.

"The worst way," said Connell.

"He *raped* them?"

Baird nodded.

"The men and the women who worked in the hotel, ma'am. I think he made a sport of it. And he could do what he wanted, because he was—"

"Gregory Brightwell," Briggs finished for him, nodding sadly.

"And because he knew Carl would cover for him," said Connell. "Denton always put his guests first, especially ones like Greg. In here, they were untouchable."

"But oot there, they weren't," said Baird.

"Why didn't they report him?" said Briggs. "Why didn't they tell somebody?"

"I think Denton recruited his staff through his therapy rooms," said Baird. "He picked them because they were vulnerable, because they were desperate, and some of them came from a background of sex work. He offered them a new start, he just didnae tell them it was the same as the old start."

"He picked the ones who wouldn't know how to ask for help," said Connell. "So they helped themselves."

A shiver ran through Baird, hard enough to make his bones rattle, but his paramedic had gone to help the others as they loaded Bethany onto a stretcher. She'd been fitted with a neck brace and secured on a spinal board, everything wrapped up tight. Even though her lips moved like she was speaking, nothing came out except clouds of breath. Her bloodshot eyes rolled in their sockets, finding Baird. Despite everything, he almost felt a pang of sympathy for her.

"You can see why they did it," he said.

A fire door crunched open in the back of the building, everyone turning as a woman ran onto the lawn. It was Marie, Baird saw when she stepped into the light. She sprinted towards the paramedics, and every copper on site ran to intercept her with a chorus of booming shouts.

"Get on the floor! Now!"

"Beth!" Marie screamed, ducking beneath a PC's arms and making it all the way to where Bethany lay on her stretcher. She touched the other woman's face. "Beth? Oh God."

"Get down!" roared a constable, running over, but Briggs held up her hand to stop him.

"Is she going to be okay?" asked Marie. She turned to Baird, her fury evident in every line in her face. "What did you do to her?"

"She fell."

"Fell?" said Marie, looking up. The second floor of the building looked impossibly far away, drowning in the dark.

"I need to know how many of you are inside," said Briggs. "And if you're planning on fighting back. Because my tactical officers won't go easy."

"We're done," said Marie, stroking Beth's vacant face. "It's over. We never wanted to hurt anyone else."

"Just Greg," said Baird, and she nodded. "How did it happen?"

Marie sniffed, standing back as the paramedics wheeled Bethany's stretcher towards the ambulance.

"It's my fault," she said.

"You shot him?" asked Briggs.

Marie shook her head, wiping her eyes with her sleeve.

"I don't suppose it matters now," she said. "After this."

She took her time, though, a good twenty seconds passing before she found the strength to talk again.

"I got him to the woods. On Friday. I was the one he trusted most, out of all of us. You know about the film he was going to do? *The Court of Avalonia*?"

Baird nodded.

"He never stopped going on about it. He was obsessed with it. Told me all about the woods where they were going to film it, right down the road from the hotel. Beth had the idea, that we could... we could get to him there. But he wouldn't have gone with anybody else."

Marie stopped, staring at the streak of blood Bethany had left on the grass. In the light from the cars, it looked too vibrant to be real.

"So I told him I wanted to see them. The woods. I wanted to be there with him. You know? So we drove out, Friday night."

"In Greg's car?" said Baird.

"Yeah, it was always his car. He kept his... his kit there."

"His kit?"

Marie wrapped her arms around herself, as if worried somebody might start punching her.

"Ropes," she said quietly. "Knives. Chokers. All his other shit. That's what he liked most. He liked it when you were tied up, he liked it when you were in pain."

Baird blew out a long breath to try to diffuse the anger.

"We'd already made a plan," Marie went on. "Beth's plan. She was out there already, waiting."

"With the bow and arrow?"

"Yeah. We got to the woods, and Greg did his thing. I knew he was going to try to... try to hurt me. He didn't even bother to get dressed. He just came out in his robe, he was that desperate to... you know. He tied my wrists, he had me on the ground, and... I didn't think Beth was there, it took her so long... I thought he was going to..."

The memory seemed too awful for her to speak it aloud, but she struggled on.

"Then Beth jumped him. She shot him, got him in the side, and... fuck, it didn't do anything. He got up, ran at her, the arrow in him and everything. She hit him again, in the gut, and he still wouldn't go down. I thought he was going to kill her, but she's a good shot, she kept her calm. She had to get four arrows in him before he dropped."

Her expression was of somebody caught in a nightmare, her eyes staring at a horror that only she could see.

"We used his own ropes to tie him to the tree. He still wasn't dead, not properly, but he was too far gone to fight back. He was... he was still talking, asking us for help. And Beth was going to shoot him again, kill him proper, but then she asked me if I wanted to."

Marie lifted her head to the dark sky, her tears bright in the headlights.

"You must think we're all monsters, but you've never been there, never been... You didn't see what he did to us."

"You could have told somebody," said Connell. "You could have walked away."

"Yeah?" she said, although the truth was written into her face.

Some people don't get to walk away.

"We would have helped you," Connell said.

"You can help me now," Marie said, wiping away more tears.

"Too late," said Briggs, extinguishing her cigarette beneath her heel. "You tried to kill three of my officers. The *good cop* train left the station this evening. You get to ride the bad cop wagon all the way to deep shit canyon."

Marie hung her head, sighing.

"You took the shot?" said Baird. "At Greg?"

He didn't think she was going to answer, but she did.

"Yeah. I shot him. Beth pulled out three of her arrows, she let me have one. I took the shot while Beth brought his car to the hotel, picked up a couple of the others so they could have a go. One shot each. I drove them back to work after, did the next round. Not much room in that car but we piled in. It's not far. We made sure there were always plenty of us at the club, so nobody would notice, made sure we were on the cameras. But we all did our bit."

"You used Savlon," said Baird. "Disinfectant. Why?"

She spat out a laugh.

"Because he always did. When he hurt us. He liked it because it stings."

"Who cut off his heid?"

"Beth," she said, without hesitation. "That was her idea, too. She knew this story, about Saint Edmund. Carl had told it to her. He was obsessed with English kings, he had new windows done for the chapel, Edmund was in one of them. Beth figured if we made Greg's death look like something like that, it would point away from us."

"And towards Carl," said Baird.

She nodded.

"It was her idea for us all to defend him. She said it would make him look more guilty. Her idea for us to say Greg was a nice guy, too. Take any suspicion away from us."

"Clever," said Baird.

"And the figurines?" asked Briggs. "The animals?"

"Gifts from Greg," Baird told her. "He gave them to everyone, aye?"

"A souvenir," spat Marie. "A little piece of Greg, so we wouldn't forget our time with him. Not that anyone ever could. He made you keep them, made you show him your animal every time you came to his room. He'd punish you if you didn't have it."

She shuddered again.

"Sounds stupid, right? We wanted to bury him with all those little pieces of *us*, so he'd always remember his last moments. All the pain, all the blood. All his screams, all those promises he tried to make. So he'd always know that we won. We were all supposed to throw them in the box. Twelve of us. I didn't even know Tracey had kept hers. So bloody stupid. I don't know why she kept it. She was his favourite. I was the one he trusted, but she was the one he liked most. Some of the things he did to her..."

She stared at Baird, her fury burning inside her.

"So yeah, we all did it. But I don't know when he actually died. I don't know which arrow killed him. You can't charge us all with murder."

"*Law and Order: Ipswich Division* is wrong again," said Baird. "Because we can do exactly that."

"Even though it was self-defence? Even though he deserved it?"

"You cannae just murder people, Marie," he said, adjusting his position against the cold wall to relieve the ache in his shoulder. "No matter what they've done. It disnae work like that."

She hissed out a laugh, shaking her head.

"You don't understand. How could you? The wounds that men like him give you, they never close. It doesn't matter how much time you have, doesn't matter what you do to try to fix yourself, you can never truly heal. He deserved it."

Baird didn't reply.

"He deserved what happened," Marie said again. "Say it."

The seconds ticked by like gunshots.

"Aye," said Baird, after a small eternity. "He deserved it."

For the briefest of seconds, a tired smile landed on Marie's lips. Then the paramedics slammed the ambulance doors on the far side of the lawn, and her head jerked up.

"Wait," she said, struggling over the grass. "I have to go with her, she can't be on her own."

Briggs nodded to the waiting PCs, who tackled Marie to the lawn before she could reach the ambulance. The woman struggled beneath them, screaming her fury into the dirt.

"It's not right! It's not right!"

"Come on," said the paramedic who'd spoken to Baird before. "Let's get you in an ambulance. You want a stretcher?"

"A motorised scooter'll do me," he said, letting her help him up. Briggs took his other arm, holding him a little too tight. The pain in his shoulder flared. "Ach, ma'am, that's tender."

"I know," she said, giving him a not-so-gentle tug.

He walked past Marie as she was being helped back to her feet, her wrists handcuffed, and here he stopped.

"There's one thing I dinnae understand," he said. "You killed Greg on Friday night. Why did you go back on Saturday? You were in the woods in the morning, aye?"

Marie nodded, trying to scrub away the tears on her shoulders.

"Why do you think?" she asked.

It took him a moment to realise he'd known the answer all along.

"The dug? You took her with you?"

"Tracey did. She didn't dare leave Dizzy in the hotel. Carl hates animals, if he'd found the dog he'd... I don't know. It wouldn't have been good. She always managed to hide her, when she was on duty. We all helped. Beth kept the SIM card in her collar because she knew nobody would find it there. But Trace was too scared to leave without the dog. So she brought her, and somewhere in the... in the frenzy, she vanished. It was too dangerous to stay and look for her, in case somebody came, and we thought she might make her own way back. When she didn't show up, I went back to find her in the morning. Found a bunch of people instead."

"You attacked one of them. A girl called Flora. Why?"

Marie frowned.

"A girl?" she said, shaking her head. "No, I didn't."

"Somebody from the hotel did," said Baird. "She stumbled onto Greg's body, and one of yous knocked her oot so she wouldnae talk. Put her in the hospital."

"It wasn't us," she said. "I was the only one there, and I left as soon as I saw them."

The PCs started to steer her towards a police car, but she resisted them.

"The young woman, Flora, she was there with a guy, right? I saw them together."

"Aye," said Baird.

Marie spat out a bitter laugh.

"Then you don't need me to tell you what happened. Open wounds. We're all so full of them, it's a wonder any of us survive."

And with that, she was gone—shepherded into a police car, the door closing behind her.

"What a chuffing mess," said Baird.

There was another clatter as the fire door opened, a tactical officer appearing. He had his rifle stowed, and he pulled up his visor as he shouted across the garden.

"We've got ten in custody," he said. "We expecting any more?"

Before anyone could answer, a tiny ball of fuzz burst between his legs, thundering across the grass like a rocket. The little chihuahua made a beeline for the ambulances, but she must have caught wind of something because she suddenly cut right, her legs a blur as she ran towards Baird.

"Diana!" he cried out. "Here, girl."

The dog practically leapt into his arms, her eyes bulging, her tail thumping. He held her tight, laughing even though it hurt to do so. The dog's tongue flapped over her crooked teeth, licking his lips, his nose, his eyes.

"Alright, alright," he said, still giggling. "No in public, Di. There's people watching."

The dog started licking his neck, too, trying to get to the bloody wound in his shoulder. He pulled her away.

"Hey! I'm no a snack!"

"Come on," said Briggs, steering Baird over the manicured lawns. "You can snog the dog in the morning. You, Harrison, need to get to hospital. Then I'm going to stick you on a cattle train back to Aberdeen, because in three weeks you've caused more mayhem in our quiet corner of the world than we've seen in twenty odd years."

"Sounds good, ma'am," he said, clinging onto the wriggling dog. "Southwold's too dangerous for a quiet guy like me."

They rounded the corner of the hotel and he saw the driveway ahead, full to bursting with emergency vehicles. He was about ready to keel over, and the thought of a cup of tea and a slice of buttery toast in a hospital bed was like heaven. But when he glanced at Connell, he saw the same thoughts on her face that were circling his brain.

"He wasn't just taking photos, was he?" she said.

"Nut," said Baird. "Can it wait?"

"Justice doesn't wait," she said, socking a fist into her free hand.

"Good lord, Connell," barked Briggs. "You're not MacGyver. Baird. Hospital. Now."

"I'm going, ma'am," he said. "But if you dinnae mind, there's something we need to do on the way."

THEY MUST HAVE MADE some sight, walking down the path of the semi-detached house on the south side of Southwold. Baird took the lead, his wound bandaged by the paramedics but his shirt drenched in blood. Behind him was Connell, caked in dirt, her hair bristling with fronds of ivy. DCI Briggs trod on their heels, sucking on another cigarette like a diver chugging air after almost drowning.

Behind all of them were four uniformed PCs, armed with Tasers.

Baird pounded on the front door, and a few seconds later it opened. A familiar greasy face stared up at him, about as flabbergasted as anyone Baird had ever seen. The young man was wearing a set of blue, striped pyjamas and bright red socks, and in his hand was a three-foot wooden pole that looked like it had been waxed to within an inch of its life. The smell of lemons wafted out of the hallway, strong enough to make Baird's mouth water.

"Lucas," said Baird. "You remember me?"

"Uh..." said the young man, staring at Baird's shoulder. "What's going on? Is that *blood*?"

"Aye, it belonged to the last bawheid who pished me off. You ken why we're here?"

"Uh... No. I was released. You're not allowed to charge me again."

He lifted the stick like he was planning on hitting somebody with it, and Baird tugged it out of his chubby hand.

"Is this your pizzle stick, you sad wee man?" he said.

Lucas nodded. Baird sniffed it, the scent of citrus even stronger.

"Lemon wax, am I right?"

He passed the stick to Connell, then gave Lucas the wildest, loon-eyed, nostrils flared and teeth bared grin he could muster. It must have worked, because the boy shrank back into the front hall of his house. A middle-aged woman appeared at the end of the corridor, wearing a pink dressing gown and holding a mug. She just about keeled over when she saw the legion of police at the door.

"Luke?" she said. "What's going on?"

"Nothing, Mum," said Lucas, just a squeak. "Listen, I told you, taking photographs of people isn't illegal, I—"

"You want me to tell you what *is* illegal, son?" said Baird, stepping into the house and looming over him. "Smacking a woman around the heid, knocking her oot, and assaulting her."

"I didn't assault her!" Lucas said. "There wasn't time!"

He clapped his soft hands to his mouth as if he could shove the words back inside.

"Lucas!" said the woman.

Baird grabbed the young man by the collar of his pyjama top, hauling him through the door like a bag of wet mince.

"Lucas Bude, you are under arrest—again—for GBH and sexual assault."

He hurled the boy to the nearest PC. The cuffs were on in a heartbeat, and he was dragged up the path in his stocking feet to the IRVs parked outside.

"And for being the stickiest wee jobbie on the planet. You dinnae have to say anything, but... Och, you must remember the rest of it from this morning."

Baird watched as the lad was shoved into the back of an IRV, then he flashed Connell a tired smile. He got one right back.

"We did good, sir," she said.

"Aye, Connie, we did," he replied, the world swaying around him like he was a kid again, being swung in mad circles by his da. He planted a hand on the wall, belching acid. "But do you mind if I pass oot now?"

CHAPTER THIRTY-SEVEN

Wednesday

Three days after he unceremoniously keeled over on the Bude family's doorstep, Baird made his way gingerly up the steps that led to Southwold Constabulary's seaside headquarters. He had to stop at the top, because his ribs still ached so much he couldn't get a breath in. The wound in his shoulder had improved thanks to a few nights in hospital, but it still hurt to lift his arm higher than his waist.

Still, it was braw to be alive.

He opened the door, taking a step inside before an invisible, mullet-scented mallet smacked him right in the face. He gagged, trying not to inhale the fishy stench of whatever was bubbling inside the kitchen. He didn't have to ask what it was. DI Henry Crump stood by the cooker, wearing an apron and using a wooden spoon to poke at a saucepan like he was trying to ward off an evil spirit.

"That fish stew should be illegal, pal," Baird said as he made for the Incident Room. "I'm about to pass oot, *again*."

"It's not fish stew," said Crump, frowning. "It's spaghetti bolognaise."

"*How?*"

He pushed through the door, slamming it behind him and leaning against it. DCI Briggs sat at the dining table, a steaming mug of tea beside her. DC Connell stood on a chair, pulling photographs and documents from the wall. Baird was surprised to see PC Tall Paul here as well, leaning against the wall by the window. He was dressed in tracksuit trousers and trainers, the bandages visible beneath his T-shirt.

Diana the dog lay on her back on a pile of blankets, her eyes closed, her tongue hanging so far past her overbite that Baird wasn't sure if she was sleeping or dead.

Either way, the smell of her was doing its bit to counter the aroma from the kitchen.

"Does everything that man cooks stink of fish?" Baird asked, hobbling to a spare chair.

"Yes," said Briggs. "Don't ever try his custard."

She watched Baird take his seat like a hawk watches a sparrow land on a branch.

"How are you feeling, Harrison?"

"No bad," he said, wincing as he sat back. "Considering I was shot with an arrow."

"Technically, you weren't actually *shot*," said Tall Paul, rubbing his chest. "You were grazed."

"Same thing!" Baird protested.

"Not really, sir," said Connell, stepping clumsily down from her chair.

"I had an arrow *inside* me," said Paul. "Two inches to

the left and it would have pierced my heart. You got a scratch on the shoulder."

"I got shot!" he said.

"Paul has been signed off on injury leave," said Briggs. "He just came by to hand in his paperwork."

"Can I get signed off?" said Baird.

"No," she said.

Baird slumped in his chair hard enough to scrape it backwards. The noise woke Diana, who sat bolt upright like Dracula, one eye checking the ceiling, the other finding him. She scrabbled to her feet with all the grace of a clockwork toy that's been through a blender, skittering over with a couple of sneezing barks. He lifted her onto his lap, rubbing her belly when she rolled over. Connell had bought her a new collar, black leather studded with diamanté. A little silver bone tag hung from it.

"You believe me, right?" he said to the dog. "I was shot."

"Keep me updated," said Briggs as Tall Paul made his way to the door.

"Will do, ma'am," he said, stepping outside and flashing Baird a smile. "Good luck with the scratch, sir."

He'd closed the door before Baird could think of a reply.

"In all seriousness," said Briggs, lifting her tea. "How are you. Graze or not, you went through a horrific ordeal."

He didn't answer immediately, scratching the dog behind her ears, enjoying the Hoover-in-the-bath sound she always made when she was getting a fuss.

"I'm no gonna say I'm alright, ma'am," he said eventually. "But I will be, in time. Aye, Connie?"

"I hope so, sir," Connell said, putting down the stack of papers and dropping into the chair she'd been standing on.

She looked older than she had before the weekend, the lines on her forehead more pronounced, her eyes dulled.

He'd seen it before, of course. In himself, in every other polis officer. It's what the job did to the poor folk who were crazy enough to do it.

"Well, for what it's worth, I think you saved some lives," said Briggs. "From what we've been able to gather from our interviews with the staff involved in Greg's murder, he wasn't the only person they planned to kill."

"No?" said Baird.

"No. The twelve of them had agreed that if they got away with this execution, they were going to target some of the other residents of the hotel. You were right, Connell, it was a cabal, of sorts. A cult. Bethany was the leader, but they were all willing participants."

"Bethany's awake?" asked Baird.

Briggs nodded, taking another swallow of tea.

"She's not said much, but Marie's doing the talking for her. I think she takes some kind of pride in what happened. They did a terrible thing, but she's convinced it was for the right reason."

"Maybe she's right, ma'am," said Connell. "Gregory Brightwell really was a monster. We raided his house yesterday, found his secret trove of... of..."

She obviously couldn't find the word.

"He filmed most of his encounters with the staff," Briggs went on. "Used the tapes to blackmail them into silence. And not just them, either. He abused people all over the world, dozens of them. You know the china animals came from Serbia? We've been in touch with the police in Belgrade. Brightwell was there filming the Doolittle thing, and his visit coincided with some of the worst attacks on sex workers they've ever seen. It's vile."

"His wife had no idea?" asked Baird.

"She idolised him," said Connell. "*Everyone* idolised

him. It made him a god, meant he could do anything he wanted, to anybody, with impunity."

"Until he got his heid cut off," said Baird.

"Indeed," said Briggs. "Needless to say, it's all going to come out. Brightwell's dead, and his legacy will be too."

"They're going to be charged?" Baird asked. "All twelve of them?

"Yes, although I doubt we'll be able to successfully prosecute every individual. Nor should we. There are some extremely vulnerable members of the group."

She sighed, shaking her head.

"Disnae seem right, ma'am," said Baird. He pictured Bethany, driven mad by the violence of her past. Marie and Tracey too. He wondered what he would have done in their situation.

When he looked at Connell, he saw the same doubts written large over her round face.

"It doesn't," said Briggs. "But thankfully it isn't our job to decide what's right and what's wrong. It's our job to stop the bad things from happening."

"Justice," said Connell, slapping a fist into the palm of her hand so hard that Diana fell off his knee in shock. The little dog shook herself, skittering beneath the table.

"Speaking of which, what's happened to our other suspects?" he asked.

"Bruce Fishbourne and Karen Kirby have both been released," said Briggs.

"Although if you ask me," added Connell, "Bruce committed the worst crime of all, betraying his readers."

"Is that really worse than cutting somebody's heid off?"

She nodded decisively.

"And what about Denton?" asked Baird, although he had a feeling he wouldn't like the answer.

"Also released," said Briggs.

"From a catapult?"

"We had no choice, Harrison. He claims Bethany called him on Friday night, just before midnight, asking him to meet her north of the Benacre woods. Phone records confirm it. I think she probably told him it was a drug-related matter, which is why he didn't tell us. She wasn't there when he arrived, so he went straight back."

"Which meant he didnae have an alibi," said Baird. "But his car would have been spotted at the scene of the crime. Clever."

"Too clever," said Briggs. "They've given him exactly what you said he liked, Connie, plausible deniability. He claims to know nothing about the drugs, or the abuse. It was Bethany who called Carl from Greg's phone, too. He was already dead by then. CPS want to focus their energies on Bethany and the others."

"That hardly seems fair," said Baird.

"The good news is that thanks to the SIM you found, we have a list of every guest of the hotel who bought narcotics or other services from the staff. They'll all be questioned. At the very least, Denton's Club is finished."

"Better than a kick to the bawbag, I suppose," he said. "But no as good as a kick to *his* bawbag."

"I'd like you to leave his *bawbag* well alone," Briggs told him. "One of these days, he'll mess up, and when that happens you can do whatever you like with his testicles."

Baird grimaced.

"Until then," she went on, "we need to decide what to do with *you*. Despite the chaos you've caused, that's two cases successfully put to bed. You and Connell make a damn good team. So are you staying, or are you going?"

Baird puffed out a breath, trying to work out how long it

would be until he could pop another painkiller. It took him a while to find an answer.

"You ken, I've come closer to death more times in this wee toon than during my entire career with Police Scotland, and I've only been here three weeks. I've been chased with guns, shot with arrows—"

"Grazed," said Connell.

"I've almost drooned in the North Sea—twice—and in a duckpond to boot, thanks to Connell and her pedalo. I've been run off the road, half of Suffolk's had a swing at me, and worst of all, you keep trying to make me eat Henry's food. This place is hazardous to my health."

Diana wandered out from beneath the table, snoofling at his shoe.

"But if I leave now, who's gonna take care of my dug?"

Briggs laughed.

"I told you, ma'am," said Connell, grinning. "Check the tag, sir."

Baird plonked the dog back onto his lap, lifting the silver, bone-shaped fob to see his surname and his brand new mobile number. On the other side was a single word: *Diana*. His laugh filled the room.

"I don't think she can be called anything else now, sir," said Connell. "And she can't go back to her old owner. Whether Tracey goes away or not, she didn't exactly take good care of her."

"Will you do it?" asked Briggs.

"Look after this daft potato?" said Baird, running his hand down the bumps of the dog's spine. "I dinnae think she'll get on with my cat. But I suppose so, if nobody else will."

Diana barked, although he didn't know if it was a celebration or a protest.

"I meant will you *stay*?" said Briggs with a weary sigh.

"It's... it's complicated, ma'am," he said.

"Well uncomplicate it," she told him, pointing to the lone poster which remained on the stark, staple-strewn wall. "We need you for dodgeball, remember. If you can be grazed by an arrow and still walk, you can take a ball to the face."

"Shot!" Baird protested. "She bloody shot me!"

The door to the Incident Room opened and DI Crump walked in, wearing a cloak of smoke and fish-fumes.

"Somebody at the door for you, Harry," he said.

"Who?"

"Old geezer, looks a bit like you would if you spent a couple of weeks in the tumble drier."

"Christ," said Baird. He lowered the dog to the floor and pushed himself out of his chair, flexing his shoulder to try to ease the pain.

"Who is it?" Briggs asked.

"Like I said, it's complicated."

He set off for the door, looking back when he reached it.

"I'll give you my decision by the end of the month, aye?"

Briggs nodded. Connell held up a slim, black lead.

"Since you're on your way out, sir, can you take your dog for a wee?"

"A wee what?" he asked.

HE KNEW who would be waiting for him at the front door of HQ, but seeing the old man there was still like a punch to the throat.

Dougie Baird looked like a rodent that had spent too long in an underground lab before being released into the world. He cowered just outside the threshold, his skinny body bent almost double. He had one hand to his balding head to shield his face from the sun, and through his shadow his expression was one of profound anxiety. He jerked around when he heard Diana barking, flinching at the sight of Baird as he walked up the corridor.

"They let you oot?" asked Baird.

"It's not a prison," he said. "I'm allowed out anytime, I just don't like it. Too fucking bright out here. Too many arseholes."

"It's England," said Baird as an explanation.

He walked outside, waiting for the dog to trip over the step before closing the door behind him. Diana sniffed at his da's foot, then sneezed so hard she fell onto her haunches.

"You allergic to bullshit too?" Baird asked her.

"What?" said Dougie, trying to stroke the chihuahua's face with his trainer. "Still got your bug-eyed mirkin, then? You know, you always wanted a dog when you were a kid. You remember the one we got you?"

"Nut," said Baird, setting off towards the street. "We had a dug?"

Dougie followed, bow-legged and struggling with every step.

"Yeah, I got you one. You and Elspy. Lovely wee thing it was, no trouble."

"A *dug*?" said Baird. He couldn't remember it, but then most of his childhood was a black gulf of missing things—his father being the main one.

"Aye, Harry, a dog." Dougie frowned. "Well, it was dog-*like*. Close enough that you believed it was a dog. More of a dog than the toad you've got now, for sure."

"You mean Sampson?" said Baird. "The guinea pig? I kent that wasnae a dug, Da."

"Oh," said Dougie, using the gate as a crutch as he limped through it. "Well, the point is..."

He stopped walking like his batteries had run out, cocking his head. Even after everything, it hurt Baird's heart to see his old man like this, to see the way he struggled to keep his train of thought. It was like somebody had opened his head and pulled out half the stuffing.

"What are you doing here, Da?" said Baird.

He walked slowly south along the coastal road, letting the dog lead the way. She rooted in every piss-splattered weed and flinched at every car that drove past. It was mid-afternoon, the slim beach packed with kids on their way home from school. The gulls soared overhead, diving every time they saw a lobbed chip, their cries imitating the shouts and laughter from below. The sea was a slab of solid silver, flecked with gold from the sun overhead. As always, the horizon looked close enough to swim to, and too good to be true.

"Just wanted to say hello," said Dougie, finally answering the question.

"Twenty-four years you managed no to say hello, and now you're so desperate to do it you get a taxi from the home?"

"Come on," whined Dougie, trying to keep up.

"You didnae want to say hello when I was in the hospital all week? At death's door?"

"You were in the hospital? How was I supposed to know that, Harry? What happened?"

"I was shot," he said.

"With a *gun*?"

"A bow and arrow, Da."

"Oh," said Dougie, sniffing. "Don't think that counts. You alright?"

"Aye," he said, well aware that his da didn't know him well enough to see the lie.

He crossed the quiet street, heading down the slope onto the promenade. His shoulder was killing him from holding the lead, so he unclipped Diana and let her go. She tore down the steps onto the beach, making it all of ten yards before face-planting in the sand. She didn't seem bothered, running in mad circles as she tried to catch the flapping gulls.

"Careful, quine, they'll eat you whole," Baird called after her. "What do you really want, *Dougie*?"

His da sniffed again, shuffling along like a zombie. He looked over his shoulder before answering, like he was expecting somebody to be there.

"Just wondered if you'd thought about what I told you the other day," he said.

Baird hadn't stopped thinking about it, but he didn't want to give him the satisfaction of knowing that.

"You'll have to remind me."

"Come on, mate," said Dougie. There was something in the tone of his voice that reminded Baird of a junkie trying to negotiate a discount from his dealer, and he felt the slow burn of his anger.

"*Mate*?" he said, looking back to where his da limped after him. "I'm your mate now, am I? Now that you need me for something?"

"It's not like that, Harry. You're getting all mixed up. Look, you're losing your rag with the wrong person. I didn't do this to us, remember? It was *him*."

"So you keep saying," muttered Baird, kicking pebbles off the promenade. He didn't know where he was going, he just felt like he had to keep moving so that his father wouldn't catch up. "And what do you need me to do, exactly?"

"Nothing," said Dougie, wheezing now. "Just look into it, yeah? Just see what you can find out about him."

"About Robert Kett," said Baird, and it wasn't a question. He thought about the board he'd made in his flat, about everything Norman Balls had told him. "I've found oot plenty, Da. I dinnae want any part of him, or of this."

"Look," Dougie said again. He grabbed the sleeve of Baird's jacket, pulling hard enough to stop him. He turned to face his father—or the poor imitation of his father who stood there, hollowed out and half-formed. "Son, I wouldn't ask if I didn't think you could do something. He stole from us, he stole all those years, all those memories. Don't you think he owes us? Eh?"

"You want *money* oot of him?" said Baird, spitting a laugh. "That it, Da?"

Dougie stepped back, shaking his head. He looked like he was melting in the sun, his scalp slick with sweat, his face dripping. He smelled bad, like rubbish left out for too long. Beneath that, beneath the old man reek of him, Baird could still make out the same aftershave he'd always used—just the faintest trace, but enough that it could have knocked him off his feet.

"I want him to pay," said Dougie. "Not money, Harry. It's not about money. But I want him to pay for what he did."

"It's an open wound, Da," said Baird. "Sometimes it's better to let them heal."

"I can't," he said. "That's the whole fucking point. I can't fix anything until he's..."

He gritted his yellow teeth, jutting out his chin, leaving it unsaid.

"Fuck's sake," said Baird, turning away and carrying on down the promenade. His shoulder was throbbing something wicked, the pain rolling down his injured ribcage and settling in his back.

"You need to find Kett, Harry," Dougie went on. "You need to meet him."

"I do, do I?"

"It's the only way you'll know. You need to look him in the eye. Look him in the eye and let him see."

"Let him see what? That I want to take him for dinner? Have his babies? I'm no staring him in the eyes, Da."

"Let him see that we know the truth," Dougie went on, undeterred. "That we know what he did, know who he killed. Let him feel the same fear that I did, all them years ago. Every fucking year since. You'll know, Harry. As soon as you look him in the face, you'll know he's guilty."

Down on the beach, Diana was barking at the shallow waves like she could turn back the tide. Baird called her and she trotted back up onto the walkway. She looked as wide-eyed and out of breath as his da did.

"Fine," he said, still walking. "I'll meet him."

"Aye?" said Dougie, letting out a hoarse laugh. "You'll do it? Good lad. How you gonna make it happen?"

"Leave that with me," he said.

The dog contorted herself into a crooked squat, her eyes bulging like a balloon animal. Baird patted his pockets, realising he didn't have any bags.

"Least you know which end's the head now," said Dougie.

He gave his da the visual equivalent of a strong slap. Dougie stepped back, his hands up in surrender. He seemed to have shrunk even in the little time they'd been strolling down the beach, like he was a kid and Baird was a parent.

He suddenly pictured his old man as a boy—full of quiet hope the way all kids were, no idea of the tragic life that was ahead of him—and he hated the wave of sympathy that rolled through him. Because he saw *himself* there too, so like his father, so unlike him.

"Fuck's sake," he said again. "Look, Da, I'm gonna walk doon the beach a bit, get some air. You're welcome to come, as long as you leave the past where it is. Aye?"

Dougie shrugged, staring out to sea.

"You're alright, mate," he said, talking to the water. "Got some stuff to do."

"Aye, you got what you want from me. Now it's time to fuck off. I'll see you in, what?" He checked his watch. "2048?"

His dad turned back, pulling a face like he'd stepped in Diana's mess.

"Doesn't suit you, Harry, all the moaning. You're your mother's son, for sure."

"Aye, and thank God for that, *mate*," said Baird, who was resisting every urge to drown his father in the North Sea.

Dougie turned about like a drunken sailor, heading back up the walkway.

"Get it fixed, Harry," he shouted back.

"I'll get you fixed, you old fart," Baird muttered.

He used a receipt to collect Diana's Malteaser-sized turd, posting it into a bin as he carried on walking. He focussed on putting as many steps as he could between him and Dougie, the town shrinking away behind him, the land opening up into the sandy meadows that edged the harbour. Only here did he start to feel calmer, but even the breeze that blew in from the water did little to dampen the anger.

It wasn't just his father, he knew. It was everything that

had happened since he'd arrived here. First Sophie Keeble, locked away for trying to protect her family. Now Bethany and Marie and the others, whose only crime was trying to heal a wound that had been torn open by a properly evil bastard. They got to spend the best part of their lives in prison, while Carl Denton enjoyed his freedom with impunity, and Gregory Brightwell got to sleep beneath the dirt, oblivious.

"It's no fair, is it, pal?" he asked the little dog, who was close to collapsing from the effort of the walk and the heat of the sun.

He picked her up, letting her rest her head on his shoulder and patting her backside like she was a baby. The sea whispered over the beach, a soft conversation that was picked up by the shifting sand as it was lifted by the breeze, then by the stalks of seagrass who seemed to shiver in delight at whatever news they'd just heard. It confirmed what he already knew: that as beautiful as it was here, this was a place of secrets, of dark truths and quiet horrors.

All the more reason to head north, he thought.

To go home.

"Come on," he said, spluttering out a sigh. "I ken what'll cheer us up."

He carried Diana to the road, heading into the car park at the harbour. There was a small queue outside Samara's ice cream shack, and he joined the back of it. They were mostly school kids who went gaga at the sight of the chihuahua, coming close for a tickle. She seemed to enjoy the attention a little too much, because when he finally reached the counter he realised she'd left a damp patch on his shirt.

"I think your dog's peed on you," said Sam.

"Aye," he said. "I thought it might cool me doon."

The dog was struggling to get away, and when Sam held out her hands he passed her over. She hugged the chihuahua to her chest, giving her kisses and laughing when Diana gave them back.

"You ever find out who she belongs to?"

"Apparently, it's me," he told her. "Diana Baird. It's got a nice ring to it."

Sam plopped the dog down, then lifted the hatch.

"You want to get out of the sun?"

"For a minute," he said, stepping into the welcome shade of the building.

"I know, don't worry," she said, closing it behind him. "You're not hanging around."

There was nobody else waiting, so she opened the door and they stepped into the dark interior together. Baird rubbed his aching shoulder, feeling the padded ridge of the bandage beneath his jacket.

"What's your poison?" Sam asked, filling a bowl in the sink and putting it down for the dog. Diana just about fell into it in her desperation to rehydrate.

"I'm braw, honest," he said.

She opened the fridge and pulled out a Diet Coke anyway, offering it to him. He took it, enjoying the ice-cold bubbles for as long as it took for them to hit his head.

"Urgh," he said. "Brain freeze."

"Suck your thumb," said Sam.

"Huh?"

"Your thumb," she said. "Press it against the roof of your mouth. Best cure for brain freeze. Trust me, I'm an ice cream salesperson."

He did as she said, tasting sand and saltwater and wondering if he should have washed his hands first. Sure enough, though, the pain began to ebb.

"The only downside is you're now a grown man sucking his thumb," she said with a laugh.

He laughed too, wiping his hand on his trousers. Diana finished drinking, jumping onto the couch with no small effort. She plodded in circles for a moment before dropping into what looked like a coma. Sam peeked through the door to make sure nobody was in the queue, then turned back.

"Look, I'm sorry about the other day," she said. "All the stuff I said. I... you didn't need to know all that."

"Dinnae be sorry," he told her. "I'm glad you told me."

"It's just..." She swung her arms like she didn't know what to do with them. "When you mentioned him, Carl, it all came back, you know? And..."

She spluttered out a long breath.

"He's always there. Lives rent free inside my head. Sometimes I can, you know... hide him, behind other stuff. I can rearrange it all so he doesn't seem so big. But he's always there. He got arrested, right?"

Baird nodded.

"He's going away?"

The hope on her face was almost unbearable.

"No this time," he said. "I'm sorry, Sam."

Her expression crumpled, but only for a heartbeat. She nodded, her arms still swinging, then she forced her face into a smile she obviously didn't feel.

"Hey," said Baird, putting down the Coke.

He caught her hands as they swung up, and he held on tight.

"Sam, you're alright," he said. "Carl's a free man, but he's finished. The hotel is done, it'll close. He's no gonna hang around in Southwold."

"Yeah, he will," she said, pulling one hand free to wipe

away a tear. "But it's okay. I'll be okay. Survived this long, haven't I?"

She went to pull her other hand free, but he held on.

"Don't, Harrison," she said. "I'm no good at saying goodbye."

"Me neither," he said. "So maybe I'll hang aboot for a while."

All those reasons to leave, all those reasons to head back to Aberdeen.

Maybe he only needed one good reason to stay.

"Yeah?" said Sam, squeezing his hand.

"Aye," he said.

There was a knock from outside, a teenage boy's voice.

"Yo! Ice cream lady! Where you gone?"

Sam reached up and touched Baird's face, her fingers hot. When she pulled away again, after what could have been seconds or could have been years, she seemed to take the warmth of the day with her.

Baird picked up Diana, who didn't even stir from her slumber, and opened the back door of the shack. Sam watched him go.

"So I'll see you around, then, Harrison Baird?" she asked.

He smiled.

"Aye. I think you will."

CHAPTER THIRTY-EIGHT

Saturday

"ARE YOU SURE YOU'RE UP FOR THIS, HARRISON?"

Baird sat in the café at Norwich Sportspark, a huge leisure centre next to the city's sprawling university. It was mobbed in here, a hundred or so people milling between the tables and most of them in the queue. The noise was out of this world, a thunder of voices and laughter that would have been intimidating if Baird didn't already know that everybody here was police. It was so loud that he didn't realise DCI Briggs was speaking to him until she tapped him on the arm.

"Earth to DI Baird. Are you going to be okay?"

"Aye," he said, looking at her across the table. She was dressed in a velvet burgundy tracksuit. Even though he couldn't see it right now, because she was sitting down, he knew it had the word 'Juicy' sequinned across the bum. "I'm braw."

That was a lie, of course. He felt like a piñata after a birthday party, beaten into chunks then thrown in the bin. It had been a couple of weeks since that night in Denton's hotel, and the wound in his shoulder—which had, in the end, been little more than a graze—still stung something terrible. The last thing in the world he needed to be doing right now was taking part in the East Anglian Constabulary's Annual Dodgeball Tournament.

And yet here he was.

"Braw?" said Connell, who sat in the chair beside him wearing what could only be described as a school PE kit: a yellowing white polo shirt, a pleated black skirt and plimsols that looked older than she did. "You mean hungry? Shall I get you something, sir?"

She glanced at the line, which stretched as far back as the doors.

"It might take a while."

"I'm fine," he said.

"You just seem a little distracted," said Briggs, and she clicked her fingers in his face. "I need focus, Baird. I'm not planning on losing today."

Baird glanced at Briggs in her Juicy leisurewear, then at Connell, and finally at DI Crump on the opposite side of the table, who seemed to have fallen asleep in his chair halfway through eating a tuna sandwich. Only the two constables who'd accompanied them here from Lowestoft HQ seemed like they'd know what to do with a dodgeball, but they'd both vanished.

Like rats from a sinking ship, he thought.

"I wouldnae worry, ma'am," he said. "This is a team of champions for sure."

He *was* distracted, though. How could he not be when

he knew for a fact that somewhere in this building, somewhere in the sprawling crowds, *he* was here.

Robert Kett.

Baird had seen his name on the team roster that had circulated earlier in the week, and even that had stopped his heart dead. The thought of meeting him, of coming face to face with the man who—according to his da, at least—had turned his childhood into a dumpster fire, made him feel like something inside him had come loose.

"I'm fine," he said again.

He pulled out his phone, Diana's squashed muffin of a face on his home screen giving him a moment of happiness for the second or two before he noticed the time.

"Shite," he said. "We'd better move, we're due on court."

Briggs shot up, her sequinned buttocks leading him through the throng and into a corridor that was equally busy. A bunch of coppers were walking out of a door, most of them sweaty and bruised, some bleeding. Baird squeezed past them, entering a large gymnasium that had been partitioned into three courts. The stacked seating was packed with the families of everyone who'd come to take part, the sound of it enough to rattle his bones.

"Christ," he said. "I had no idea dodgeball was so popular."

"It's not the game," explained Connell, "it's the chance to kick the butts of the other constabularies. It's basically a bloodsport."

The two Suffolk constables were waiting for them in the middle court, both big enough and scary enough that they might have been better off competing by themselves. There was a woman there too, dressed in the striped uniform of a referee. Briggs went to talk to her, while Connell began a series of warm-up exercises that looked like a pigeon choking on a breadstick.

Baird took the opportunity to search the room, unsure if he was relieved or disappointed when he didn't see Kett amongst the crowd.

What he did see, though, was a group of what might have been pro-wrestlers walking towards them from the door. The five men and one woman were all wearing matching red and black outfits, including sweatbands around their beefy foreheads, and they looked like they were here to evict somebody.

"Oh crumbs," said Crump, who was still eating his sandwich. "Essex have sent their tactical team again."

"Please tell me we're no up against them?" said Baird.

There was no need for anybody to answer, because the troop of Special Forces Neanderthals marched to the other side of the central court. There they proceeded to do a foot-stamping, arm-waving, tongue-poking version of the Haka which was as intimidating as it was offensive.

"Christ," said Baird. "It was nice knowing you all."

"Don't worry, we've got a secret weapon," said Briggs, walking back over. She flashed Baird a knowing grin. "Connie."

Baird looked at Connell, who was trying and failing to crack her knuckles.

"*That* Connie?"

The referee blew her whistle, the crowd breaking into a round of cheers and whoops that felt loud enough to carry Baird out the door. The Essex team collected their balls, moving into a tight formation that smacked of months of training.

"I want a clean fight," said the referee. "No kicking, no punching, no biting."

"What?" said Baird.

"Any shots to the crotch will be deemed fair, but any ruptures must be declared immediately. I'm not having a repeat of last year's grape crush."

"*What*?"

"Take your balls!" she hollered.

"Take them where? A vault?"

"*Dodge*balls," explained Briggs.

"Christ," muttered Baird, collecting a hard ball from the side of the court. He held it in one hand and placed the other defensively over his groin. "Is it too late to—"

The referee blew her whistle, and a storm of orange missiles sailed across the court. Baird screamed, twisting his body out of the way as one shot past his nethers. Crump wasn't so lucky, mainly because he was facing the wrong way. One ball smacked him in the back of the head so hard that if he'd had false teeth they would have been up in the stands. He dropped onto his hands and knees with a sound like a walrus giving birth.

"Out!" screamed the referee.

The Essex team had already reloaded, another wave of balls breaking the sound barrier as they cut across the court. Baird ducked, sheer dumb luck keeping him safe from the barrage. He was having flashbacks to being shot at in the hotel, his palms so sweaty that when he went to throw his own ball it slipped out of his fingers.

"Shite!"

He scooped it up, lobbing it at one of the cavemen as hard as he could and missing by about twelve feet. He reached for another ball but Connell beat him to it, holding it beneath her chin as she moved evasively back and forth. Her eyes scanned the opposing team, as serious as Baird had ever seen them. She locked onto a target, drew the ball back, then launched it.

"Hai ya!" she shouted, sounding exactly like Miss Piggy.

The ball curved across the court like a David Beckham free kick, smacking one of the Essex team right between the legs. He dropped like a KO'd boxer, his gargled cry louder than the screaming crowds.

"Connie!" exclaimed Baird.

And he would have said more, if he hadn't looked past her at the exact moment Robert Kett walked by the door.

He was gone in an instant, but there was no doubt at all in Baird's mind who he'd just seen. He'd studied that face enough times over the last month, he knew it better than he knew his own. There was no doubt because as soon as he'd seen him, a klaxon of panic had sounded, his heart imploding.

He started walking before he could talk himself out of it, ignoring Briggs and Connell as he left the court. He broke into a jog, almost taking out a member of staff as he crashed through the door. There were so many people out here he almost didn't see where Kett had gone. Then there he was, walking through another door with a bunch of coppers and what looked like three young girls in tow.

Baird hesitated, feeling like he was standing on a ledge before a bungee jump. He didn't know what to do. Behind him, through the open door, he saw Briggs and Connell trying to fend off the Essex team. Back there, he knew, was something that had become familiar, and welcome, and safe. He could run to them now, he could forget all about his father's bullshit.

He could let the wound heal.

But his da was right. This was the only way he'd know for sure.

The room next door was another cavernous gymnasium, as busy as the one he'd just left. Teams were warming up next to the courts, the drum of balls and the noise of the crowd riotous. It took him a moment to find Kett again. He'd moved to the edge of the room, putting down his bag and pulling off his hoodie. He wore black shorts and a black T-shirt over his lean frame.

He looked older than Baird had been expecting, older than anyone should look at his age. It wasn't just the years, he knew. He looked like a man who was weighed down by a lifetime of baggage.

Or a lifetime of guilt.

There were a bunch of people with Kett, and Baird realised he knew one of them. It was Norman Balls, dressed in cricket whites—including leg defenders, a helmet, and the biggest groin box Baird had ever seen. There was another man wearing what looked like blue and gold pyjamas, chatting on his phone, plus a couple of younger people dressed in black: a muscly fella with a beard who had one arm around a serious-looking woman with a pixie cut. An older man in a shite-coloured tracksuit stood in the middle of the group, managing—somewhat impressively—to spew out a constant stream of obscenities at the same time as cramming Bounties into his mouth.

When the man had finished shouting, Kett returned to his daughter—down on one knee, helping her fix her ponytail. She must have been seven or eight, and the way she gazed at her father as he sorted her hair did strange things to Baird's stomach. It had been a long time since he'd seen a look so full of love.

There were two other girls. One was older, a teenager, and she'd dropped into a chair to stare at her phone. Next to her was a woman in a blue dress with honey-coloured hair, whose attractive face was creased with worry. The youngest child was tearing about like a curly-haired gremlin, picking up loose balls and hurling them in random directions. She lobbed one at the teenager hard enough to send her phone flying, and the resulting scream of rage caused the gym to fall silent for a second or two.

Kett gathered the two younger girls into a hug, speaking to them. He beckoned to the older one and she grudgingly joined them, their arms wrapped around each other. It hurt Baird's heart to see them like that, and for a moment he didn't know why.

Then they parted, and the girls laughed at something their father had said, and the sudden understanding was worse than the not knowing.

Because Baird had looked at *his* father that way, a million years ago—with that same unconditional devotion. He'd loved his da with every atom of his being, and when Dougie had upped and left it had cut a hole in him that nothing had been able to fill.

Nothing except the anger.

He felt it now, every single part of him on fire. And it must have burned bright, because Kett finally turned to the door and saw him there.

They locked eyes, and nothing else in the world existed. There was just him and Kett and that awful, unspeakable truth of what had happened. Baird didn't look away, he held the other man's eyes until Kett dropped his head, frowning. Was that an expression of recognition on his face? Did he *know*? Had he been waiting for this day as long as Baird had?

For judgement?

Norman Balls had spotted Baird in the door, and he touched Kett's arm, whispering something into his ear.

Then Kett was moving, heading towards Baird with more than a little purpose in his stride.

"Oh, shite," said Baird, realising he had absolutely no idea what to do now. He backed into the corridor, hitting the wall just as Kett walked out of the door.

He was taller than he'd looked from a distance, and there was something in the way he held himself that made him look even bigger. Even though he moved with obvious discomfort, even though there was pain etched into every line of his face, he seemed like a giant. Kett didn't stop until they were practically chest to chest, forcing Baird back against the cold wall. He felt like a child next to the older man, and he wondered if this is how his da had felt too, all those years ago, when Kett had knocked on his door.

"I hear you've been asking about me," said Kett. His blue eyes were so intense they could have been lasers.

"Ach, dinnae flatter yourself, pal," said Baird, trying to keep his cool. "I'm in a happy relationship with my Diana."

He pushed forward a little, putting Kett on the back foot. The other man didn't retreat, though, closing the gap again. Baird's heart was practically galloping on his tonsils.

"I am curious, though, Robert," he said. "Because I think you kent my father, back in London."

Kett didn't reply, he just waited.

"Dougie Baird," he went on. "Used to work for a fella called Nigel Topper, back when you were under John Cooper in the Met. Ring any bells?"

It rang bells alright. Kett looked like he'd been slapped. His face tightened, his eyes narrowing. When he spoke again, it was in a low, dangerous growl that sucked every ounce of warmth from Baird's body.

"Did you not get the message? You lot are done. You come at me again, I'll fucking bury you."

"*What*?" said Baird, barely able to get the word out.

"You heard me," said Kett. "And I'm going to say this once, Harrison."

Hearing his name come out of Kett's mouth was like taking a bullet.

"Just once. You've been asking questions about me, so you've probably got some answers, too. And if even a fraction of what you've learned about me is true, then do you really think you should keep pushing?"

Baird had shaken his head before he even knew he was doing it.

"Tread carefully," said Kett. "Understood? Or you're a fucking dead man."

Kett pushed a finger into Baird's shoulder, right where he'd been grazed by the arrow, and the pain nearly floored him. The world flashed white, and by the time he could see again the other man was walking away, heading back into the gymnasium. Baird watched as he gathered his girls into another hug, as he made a joke to the rest of his team, as he went back to the life he'd stolen.

Then he turned away.

"Aye, I'll tread carefully, you gobshite," he muttered, his shoulder throbbing as he pulled out his phone. "I'll tread on your fucking heid."

He found the number for his old DCI in Police Scotland, pushing through the fire door into the warm afternoon in order to escape the crowds.

"Harrison," said McLean. "How's life in Hell? Pished off any more locals yet?"

"Aye," he said. "Most of them. Listen, sir, I need a favour."

"What, Baird? I'm up to my eyeballs in liquid shite."

"It'll no take long. I just need you to find a man called

Nigel Topper for me. Ex-con, probably doon in London. Went by Mad Dog."

"I can do that," said McLean, although he didn't sound happy about it. "Why?"

Baird took a breath, turning to the ceiling. He could let the wound heal, he knew, simply by walking away.

Or he could open it up again, and risk everything that came with it. The blood. The pain.

The death.

In the end, he knew, he didn't really have a choice. He'd met Kett, after all. He'd seen the truth on his face, just like his da had told him he would.

"I need a word with him, sir," he said, taking another hitching breath. "Something tells me he'll want to find oot who murdered his son."

DI Harrison Baird will return in

Mad Dogs

May 2026!

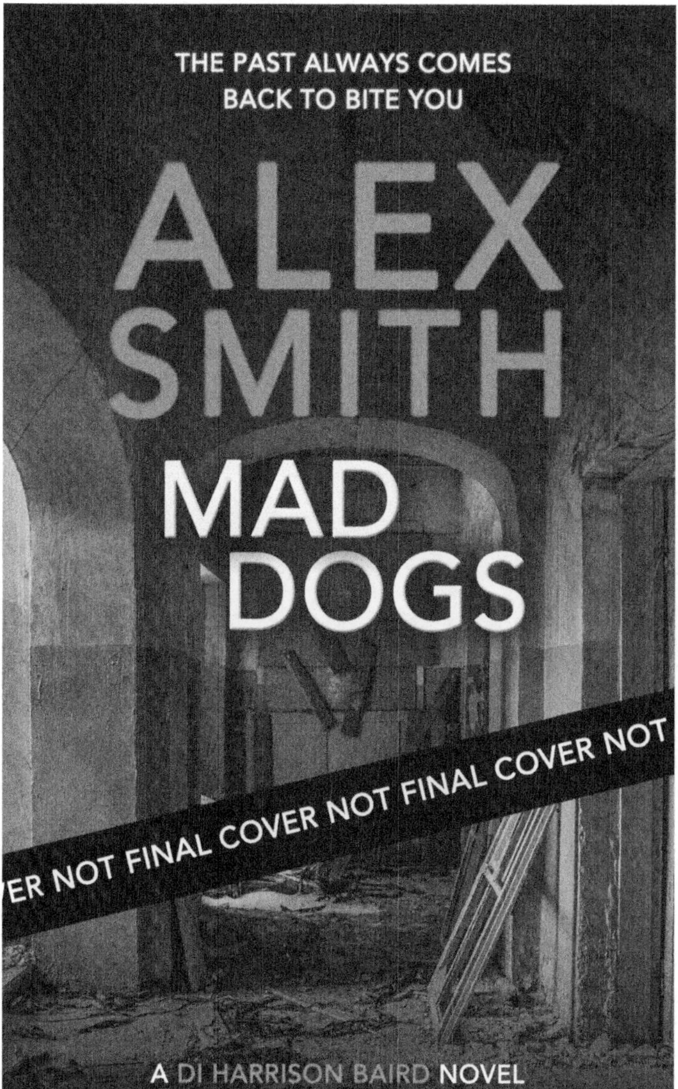
THE PAST ALWAYS COMES
BACK TO BITE YOU
ALEX
SMITH
MAD
DOGS
VER NOT FINAL COVER NOT FINAL COVER NOT
A DI HARRISON BAIRD NOVEL

PAPER GIRLS
ALEX SMITH
BAD DOG
ALEX SMITH
THREE LITTLE PIGS
ALEX SMITH
WHIP CRACK
ALEX SMITH
RUN RABBIT RUN
ALEX SMITH
STONE COLD DEAD
ALEX SMITH
EVERY MOTHER'S SON
ALEX SMITH
SWEET BRIAR ROSE
ALEX SMITH
JAW BREAKER
ALEX SMITH
KNOCK KNOCK
ALEX SMITH
KING RAT
ALEX SMITH
KNUCKLE BONES
ALEX SMITH
LUCKY NUMBER SEVEN
ALEX SMITH
UNHOLY SAINTS
ALEX SMITH
TRULY MADLY DEADLY
ALEX SMITH
EVERY LAST DEVIL
ALEX SMITH
RED LINE
ALEX SMITH
COLD IRON KILLS
ALEX SMITH
READ THE DCI KETT BOOKS NOW!

ABOUT THE AUTHOR

Alex Smith wrote his first book when he was six. It wasn't particularly good, but it did have some supernatural monsters in it. His latest books, the DCI Robert Kett and the DI Harrison Baird thrillers, have monsters in them too, although these monsters are very human, and all the more terrifying for it. In between, he has published fourteen novels for children and teenagers under his full name, Alexander Gordon Smith—including the number one best-selling series Escape From Furnace, which is loved by millions of readers worldwide and which is soon to become a motion picture. He lives in Norwich with his wife and three young daughters.

Find out more at alexsmithbooks.com

RELENTLESS
MEDIA

Printed in Dunstable, United Kingdom

83265096R00262